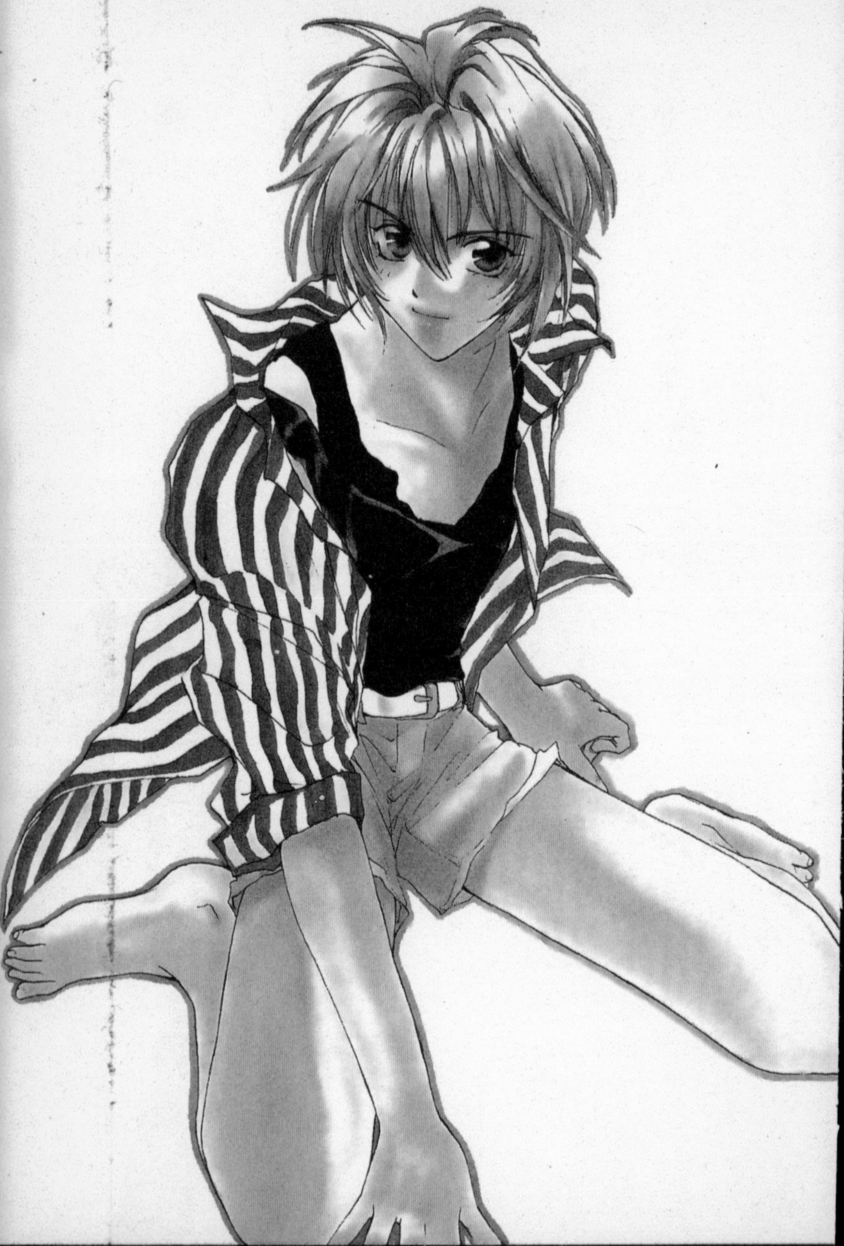

GRAVITATION

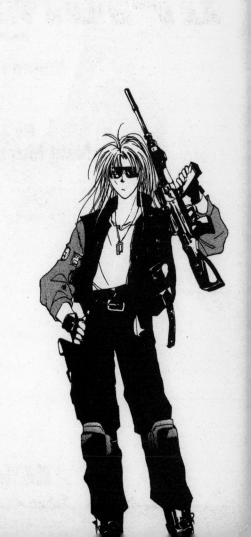

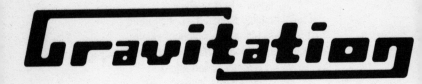

Volume 6

By
Maki Murakami

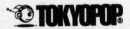

Los Angeles • Tokyo • London • Hamburg

Translator - Ray Yoshimoto
English Adaptation - Jamie S. Rich
Copy Editor - Tim Beedle
Retouch and Lettering - Tina Fulkerson and Yoohae Yang
Cover Layout - Raymond Makowski

Editor - Paul Morrissey
Digital Imaging Manager - Chris Buford
Pre-Press Manager - Antonio DePietro
Production Managers - Jennifer Miller and Mutsumi Miyazaki
Art Director - Matt Alford
Managing Editor - Jill Freshney
VP of Production - Ron Klamert
President & C.O.O. - John Parker
Publisher & C.E.O. - Stuart Levy

Email: info@TOKYOPOP.com
Come visit us online at www.TOKYOPOP.com

A 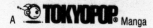 TOKYOPOP® Manga

TOKYOPOP Inc.
5900 Wilshire Blvd. Suite 2000
Los Angeles, CA 90036

Gravitation Vol. 6

ISBN: 1-59182-338-2

First TOKYOPOP printing: June 2004

10 9 8 7 6

Printed in the USA

THE MEMBERS OF THE GRAVITATION BAND

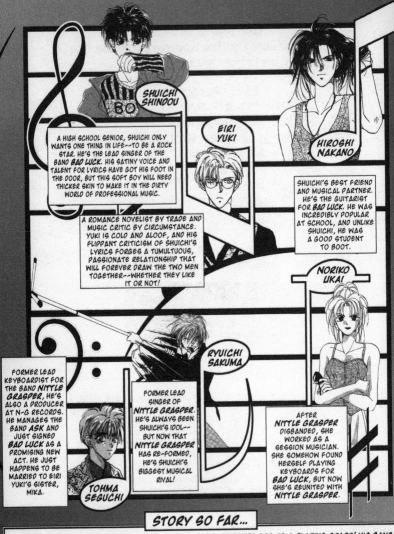

SHUICHI SHINDOU
A HIGH SCHOOL SENIOR, SHUICHI ONLY WANTS ONE THING IN LIFE--TO BE A ROCK STAR. HE'S THE LEAD SINGER OF THE BAND BAD LUCK. HIS SATINY VOICE AND TALENT FOR LYRICS HAVE GOT HIS FOOT IN THE DOOR, BUT THIS SOFT BOY WILL NEED THICKER SKIN TO MAKE IT IN THE DIRTY WORLD OF PROFESSIONAL MUSIC.
HIROSHI NAKANO
SHUICHI'S BEST FRIEND AND MUSICAL PARTNER. HE'S THE GUITARIST FOR BAD LUCK. HE WAS INCREDIBLY POPULAR AT SCHOOL, AND UNLIKE SHUICHI, HE WAS A GOOD STUDENT TO BOOT.
EIRI YUKI
A ROMANCE NOVELIST BY TRADE AND MUSIC CRITIC BY CIRCUMSTANCE. YUKI IS COLD AND ALOOF, AND HIS FLIPPANT CRITICISM OF SHUICHI'S LYRICS FORGES A TUMULTUOUS, PASSIONATE RELATIONSHIP THAT WILL FOREVER DRAW THE TWO MEN TOGETHER--WHETHER THEY LIKE IT OR NOT!
NORIKO UKAI
AFTER NITTLE GRASPER DISBANDED, SHE WORKED AS A SESSION MUSICIAN. SHE SOMEHOW FOUND HERSELF PLAYING KEYBOARDS FOR BAD LUCK, BUT NOW SHE'S REUNITED WITH NITTLE GRASPER.
RYUICHI SAKUMA
FORMER LEAD SINGER OF NITTLE GRASPER. HE'S ALWAYS BEEN SHUICHI'S IDOL--BUT NOW THAT NITTLE GRASPER HAS RE-FORMED, HE'S SHUICHI'S BIGGEST MUSICAL RIVAL!
TOHMA SEGUCHI
FORMER LEAD KEYBOARDIST FOR THE BAND NITTLE GRASPER, HE'S ALSO A PRODUCER AT N-G RECORDS. HE MANAGES THE BAND ASK AND JUST SIGNED BAD LUCK AS A PROMISING NEW ACT. HE JUST HAPPENS TO BE MARRIED TO EIRI YUKI'S SISTER, MIKA.

STORY SO FAR...

SHUICHI SHINDOU IS DETERMINED TO BE A ROCK STAR...AND HE'S OFF TO A BLAZING START! HIS BAND, ***BAD LUCK***, HAS JUST BEEN SIGNED TO THE N-G RECORD LABEL, AND THEIR FIRST SINGLE IS BURNING UP THE CHARTS! WITH THE ADDITION OF HIS NEW MANAGER--THE GUN-TOTING AMERICAN MANIAC NAMED "K"--SHUICHI IS POISED TO TAKE THE WORLD HOSTAGE! BUT THINGS ARE THROWN INTO DISACCORD WHEN THE LEGENDARY BAND NITTLE GRASPER ANNOUNCES THEY ARE REUNITING! NOW SHUICHI WILL HAVE TO GO HEAD-TO-HEAD WITH HIS IDOL, RYUICHI SAKUMA. ALL THE WHILE, SHUICHI IS DESPERATE TO KEEP HIS ROLLER-COASTER RELATIONSHIP WITH THE MYSTERIOUS WRITER EIRI YUKI RED-HOT. BUT LOVE IS NEVER EASY. ARE SHUICHI AND YUKI DESTINED TO DRIFT APART, OR WILL THEY REMAIN INEXORABLY INTERTWINED, HELD TOGETHER BY A FORCE AS STRONG AS GRAVITY?

CONTENTS

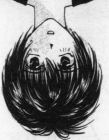

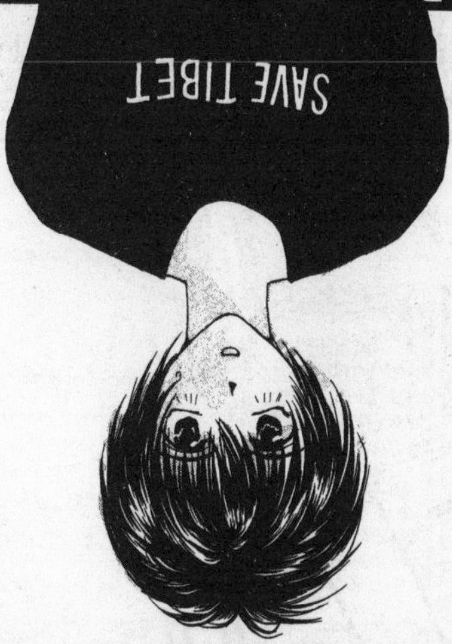

SAVE TIBET

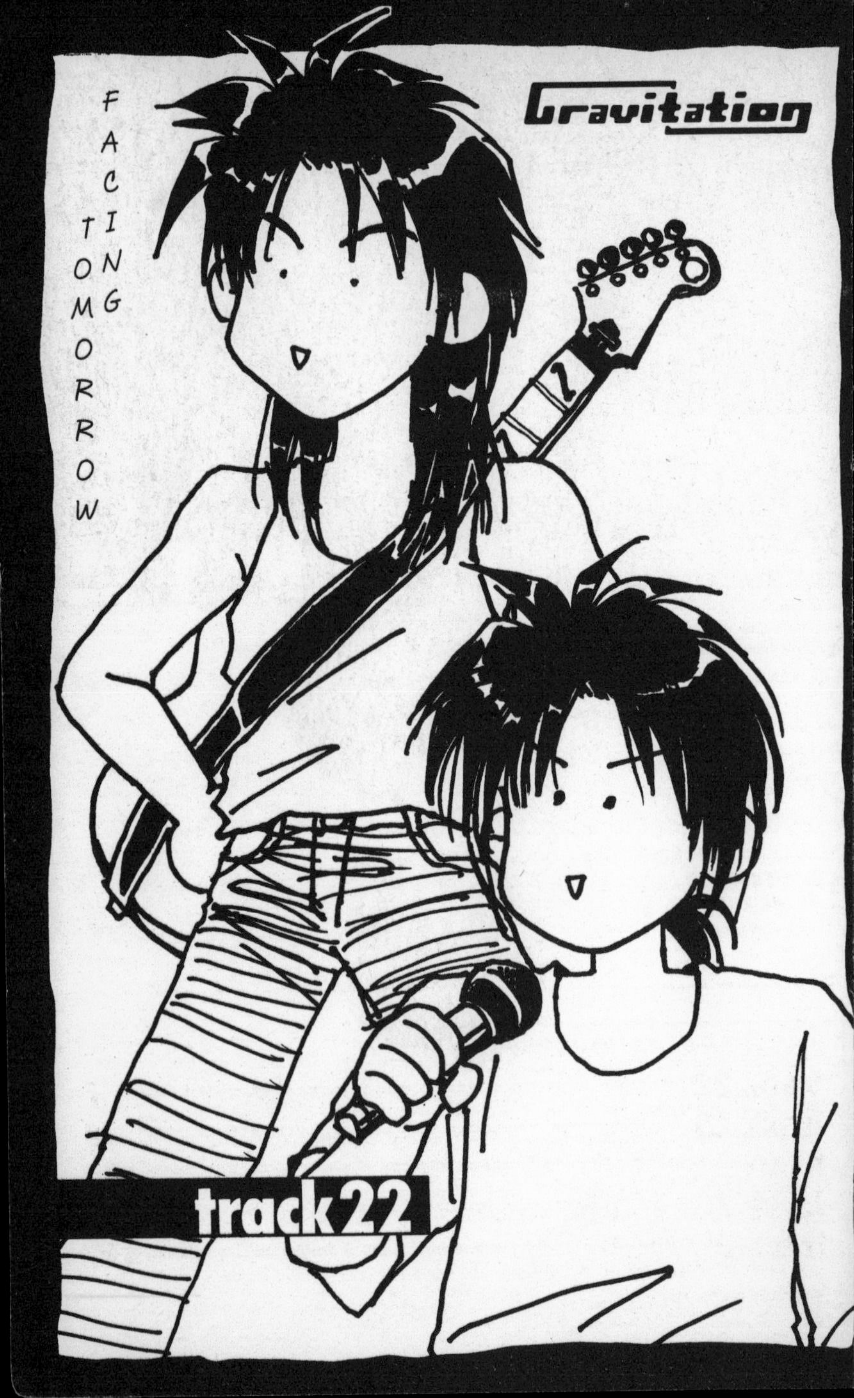
Gravitation
FACING TOMORROW
track 22

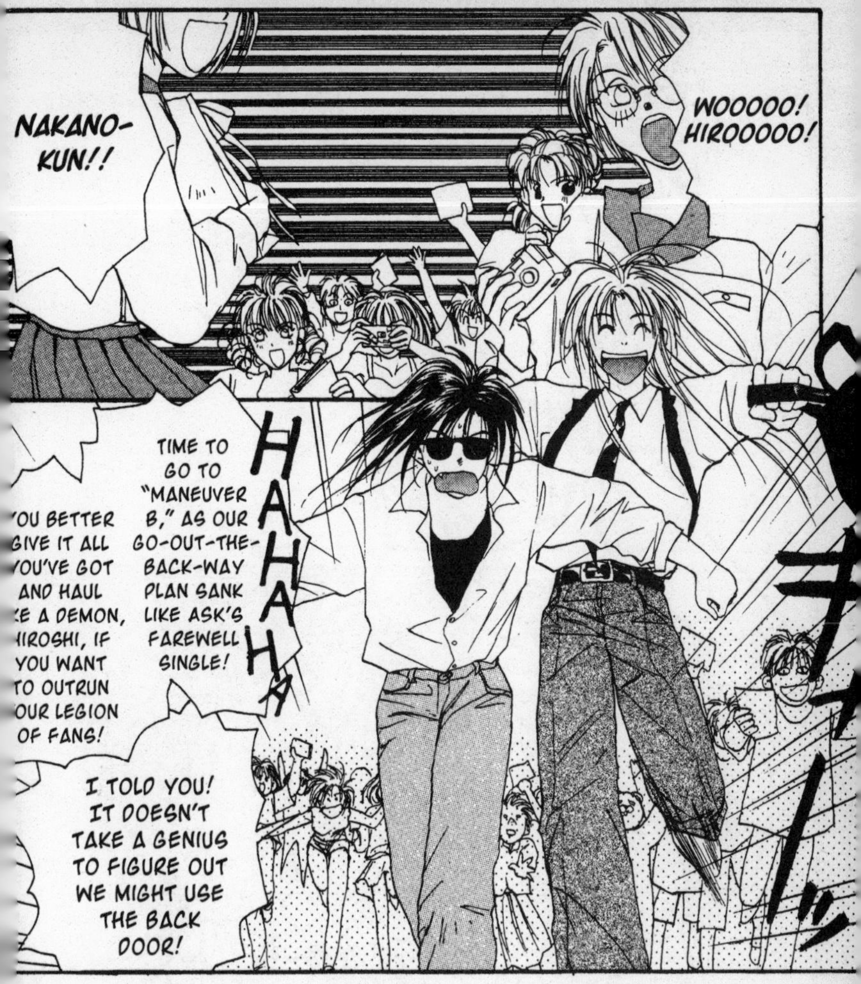
WOOOOO! HIROOOOO!
NAKANO-KUN!!
HAHAHAHA
TIME TO GO TO "MANEUVER B," AS OUR GO-OUT-THE-BACK-WAY PLAN SANK LIKE ASK'S FAREWELL SINGLE!
'OU BETTER GIVE IT ALL 'OU'VE GOT AND HAUL :E A DEMON, IIROSHI, IF YOU WANT TO OUTRUN 'OUR LEGION OF FANS!
I TOLD YOU! IT DOESN'T TAKE A GENIUS TO FIGURE OUT WE MIGHT USE THE BACK DOOR!

ABOUT GRAVITATION TRACK 22

We're getting into it now. This is the meaty center of the Gravitation saga. So, how has life been treating you all? You can tell little ol' Murakami. In my world, Bad Luck's popularity has been on the rise. Take a look at the opening of this book! Girls are chasing them down the street! Rock on, Bad Luck! Go for it! By the way, I often use these sidebars to reveal spoilers, so it might not be a good idea to pay careful attention to them. You've been warned. I try not to reveal too much, but sometimes I just can't help myself. I'll try to exercise restraint!

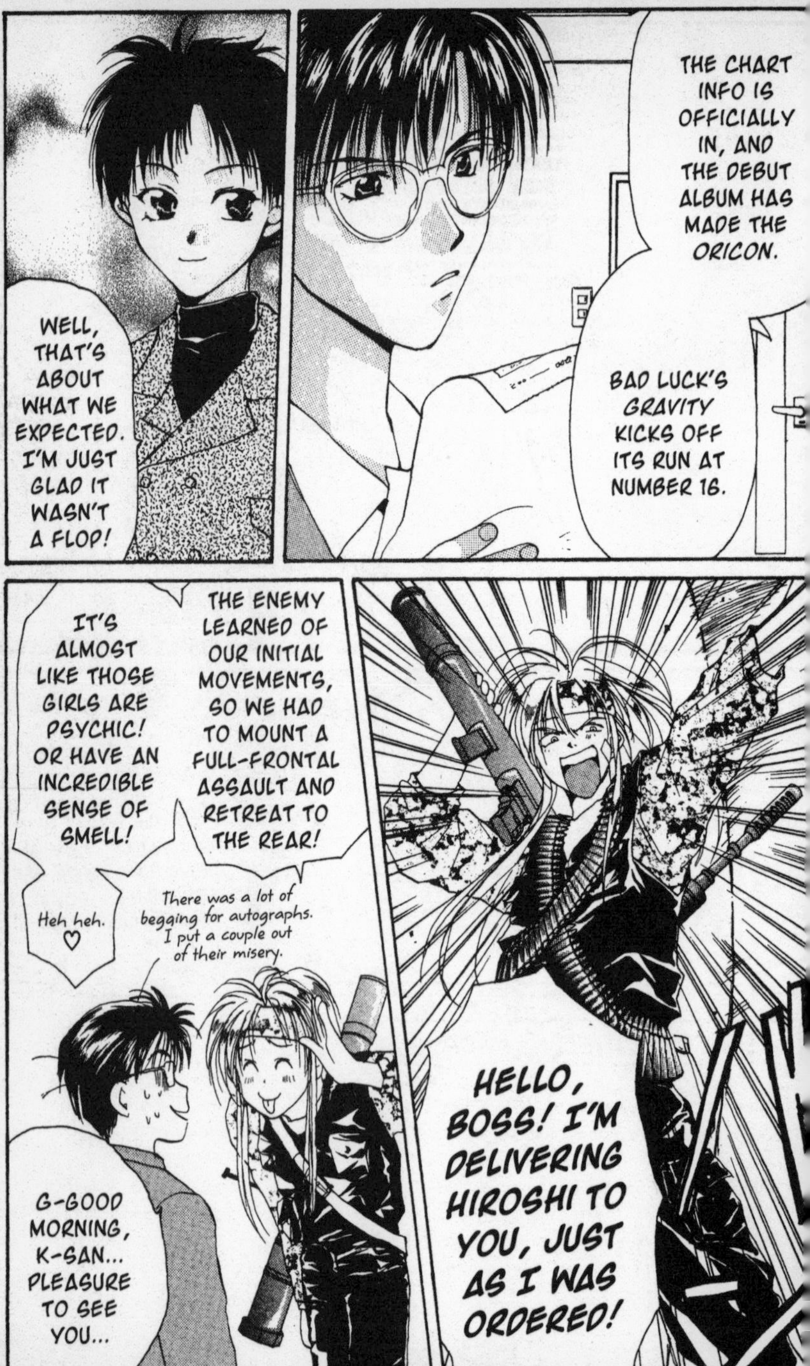
THE CHART INFO IS OFFICIALLY IN, AND THE DEBUT ALBUM HAS MADE THE ORICON.
BAD LUCK'S GRAVITY KICKS OFF ITS RUN AT NUMBER 16.
WELL, THAT'S ABOUT WHAT WE EXPECTED. I'M JUST GLAD IT WASN'T A FLOP!
HELLO, BOSS! I'M DELIVERING HIROSHI TO YOU, JUST AS I WAS ORDERED!
THE ENEMY LEARNED OF OUR INITIAL MOVEMENTS, SO WE HAD TO MOUNT A FULL-FRONTAL ASSAULT AND RETREAT TO THE REAR!
IT'S ALMOST LIKE THOSE GIRLS ARE PSYCHIC! OR HAVE AN INCREDIBLE SENSE OF SMELL!
There was a lot of begging for autographs. I put a couple out of their misery.
Heh heh. ♡
G-GOOD MORNING, K-SAN... PLEASURE TO SEE YOU...

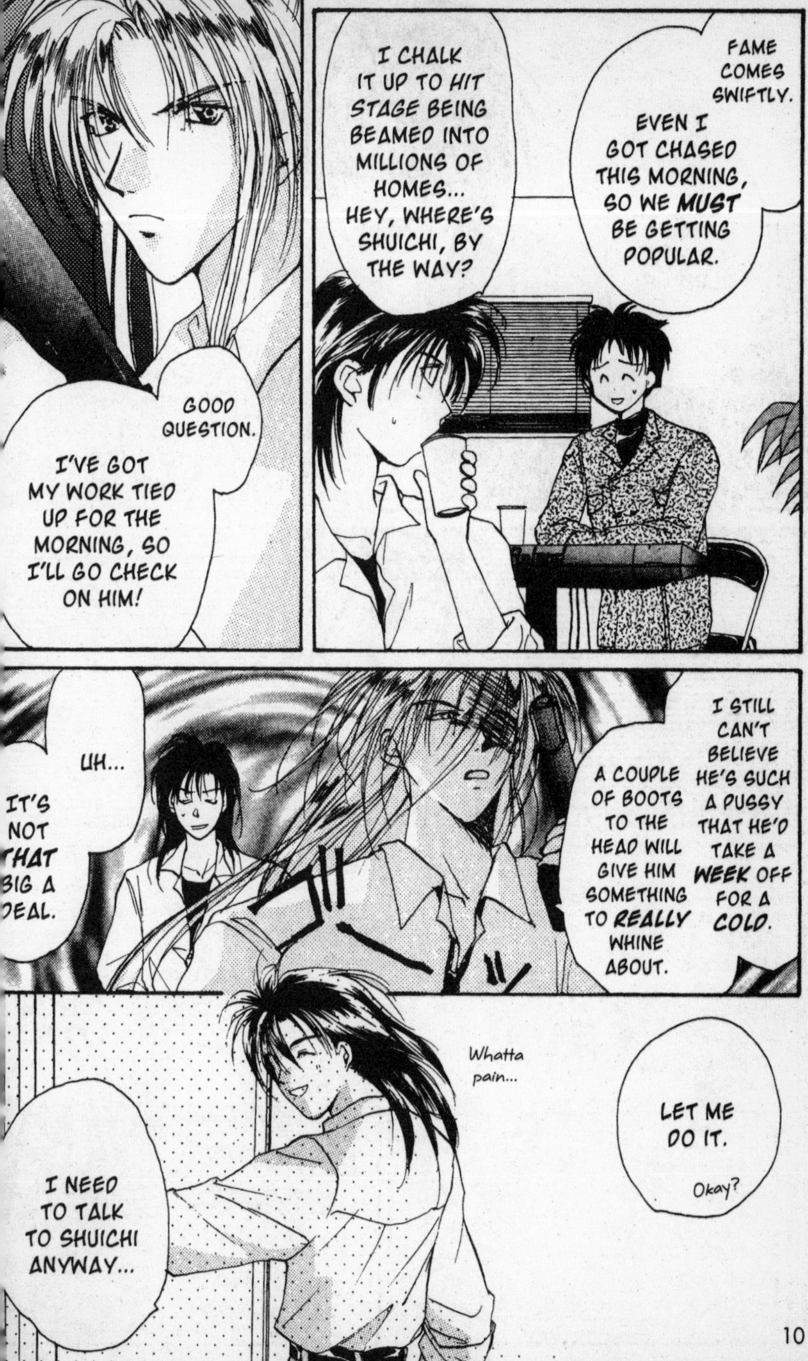
FAME COMES SWIFTLY.
EVEN I GOT CHASED THIS MORNING, SO WE **MUST** BE GETTING POPULAR.
I CHALK IT UP TO HIT STAGE BEING BEAMED INTO MILLIONS OF HOMES... HEY, WHERE'S SHUICHI, BY THE WAY?
GOOD QUESTION.
I'VE GOT MY WORK TIED UP FOR THE MORNING, SO I'LL GO CHECK ON HIM!
I STILL CAN'T BELIEVE HE'S SUCH A PUSSY THAT HE'D TAKE A **WEEK** OFF FOR A **COLD**.
A COUPLE OF BOOTS TO THE HEAD WILL GIVE HIM SOMETHING TO **REALLY** WHINE ABOUT.
UH...
IT'S NOT **THAT** BIG A DEAL.
LET ME DO IT.
Okay?
Whatta pain...
I NEED TO TALK TO SHUICHI ANYWAY...

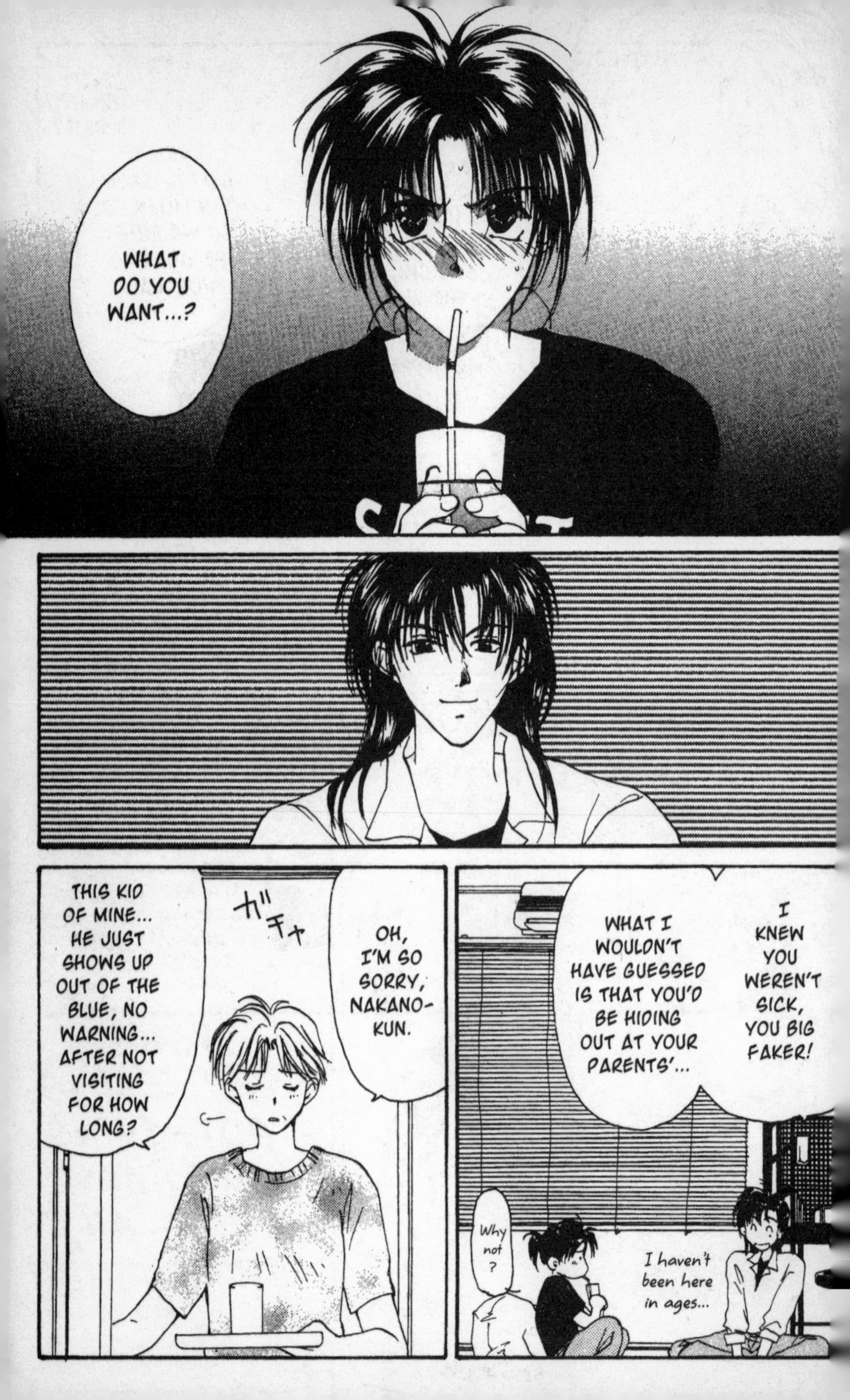
WHAT DO YOU WANT...?
I KNEW YOU WEREN'T SICK, YOU BIG FAKER!
WHAT I WOULDN'T HAVE GUESSED IS THAT YOU'D BE HIDING OUT AT YOUR PARENTS'...
I haven't been here in ages...
Why not?
OH, I'M SO SORRY, NAKANO-KUN.
ガチャ
THIS KID OF MINE... HE JUST SHOWS UP OUT OF THE BLUE, NO WARNING... AFTER NOT VISITING FOR HOW LONG?

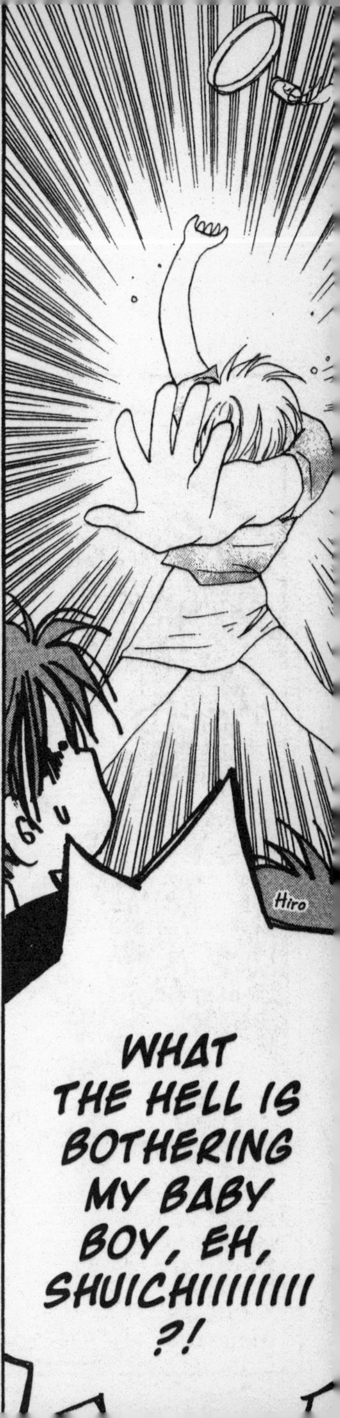

Hiro
WHAT THE HELL IS BOTHERING MY BABY BOY, EH, SHUICHIIIIIIII ?!

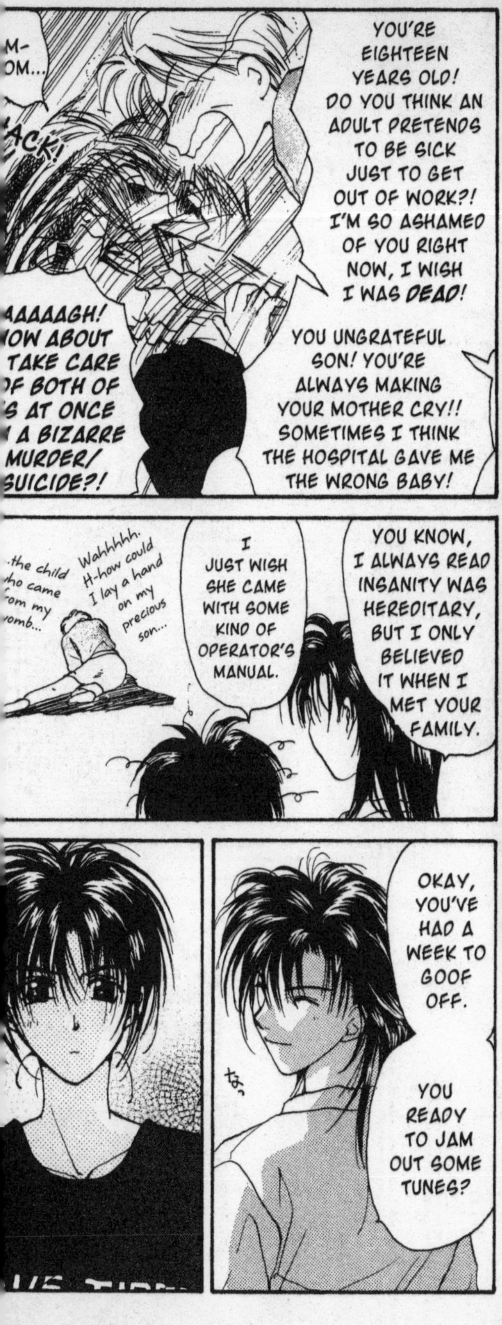

YOU'RE EIGHTEEN YEARS OLD! DO YOU THINK AN ADULT PRETENDS TO BE SICK JUST TO GET OUT OF WORK?! I'M SO ASHAMED OF YOU RIGHT NOW, I WISH I WAS DEAD!
YOU UNGRATEFUL SON! YOU'RE ALWAYS MAKING YOUR MOTHER CRY!! SOMETIMES I THINK THE HOSPITAL GAVE ME THE WRONG BABY!
M- OM...
ACK!
AAAAAGH! IOW ABOUT TAKE CARE OF BOTH OF S AT ONCE A BIZARRE MURDER/ SUICIDE?!
YOU KNOW, I ALWAYS READ INSANITY WAS HEREDITARY, BUT I ONLY BELIEVED IT WHEN I MET YOUR FAMILY.
I JUST WISH SHE CAME WITH SOME KIND OF OPERATOR'S MANUAL.
Wahhhhh. H-how could I lay a hand on my precious son...
the child who came from my womb...
OKAY, YOU'VE HAD A WEEK TO GOOF OFF.
YOU READY TO JAM OUT SOME TUNES?

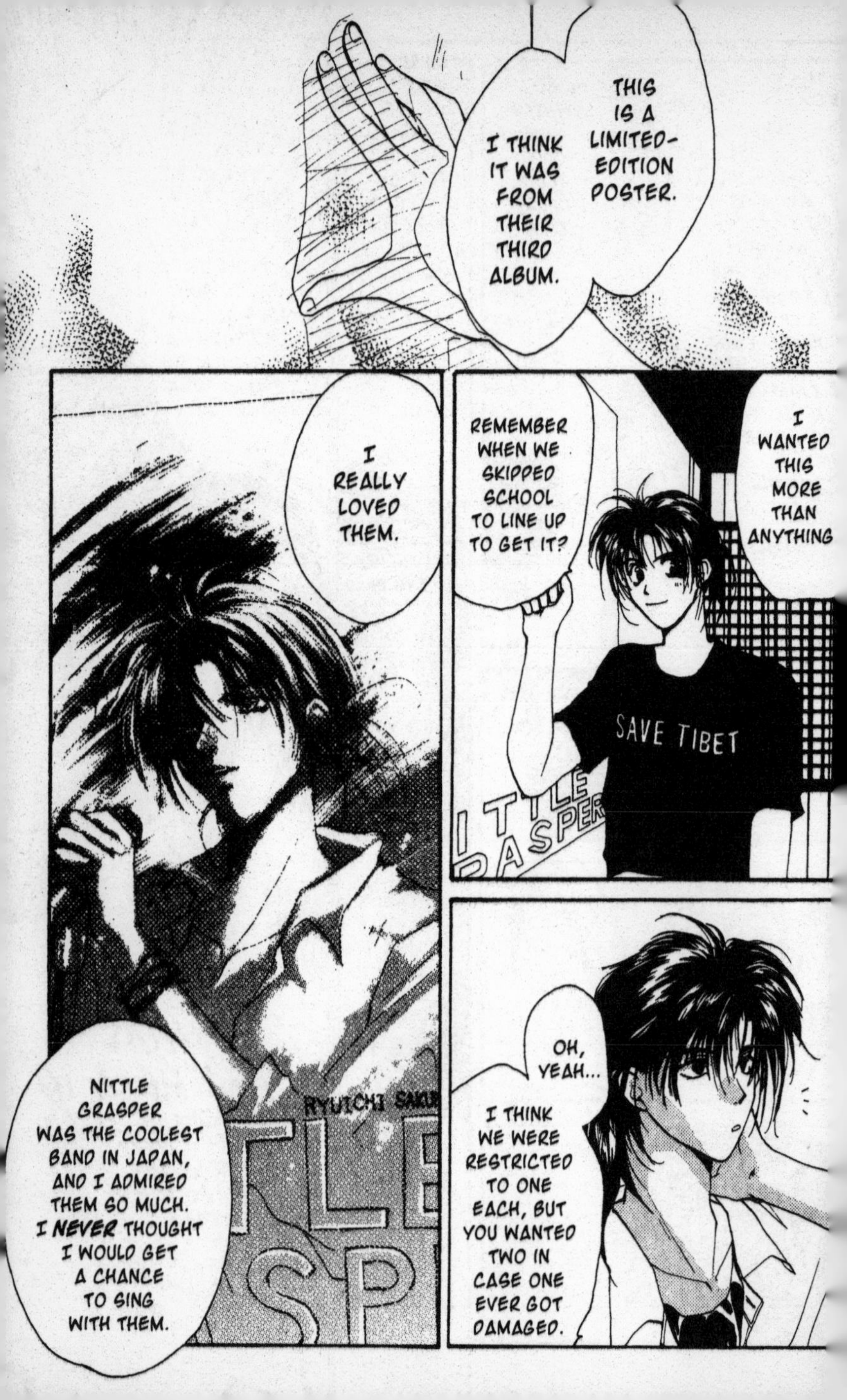
THIS IS A LIMITED-EDITION POSTER.
I THINK IT WAS FROM THEIR THIRD ALBUM.
I WANTED THIS MORE THAN ANYTHING
REMEMBER WHEN WE SKIPPED SCHOOL TO LINE UP TO GET IT?
SAVE TIBET
OH, YEAH...
I THINK WE WERE RESTRICTED TO ONE EACH, BUT YOU WANTED TWO IN CASE ONE EVER GOT DAMAGED.
I REALLY LOVED THEM.
NITTLE GRASPER WAS THE COOLEST BAND IN JAPAN, AND I ADMIRED THEM SO MUCH. I *NEVER* THOUGHT I WOULD GET A CHANCE TO SING WITH THEM.

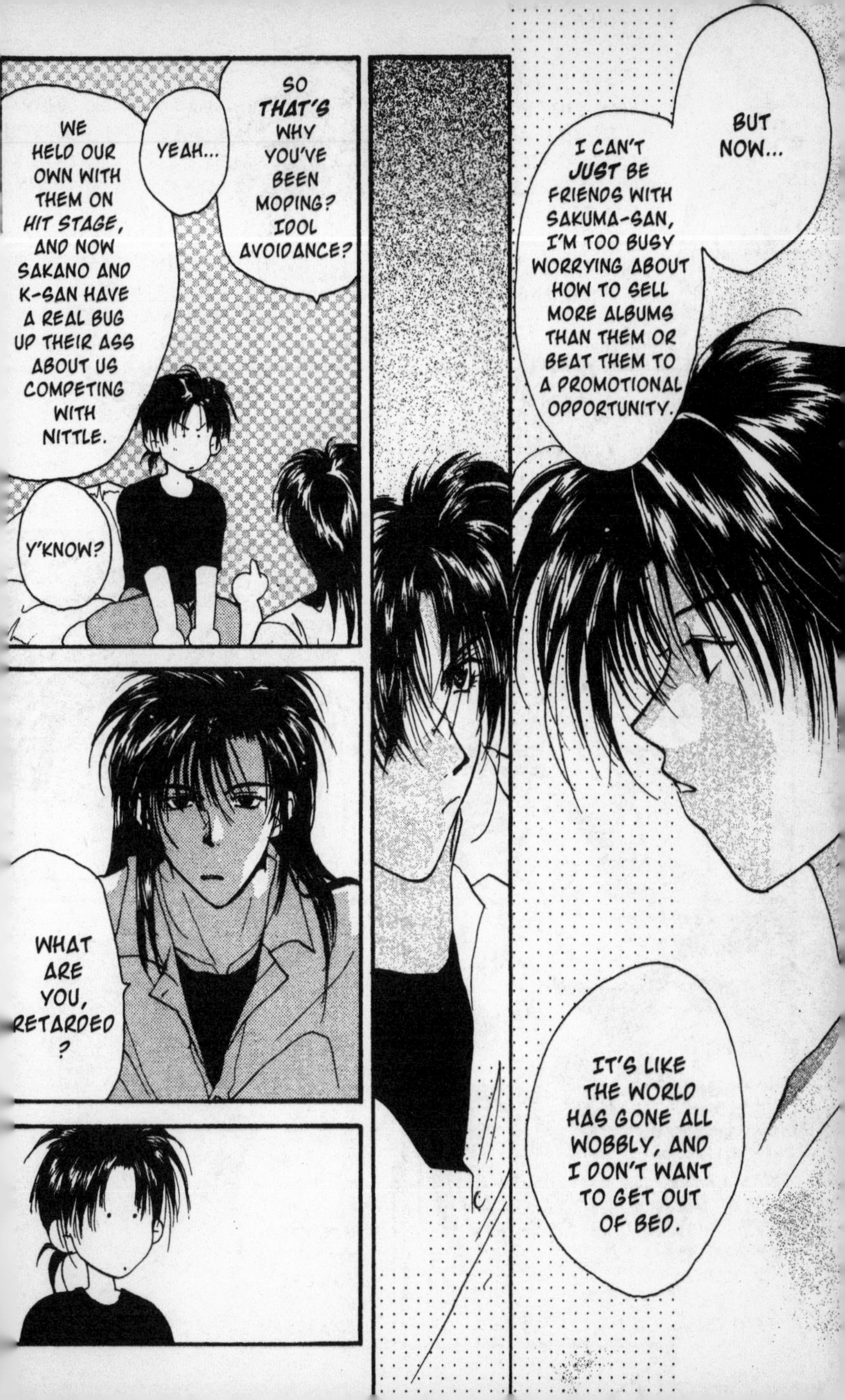
BUT NOW...
I CAN'T JUST BE FRIENDS WITH SAKUMA-SAN, I'M TOO BUSY WORRYING ABOUT HOW TO SELL MORE ALBUMS THAN THEM OR BEAT THEM TO A PROMOTIONAL OPPORTUNITY.
IT'S LIKE THE WORLD HAS GONE ALL WOBBLY, AND I DON'T WANT TO GET OUT OF BED.
SO THAT'S WHY YOU'VE BEEN MOPING? IDOL AVOIDANCE?
YEAH...
WE HELD OUR OWN WITH THEM ON HIT STAGE, AND NOW SAKANO AND K-SAN HAVE A REAL BUG UP THEIR ASS ABOUT US COMPETING WITH NITTLE.
Y'KNOW?
WHAT ARE YOU, RETARDED?

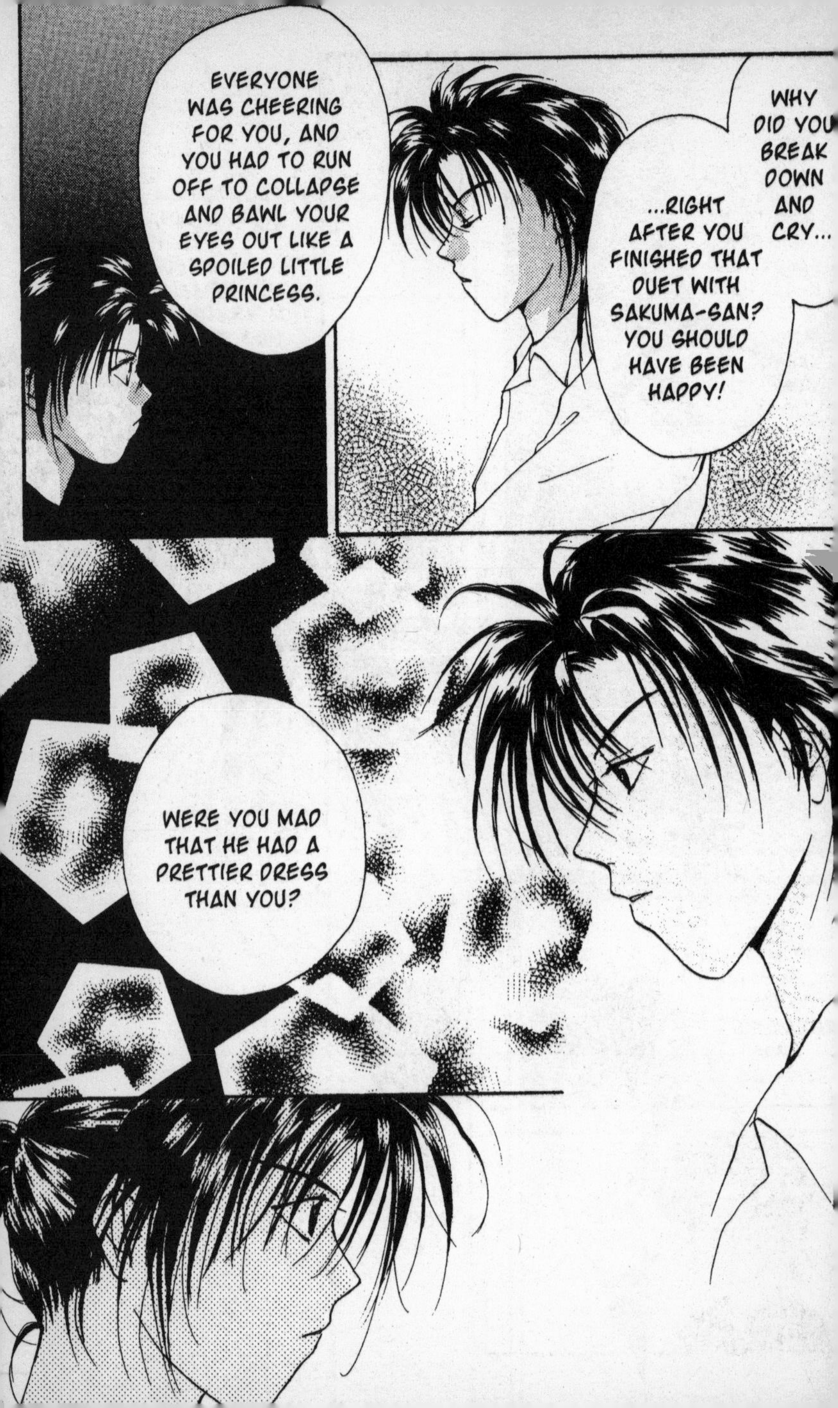
WHY DID YOU BREAK DOWN AND CRY...
...RIGHT AFTER YOU FINISHED THAT DUET WITH SAKUMA-SAN? YOU SHOULD HAVE BEEN HAPPY!
EVERYONE WAS CHEERING FOR YOU, AND YOU HAD TO RUN OFF TO COLLAPSE AND BAWL YOUR EYES OUT LIKE A SPOILED LITTLE PRINCESS.
WERE YOU MAD THAT HE HAD A PRETTIER DRESS THAN YOU?

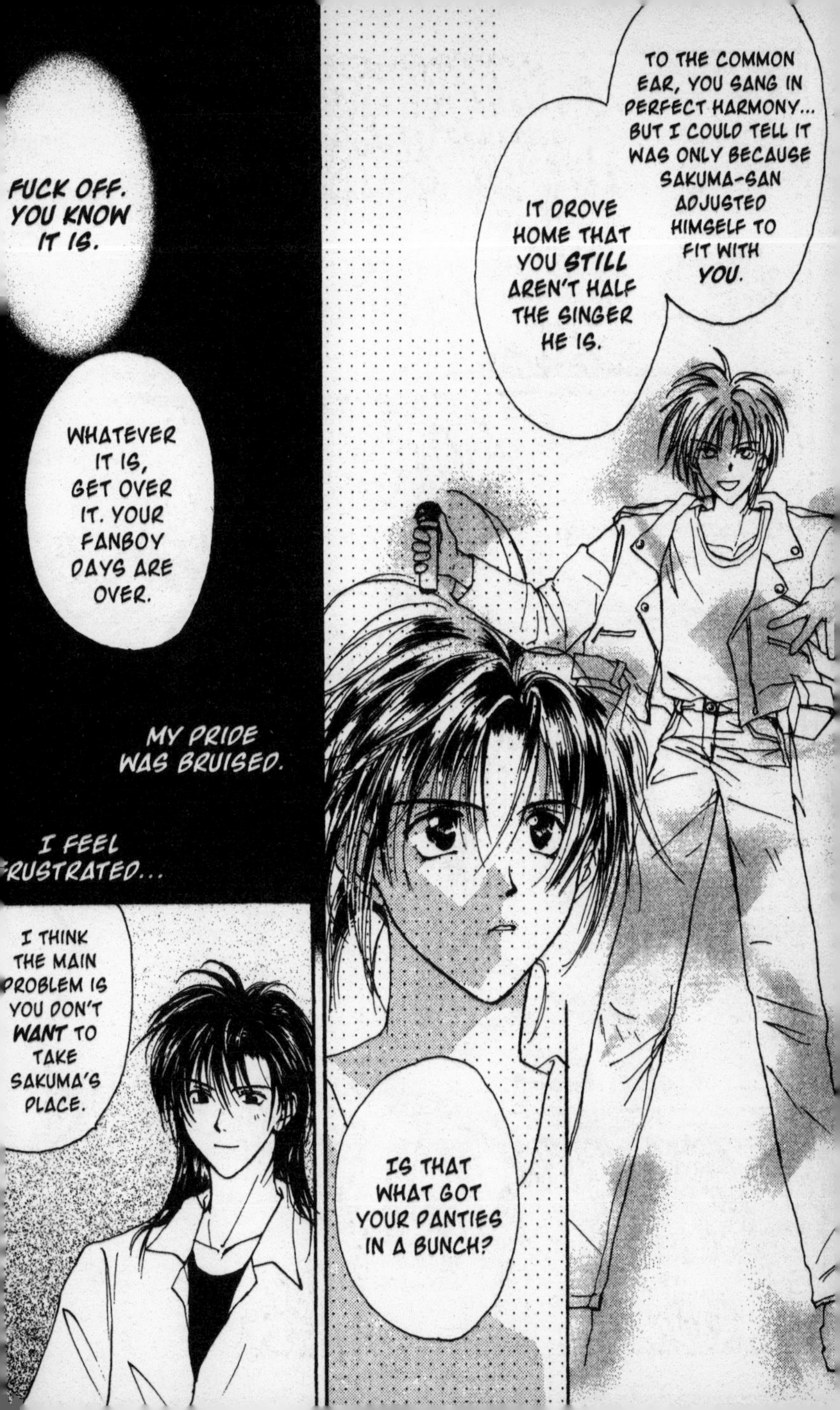
TO THE COMMON EAR, YOU SANG IN PERFECT HARMONY... BUT I COULD TELL IT WAS ONLY BECAUSE SAKUMA-SAN ADJUSTED HIMSELF TO FIT WITH YOU.
IT DROVE HOME THAT YOU STILL AREN'T HALF THE SINGER HE IS.
IS THAT WHAT GOT YOUR PANTIES IN A BUNCH?
FUCK OFF. YOU KNOW IT IS.
WHATEVER IT IS, GET OVER IT. YOUR FANBOY DAYS ARE OVER.
MY PRIDE WAS BRUISED.
I FEEL RUSTRATED...
I THINK THE MAIN PROBLEM IS YOU DON'T WANT TO TAKE SAKUMA'S PLACE.

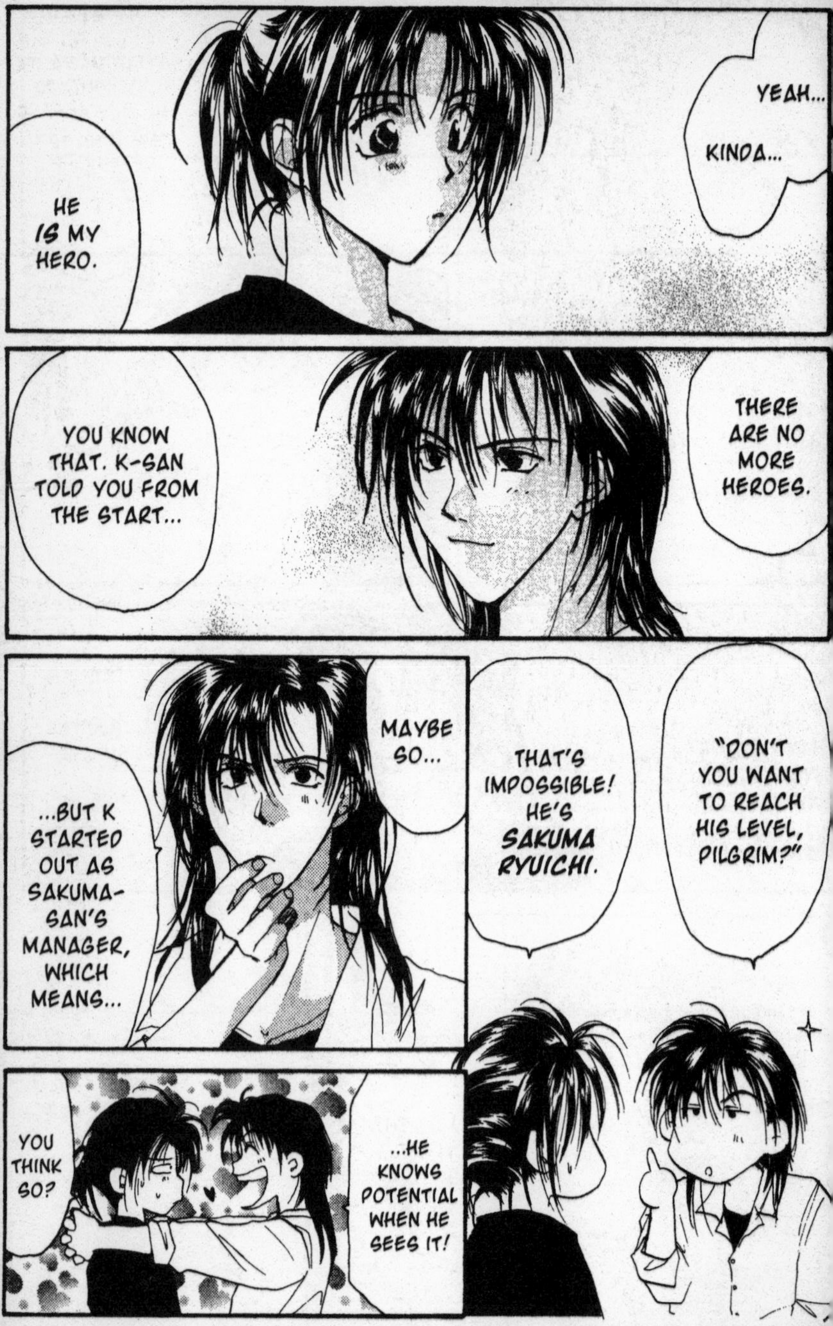
YEAH... KINDA...
HE *IS* MY HERO.
THERE ARE NO MORE HEROES.
YOU KNOW THAT. K-SAN TOLD YOU FROM THE START...
"DON'T YOU WANT TO REACH HIS LEVEL, PILGRIM?"
THAT'S IMPOSSIBLE! HE'S **SAKUMA RYUICHI**.
MAYBE SO...
...BUT K STARTED OUT AS SAKUMA-SAN'S MANAGER, WHICH MEANS...
...HE KNOWS POTENTIAL WHEN HE SEES IT!
YOU THINK SO?

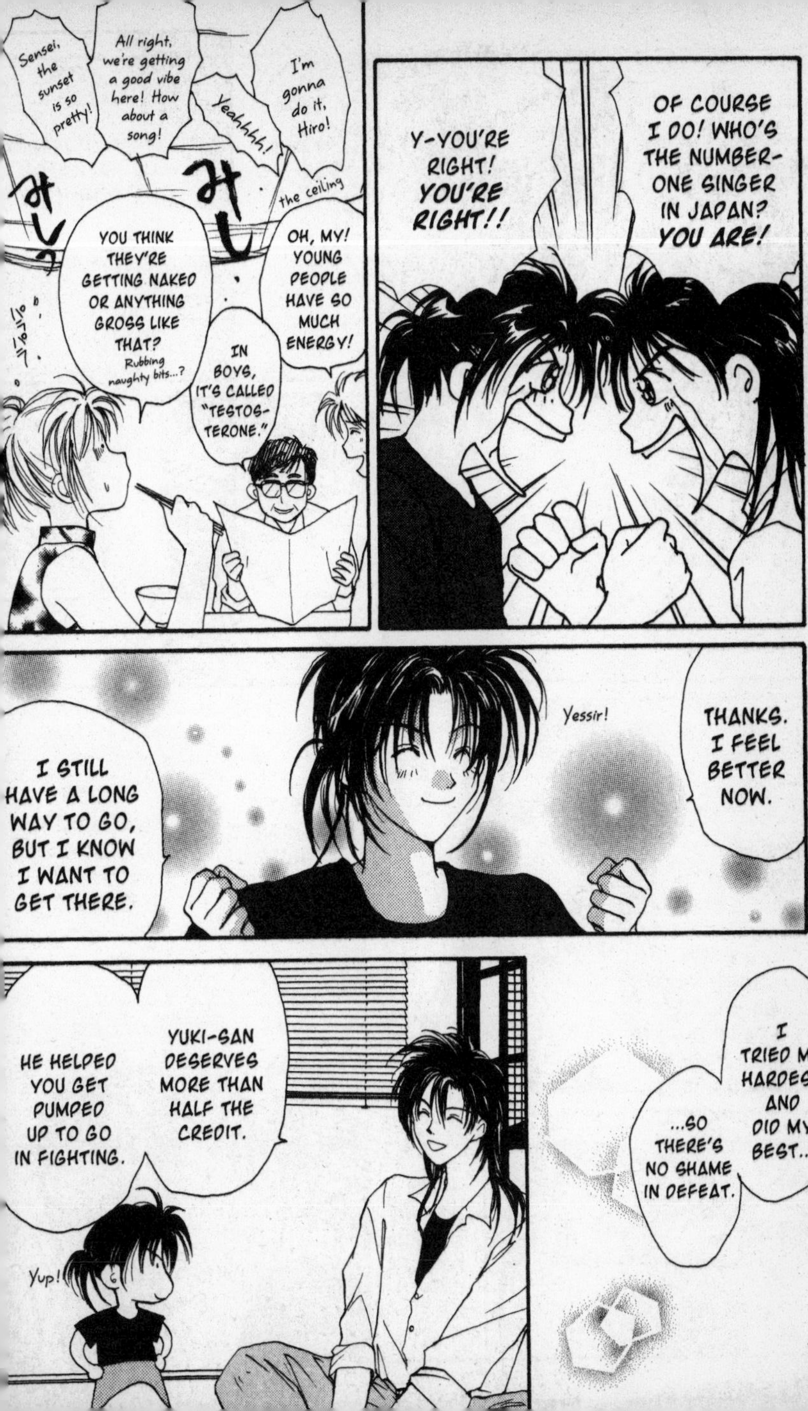
OF COURSE I DO! WHO'S THE NUMBER-ONE SINGER IN JAPAN? YOU ARE!
Y-YOU'RE RIGHT! YOU'RE RIGHT!!
I'm gonna do it, Hiro!
Yeahhhh!
All right, we're getting a good vibe here! How about a song!
Sensei, the sunset is so pretty!
みし
みし
the ceiling
OH, MY! YOUNG PEOPLE HAVE SO MUCH ENERGY!
YOU THINK THEY'RE GETTING NAKED OR ANYTHING GROSS LIKE THAT?
Rubbing naughty bits...?
IN BOYS, IT'S CALLED "TESTOSTERONE."
THANKS. I FEEL BETTER NOW.
Yessir!
I STILL HAVE A LONG WAY TO GO, BUT I KNOW I WANT TO GET THERE.
I TRIED MY HARDEST AND DID MY BEST...
...SO THERE'S NO SHAME IN DEFEAT.
YUKI-SAN DESERVES MORE THAN HALF THE CREDIT.
HE HELPED YOU GET PUMPED UP TO GO IN FIGHTING.
Yup!

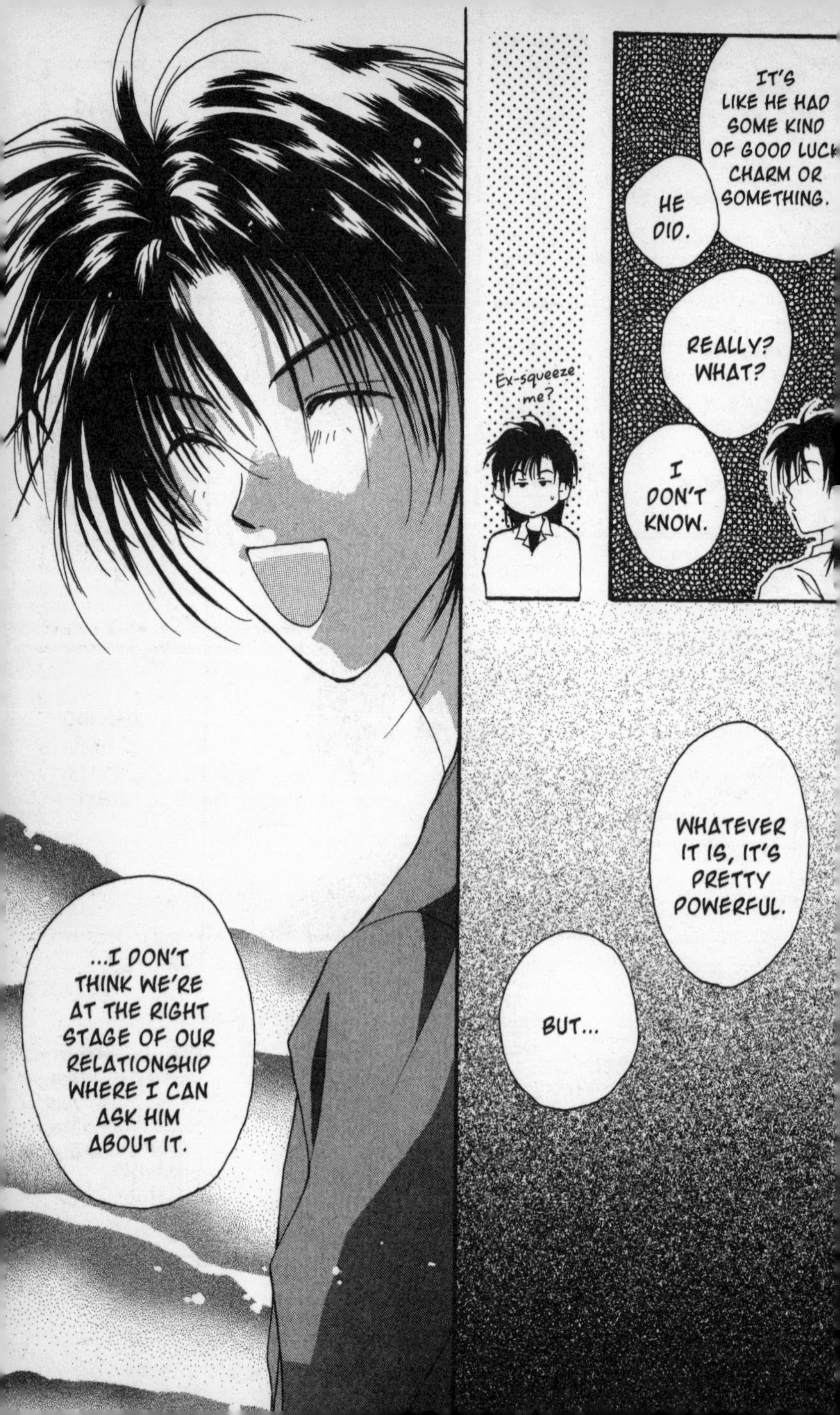
IT'S LIKE HE HAD SOME KIND OF GOOD LUCK CHARM OR SOMETHING.
HE DID.
REALLY? WHAT?
I DON'T KNOW.
Ex-squeeze me?
WHATEVER IT IS, IT'S PRETTY POWERFUL.
BUT...
...I DON'T THINK WE'RE AT THE RIGHT STAGE OF OUR RELATIONSHIP WHERE I CAN ASK HIM ABOUT IT.

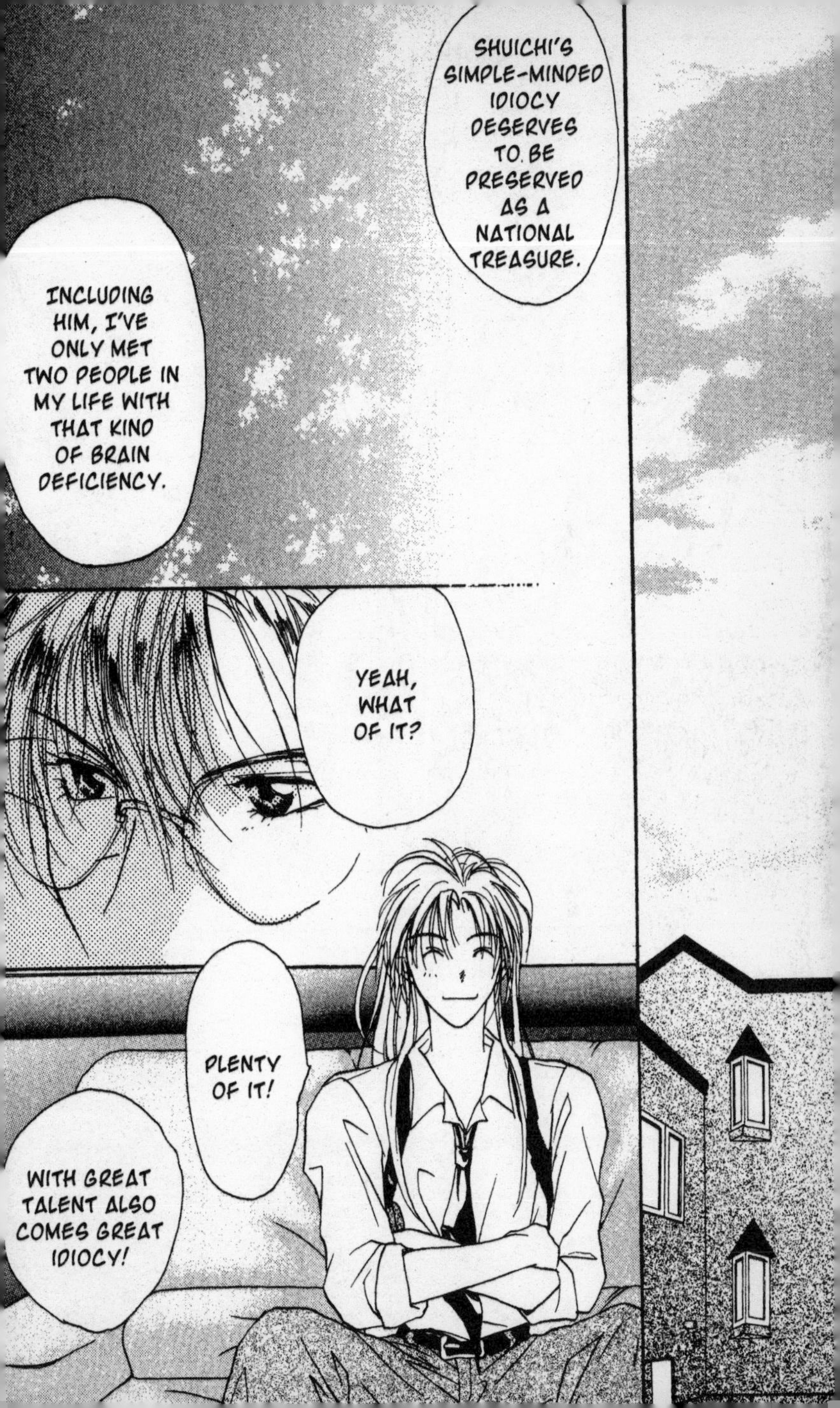
SHUICHI'S SIMPLE-MINDED IDIOCY DESERVES TO BE PRESERVED AS A NATIONAL TREASURE.
INCLUDING HIM, I'VE ONLY MET TWO PEOPLE IN MY LIFE WITH THAT KIND OF BRAIN DEFICIENCY.
YEAH, WHAT OF IT?
PLENTY OF IT!
WITH GREAT TALENT ALSO COMES GREAT IDIOCY!

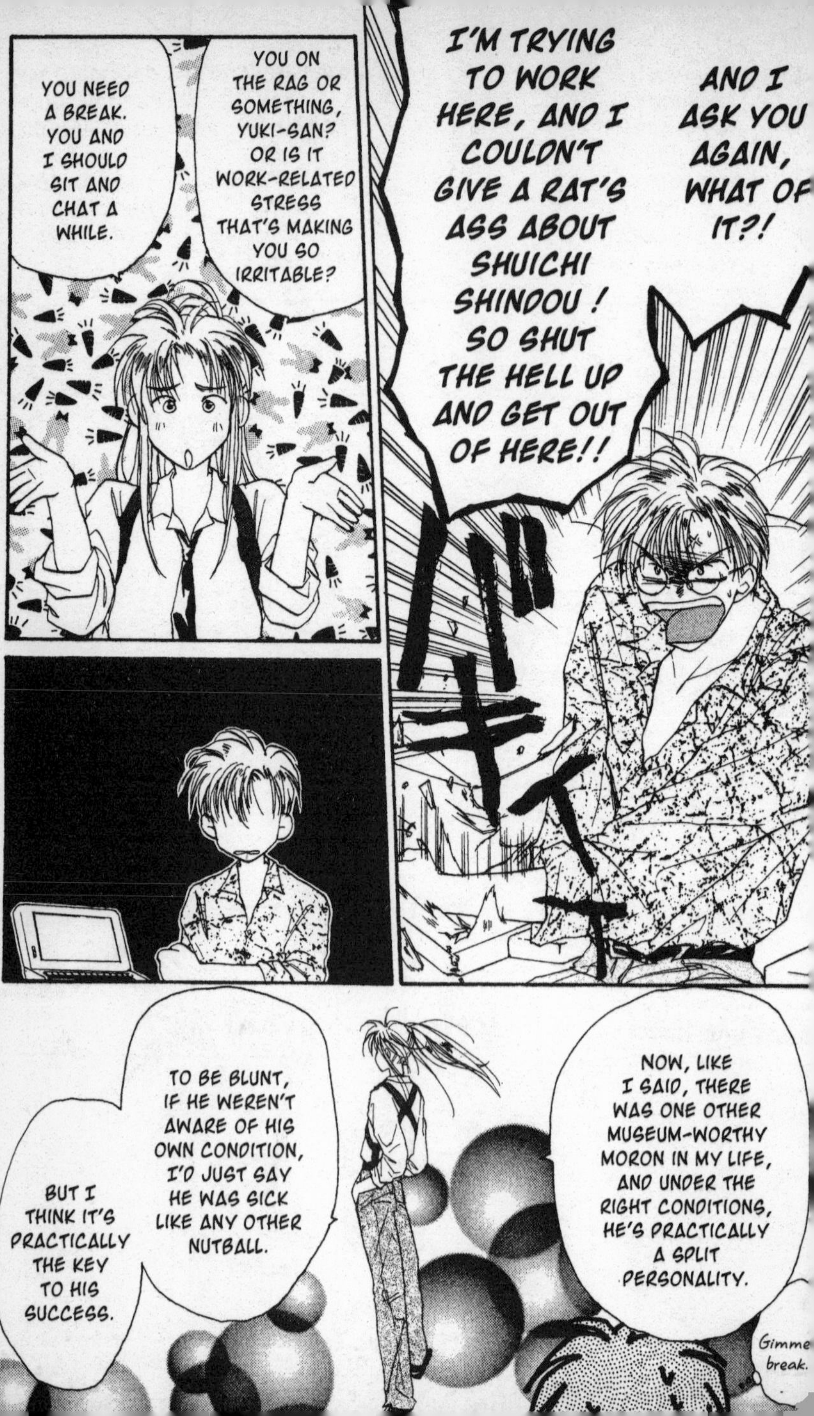
AND I ASK YOU AGAIN, WHAT OF IT?!
I'M TRYING TO WORK HERE, AND I COULDN'T GIVE A RAT'S ASS ABOUT SHUICHI SHINDOU! SO SHUT THE HELL UP AND GET OUT OF HERE!!
YOU ON THE RAG OR SOMETHING, YUKI-SAN? OR IS IT WORK-RELATED STRESS THAT'S MAKING YOU SO IRRITABLE?
YOU NEED A BREAK. YOU AND I SHOULD SIT AND CHAT A WHILE.
NOW, LIKE I SAID, THERE WAS ONE OTHER MUSEUM-WORTHY MORON IN MY LIFE, AND UNDER THE RIGHT CONDITIONS, HE'S PRACTICALLY A SPLIT PERSONALITY.
Gimme break.
TO BE BLUNT, IF HE WEREN'T AWARE OF HIS OWN CONDITION, I'D JUST SAY HE WAS SICK LIKE ANY OTHER NUTBALL.
BUT I THINK IT'S PRACTICALLY THE KEY TO HIS SUCCESS.

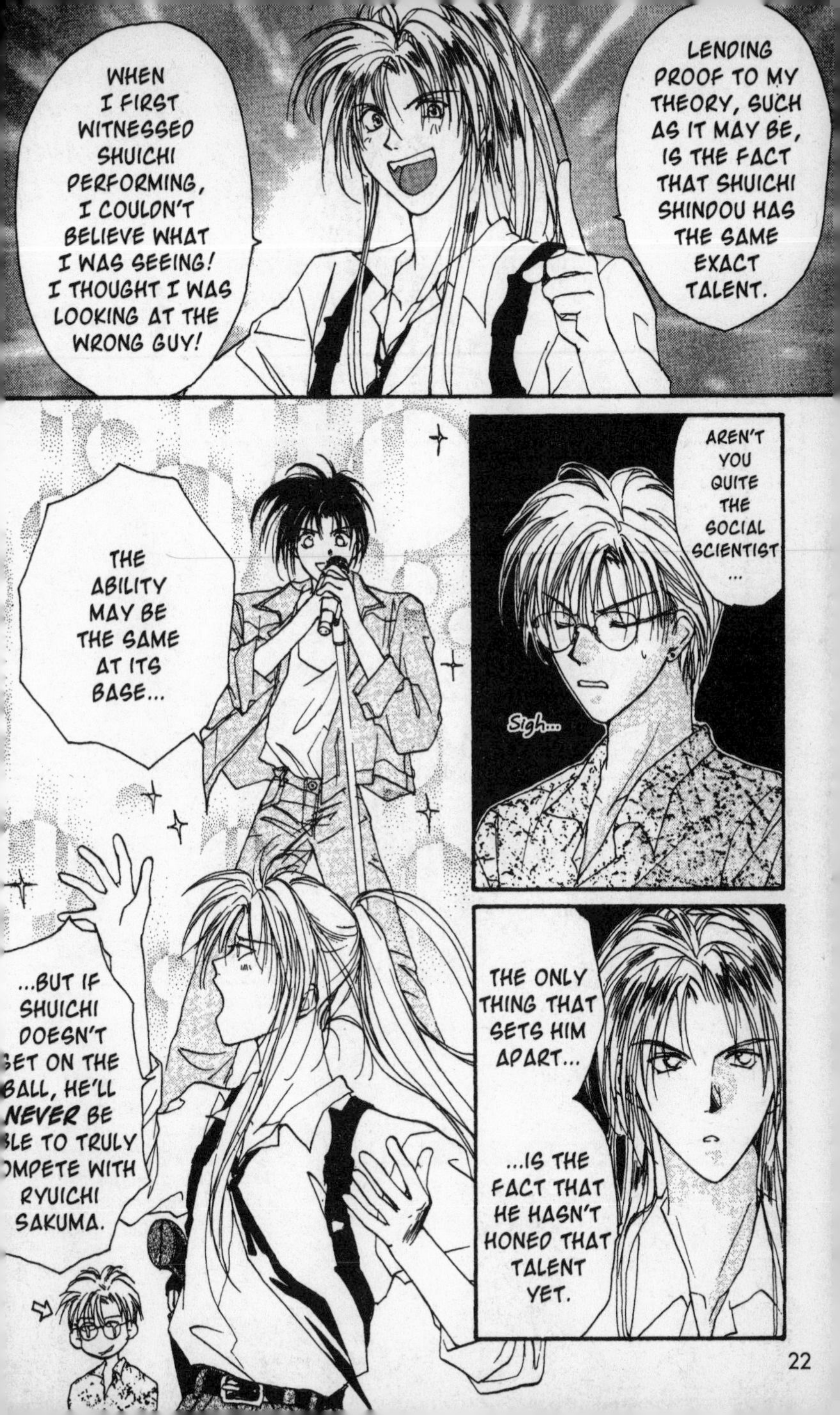
LENDING PROOF TO MY THEORY, SUCH AS IT MAY BE, IS THE FACT THAT SHUICHI SHINDOU HAS THE SAME EXACT TALENT.
WHEN I FIRST WITNESSED SHUICHI PERFORMING, I COULDN'T BELIEVE WHAT I WAS SEEING! I THOUGHT I WAS LOOKING AT THE WRONG GUY!
AREN'T YOU QUITE THE SOCIAL SCIENTIST ...
Sigh...
THE ONLY THING THAT SETS HIM APART...
...IS THE FACT THAT HE HASN'T HONED THAT TALENT YET.
THE ABILITY MAY BE THE SAME AT ITS BASE...
...BUT IF SHUICHI DOESN'T ET ON THE BALL, HE'LL *NEVER* BE BLE TO TRULY MPETE WITH RYUICHI SAKUMA.

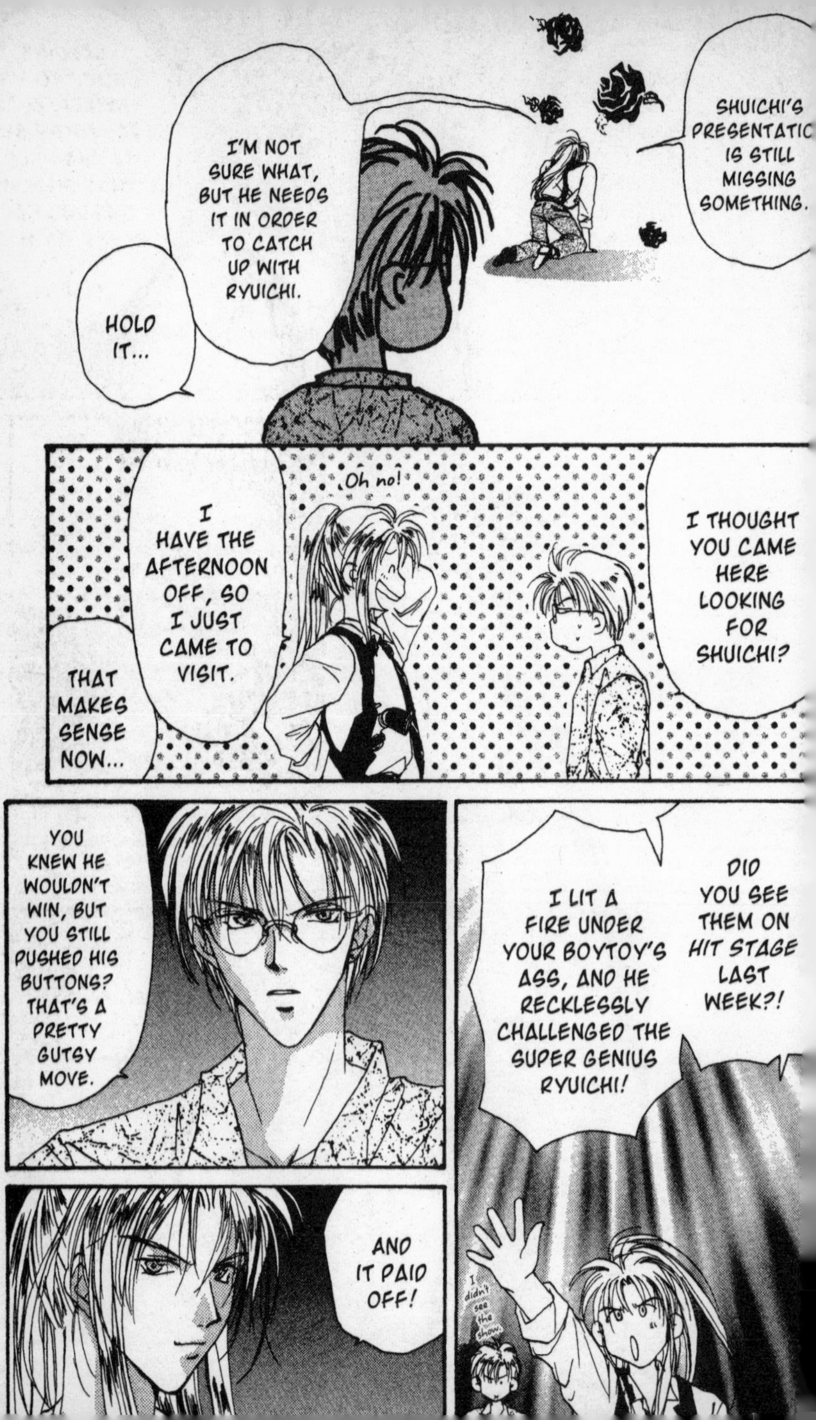
SHUICHI'S PRESENTATI IS STILL MISSING SOMETHING.
I'M NOT SURE WHAT, BUT HE NEEDS IT IN ORDER TO CATCH UP WITH RYUICHI.
HOLD IT...
I THOUGHT YOU CAME HERE LOOKING FOR SHUICHI?
Oh no!
I HAVE THE AFTERNOON OFF, SO I JUST CAME TO VISIT.
THAT MAKES SENSE NOW...
DID YOU SEE THEM ON HIT STAGE LAST WEEK?!
I LIT A FIRE UNDER YOUR BOYTOY'S ASS, AND HE RECKLESSLY CHALLENGED THE SUPER GENIUS RYUICHI!
I didn't see the show.
YOU KNEW HE WOULDN'T WIN, BUT YOU STILL PUSHED HIS BUTTONS? THAT'S A PRETTY GUTSY MOVE.
AND IT PAID OFF!

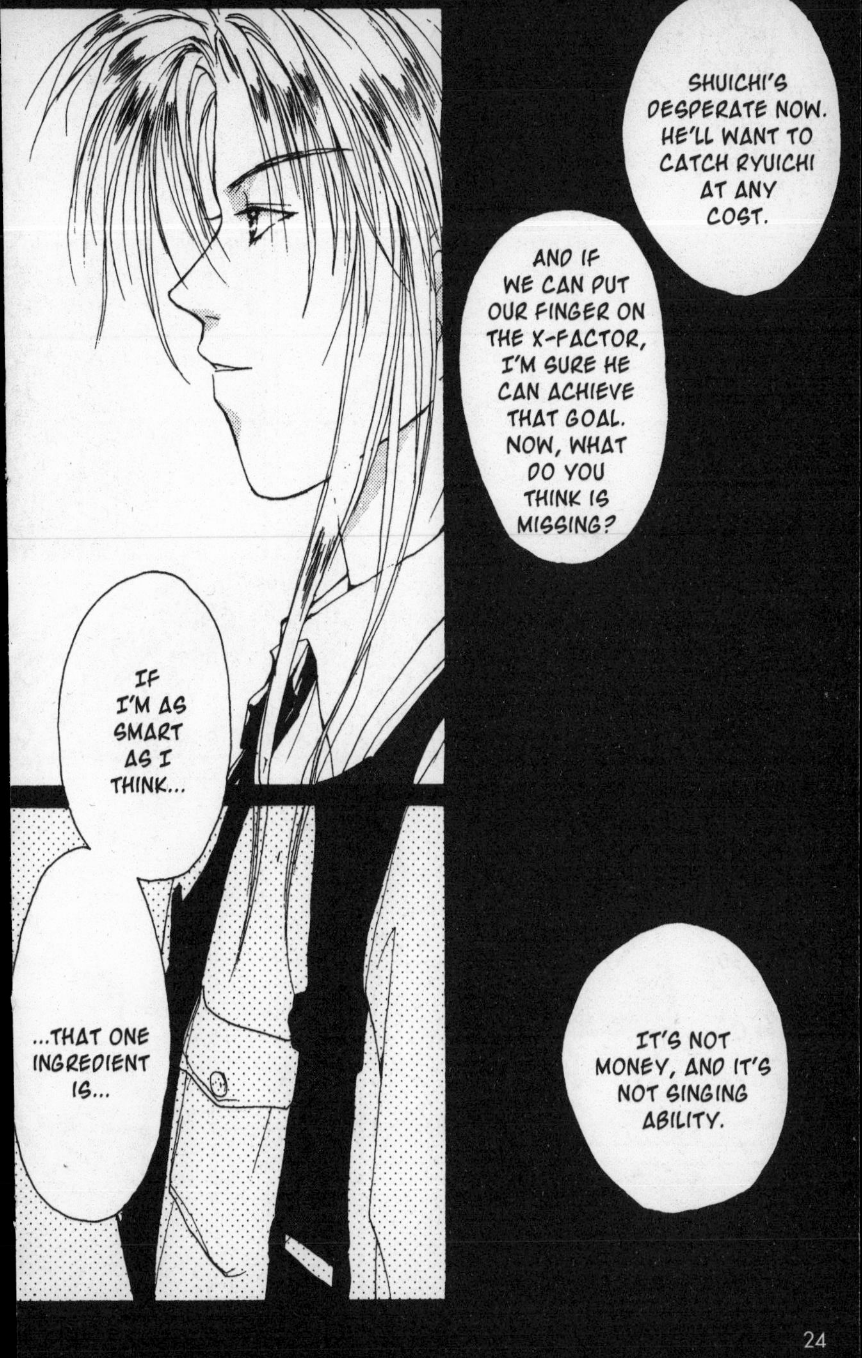
SHUICHI'S DESPERATE NOW. HE'LL WANT TO CATCH RYUICHI AT ANY COST.
AND IF WE CAN PUT OUR FINGER ON THE X-FACTOR, I'M SURE HE CAN ACHIEVE THAT GOAL. NOW, WHAT DO YOU THINK IS MISSING?
IF I'M AS SMART AS I THINK...
IT'S NOT MONEY, AND IT'S NOT SINGING ABILITY.
...THAT ONE INGREDIENT IS...

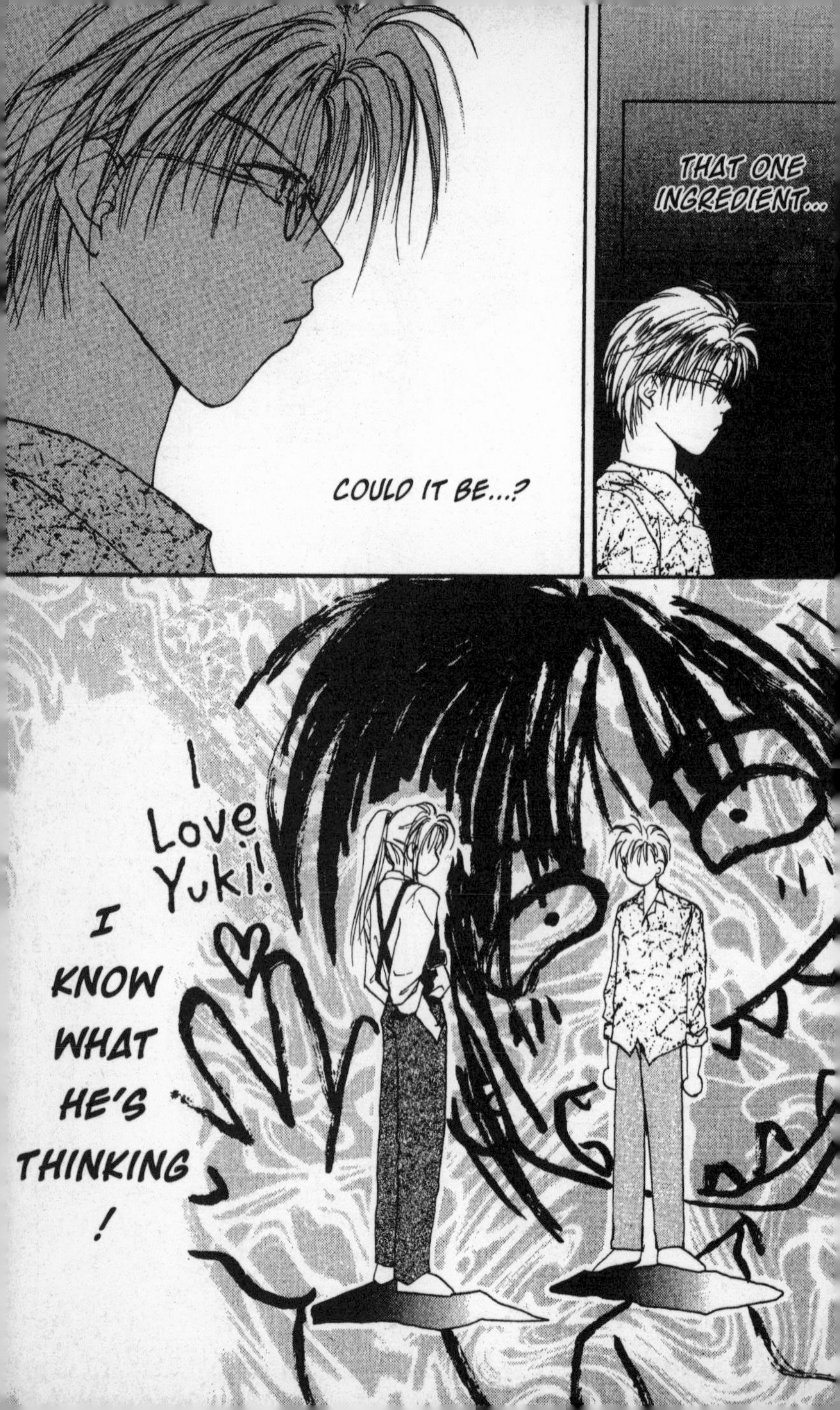
THAT ONE INGREDIENT...
COULD IT BE...?
I Love Yuki!
I KNOW WHAT HE'S THINKING!

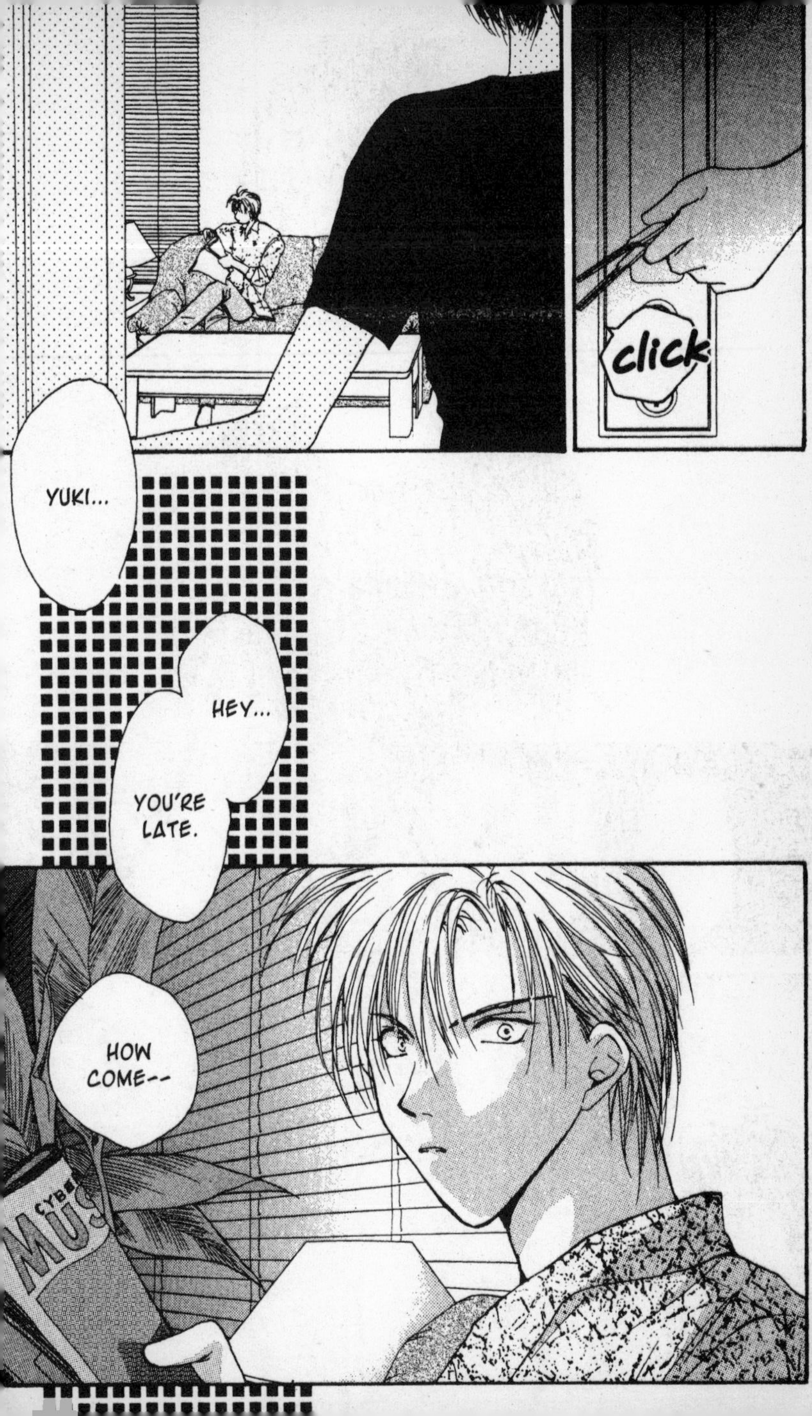
click
YUKI...
HEY...
YOU'RE LATE.
HOW COME--

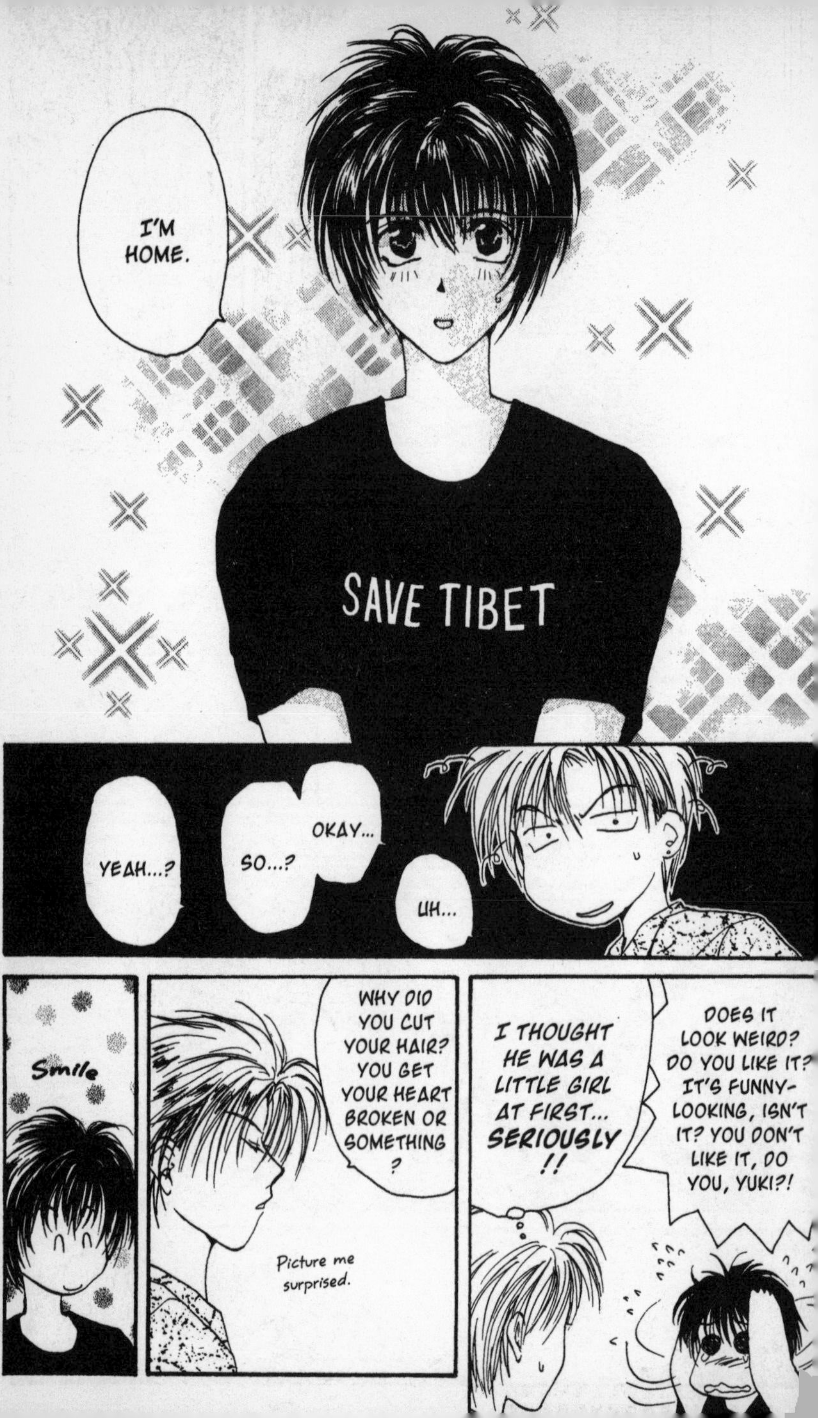
I'M HOME.
SAVE TIBET
UH...
OKAY...
SO...?
YEAH...?
DOES IT LOOK WEIRD? DO YOU LIKE IT? IT'S FUNNY-LOOKING, ISN'T IT? YOU DON'T LIKE IT, DO YOU, YUKI?!
I THOUGHT HE WAS A LITTLE GIRL AT FIRST... SERIOUSLY!!
WHY DID YOU CUT YOUR HAIR? YOU GET YOUR HEART BROKEN OR SOMETHING?
Picture me surprised.
Smile

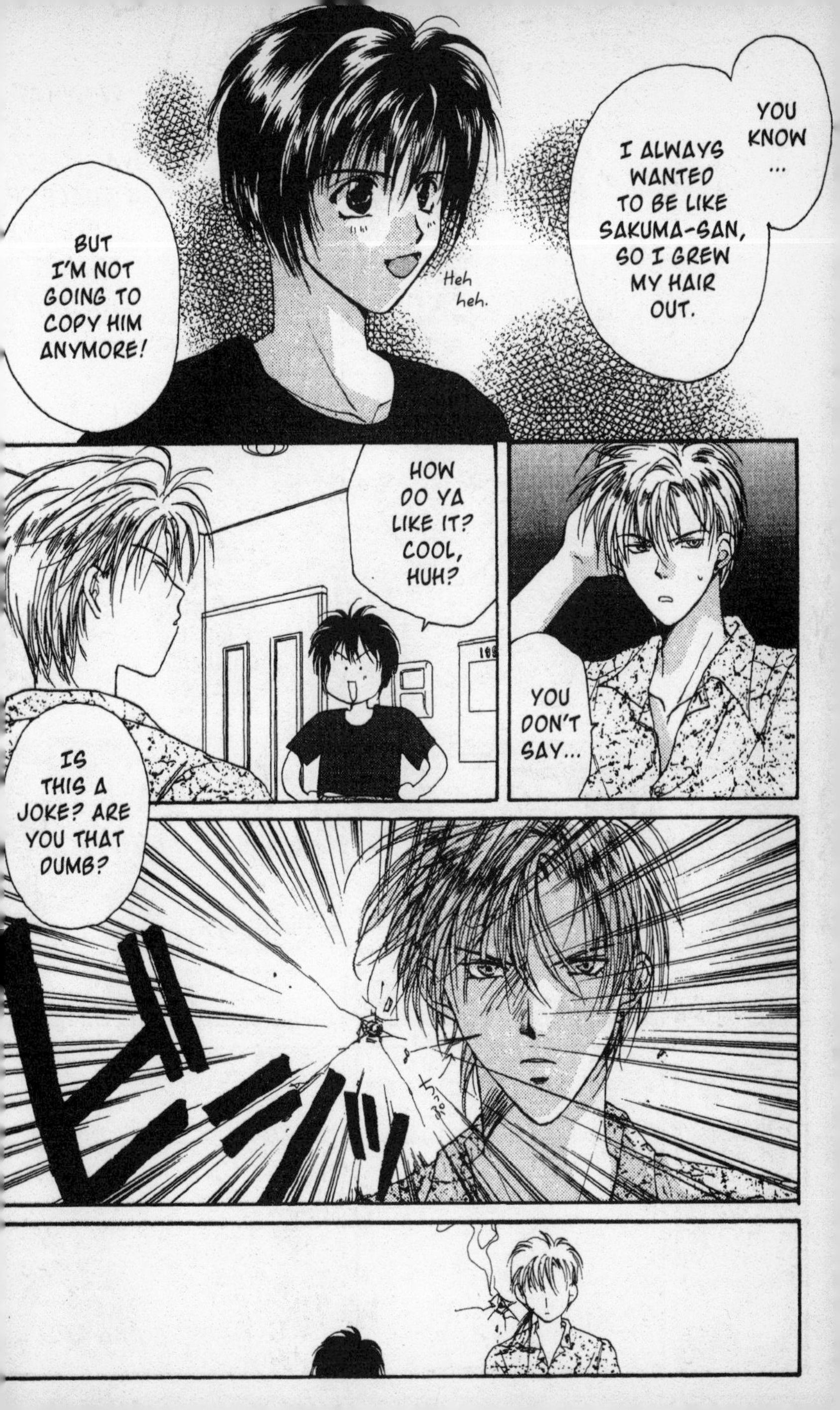

YOU KNOW ...
I ALWAYS WANTED TO BE LIKE SAKUMA-SAN, SO I GREW MY HAIR OUT.
Heh heh.
BUT I'M NOT GOING TO COPY HIM ANYMORE!
YOU DON'T SAY...
HOW DO YA LIKE IT? COOL, HUH?
IS THIS A JOKE? ARE YOU THAT DUMB?

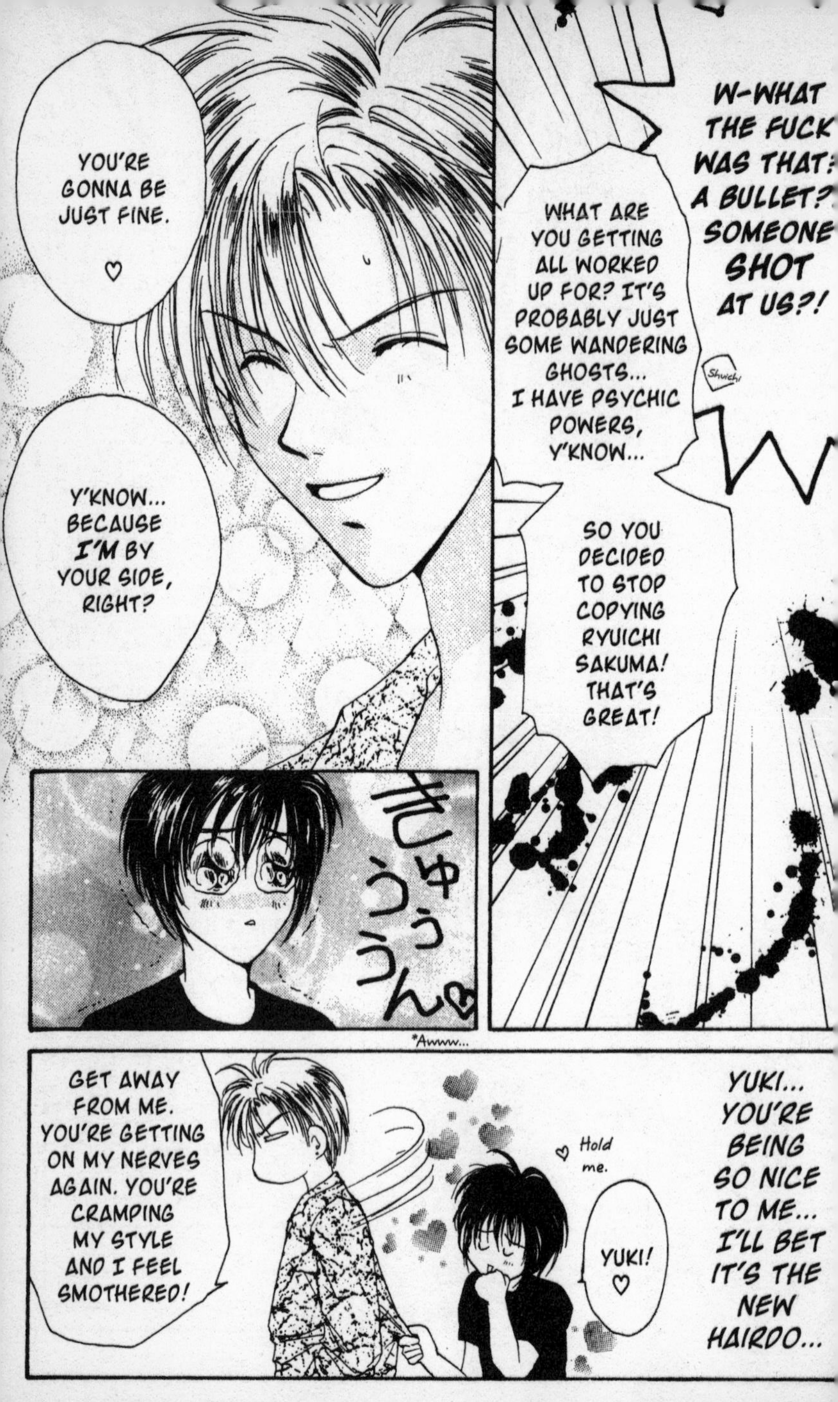
W-WHAT THE FUCK WAS THAT? A BULLET? SOMEONE SHOT AT US?!
Shuichi
WHAT ARE YOU GETTING ALL WORKED UP FOR? IT'S PROBABLY JUST SOME WANDERING GHOSTS... I HAVE PSYCHIC POWERS, Y'KNOW...
SO YOU DECIDED TO STOP COPYING RYUICHI SAKUMA! THAT'S GREAT!
YOU'RE GONNA BE JUST FINE. ♡
Y'KNOW... BECAUSE I'M BY YOUR SIDE, RIGHT?
きゅううん♡
*Awww...
YUKI... YOU'RE BEING SO NICE TO ME... I'LL BET IT'S THE NEW HAIRDO...
♡ Hold me.
YUKI! ♡
GET AWAY FROM ME. YOU'RE GETTING ON MY NERVES AGAIN. YOU'RE CRAMPING MY STYLE AND I FEEL SMOTHERED!

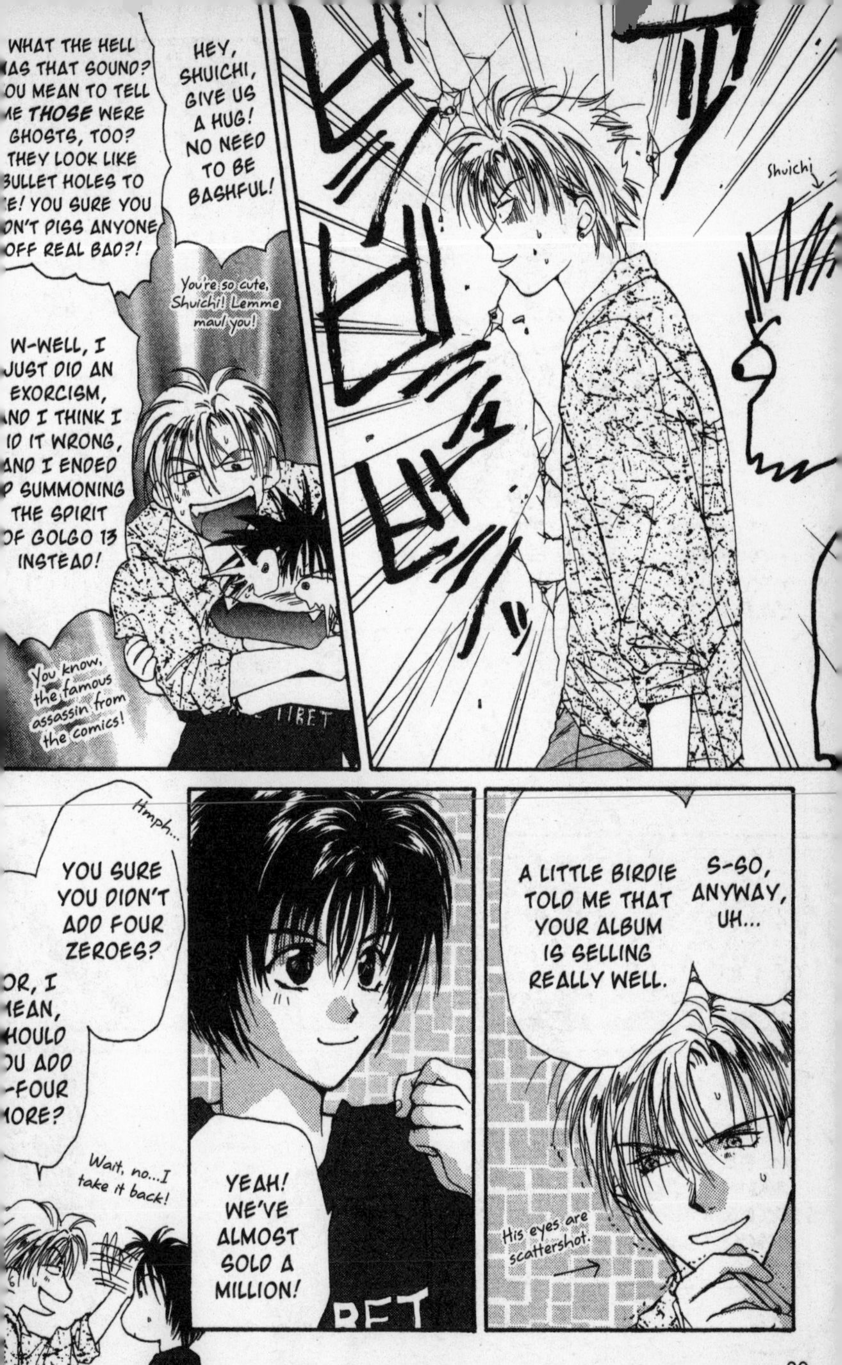
Shuichi
HEY, SHUICHI, GIVE US A HUG! NO NEED TO BE BASHFUL!
WHAT THE HELL AS THAT SOUND? OU MEAN TO TELL E THOSE WERE GHOSTS, TOO? THEY LOOK LIKE ULLET HOLES TO E! YOU SURE YOU N'T PISS ANYONE OFF REAL BAD?!
You're so cute, Shuichi! Lemme maul you!
W-WELL, I JUST DID AN EXORCISM, ND I THINK I ID IT WRONG, AND I ENDED P SUMMONING THE SPIRIT OF GOLGO 13 INSTEAD!
You know, the famous assassin from the comics!
S-SO, ANYWAY, UH...
A LITTLE BIRDIE TOLD ME THAT YOUR ALBUM IS SELLING REALLY WELL.
His eyes are scattershot.
YEAH! WE'VE ALMOST SOLD A MILLION!
Hmph...
YOU SURE YOU DIDN'T ADD FOUR ZEROES?
R, I EAN, HOULD U ADD -FOUR ORE?
Wait, no...I take it back!

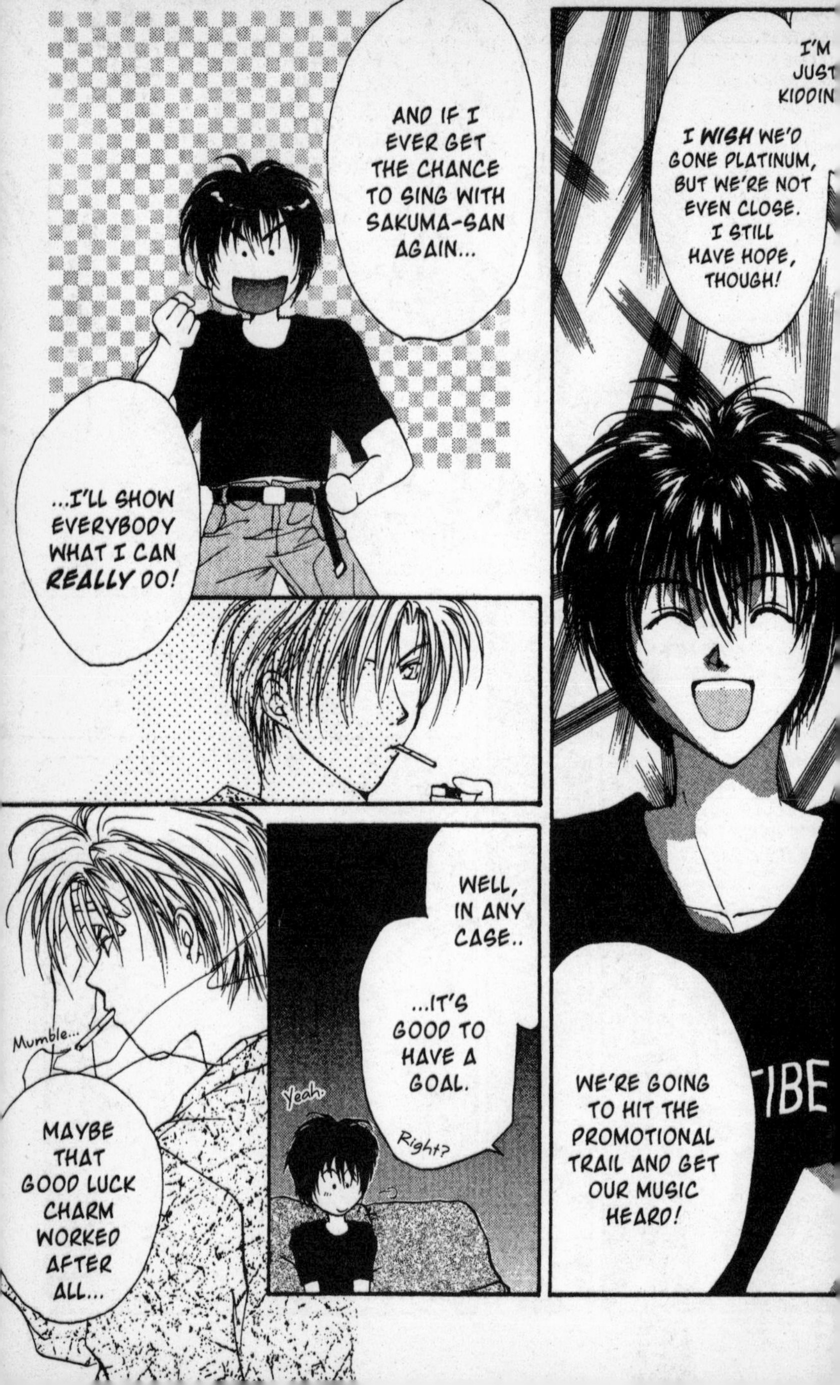
I'M JUST KIDDIN
I WISH WE'D GONE PLATINUM, BUT WE'RE NOT EVEN CLOSE. I STILL HAVE HOPE, THOUGH!
WE'RE GOING TO HIT THE PROMOTIONAL TRAIL AND GET OUR MUSIC HEARD!
AND IF I EVER GET THE CHANCE TO SING WITH SAKUMA-SAN AGAIN...
...I'LL SHOW EVERYBODY WHAT I CAN REALLY DO!
WELL, IN ANY CASE..
...IT'S GOOD TO HAVE A GOAL.
Right?
Yeah.
Mumble...
MAYBE THAT GOOD LUCK CHARM WORKED AFTER ALL...

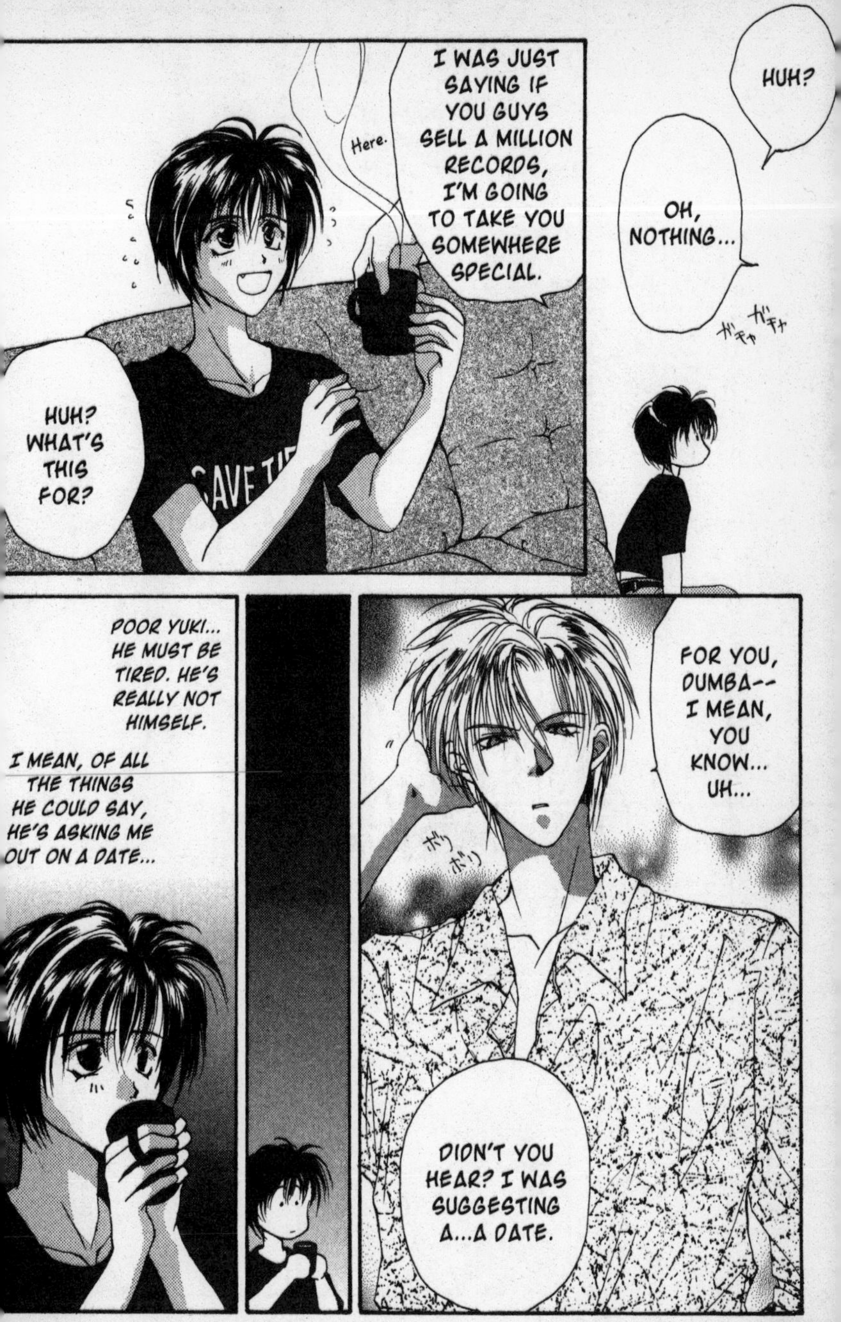

HUH?
OH, NOTHING...
ガチャガチャ
I WAS JUST SAYING IF YOU GUYS SELL A MILLION RECORDS, I'M GOING TO TAKE YOU SOMEWHERE SPECIAL.
Here.
HUH? WHAT'S THIS FOR?
SAVE TH
FOR YOU, DUMBA-- I MEAN, YOU KNOW... UH...
ボリボリ
DIDN'T YOU HEAR? I WAS SUGGESTING A...A DATE.
POOR YUKI... HE MUST BE TIRED. HE'S REALLY NOT HIMSELF.
I MEAN, OF ALL THE THINGS HE COULD SAY, HE'S ASKING ME OUT ON A DATE...

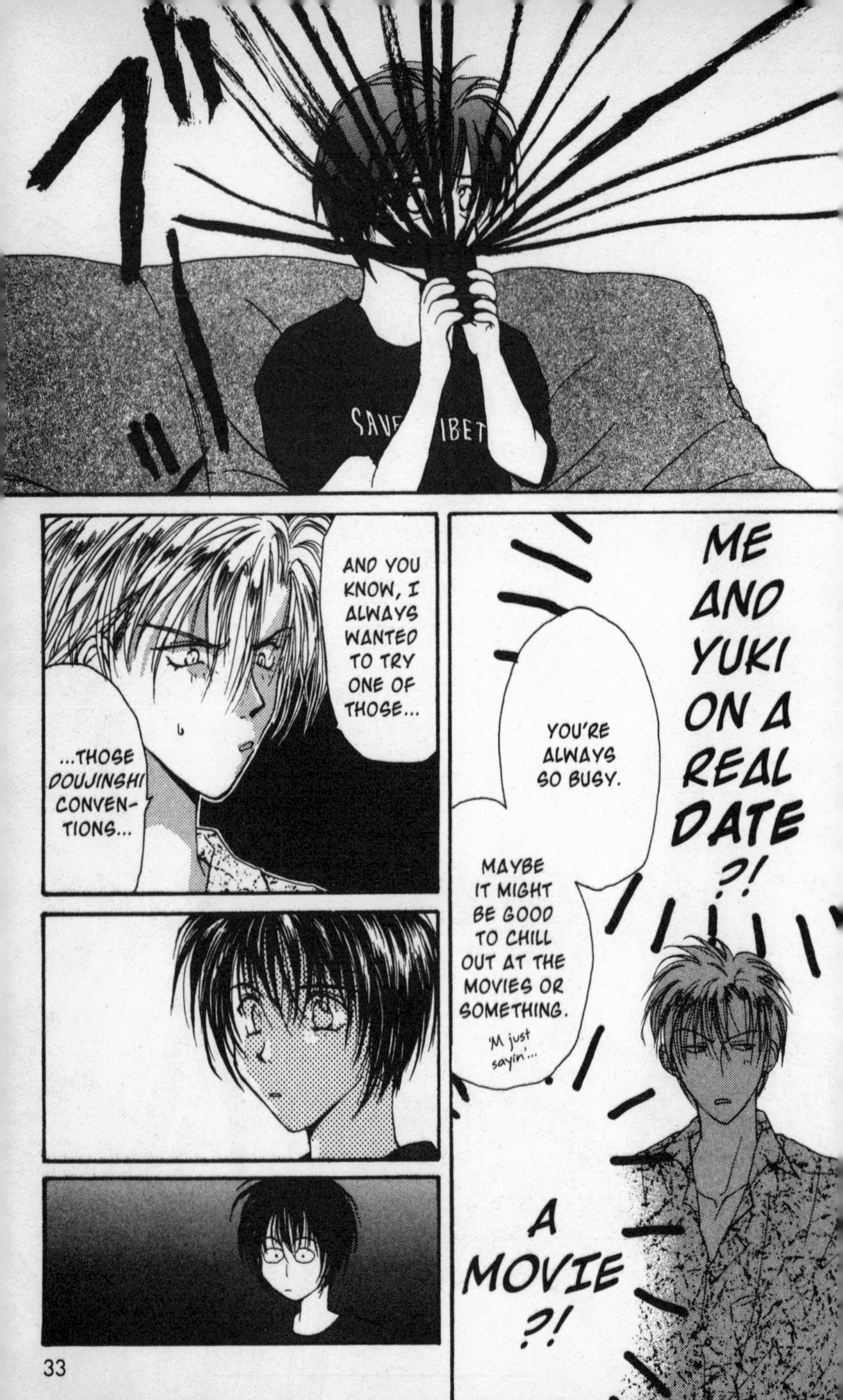
ME AND YUKI ON A REAL DATE ?!
YOU'RE ALWAYS SO BUSY.
MAYBE IT MIGHT BE GOOD TO CHILL OUT AT THE MOVIES OR SOMETHING.
'M just sayin'...
A MOVIE ?!
AND YOU KNOW, I ALWAYS WANTED TO TRY ONE OF THOSE...
...THOSE DOUJINSHI CONVEN- TIONS...

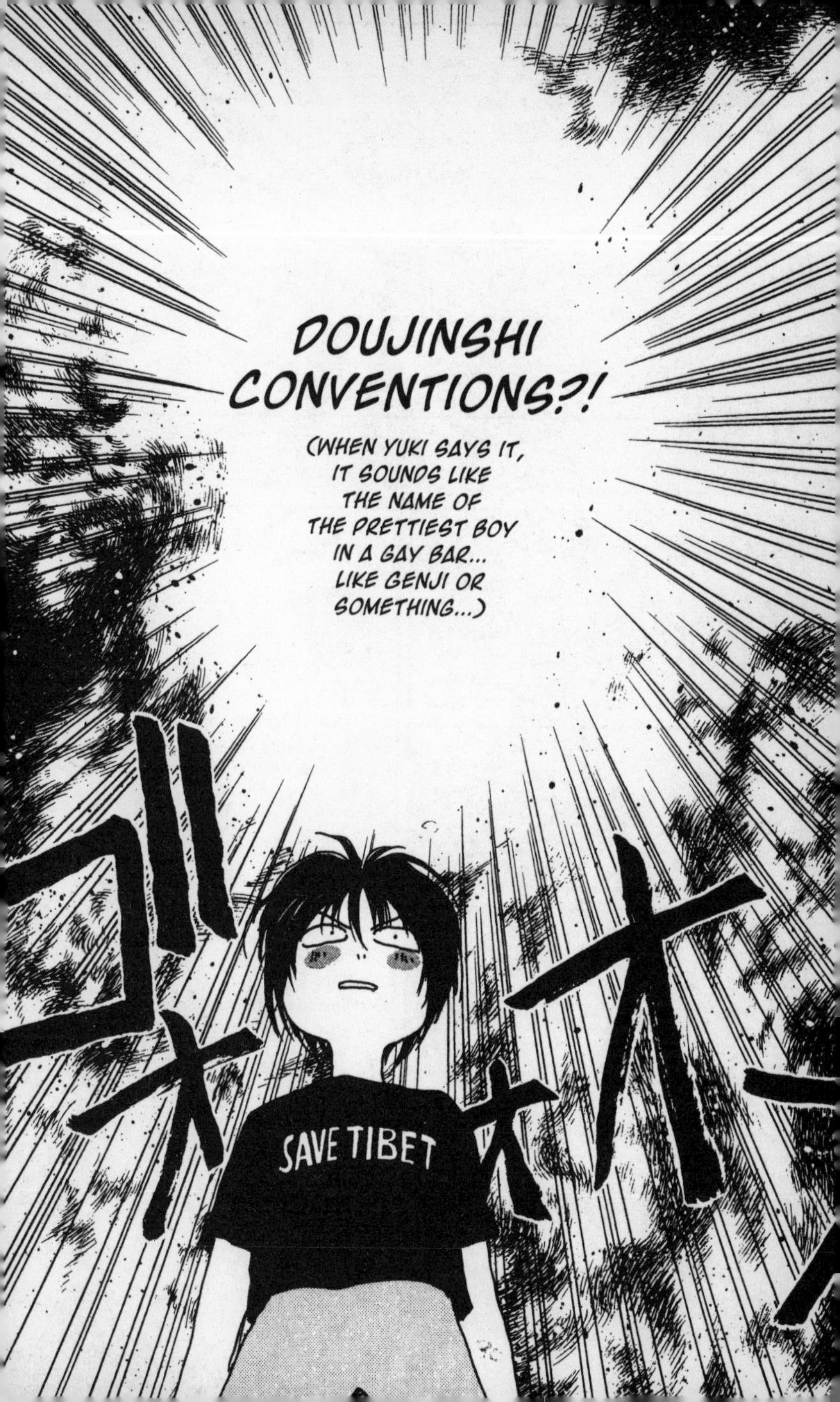
DOUJINSHI CONVENTIONS?!
(WHEN YUKI SAYS IT, IT SOUNDS LIKE THE NAME OF THE PRETTIEST BOY IN A GAY BAR... LIKE GENJI OR SOMETHING...)
SAVE TIBET

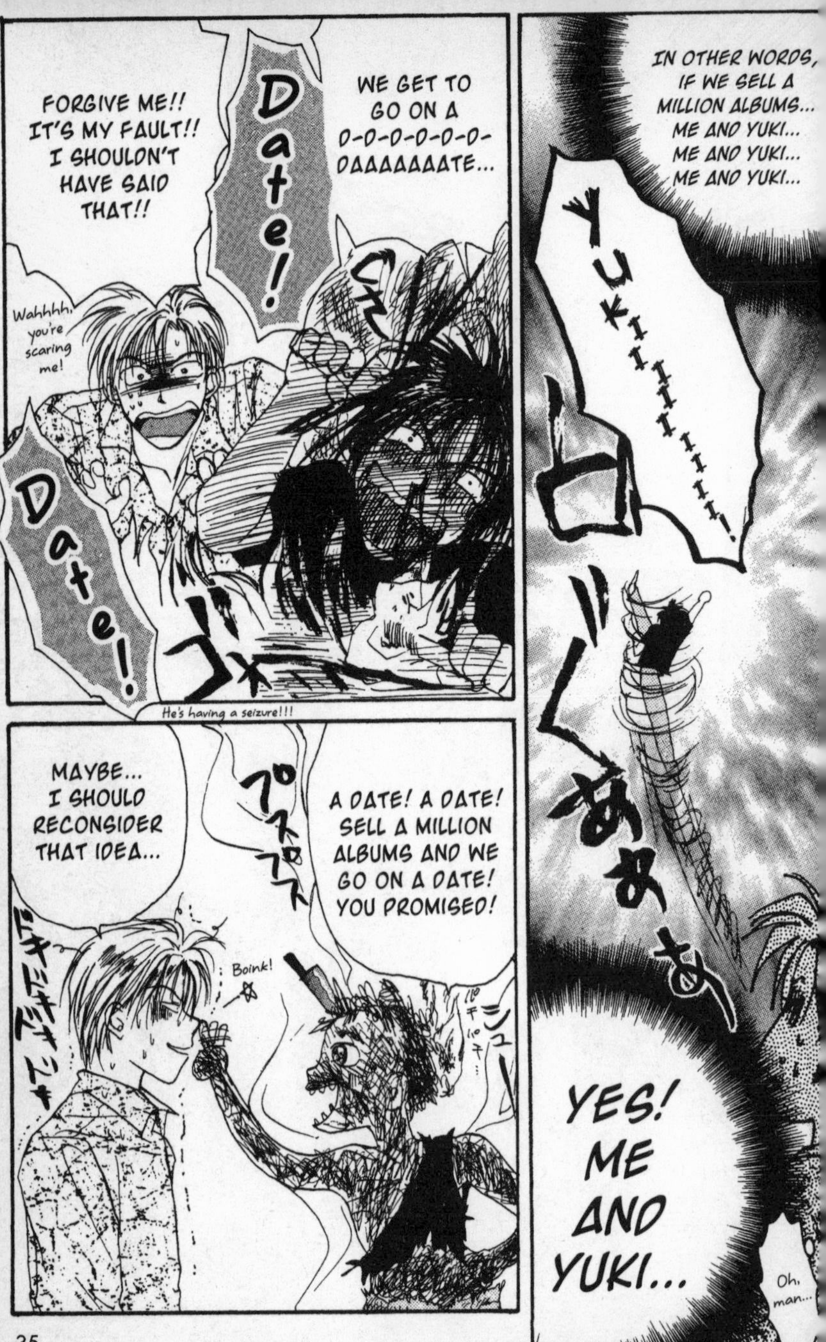
IN OTHER WORDS, IF WE SELL A MILLION ALBUMS... ME AND YUKI... ME AND YUKI... ME AND YUKI...
YUKIIIIIIIIIII!
YES! ME AND YUKI...
Oh, man...
WE GET TO GO ON A D-D-D-D-D-D-DAAAAAAAATE...
Date!
FORGIVE ME!! IT'S MY FAULT!! I SHOULDN'T HAVE SAID THAT!!
Wahhhh, you're scaring me!
Date!
He's having a seizure!!!
A DATE! A DATE! SELL A MILLION ALBUMS AND WE GO ON A DATE! YOU PROMISED!
MAYBE... I SHOULD RECONSIDER THAT IDEA...
Boink!

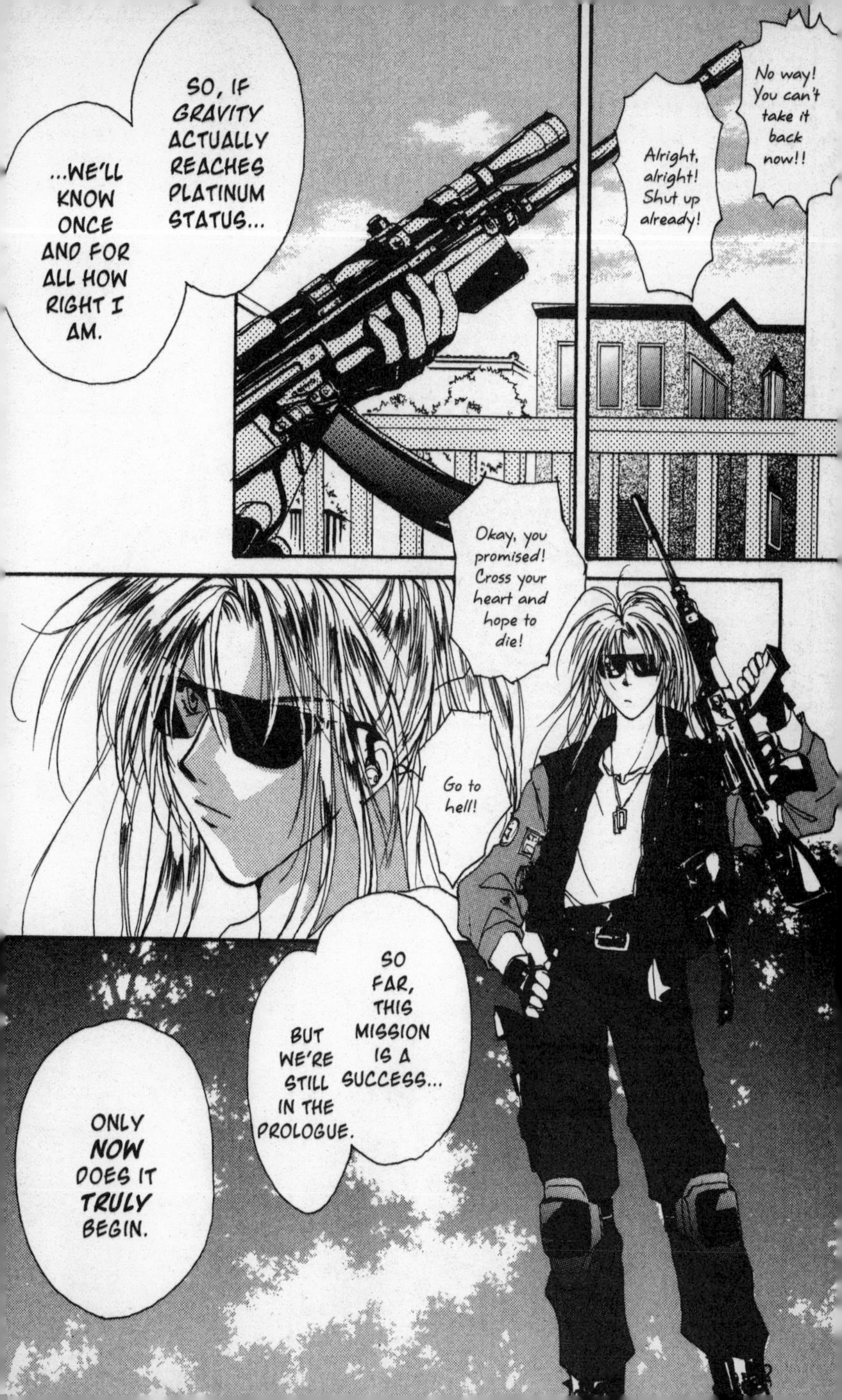
No way! You can't take it back now!!
Alright, alright! Shut up already!
SO, IF GRAVITY ACTUALLY REACHES PLATINUM STATUS...
...WE'LL KNOW ONCE AND FOR ALL HOW RIGHT I AM.
Okay, you promised! Cross your heart and hope to die!
Go to hell!
SO FAR, THIS MISSION IS A SUCCESS...
BUT WE'RE STILL IN THE PROLOGUE.
ONLY NOW DOES IT TRULY BEGIN.

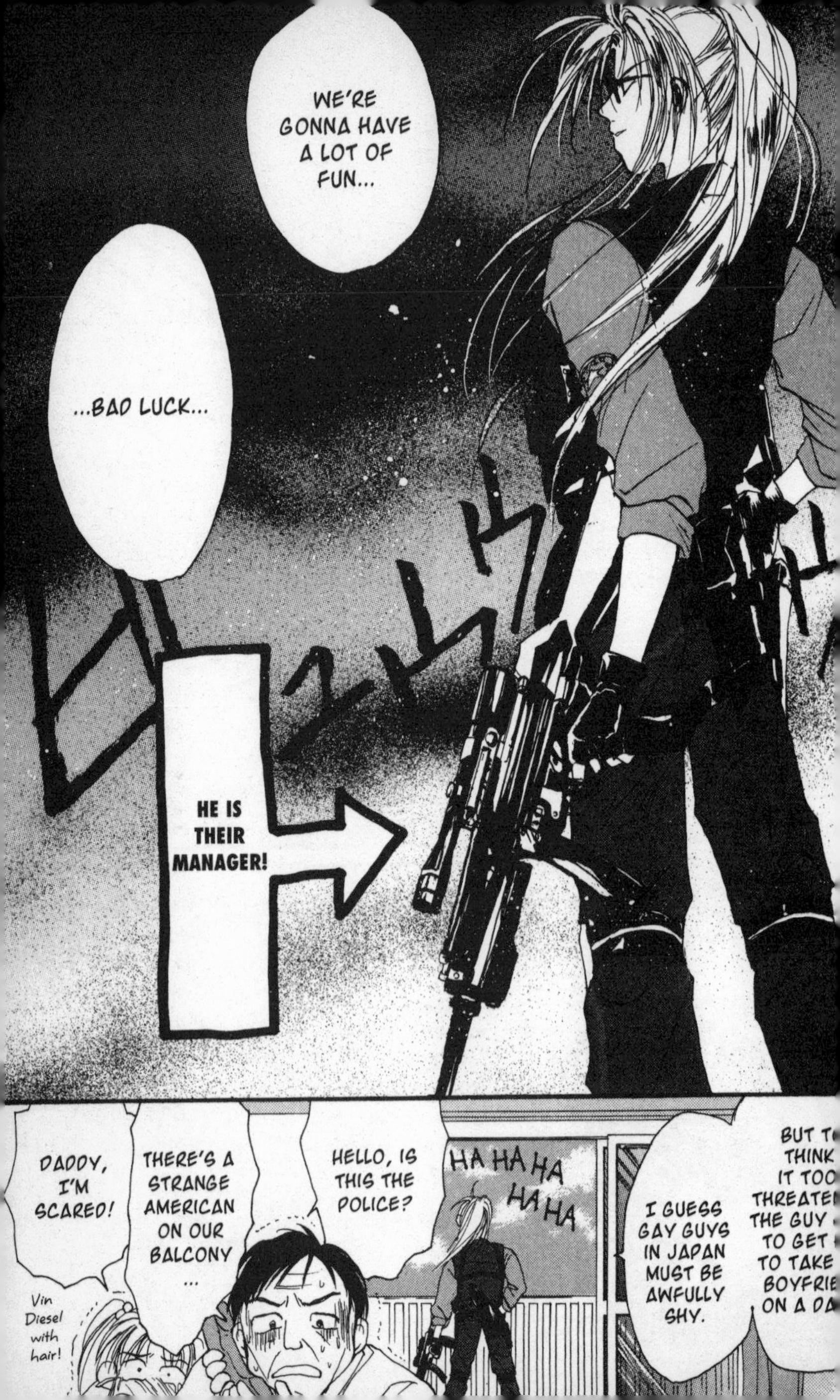
WE'RE GONNA HAVE A LOT OF FUN...
...BAD LUCK...
HE IS THEIR MANAGER!
BUT T THINK IT TOO THREATE THE GUY TO GET TO TAKE BOYFRIE ON A DA
I GUESS GAY GUYS IN JAPAN MUST BE AWFULLY SHY.
HA HA HA HA HA
HELLO, IS THIS THE POLICE?
THERE'S A STRANGE AMERICAN ON OUR BALCONY ...
DADDY, I'M SCARED!
Vin Diesel with hair!

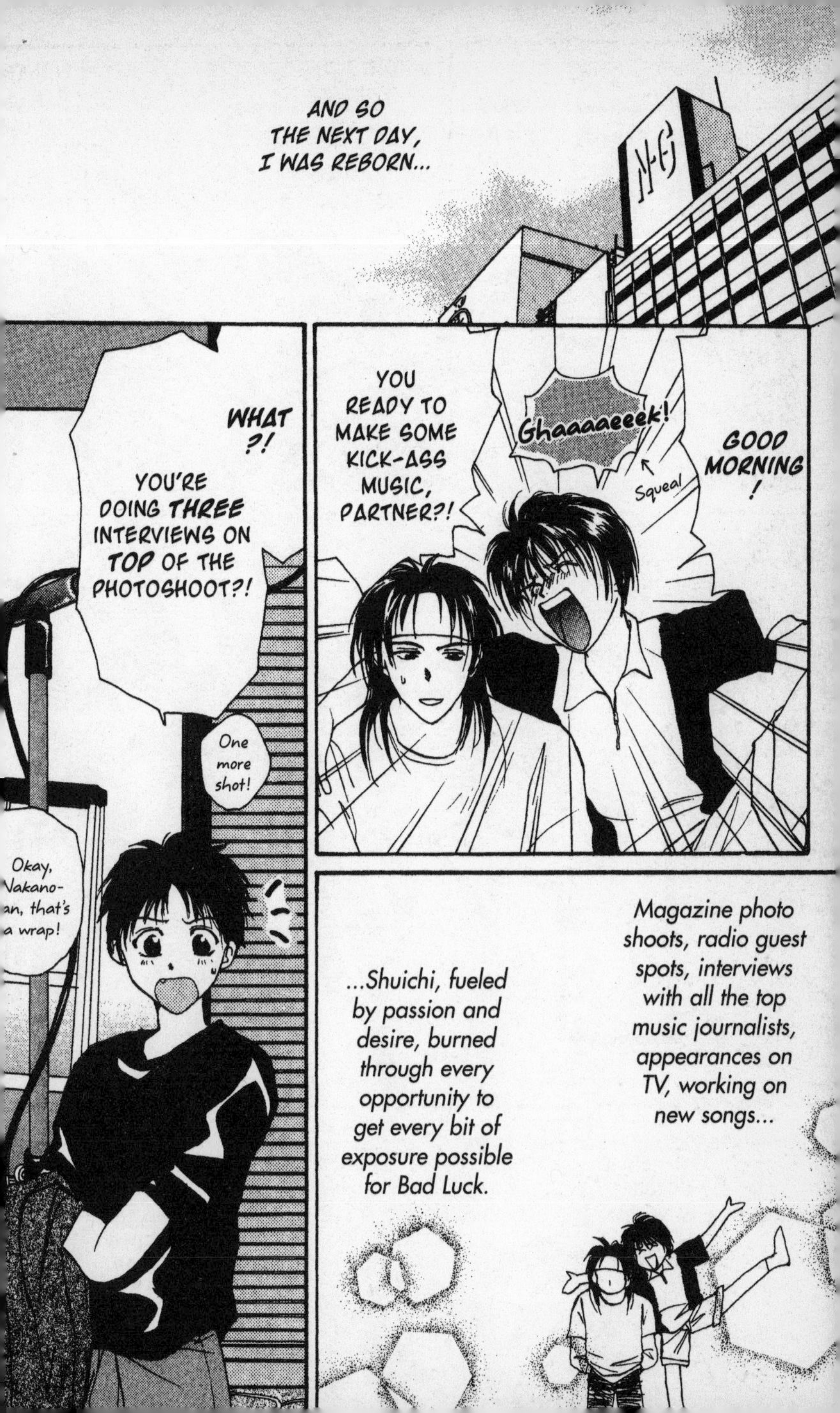
AND SO THE NEXT DAY, I WAS REBORN...
GOOD MORNING!
Ghaaaaeeek!
Squeal
YOU READY TO MAKE SOME KICK-ASS MUSIC, PARTNER?!
Magazine photo shoots, radio guest spots, interviews with all the top music journalists, appearances on TV, working on new songs...
...Shuichi, fueled by passion and desire, burned through every opportunity to get every bit of exposure possible for Bad Luck.
WHAT?!
YOU'RE DOING THREE INTERVIEWS ON TOP OF THE PHOTOSHOOT?!
One more shot!
Okay, Nakano- an, that's a wrap!

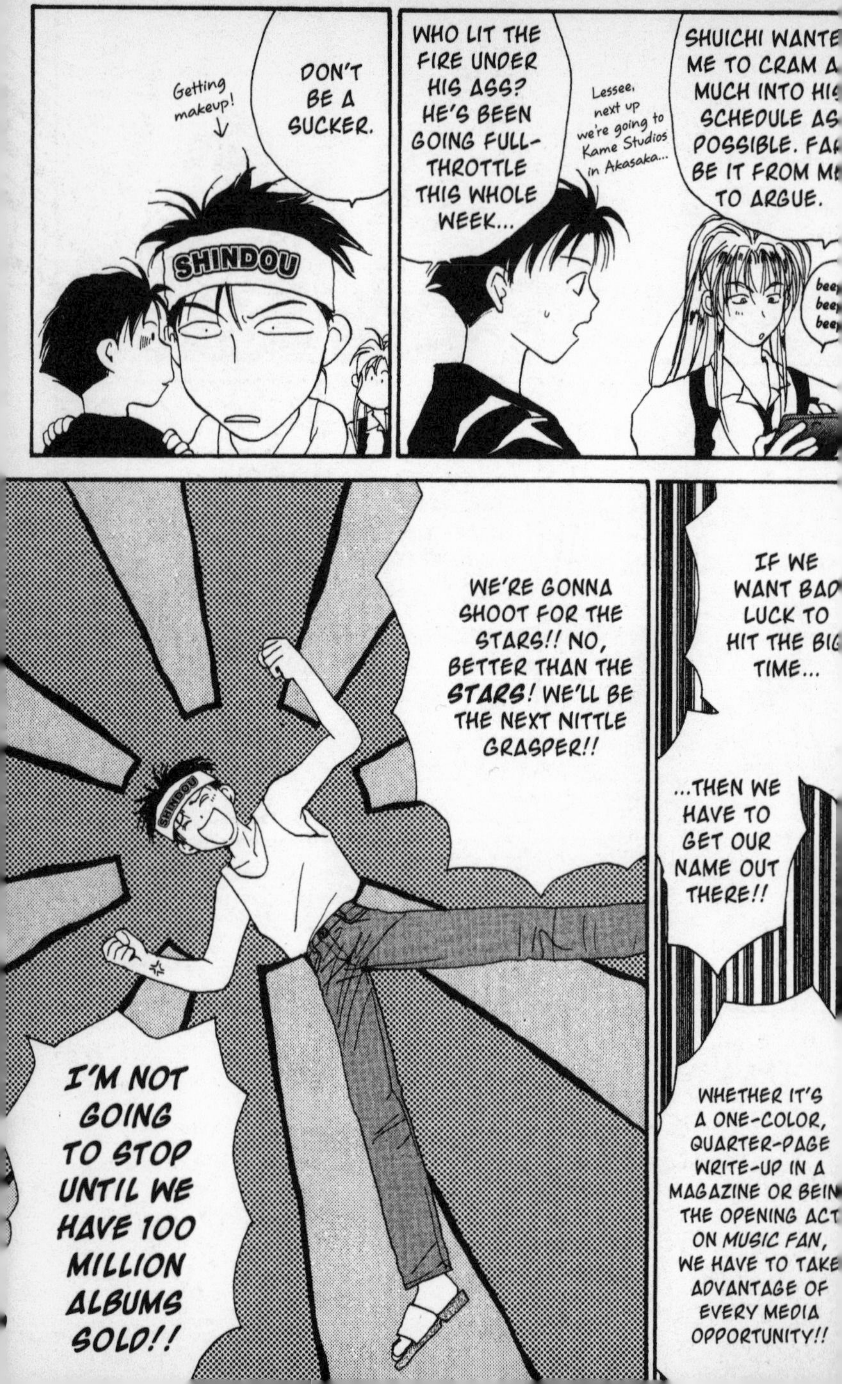
SHUICHI WANTE ME TO CRAM A MUCH INTO HI SCHEDULE AS POSSIBLE. FA BE IT FROM M TO ARGUE.
bee bee bee
Lessee, next up we're going to Kame Studios in Akasaka...
WHO LIT THE FIRE UNDER HIS ASS? HE'S BEEN GOING FULL-THROTTLE THIS WHOLE WEEK...
DON'T BE A SUCKER.
Getting makeup!
SHINDOU
IF WE WANT BAD LUCK TO HIT THE BI TIME...
...THEN WE HAVE TO GET OUR NAME OUT THERE!!
WHETHER IT'S A ONE-COLOR, QUARTER-PAGE WRITE-UP IN A MAGAZINE OR BEIN THE OPENING AC ON MUSIC FAN, WE HAVE TO TAK ADVANTAGE OF EVERY MEDIA OPPORTUNITY!!
WE'RE GONNA SHOOT FOR THE STARS!! NO, BETTER THAN THE STARS! WE'LL BE THE NEXT NITTLE GRASPER!!
SHINDOU
I'M NOT GOING TO STOP UNTIL WE HAVE 100 MILLION ALBUMS SOLD!!

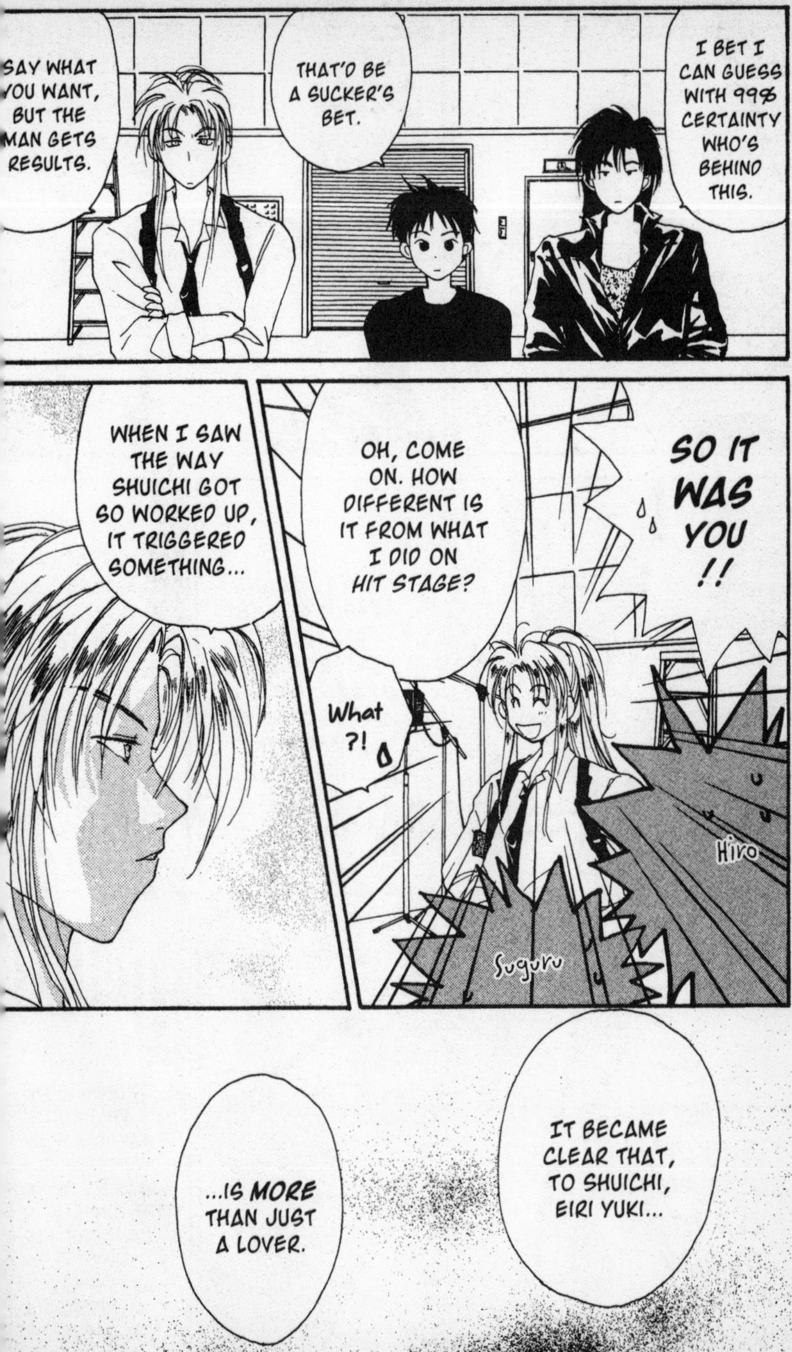
I BET I CAN GUESS WITH 99% CERTAINTY WHO'S BEHIND THIS.
THAT'D BE A SUCKER'S BET.
SAY WHAT YOU WANT, BUT THE MAN GETS RESULTS.
SO IT WAS YOU!!
OH, COME ON. HOW DIFFERENT IS IT FROM WHAT I DID ON HIT STAGE?
What?!
Hiro
Suguru
WHEN I SAW THE WAY SHUICHI GOT SO WORKED UP, IT TRIGGERED SOMETHING...
IT BECAME CLEAR THAT, TO SHUICHI, EIRI YUKI...
...IS **MORE** THAN JUST A LOVER.

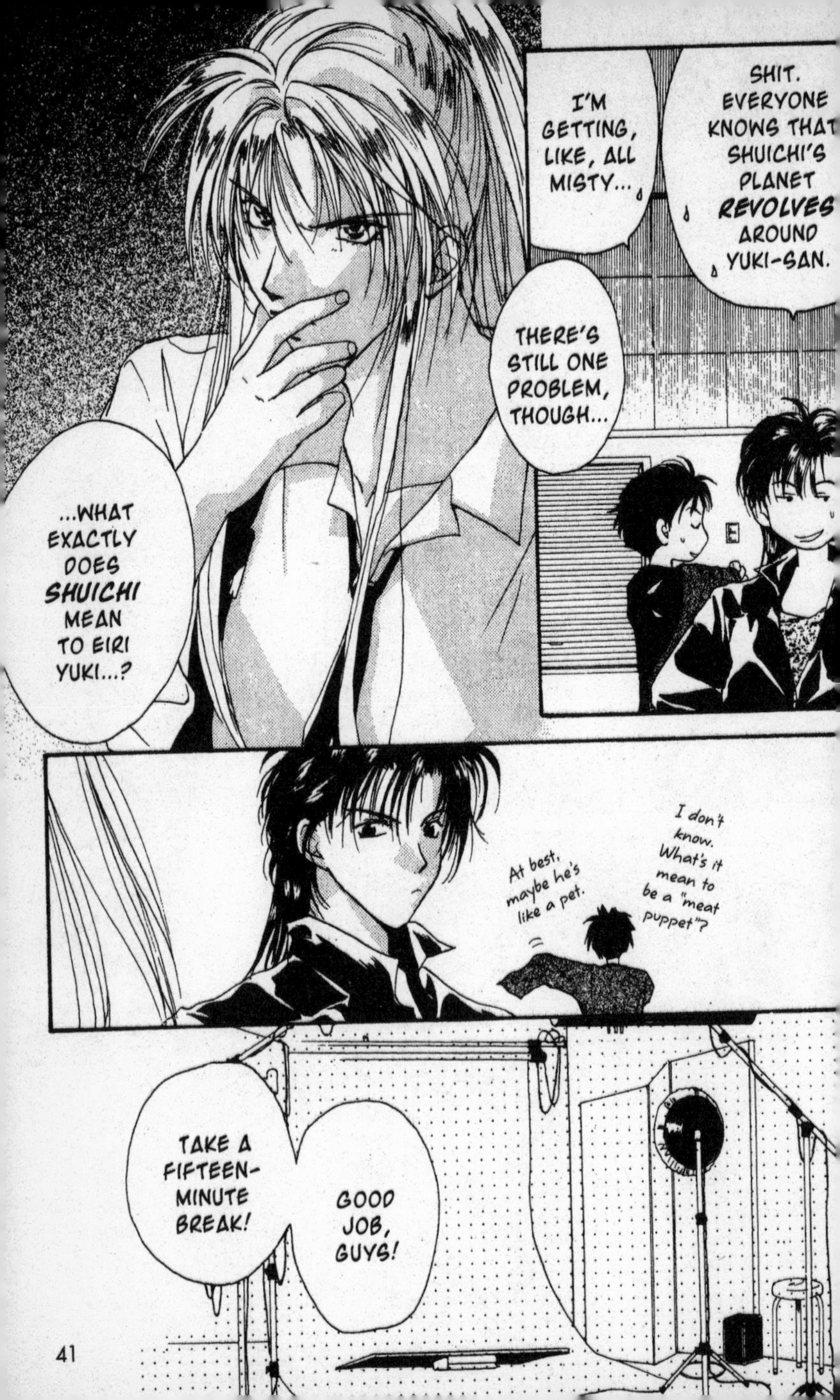

SHIT. EVERYONE KNOWS THAT SHUICHI'S PLANET **REVOLVES** AROUND YUKI-SAN.
I'M GETTING, LIKE, ALL MISTY...
THERE'S STILL ONE PROBLEM, THOUGH...
...WHAT EXACTLY DOES **SHUICHI** MEAN TO EIRI YUKI...?
I don't know. What's it mean to be a "meat puppet"?
At best, maybe he's like a pet.
TAKE A FIFTEEN-MINUTE BREAK!
GOOD JOB, GUYS!

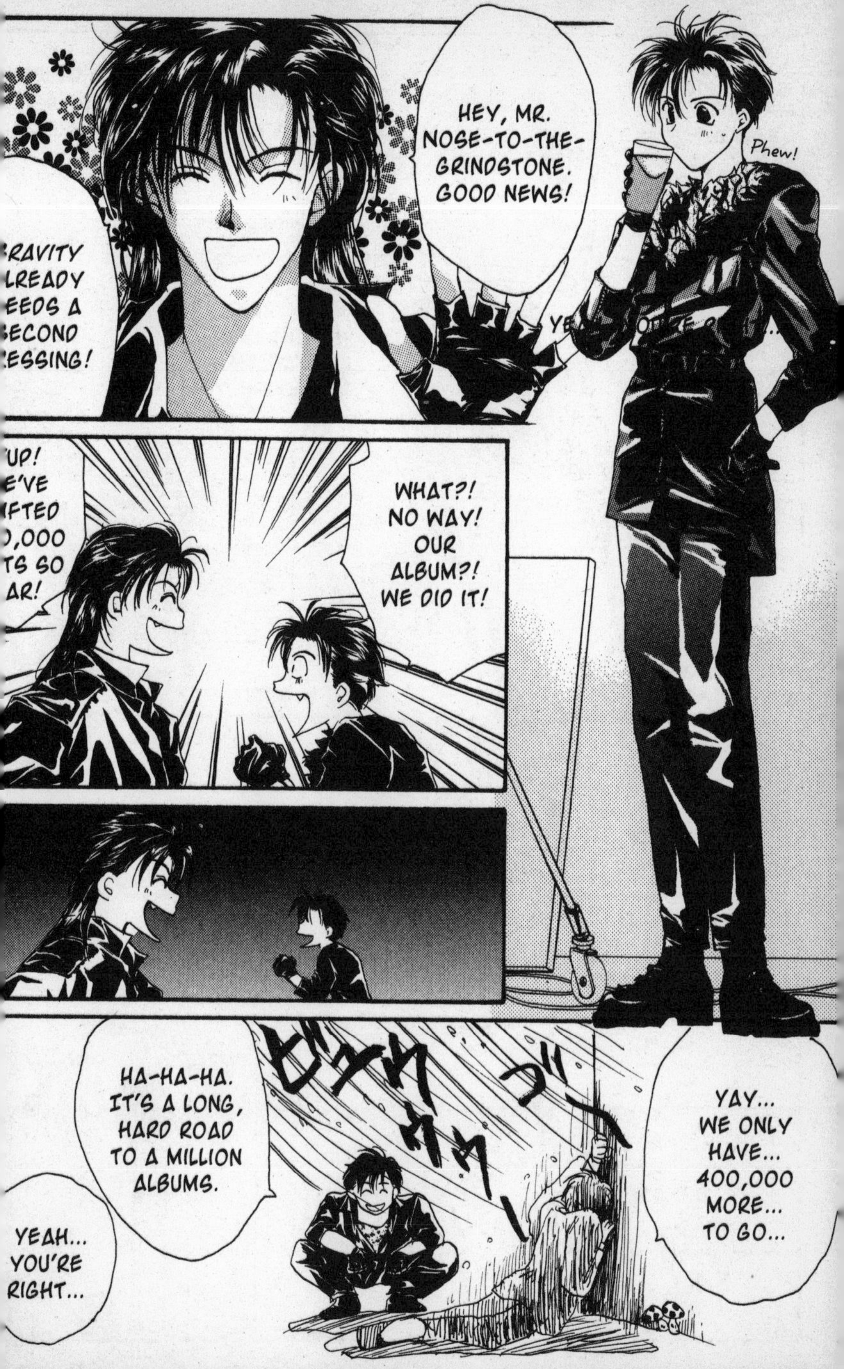

Phew!
HEY, MR. NOSE-TO-THE-GRINDSTONE. GOOD NEWS!
RAVITY LREADY EEDS A ECOND ESSING!
WHAT?! NO WAY! OUR ALBUM?! WE DID IT!
UP! E'VE IFTED ,000 TS SO AR!
YAY... WE ONLY HAVE... 400,000 MORE... TO GO...
HA-HA-HA. IT'S A LONG, HARD ROAD TO A MILLION ALBUMS.
YEAH... YOU'RE RIGHT...

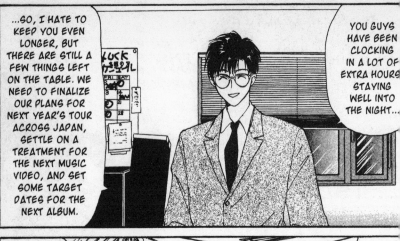

YOU GUYS HAVE BEEN CLOCKING IN A LOT OF EXTRA HOURS STAYING WELL INTO THE NIGHT...
...SO, I HATE TO KEEP YOU EVEN LONGER, BUT THERE ARE STILL A FEW THINGS LEFT ON THE TABLE. WE NEED TO FINALIZE OUR PLANS FOR NEXT YEAR'S TOUR ACROSS JAPAN, SETTLE ON A TREATMENT FOR THE NEXT MUSIC VIDEO, AND SET SOME TARGET DATES FOR THE NEXT ALBUM.
O-OKAY
ぐったり
Oh, yeah...
WANI TV IS BEGGING FOR YOU GUYS TO MAKE ANOTHER APPEARANCE...
NOT ANOTHE TV SPOT
QUIT YOUR WHINING.
YOU'RE THE ONE WHO WANTED TO WORK SO MUCH.
YEAH, I GUESS...AND I KNOW THAT EVEN THE LITTLE JOBS CAN PAY OFF IN THE END, BUT...
LOOK, THIS SHOW MIGHT BE JUST WHAT YOU NEED TO SEND YOU GUYS UP THE PLATINUM LADDER.
400,000 more?

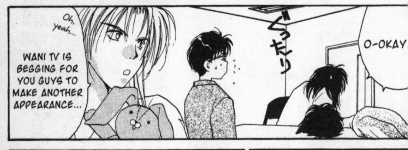

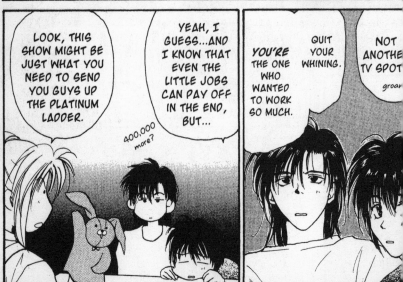

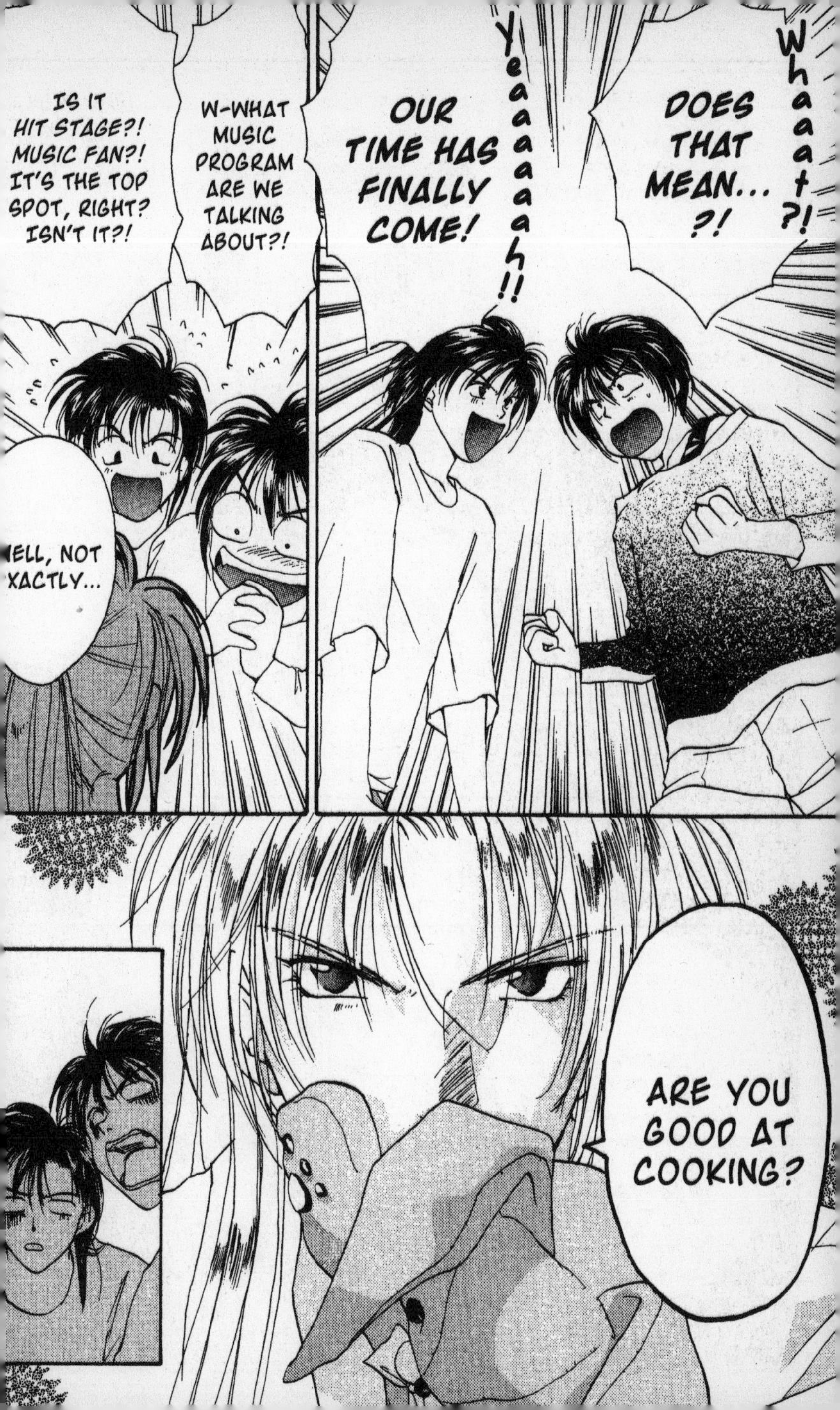
Whaaat?!
DOES THAT MEAN...?!
Yeaaaaaah!!
OUR TIME HAS FINALLY COME!
W-WHAT MUSIC PROGRAM ARE WE TALKING ABOUT?!
IS IT HIT STAGE?! MUSIC FAN?! IT'S THE TOP SPOT, RIGHT? ISN'T IT?!
ELL, NOT XACTLY...
ARE YOU GOOD AT COOKING?

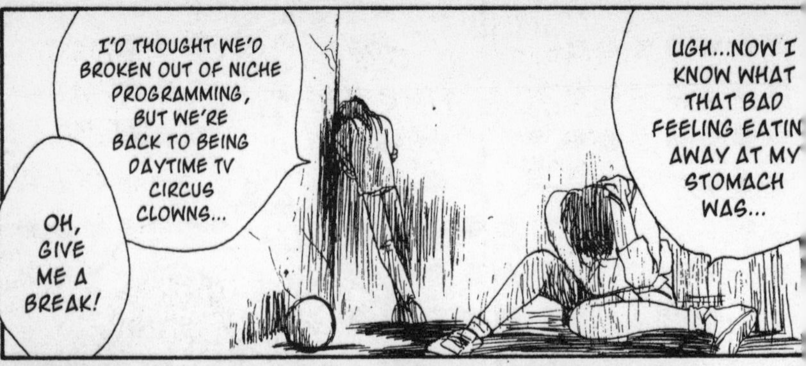
UGH...NOW I KNOW WHAT THAT BAD FEELING EATIN AWAY AT MY STOMACH WAS...
I'D THOUGHT WE'D BROKEN OUT OF NICHE PROGRAMMING, BUT WE'RE BACK TO BEING DAYTIME TV CIRCUS CLOWNS...
OH, GIVE ME A BREAK!

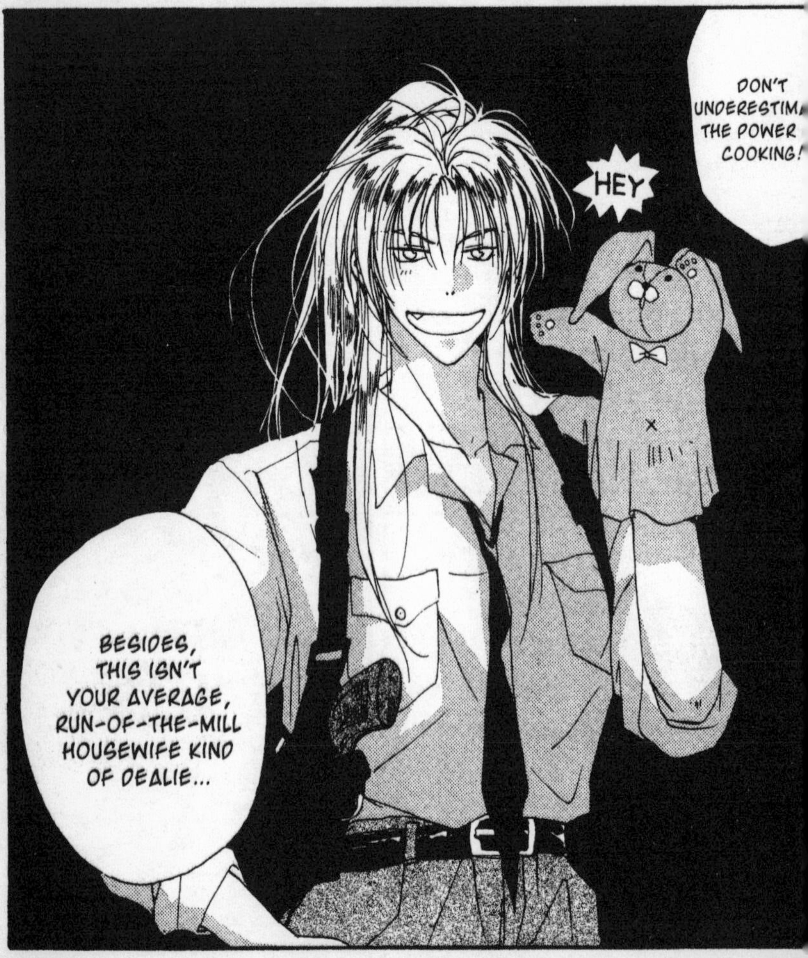
DON'T UNDERESTIM THE POWER COOKING!
HEY
BESIDES, THIS ISN'T YOUR AVERAGE, RUN-OF-THE-MILL HOUSEWIFE KIND OF DEALIE...

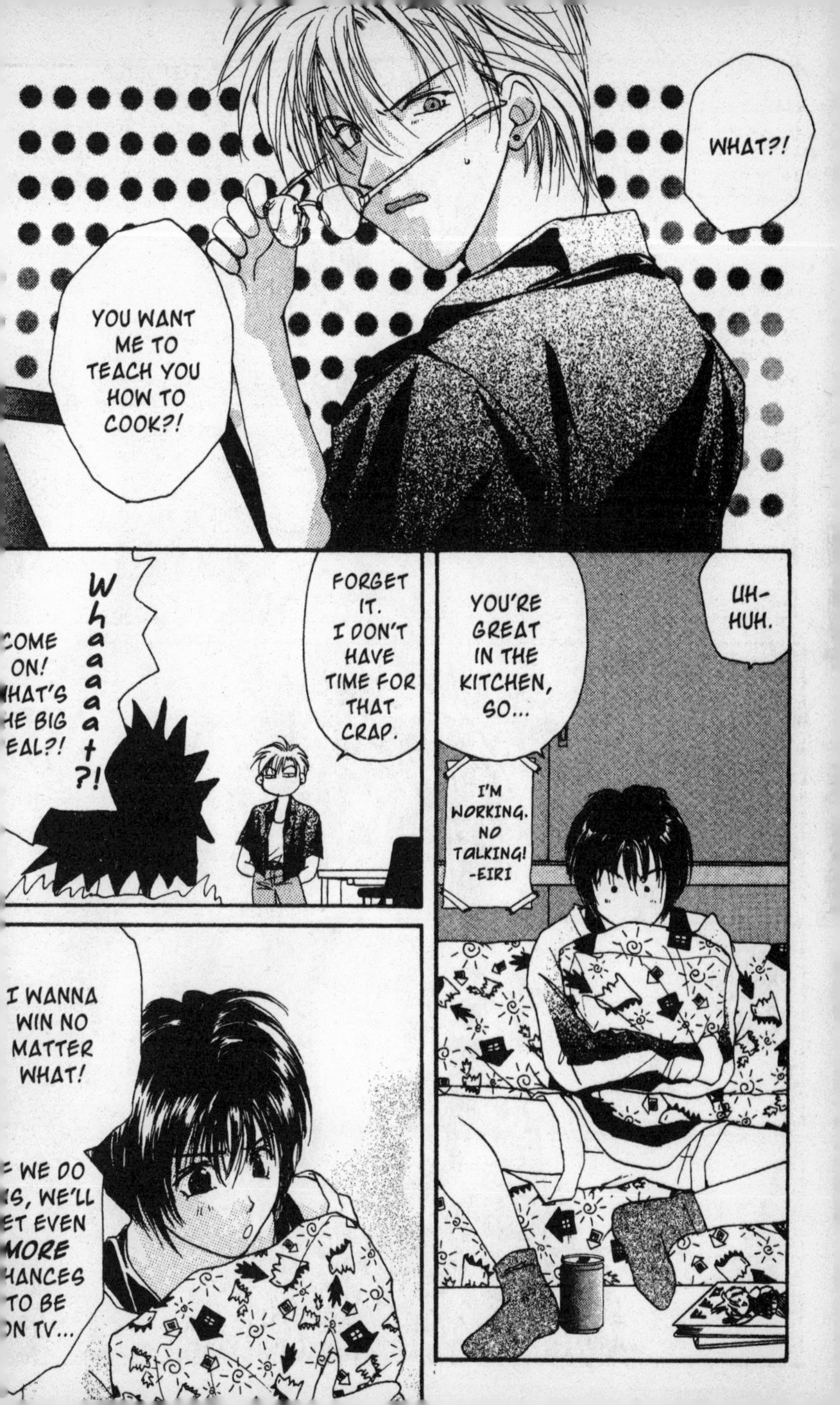
WHAT?!
YOU WANT ME TO TEACH YOU HOW TO COOK?!
UH-HUH.
YOU'RE GREAT IN THE KITCHEN, SO...
I'M WORKING. NO TALKING! -EIRI
FORGET IT. I DON'T HAVE TIME FOR THAT CRAP.
Whaaaaaaat?!
COME ON! HAT'S HE BIG EAL?!
I WANNA WIN NO MATTER WHAT!
WE DO S, WE'LL ET EVEN MORE HANCES TO BE N TV...

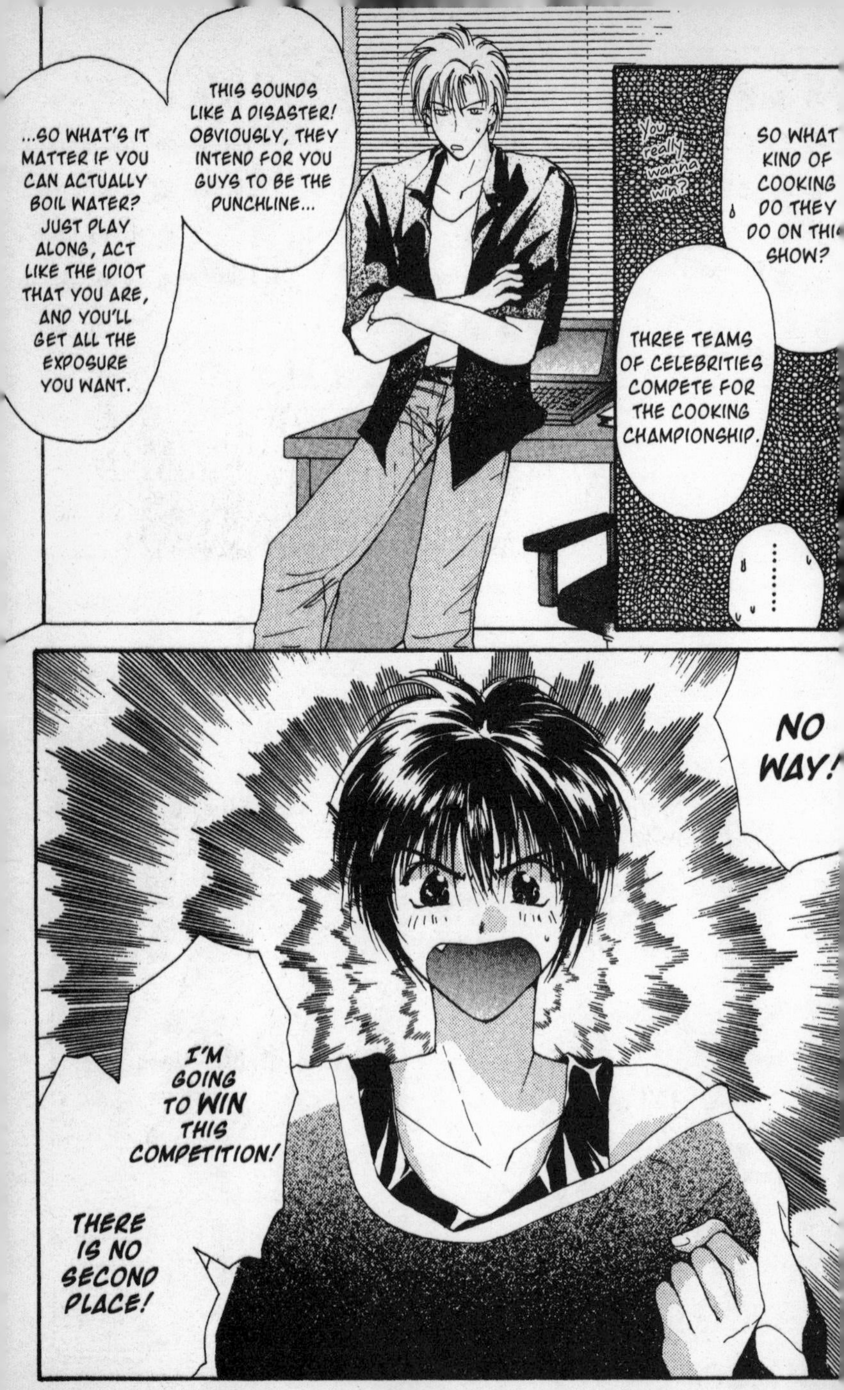
SO WHAT KIND OF COOKING DO THEY DO ON THIS SHOW?
You really wanna win?
THREE TEAMS OF CELEBRITIES COMPETE FOR THE COOKING CHAMPIONSHIP.
......
THIS SOUNDS LIKE A DISASTER! OBVIOUSLY, THEY INTEND FOR YOU GUYS TO BE THE PUNCHLINE...
...SO WHAT'S IT MATTER IF YOU CAN ACTUALLY BOIL WATER? JUST PLAY ALONG, ACT LIKE THE IDIOT THAT YOU ARE, AND YOU'LL GET ALL THE EXPOSURE YOU WANT.
NO WAY!
I'M GOING TO WIN THIS COMPETITION!
THERE IS NO SECOND PLACE!

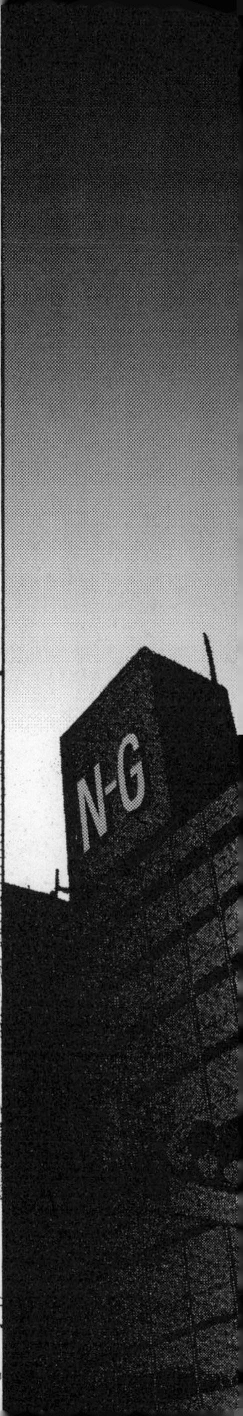
N-G

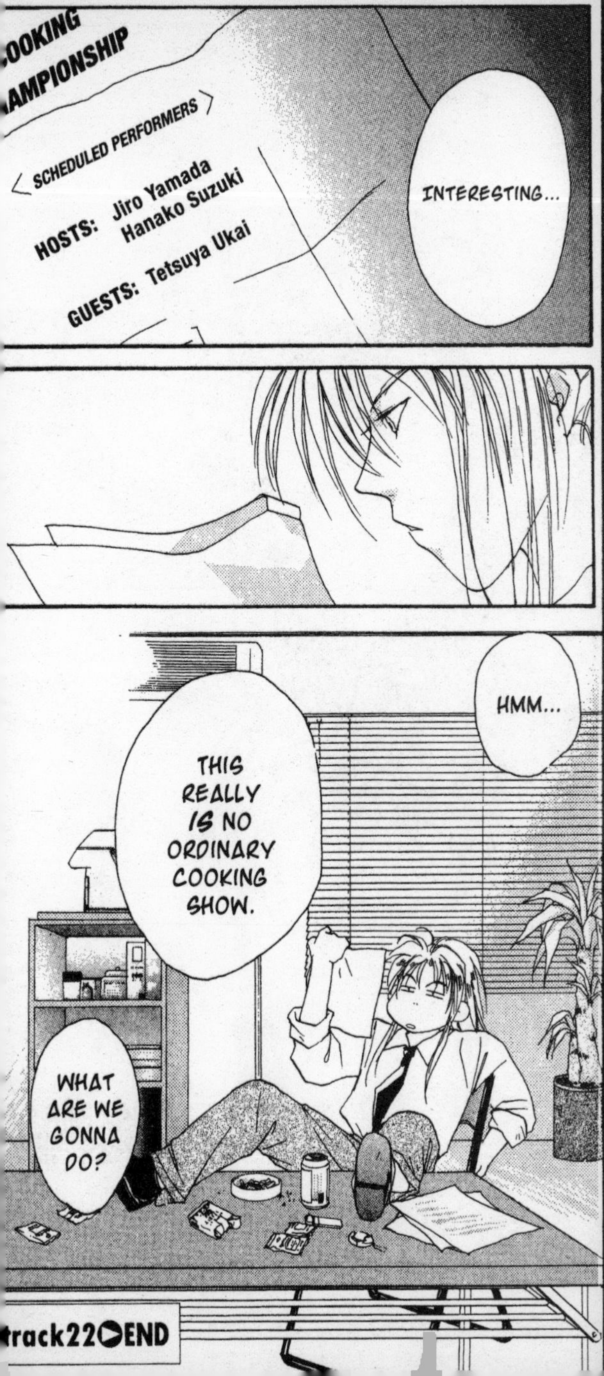
INTERESTING...
OOKING
AMPIONSHIP
< SCHEDULED PERFORMERS >
HOSTS: Jiro Yamada
Hanako Suzuki
GUESTS: Tetsuya Ukai
HMM...
THIS REALLY IS NO ORDINARY COOKING SHOW.
WHAT ARE WE GONNA DO?
rack22▶END

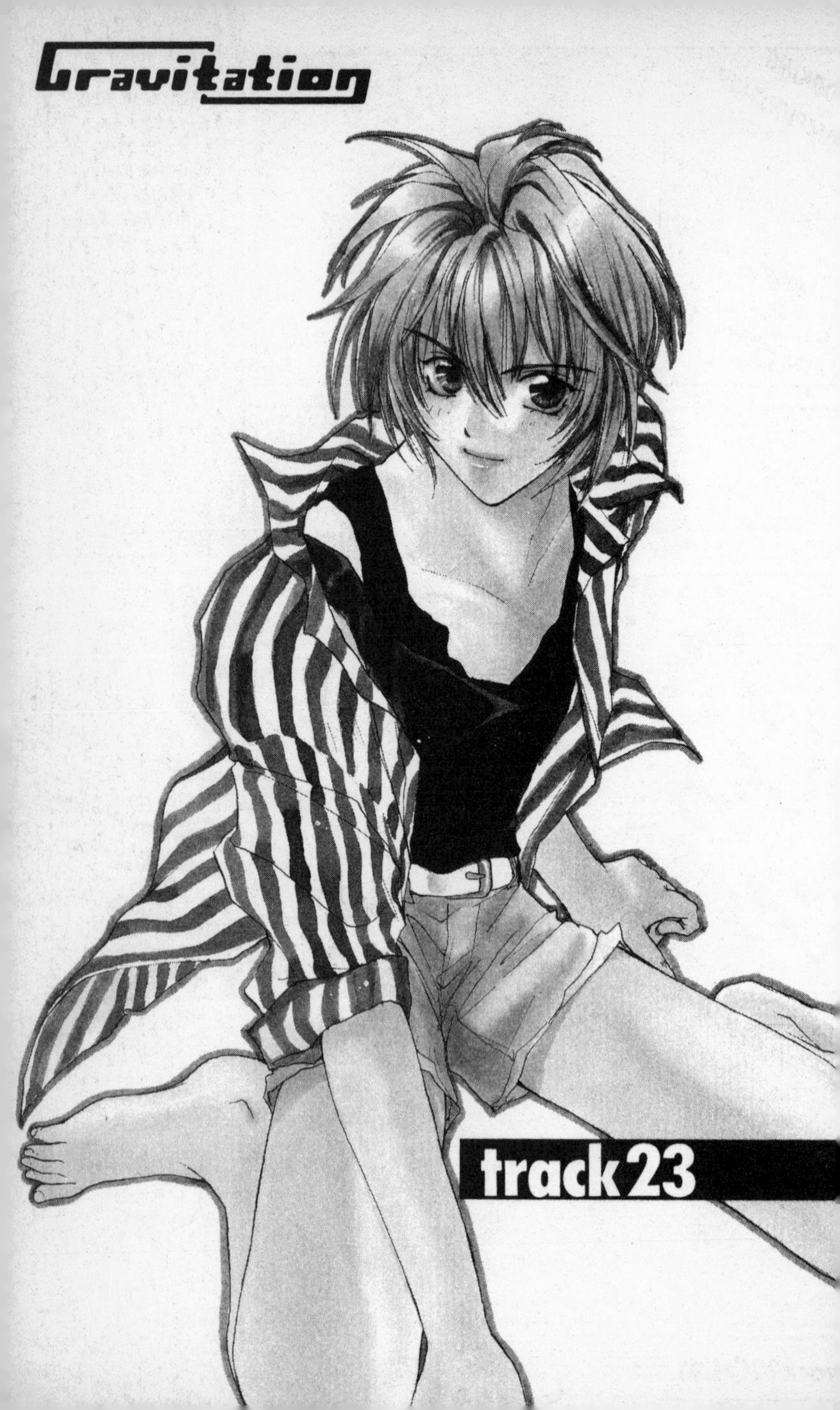
Gravitation
track 23

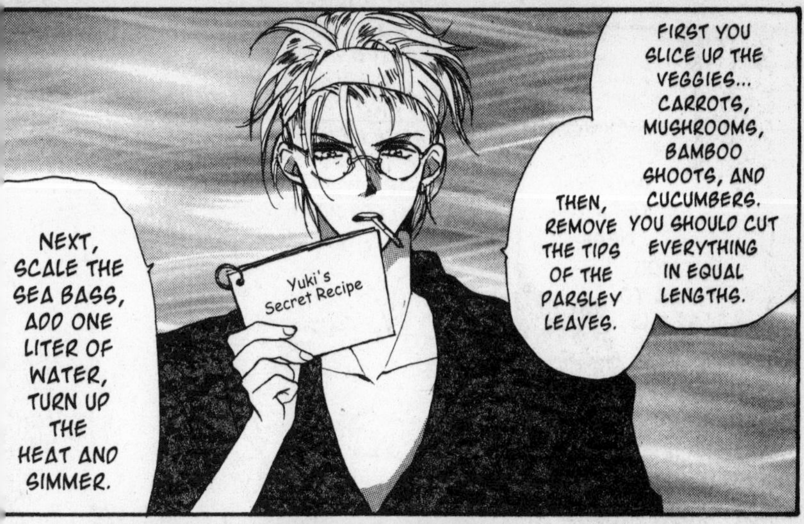
FIRST YOU SLICE UP THE VEGGIES... CARROTS, MUSHROOMS, BAMBOO SHOOTS, AND CUCUMBERS. YOU SHOULD CUT EVERYTHING IN EQUAL LENGTHS.
THEN, REMOVE THE TIPS OF THE PARSLEY LEAVES.
Yuki's Secret Recipe
NEXT, SCALE THE SEA BASS, ADD ONE LITER OF WATER, TURN UP THE HEAT AND SIMMER.
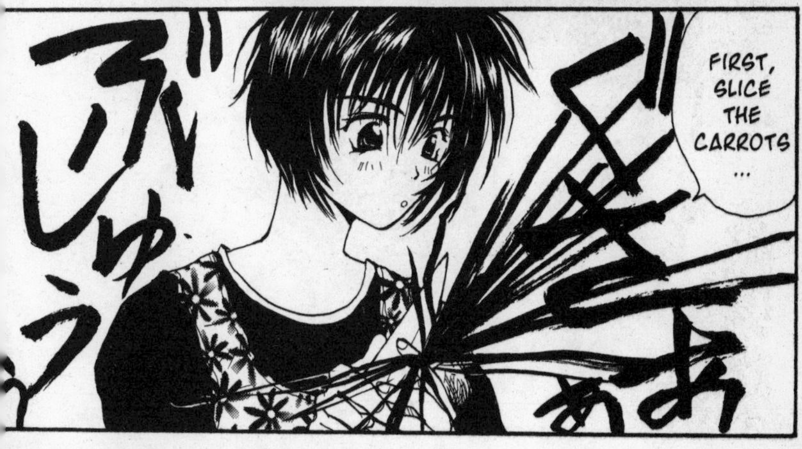
FIRST, SLICE THE CARROTS ...
ぶしゅう

BOUT GRAVITATION TRACK 23

avitation has now officially gone off track. A cooking show? I've been thinking, I never have ything important to write in this space. I wonder what the other manga artists do with eir sidebar text? Maybe they draw pictures? Is it pictures? But I don't want to do pictures, I've got a problem. I hate drawing. Ughh. And I can't really share with you my cherished mories, since I forget things after a few months if they aren't that special. And there's use in writing down stuff I bitch about. Pictures? You want pictures? All right. You want tures. So, if you're okay with me drawing pictures...?

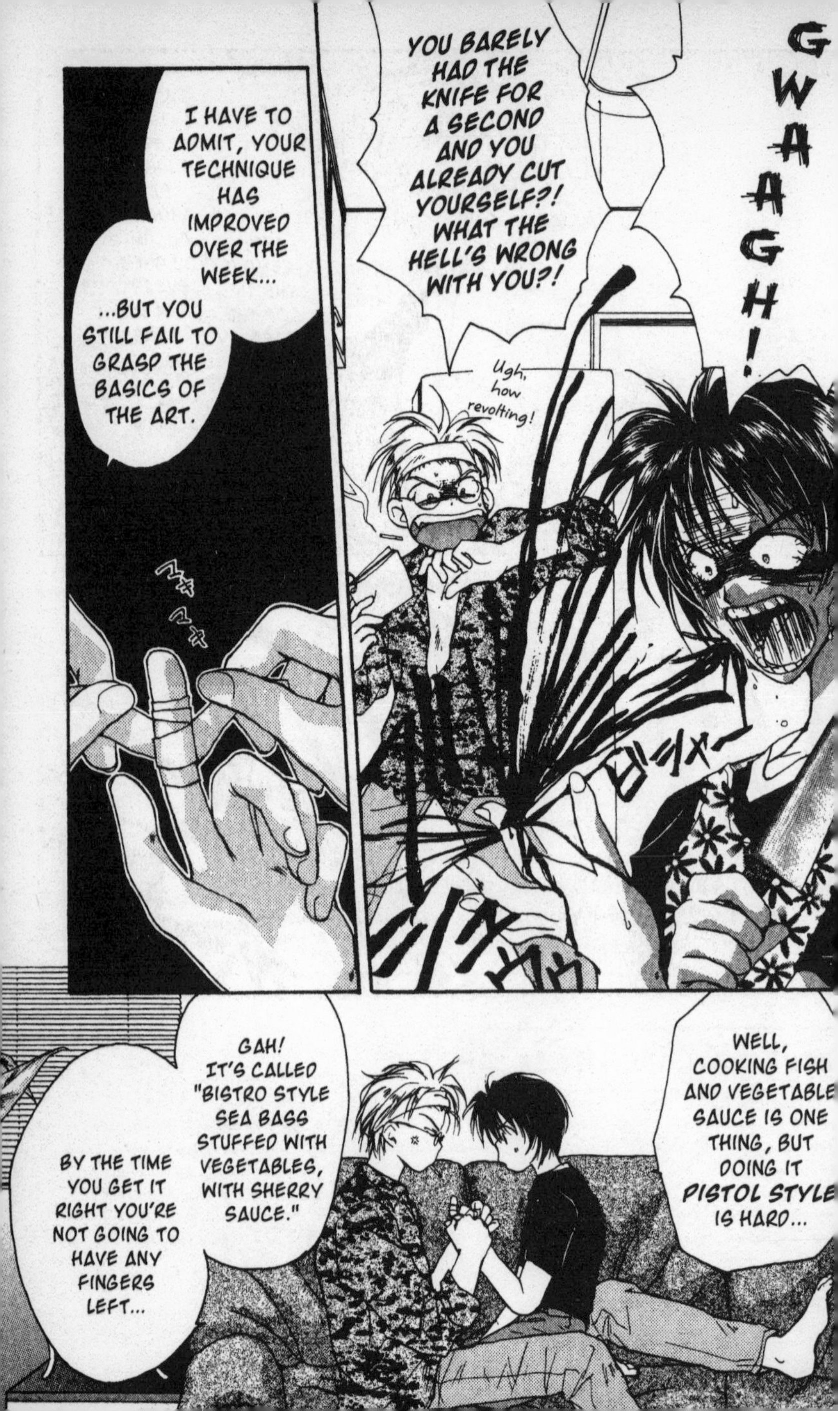
GWAAGH!
YOU BARELY HAD THE KNIFE FOR A SECOND AND YOU ALREADY CUT YOURSELF?! WHAT THE HELL'S WRONG WITH YOU?!
Ugh, how revolting!
I HAVE TO ADMIT, YOUR TECHNIQUE HAS IMPROVED OVER THE WEEK...
...BUT YOU STILL FAIL TO GRASP THE BASICS OF THE ART.
マキ マキ
WELL, COOKING FISH AND VEGETABLE SAUCE IS ONE THING, BUT DOING IT PISTOL STYLE IS HARD...
GAH! IT'S CALLED "BISTRO STYLE SEA BASS STUFFED WITH VEGETABLES, WITH SHERRY SAUCE."
BY THE TIME YOU GET IT RIGHT YOU'RE NOT GOING TO HAVE ANY FINGERS LEFT...

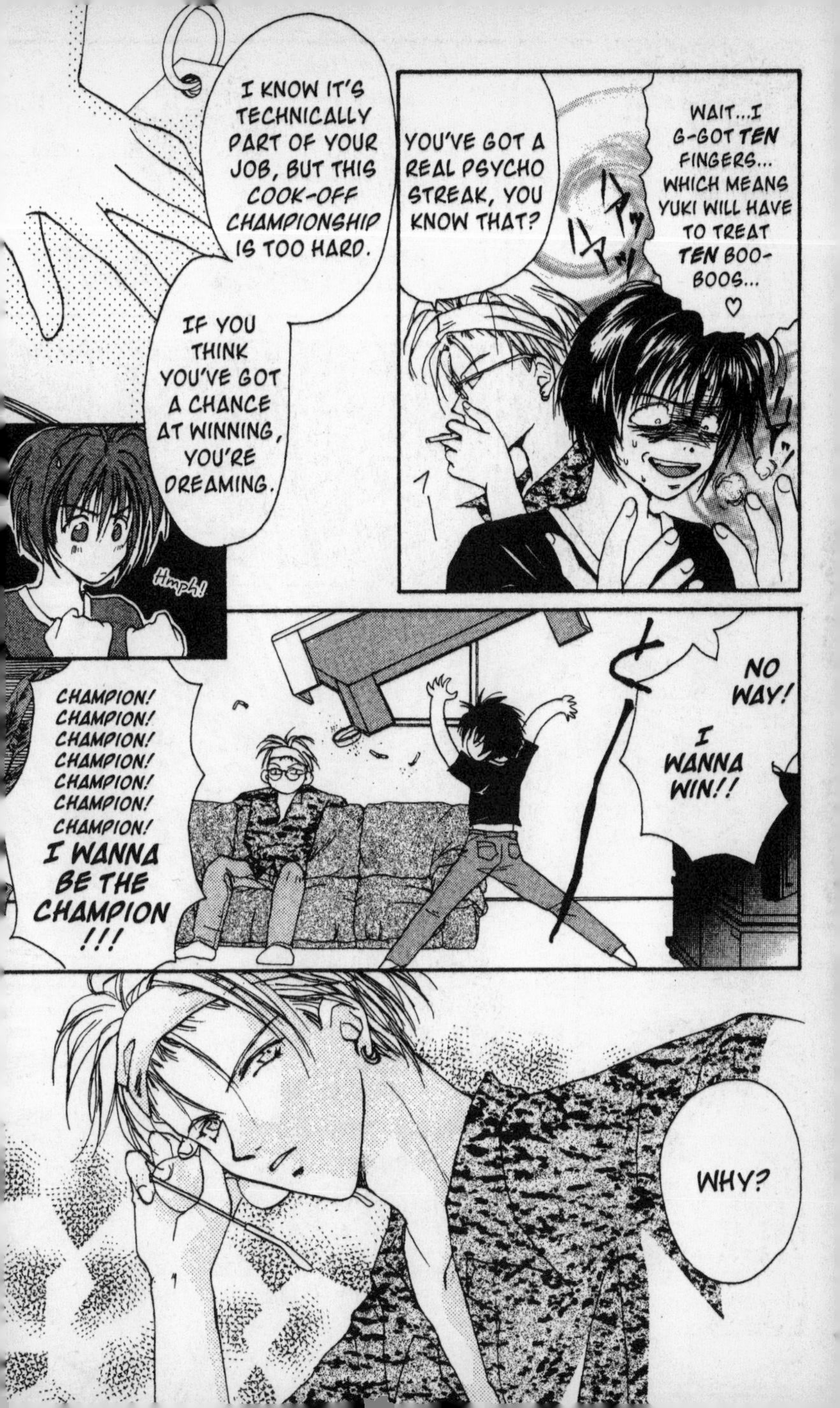
WAIT...I G-GOT TEN FINGERS... WHICH MEANS YUKI WILL HAVE TO TREAT TEN BOO-BOOS... ♡
YOU'VE GOT A REAL PSYCHO STREAK, YOU KNOW THAT?
I KNOW IT'S TECHNICALLY PART OF YOUR JOB, BUT THIS COOK-OFF CHAMPIONSHIP IS TOO HARD.
IF YOU THINK YOU'VE GOT A CHANCE AT WINNING, YOU'RE DREAMING.
Hmph!
NO WAY!
I WANNA WIN!!
CHAMPION! CHAMPION! CHAMPION! CHAMPION! CHAMPION! CHAMPION! CHAMPION! I WANNA BE THE CHAMPION!!!
WHY?

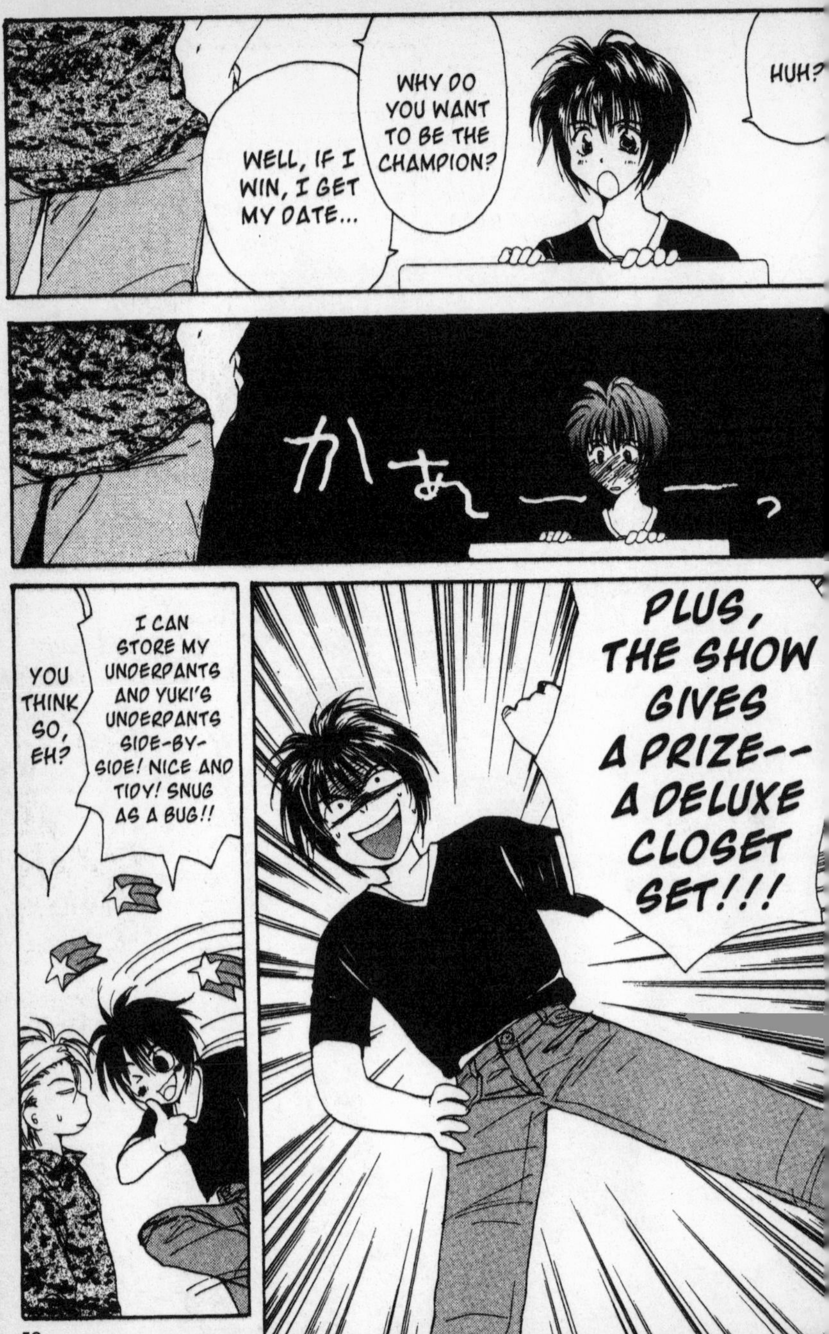
HUH?
WHY DO YOU WANT TO BE THE CHAMPION?
WELL, IF I WIN, I GET MY DATE...
かぁ――っ
PLUS, THE SHOW GIVES A PRIZE-- A DELUXE CLOSET SET!!!
I CAN STORE MY UNDERPANTS AND YUKI'S UNDERPANTS SIDE-BY-SIDE! NICE AND TIDY! SNUG AS A BUG!!
YOU THINK SO, EH?

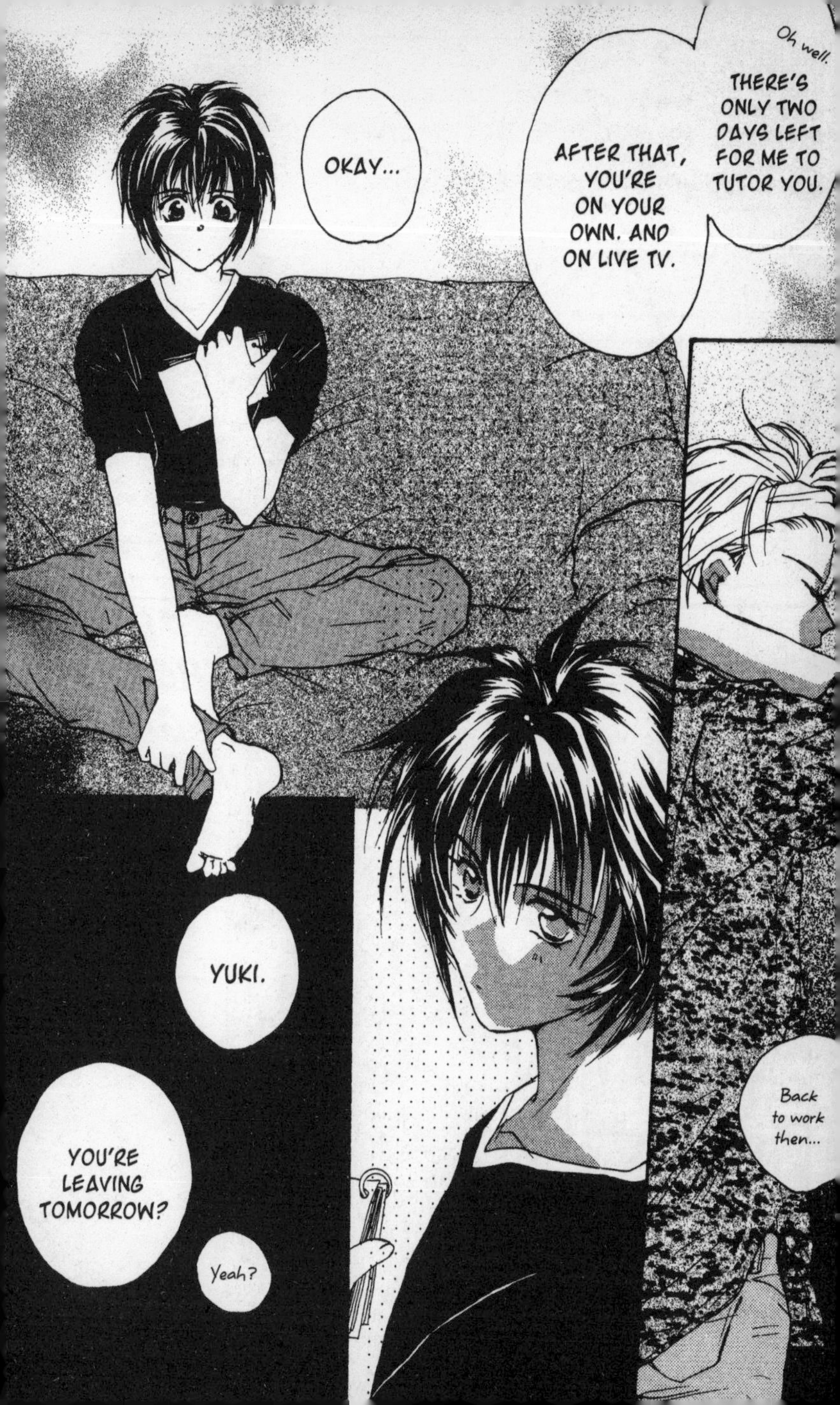
Oh well.
THERE'S ONLY TWO DAYS LEFT FOR ME TO TUTOR YOU.
AFTER THAT, YOU'RE ON YOUR OWN. AND ON LIVE TV.
OKAY...
Back to work then...
YUKI.
YOU'RE LEAVING TOMORROW?
Yeah?

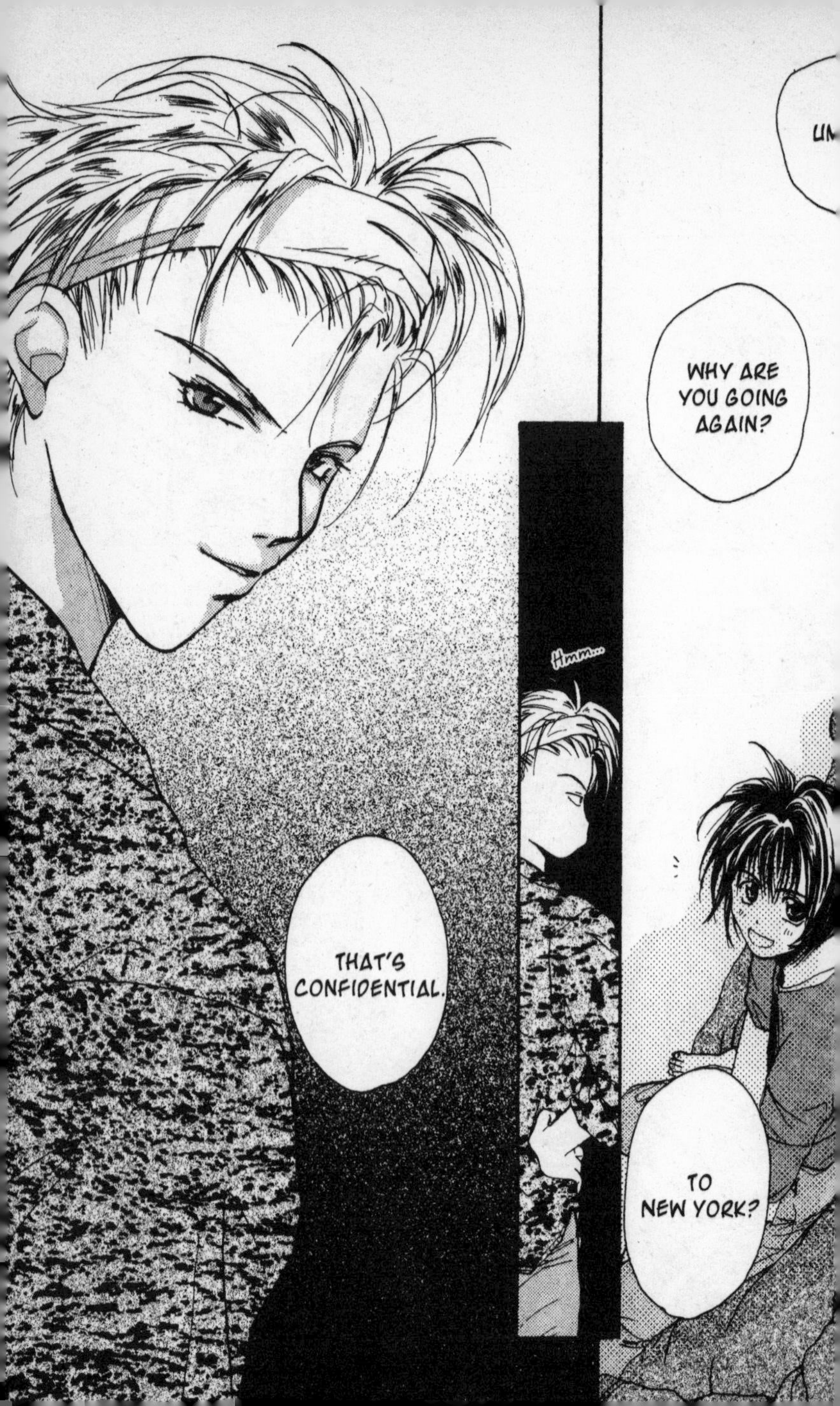
UM
WHY ARE YOU GOING AGAIN?
TO NEW YORK?
Hmm...
THAT'S CONFIDENTIAL.

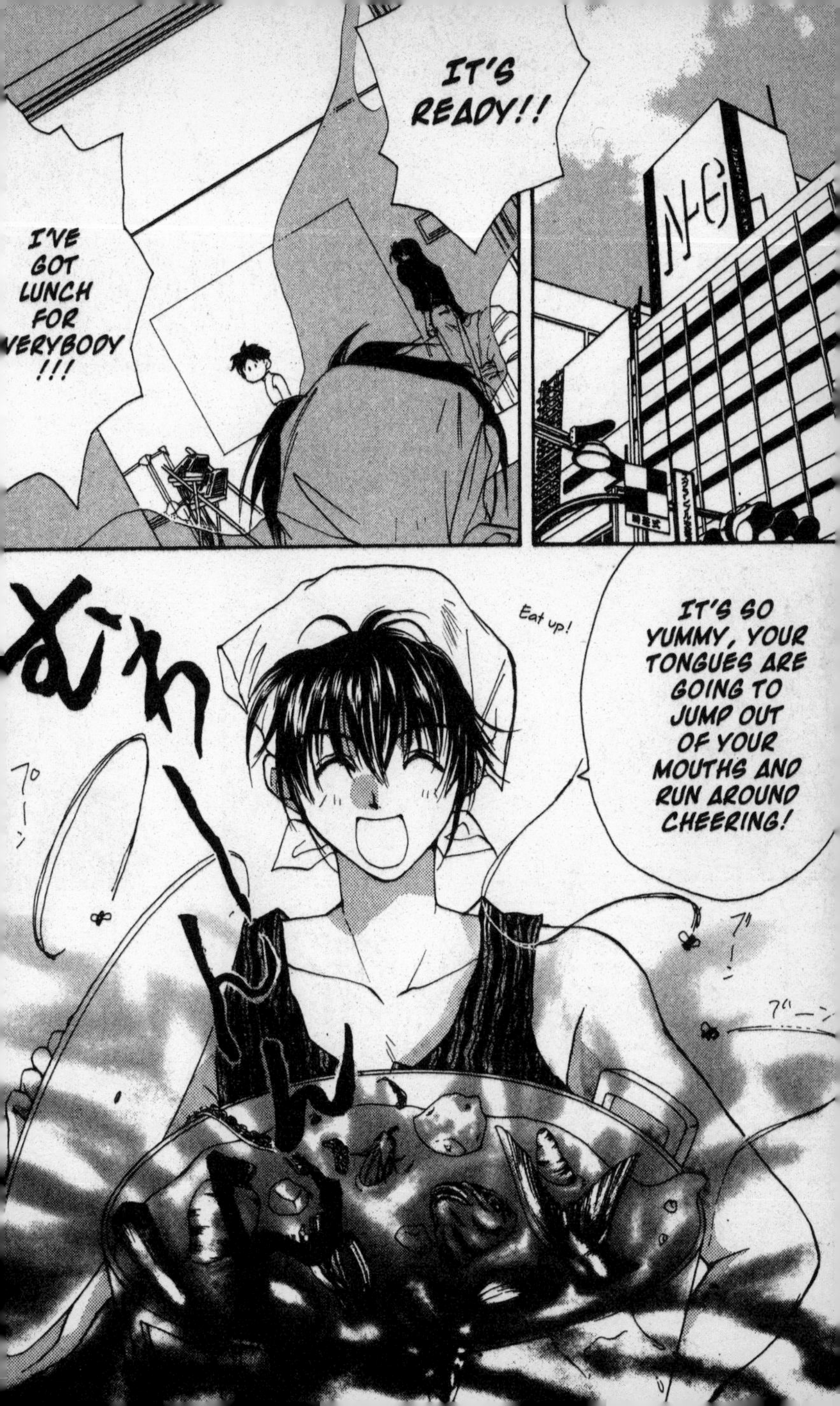
IT'S READY!!
I'VE GOT LUNCH FOR VERYBODY!!!
IT'S SO YUMMY, YOUR TONGUES ARE GOING TO JUMP OUT OF YOUR MOUTHS AND RUN AROUND CHEERING!
Eat up!

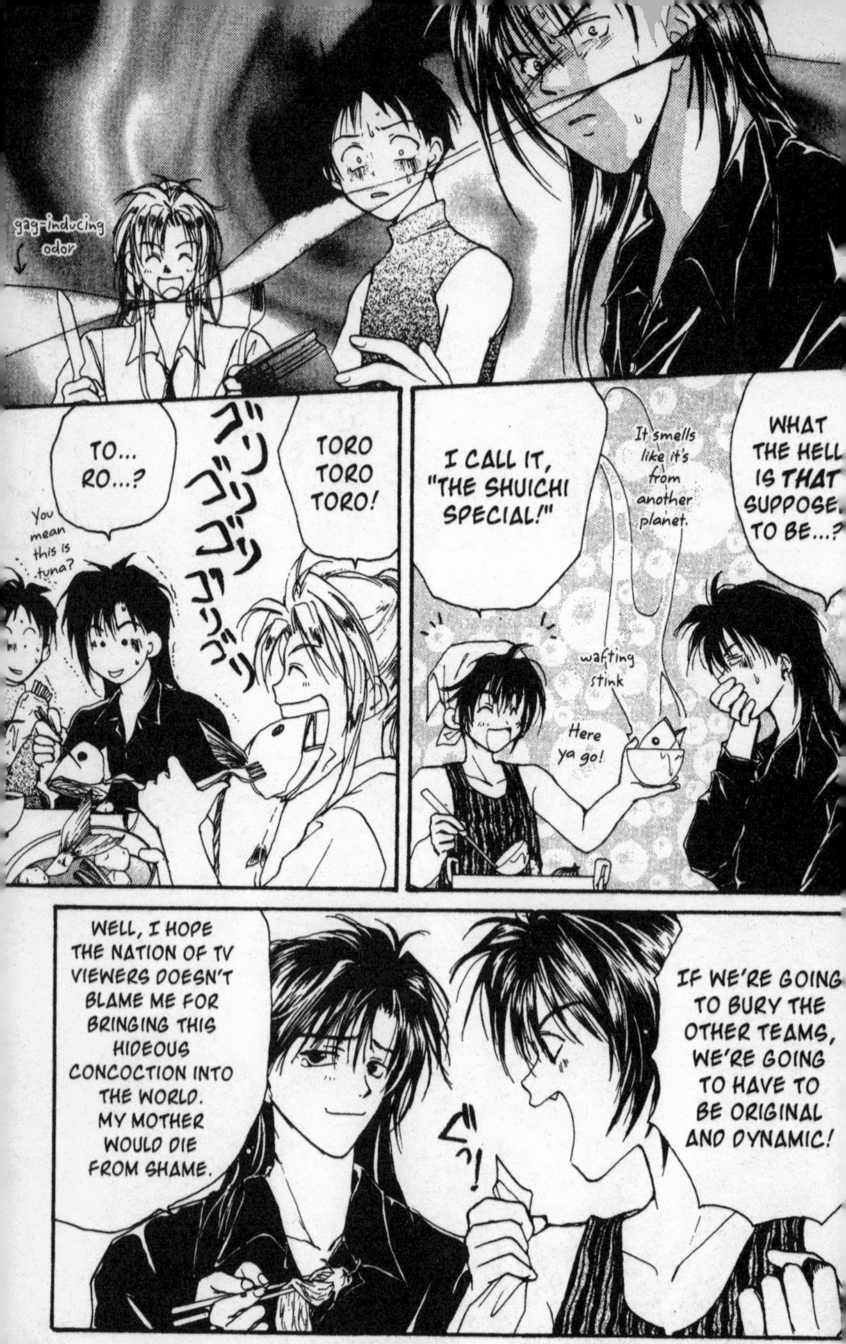
gag-inducing odor
WHAT THE HELL IS THAT SUPPOSE, TO BE...?
It smells like it's from another planet.
I CALL IT, "THE SHUICHI SPECIAL!"
wafting stink
Here ya go!
TORO TORO TORO!
ゴリゴリゴリゴリ
TO... RO...?
You mean this is tuna?
IF WE'RE GOING TO BURY THE OTHER TEAMS, WE'RE GOING TO HAVE TO BE ORIGINAL AND DYNAMIC!
ぐっ!
WELL, I HOPE THE NATION OF TV VIEWERS DOESN'T BLAME ME FOR BRINGING THIS HIDEOUS CONCOCTION INTO THE WORLD. MY MOTHER WOULD DIE FROM SHAME.

↑eggplant

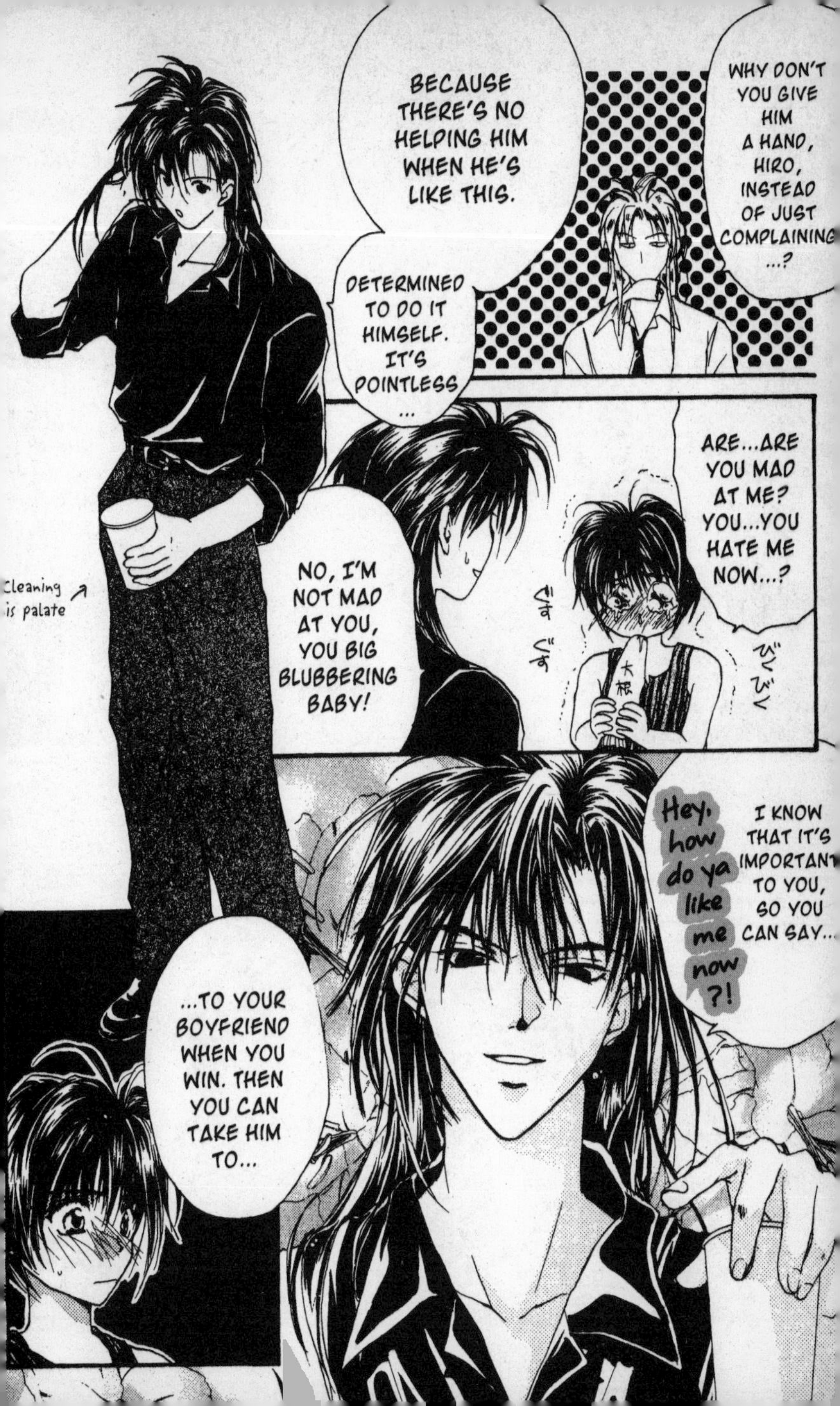
WHY DON'T YOU GIVE HIM A HAND, HIRO, INSTEAD OF JUST COMPLAINING ...?
BECAUSE THERE'S NO HELPING HIM WHEN HE'S LIKE THIS.
DETERMINED TO DO IT HIMSELF. IT'S POINTLESS ...
Cleaning is palate
ARE...ARE YOU MAD AT ME? YOU...YOU HATE ME NOW...?
びくびく
大根
ぐすぐす
NO, I'M NOT MAD AT YOU, YOU BIG BLUBBERING BABY!
I KNOW THAT IT'S IMPORTANT TO YOU, SO YOU CAN SAY...
Hey, how do ya like me now?!
...TO YOUR BOYFRIEND WHEN YOU WIN. THEN YOU CAN TAKE HIM TO...

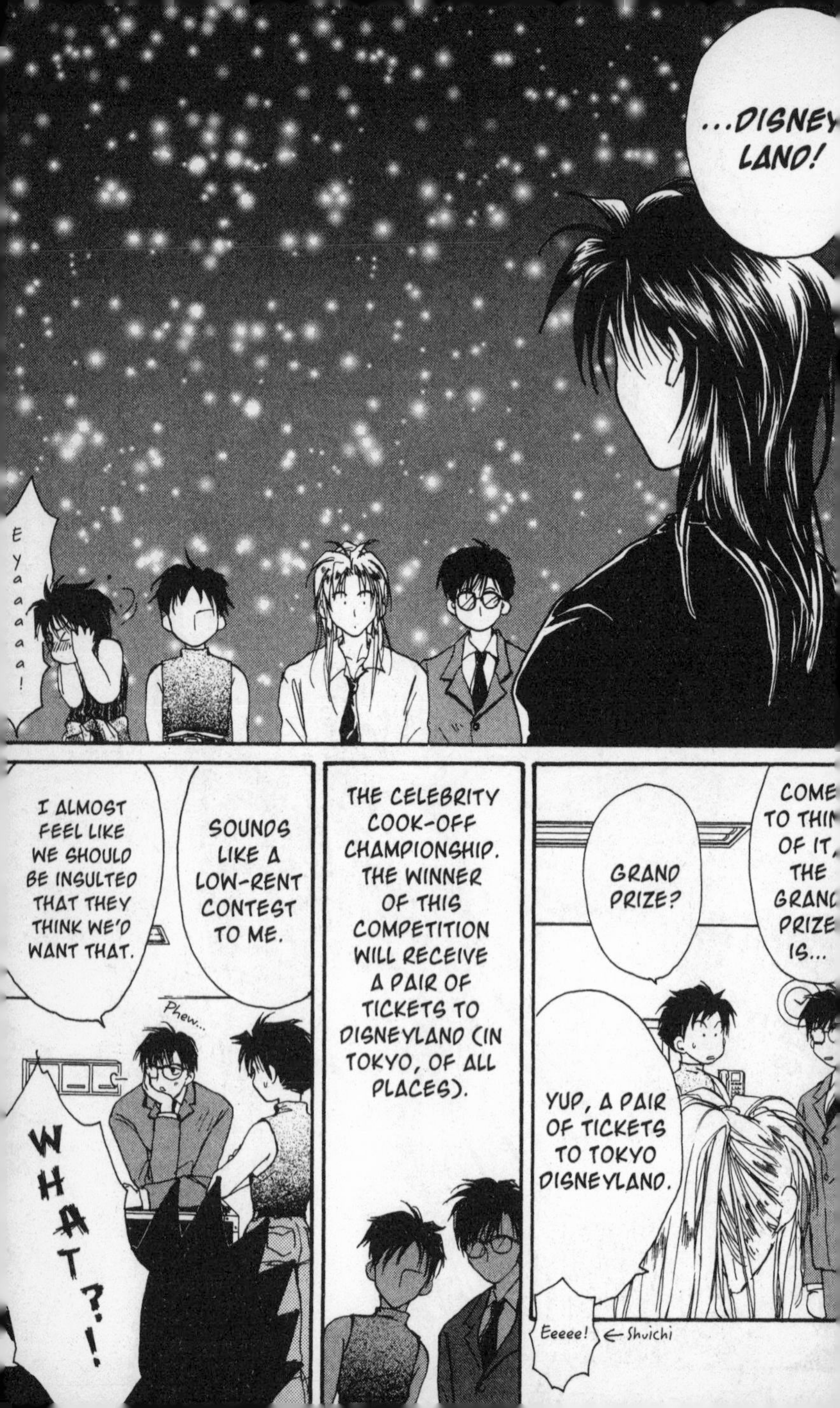
...DISNEY LAND!
Eyaaaaa!
COME TO THI OF IT, THE GRAN PRIZE IS...
GRAND PRIZE?
YUP, A PAIR OF TICKETS TO TOKYO DISNEYLAND.
Eeeee! ← Shuichi
THE CELEBRITY COOK-OFF CHAMPIONSHIP. THE WINNER OF THIS COMPETITION WILL RECEIVE A PAIR OF TICKETS TO DISNEYLAND (IN TOKYO, OF ALL PLACES).
SOUNDS LIKE A LOW-RENT CONTEST TO ME.
I ALMOST FEEL LIKE WE SHOULD BE INSULTED THAT THEY THINK WE'D WANT THAT.
Phew...
WHAT?!

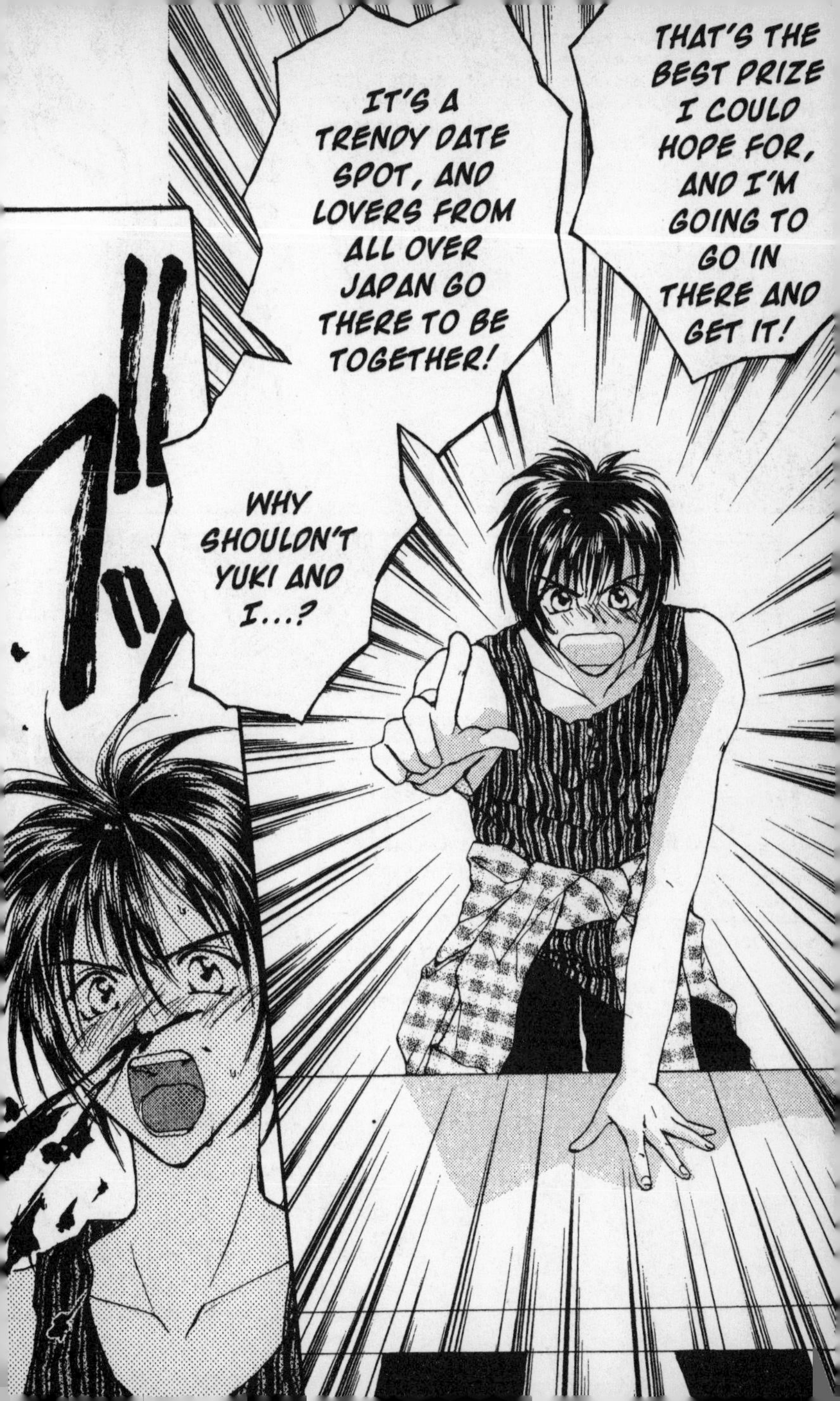
THAT'S THE BEST PRIZE I COULD HOPE FOR, AND I'M GOING TO GO IN THERE AND GET IT!
IT'S A TRENDY DATE SPOT, AND LOVERS FROM ALL OVER JAPAN GO THERE TO BE TOGETHER!
WHY SHOULDN'T YUKI AND I...?

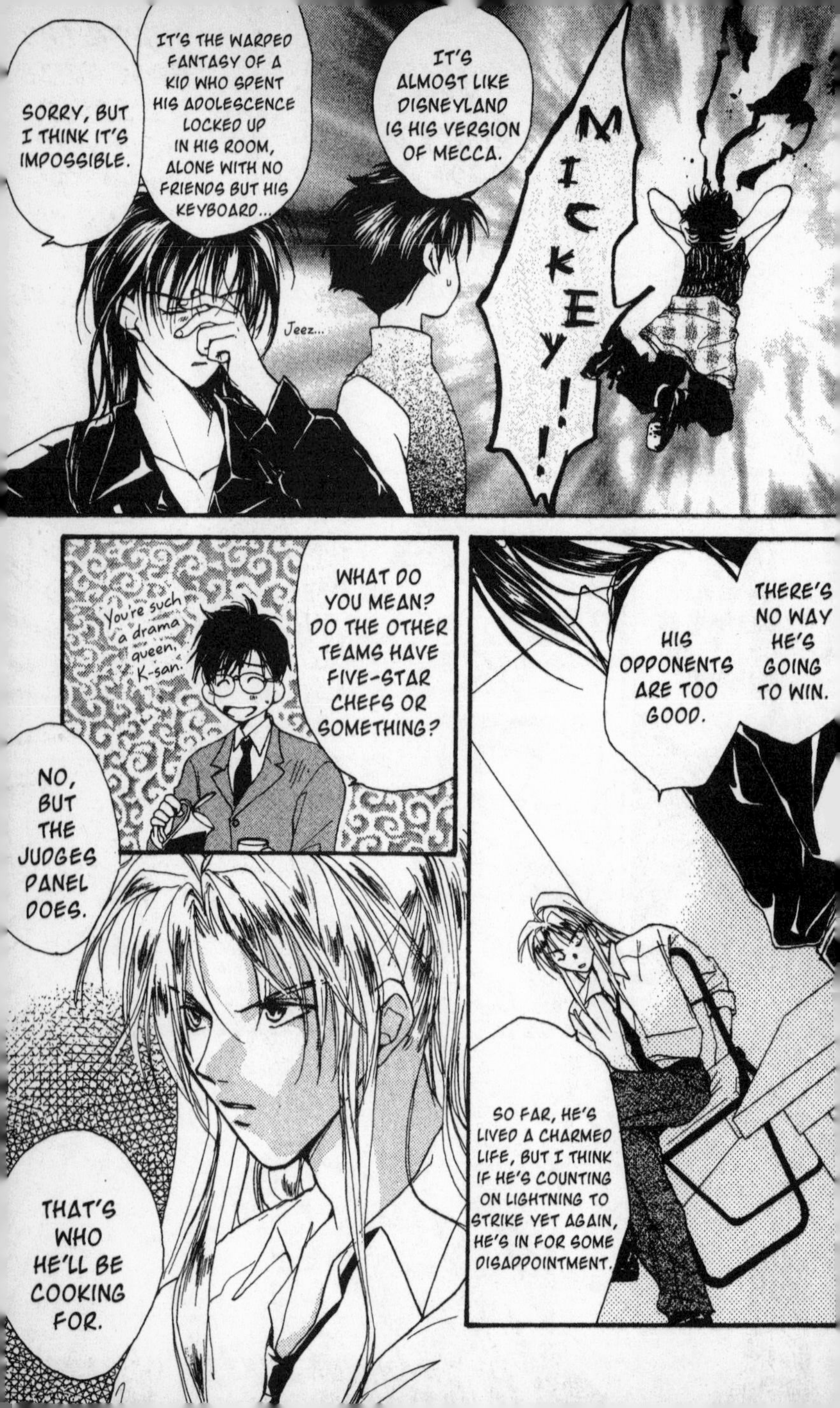
MICKEY!!
IT'S ALMOST LIKE DISNEYLAND IS HIS VERSION OF MECCA.
IT'S THE WARPED FANTASY OF A KID WHO SPENT HIS ADOLESCENCE LOCKED UP IN HIS ROOM, ALONE WITH NO FRIENDS BUT HIS KEYBOARD...
SORRY, BUT I THINK IT'S IMPOSSIBLE.
Jeez...
THERE'S NO WAY HE'S GOING TO WIN.
HIS OPPONENTS ARE TOO GOOD.
SO FAR, HE'S LIVED A CHARMED LIFE, BUT I THINK IF HE'S COUNTING ON LIGHTNING TO STRIKE YET AGAIN, HE'S IN FOR SOME DISAPPOINTMENT.
WHAT DO YOU MEAN? DO THE OTHER TEAMS HAVE FIVE-STAR CHEFS OR SOMETHING?
You're such a drama queen, K-san.
NO, BUT THE JUDGES PANEL DOES.
THAT'S WHO HE'LL BE COOKING FOR.

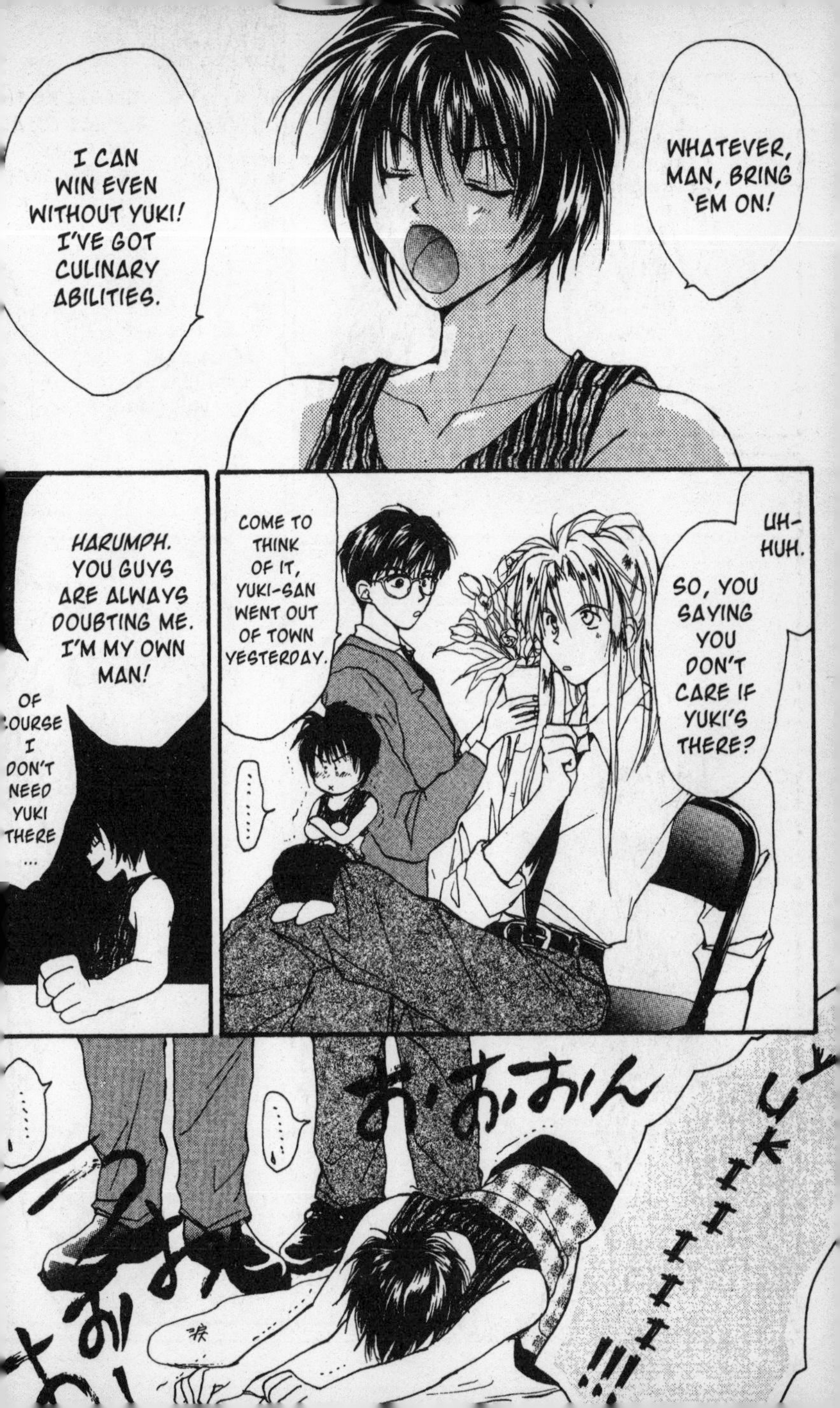
WHATEVER, MAN, BRING 'EM ON!
I CAN WIN EVEN WITHOUT YUKI! I'VE GOT CULINARY ABILITIES.
UH-HUH.
SO, YOU SAYING YOU DON'T CARE IF YUKI'S THERE?
COME TO THINK OF IT, YUKI-SAN WENT OUT OF TOWN YESTERDAY.
......
HARUMPH. YOU GUYS ARE ALWAYS DOUBTING ME. I'M MY OWN MAN!
OF COURSE I DON'T NEED YUKI THERE ...
YUKIIIIII!!!
お・お・おん
......
......

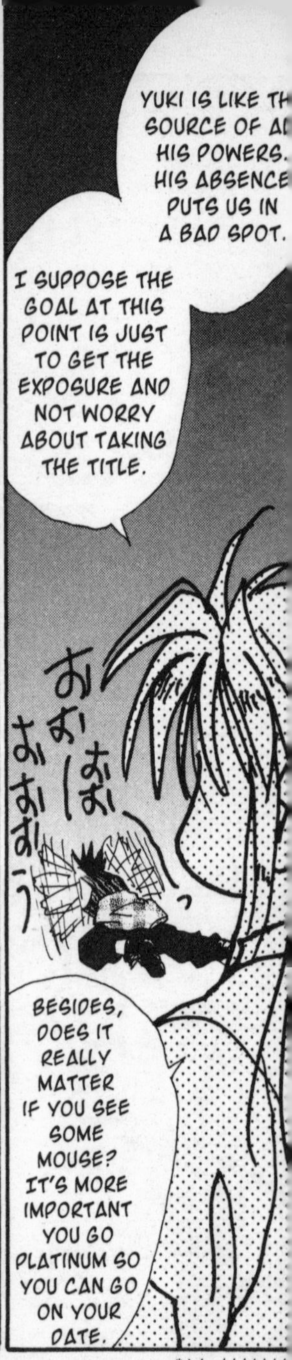
YUKI IS LIKE TH
SOURCE OF AI
HIS POWERS.
HIS ABSENCE
PUTS US IN
A BAD SPOT.
I SUPPOSE THE GOAL AT THIS POINT IS JUST TO GET THE EXPOSURE AND NOT WORRY ABOUT TAKING THE TITLE.
BESIDES, DOES IT REALLY MATTER IF YOU SEE SOME MOUSE? IT'S MORE IMPORTANT YOU GO PLATINUM SO YOU CAN GO ON YOUR DATE.

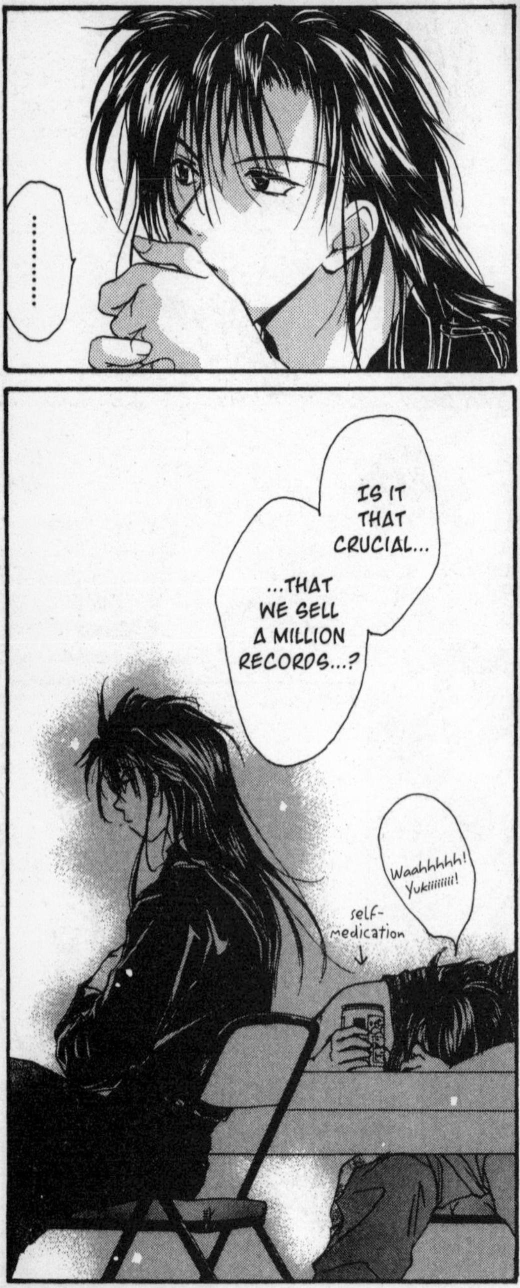
....
IS IT THAT CRUCIAL...
...THAT WE SELL A MILLION RECORDS...?
Waahhhhh! Yukiiiiiii!
self-medication

* Waahhhhhh

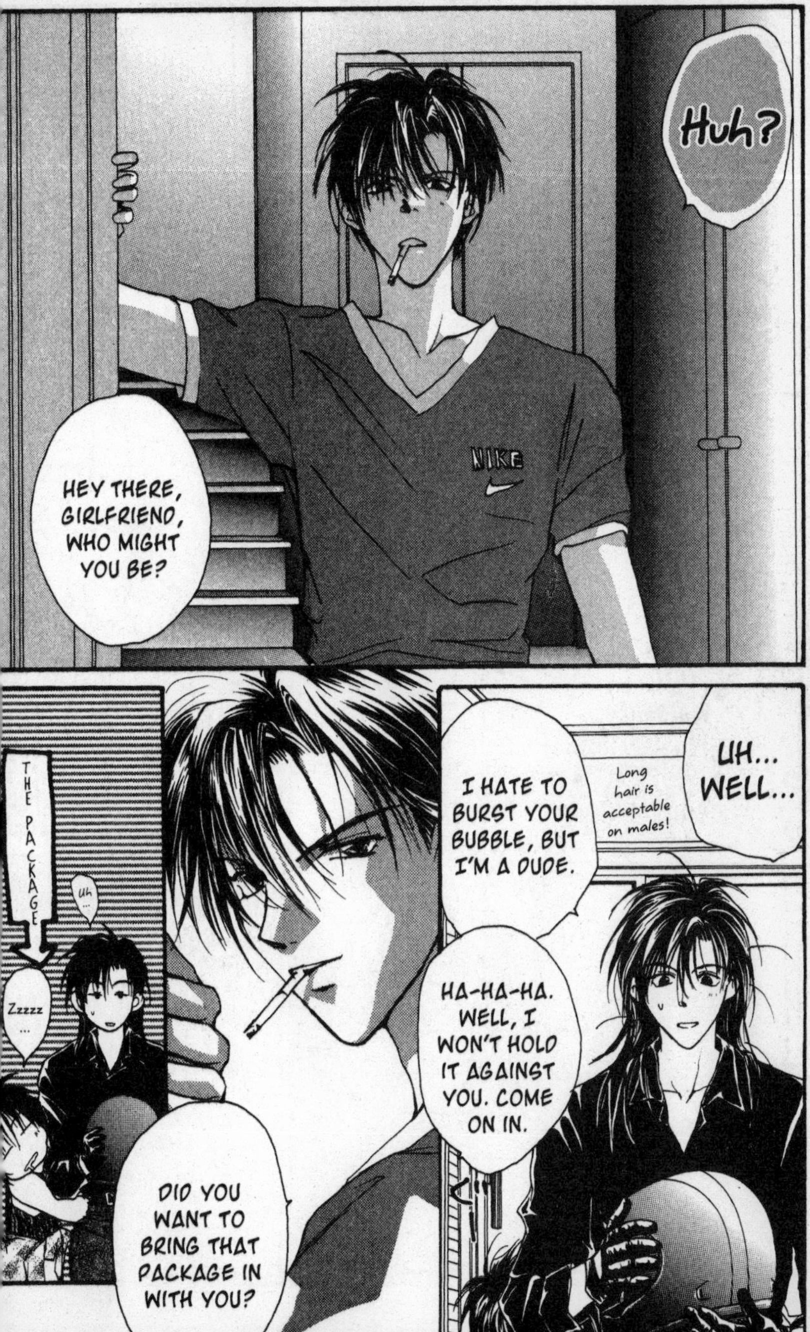
Huh?
HEY THERE, GIRLFRIEND, WHO MIGHT YOU BE?
UH... WELL...
Long hair is acceptable on males!
I HATE TO BURST YOUR BUBBLE, BUT I'M A DUDE.
HA-HA-HA. WELL, I WON'T HOLD IT AGAINST YOU. COME ON IN.
DID YOU WANT TO BRING THAT PACKAGE IN WITH YOU?
THE PACKAGE
uh...
Zzzzz...

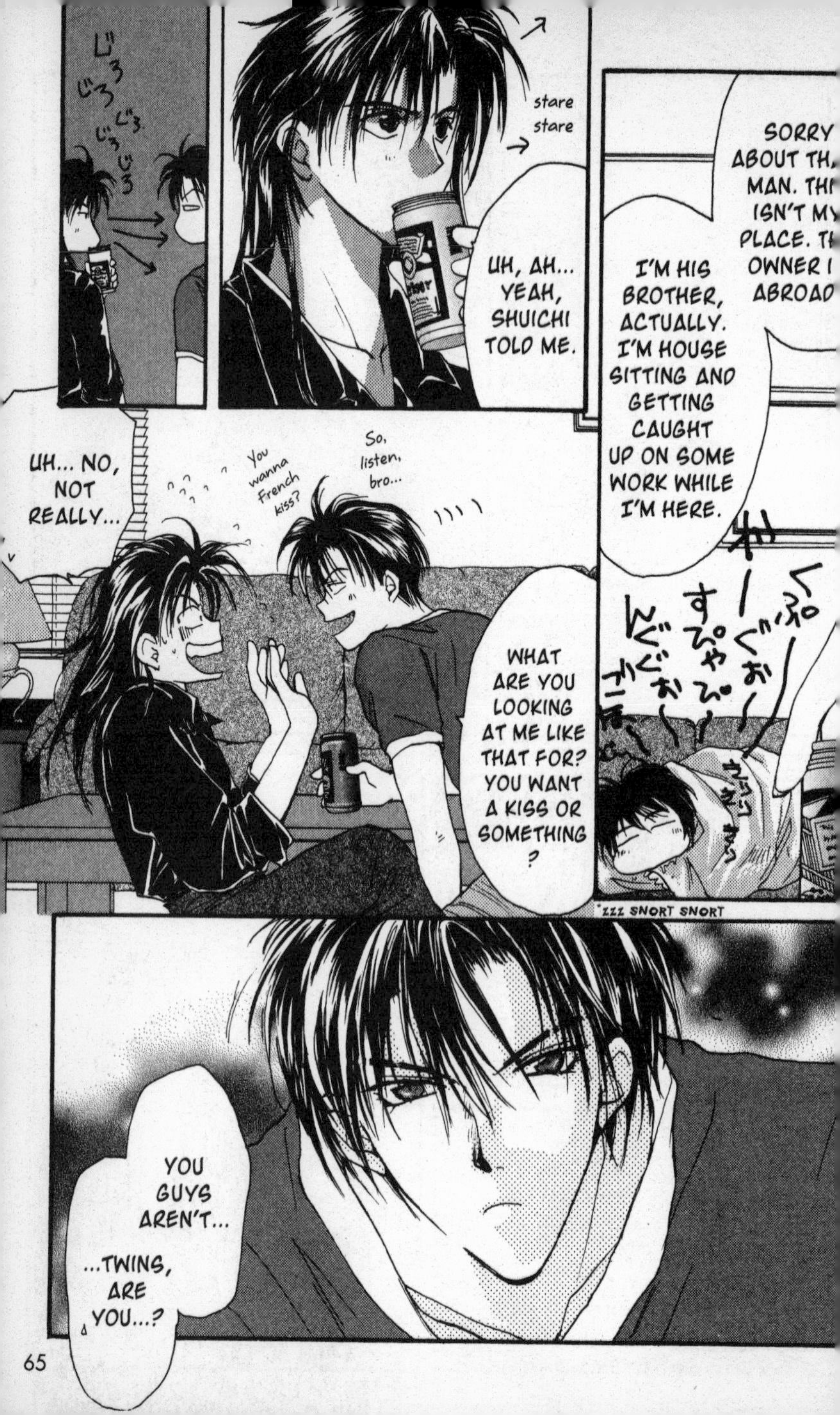
SORRY ABOUT TH MAN. THI ISN'T MY PLACE. TH OWNER I ABROAD
I'M HIS BROTHER, ACTUALLY. I'M HOUSE SITTING AND GETTING CAUGHT UP ON SOME WORK WHILE I'M HERE.
*ZZZ SNORT SNORT
stare stare
UH, AH... YEAH, SHUICHI TOLD ME.
じろじろじろじろじろ
WHAT ARE YOU LOOKING AT ME LIKE THAT FOR? YOU WANT A KISS OR SOMETHING ?
So, listen, bro...
You wanna French kiss?
UH... NO, NOT REALLY...
YOU GUYS AREN'T...
...TWINS, ARE YOU...?

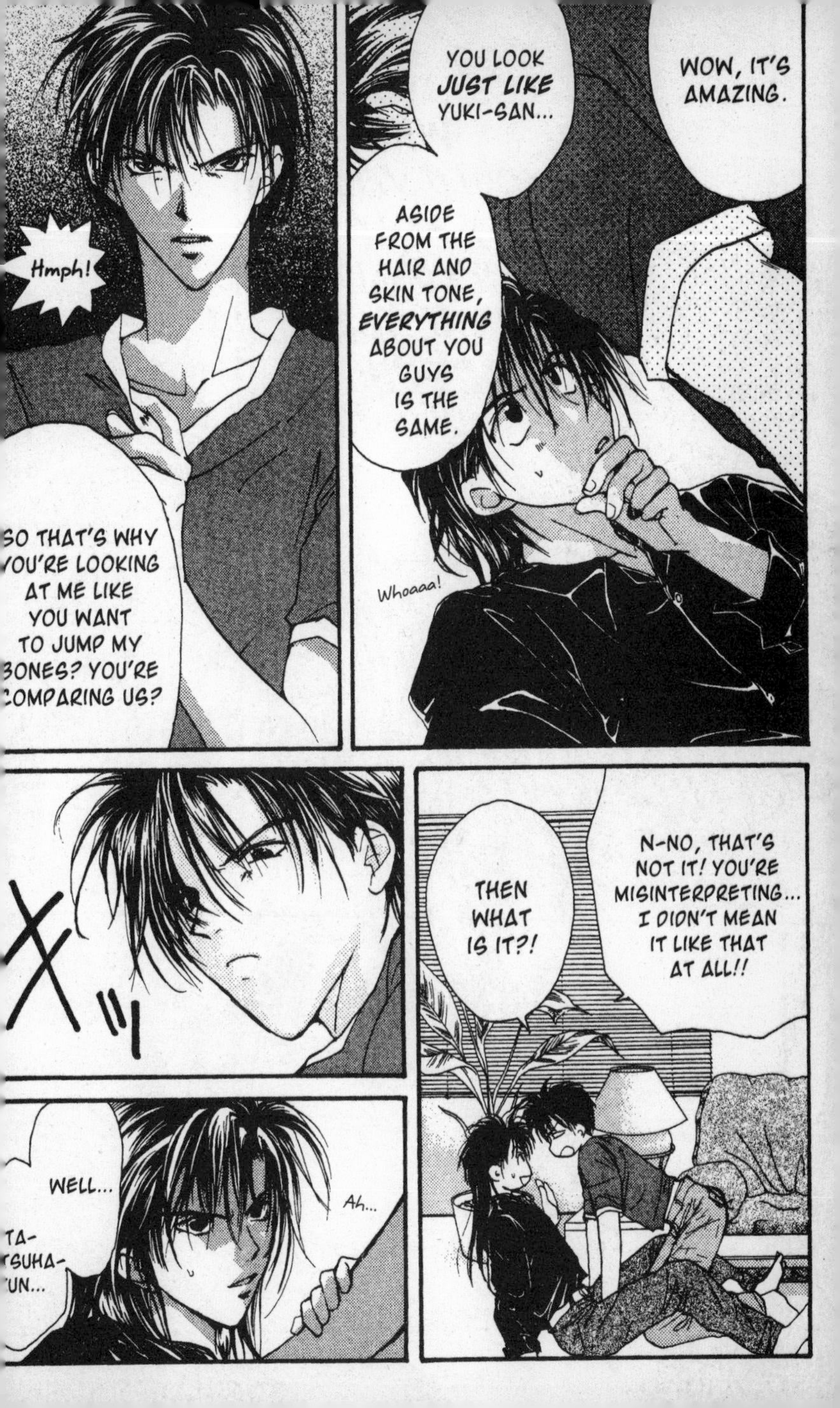
WOW, IT'S AMAZING.
YOU LOOK JUST LIKE YUKI-SAN...
ASIDE FROM THE HAIR AND SKIN TONE, EVERYTHING ABOUT YOU GUYS IS THE SAME.
Whoaaa!
Hmph!
SO THAT'S WHY YOU'RE LOOKING AT ME LIKE YOU WANT TO JUMP MY BONES? YOU'RE COMPARING US?
N-NO, THAT'S NOT IT! YOU'RE MISINTERPRETING... I DIDN'T MEAN IT LIKE THAT AT ALL!!
THEN WHAT IS IT?!
WELL...
Ah...
TA-TSUHA-KUN...

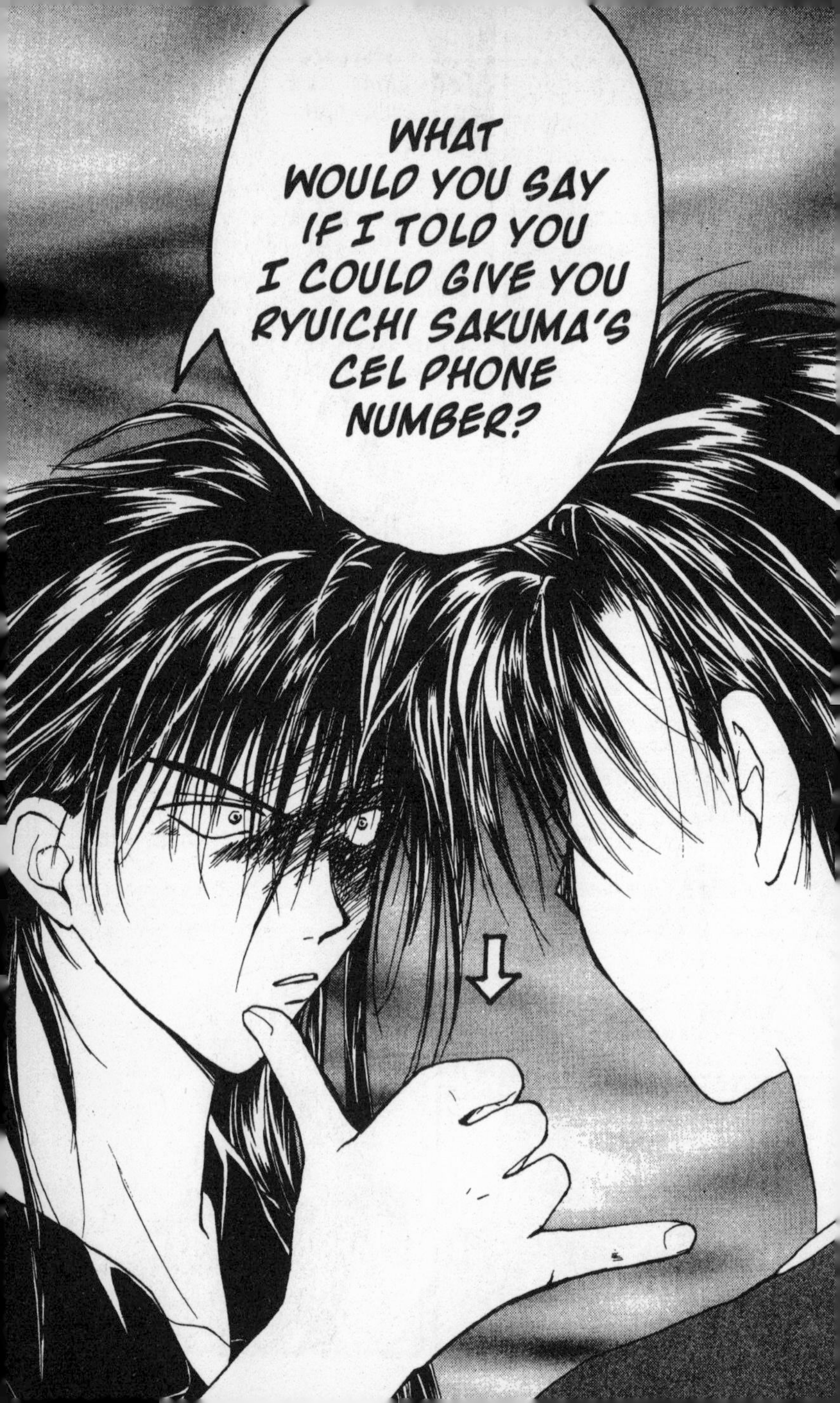
WHAT WOULD YOU SAY IF I TOLD YOU I COULD GIVE YOU RYUICHI SAKUMA'S CEL PHONE NUMBER?

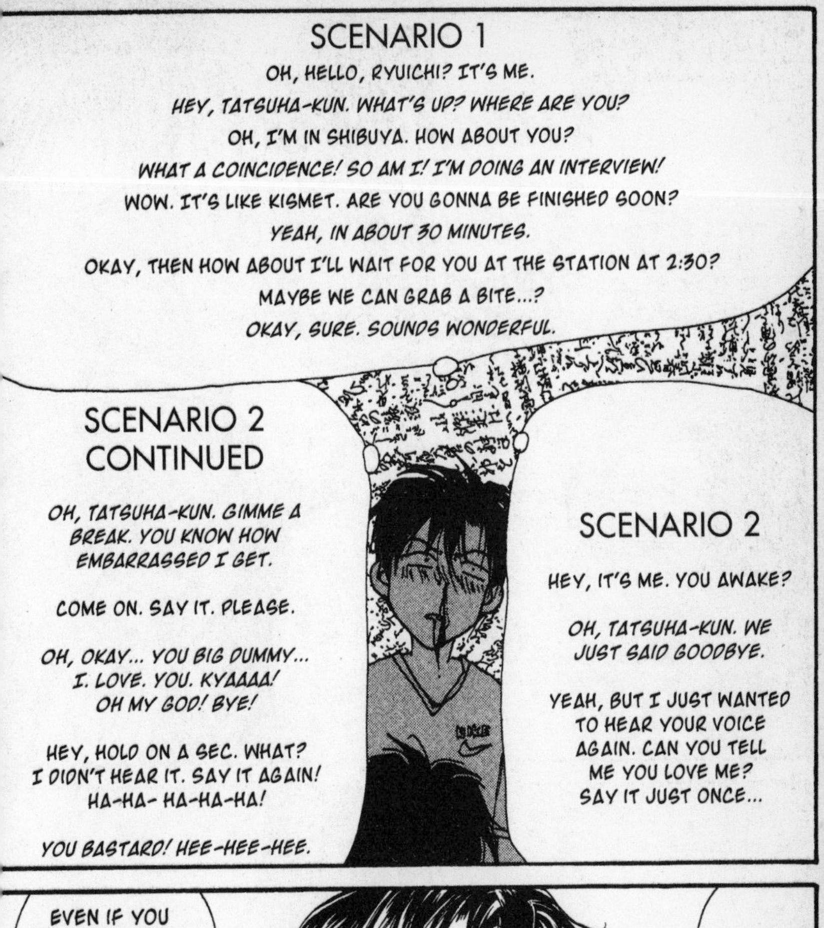
SCENARIO 1
OH, HELLO, RYUICHI? IT'S ME.
HEY, TATSUHA-KUN. WHAT'S UP? WHERE ARE YOU?
OH, I'M IN SHIBUYA. HOW ABOUT YOU?
WHAT A COINCIDENCE! SO AM I! I'M DOING AN INTERVIEW!
WOW. IT'S LIKE KISMET. ARE YOU GONNA BE FINISHED SOON?
YEAH, IN ABOUT 30 MINUTES.
OKAY, THEN HOW ABOUT I'LL WAIT FOR YOU AT THE STATION AT 2:30?
MAYBE WE CAN GRAB A BITE...?
OKAY, SURE. SOUNDS WONDERFUL.
SCENARIO 2
HEY, IT'S ME. YOU AWAKE?
OH, TATSUHA-KUN. WE JUST SAID GOODBYE.
YEAH, BUT I JUST WANTED TO HEAR YOUR VOICE AGAIN. CAN YOU TELL ME YOU LOVE ME? SAY IT JUST ONCE...
SCENARIO 2 CONTINUED
OH, TATSUHA-KUN. GIMME A BREAK. YOU KNOW HOW EMBARRASSED I GET.
COME ON. SAY IT. PLEASE.
OH, OKAY... YOU BIG DUMMY... I. LOVE. YOU. KYAAAA! OH MY GOD! BYE!
HEY, HOLD ON A SEC. WHAT? I DIDN'T HEAR IT. SAY IT AGAIN! HA-HA- HA-HA-HA!
YOU BASTARD! HEE-HEE-HEE.
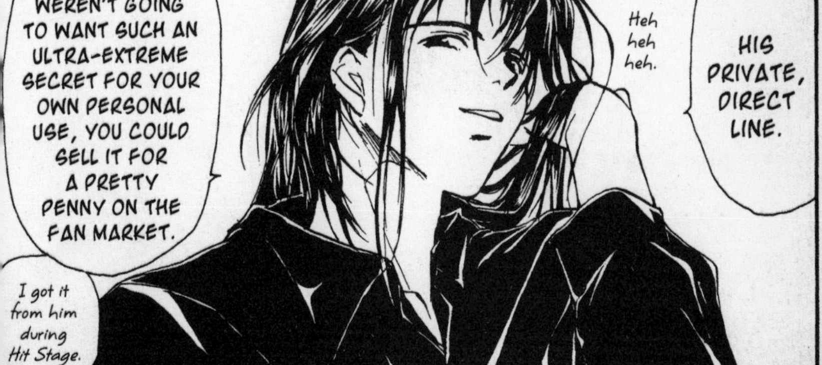
HIS PRIVATE, DIRECT LINE.
Heh heh heh.
EVEN IF YOU WEREN'T GOING TO WANT SUCH AN ULTRA-EXTREME SECRET FOR YOUR OWN PERSONAL USE, YOU COULD SELL IT FOR A PRETTY PENNY ON THE FAN MARKET.
I got it from him during Hit Stage.

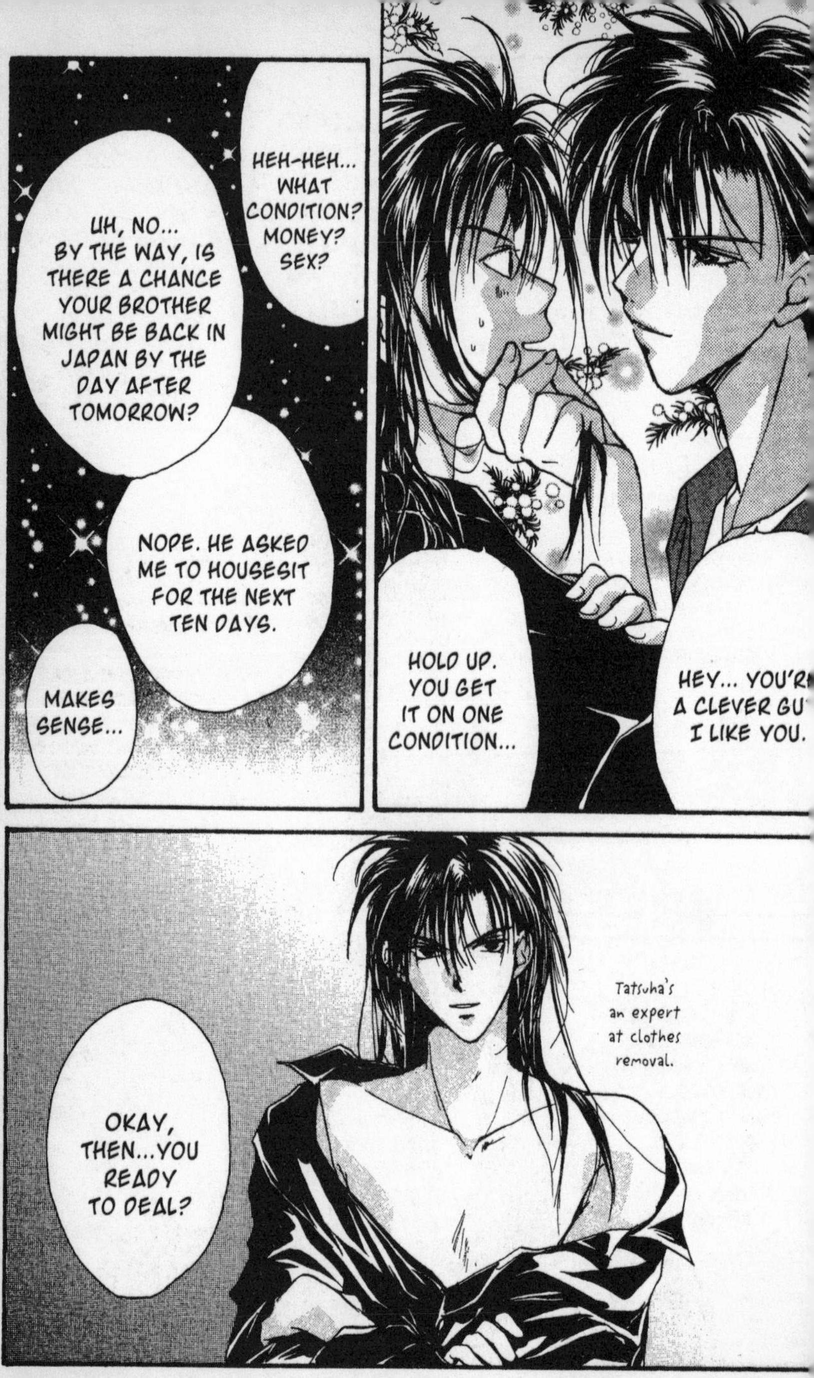
HEY... YOU'R
A CLEVER GU
I LIKE YOU.
HOLD UP. YOU GET IT ON ONE CONDITION...
HEH-HEH... WHAT CONDITION? MONEY? SEX?
UH, NO... BY THE WAY, IS THERE A CHANCE YOUR BROTHER MIGHT BE BACK IN JAPAN BY THE DAY AFTER TOMORROW?
NOPE. HE ASKED ME TO HOUSESIT FOR THE NEXT TEN DAYS.
MAKES SENSE...
Tatsuha's an expert at clothes removal.
OKAY, THEN...YOU READY TO DEAL?

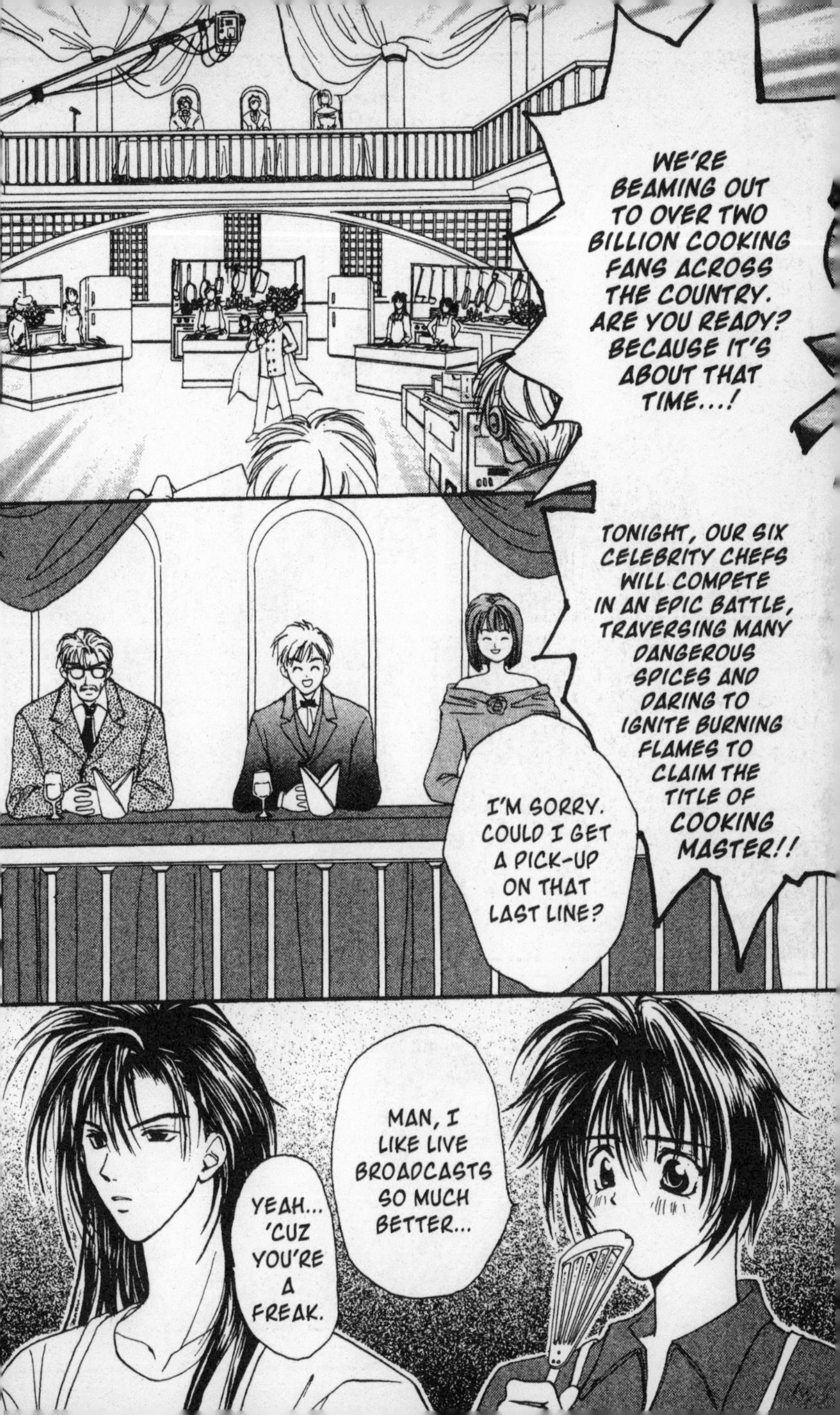
WE'RE BEAMING OUT TO OVER TWO BILLION COOKING FANS ACROSS THE COUNTRY. ARE YOU READY? BECAUSE IT'S ABOUT THAT TIME...!
TONIGHT, OUR SIX CELEBRITY CHEFS WILL COMPETE IN AN EPIC BATTLE, TRAVERSING MANY DANGEROUS SPICES AND DARING TO IGNITE BURNING FLAMES TO CLAIM THE TITLE OF COOKING MASTER!!
I'M SORRY. COULD I GET A PICK-UP ON THAT LAST LINE?
MAN, I LIKE LIVE BROADCASTS SO MUCH BETTER...
YEAH... 'CUZ YOU'RE A FREAK.

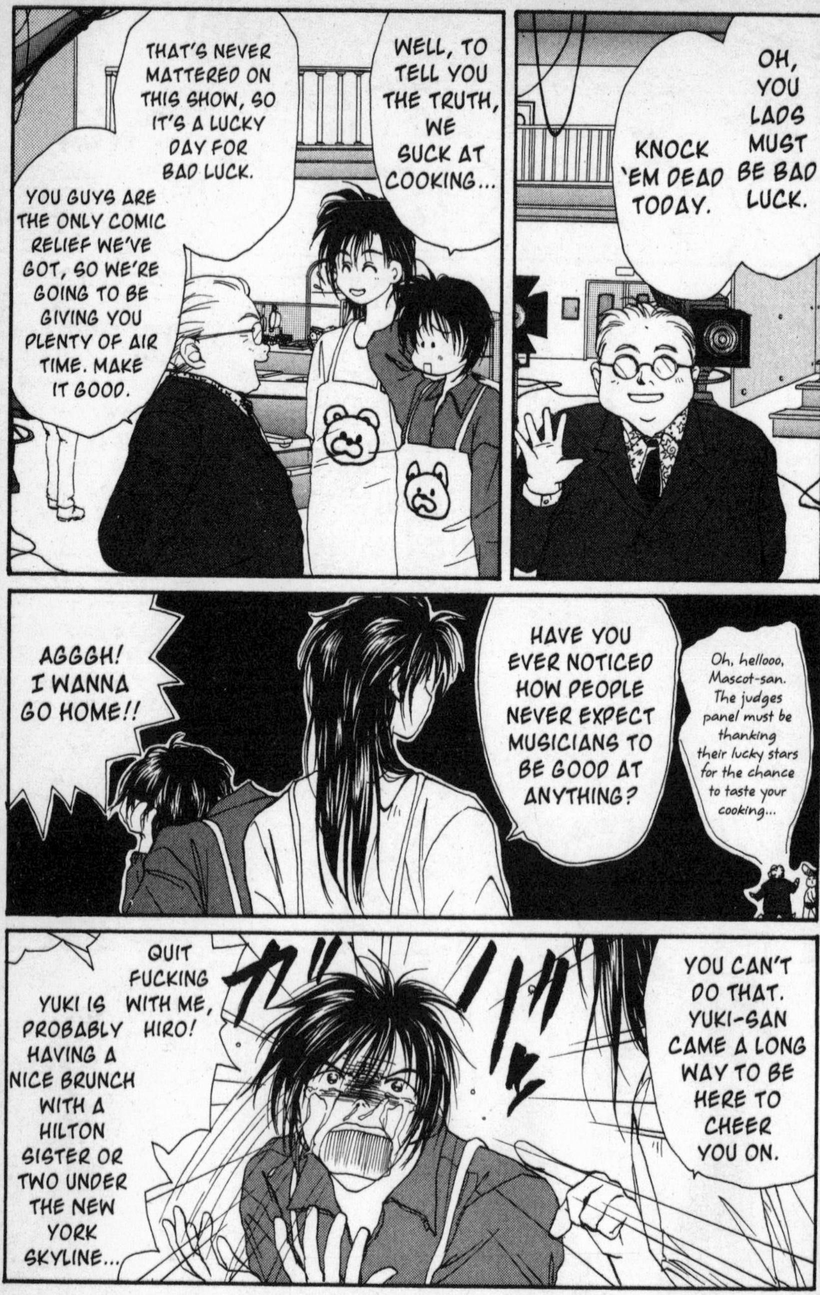
OH, YOU LADS MUST BE BAD LUCK.
KNOCK 'EM DEAD TODAY.
WELL, TO TELL YOU THE TRUTH, WE SUCK AT COOKING...
THAT'S NEVER MATTERED ON THIS SHOW, SO IT'S A LUCKY DAY FOR BAD LUCK.
YOU GUYS ARE THE ONLY COMIC RELIEF WE'VE GOT, SO WE'RE GOING TO BE GIVING YOU PLENTY OF AIR TIME. MAKE IT GOOD.
Oh, hellooo, Mascot-san. The judges panel must be thanking their lucky stars for the chance to taste your cooking...
HAVE YOU EVER NOTICED HOW PEOPLE NEVER EXPECT MUSICIANS TO BE GOOD AT ANYTHING?
AGGGH! I WANNA GO HOME!!
YOU CAN'T DO THAT. YUKI-SAN CAME A LONG WAY TO BE HERE TO CHEER YOU ON.
QUIT FUCKING WITH ME, HIRO!
YUKI IS PROBABLY HAVING A NICE BRUNCH WITH A HILTON SISTER OR TWO UNDER THE NEW YORK SKYLINE...

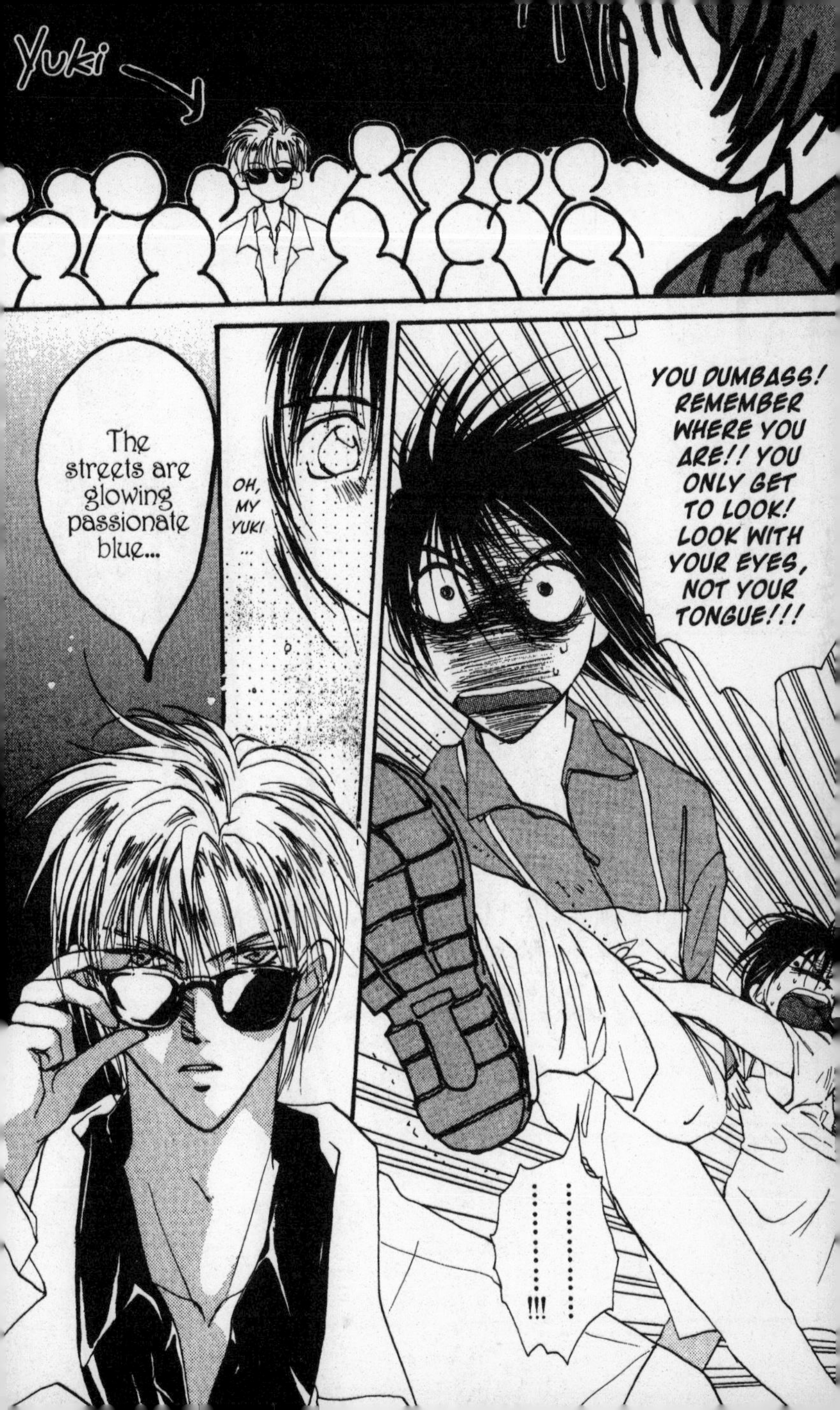
Yuki
YOU DUMBASS! REMEMBER WHERE YOU ARE!! YOU ONLY GET TO LOOK! LOOK WITH YOUR EYES, NOT YOUR TONGUE!!!
......!!!
OH, MY YUKI ...
The streets are glowing passionate blue...

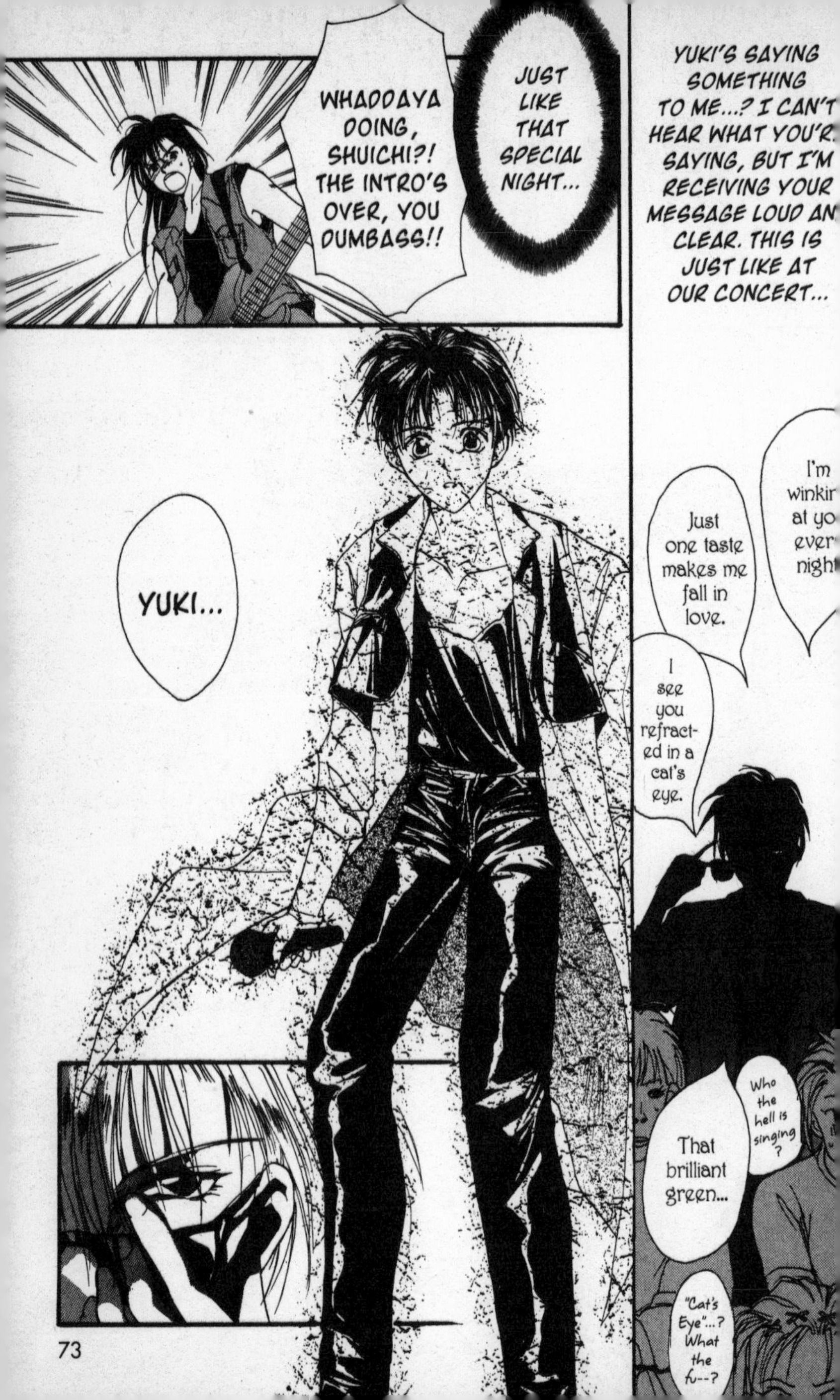
YUKI'S SAYING SOMETHING TO ME...? I CAN'T HEAR WHAT YOU'R SAYING, BUT I'M RECEIVING YOUR MESSAGE LOUD AN CLEAR. THIS IS JUST LIKE AT OUR CONCERT...
I'm winkin at yo ever nigh
Just one taste makes me fall in love.
I see you refract-ed in a cat's eye.
Who the hell is singing?
That brilliant green...
"Cat's Eye"...? What the fu--?
JUST LIKE THAT SPECIAL NIGHT...
WHADDAYA DOING, SHUICHI?! THE INTRO'S OVER, YOU DUMBASS!!
YUKI...

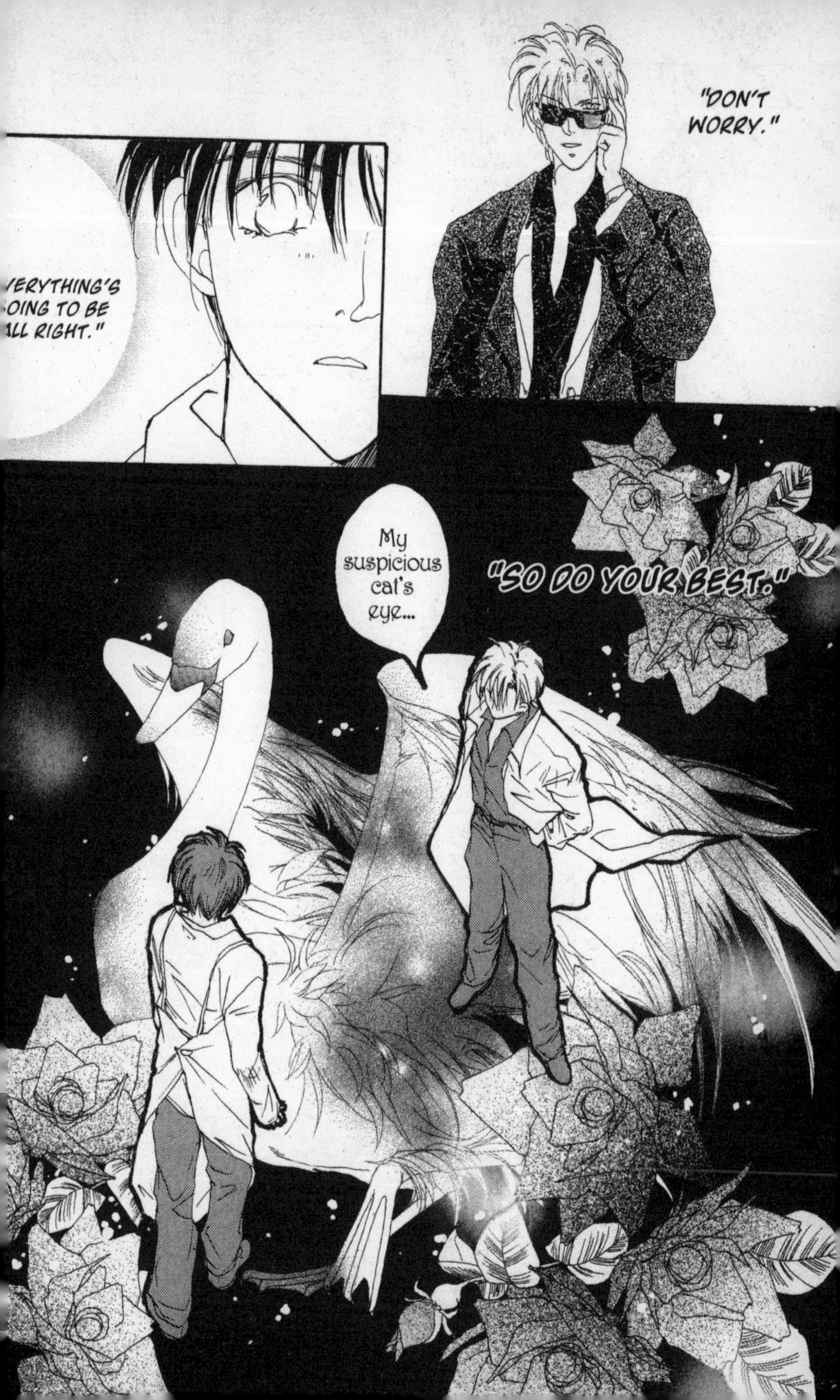
"DON'T WORRY."
VERYTHING'S OING TO BE LL RIGHT."
"SO DO YOUR BEST."
My suspicious cat's eye...

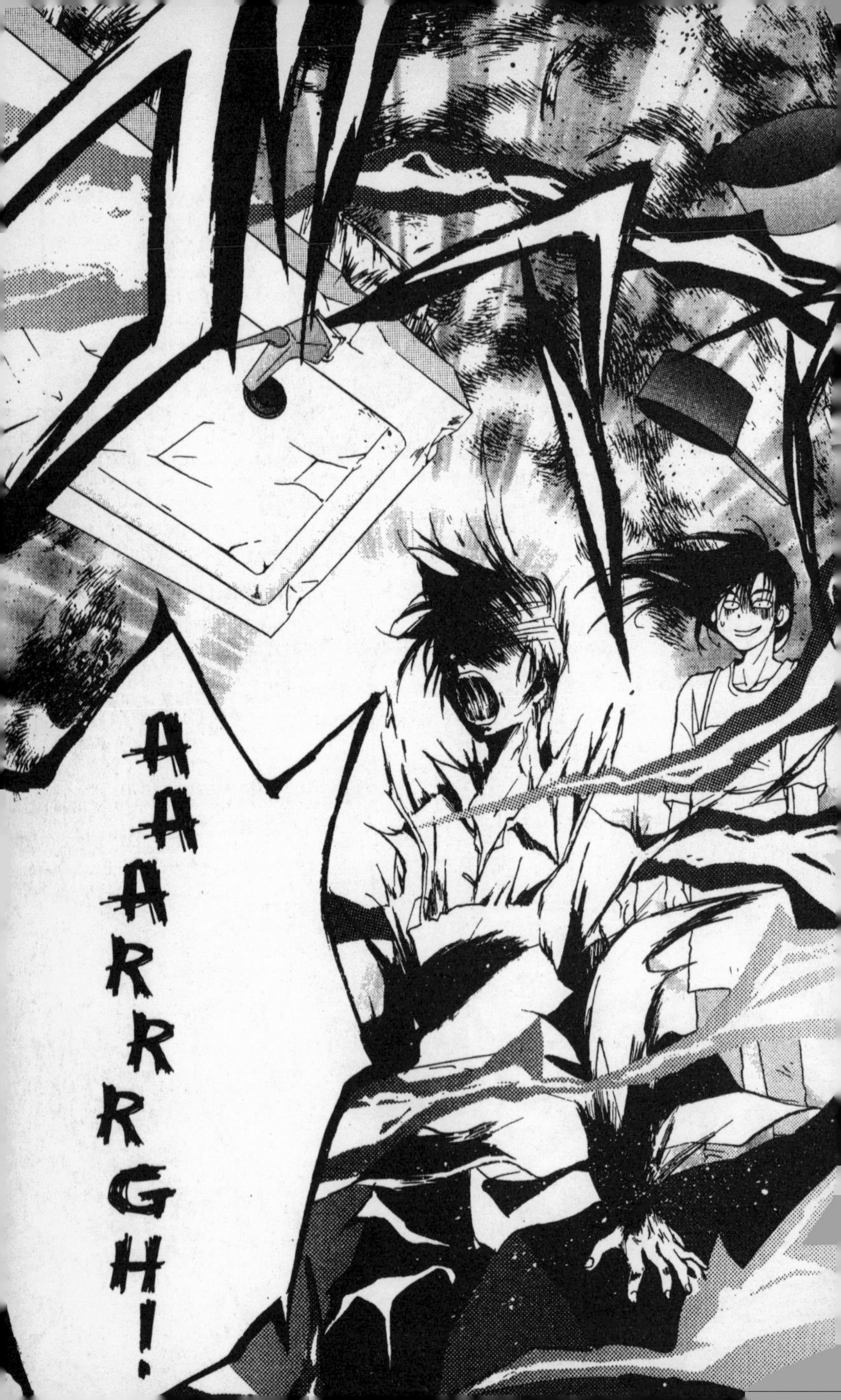
AAARRRGH!

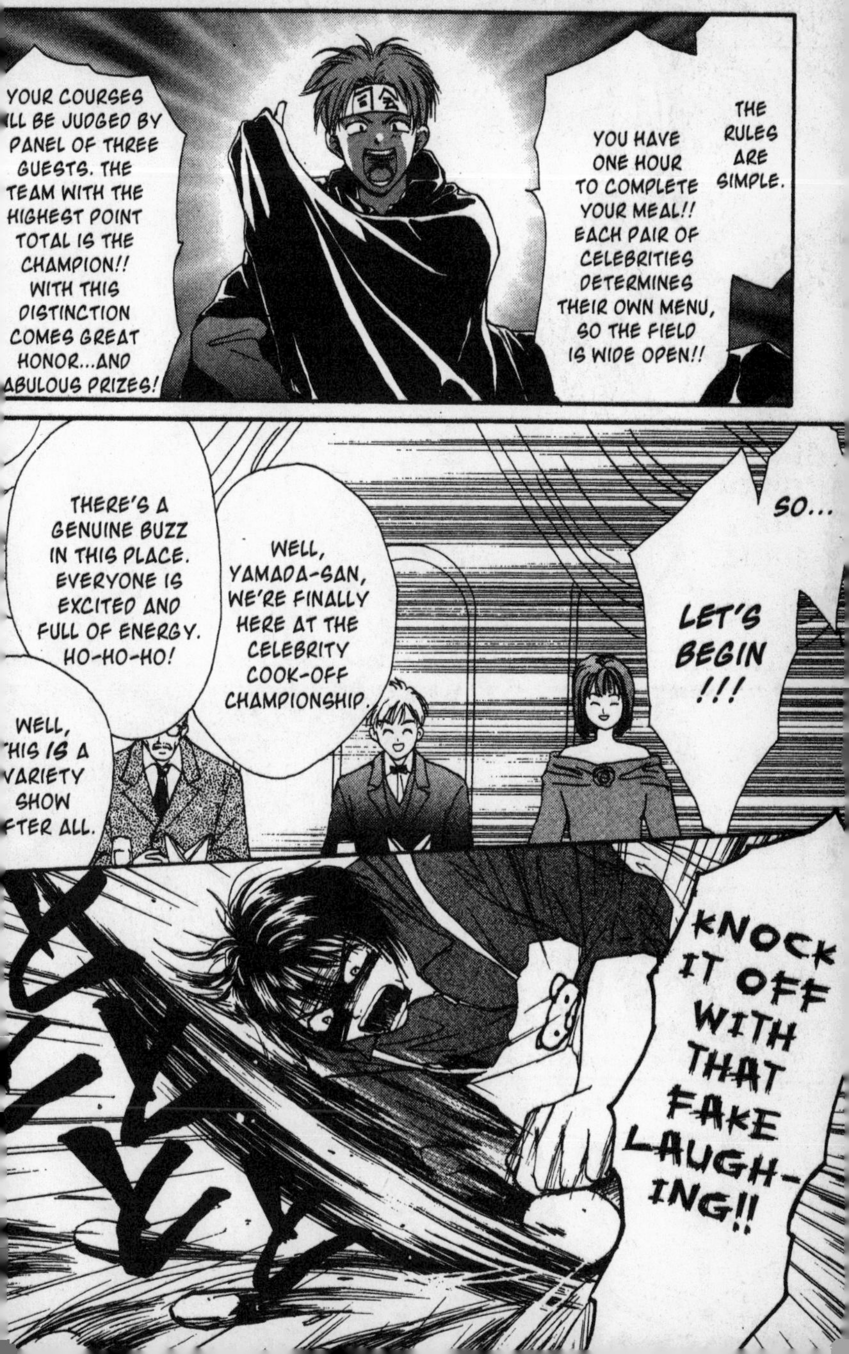
THE RULES ARE SIMPLE.
YOU HAVE ONE HOUR TO COMPLETE YOUR MEAL!! EACH PAIR OF CELEBRITIES DETERMINES THEIR OWN MENU, SO THE FIELD IS WIDE OPEN!!
YOUR COURSES ILL BE JUDGED BY PANEL OF THREE GUESTS. THE TEAM WITH THE HIGHEST POINT TOTAL IS THE CHAMPION!! WITH THIS DISTINCTION COMES GREAT HONOR...AND ABULOUS PRIZES!
SO...
LET'S BEGIN!!!
WELL, YAMADA-SAN, WE'RE FINALLY HERE AT THE CELEBRITY COOK-OFF CHAMPIONSHIP.
THERE'S A GENUINE BUZZ IN THIS PLACE. EVERYONE IS EXCITED AND FULL OF ENERGY. HO-HO-HO!
WELL, HIS *IS* A VARIETY SHOW FTER ALL.
KNOCK IT OFF WITH THAT FAKE LAUGH-ING!!

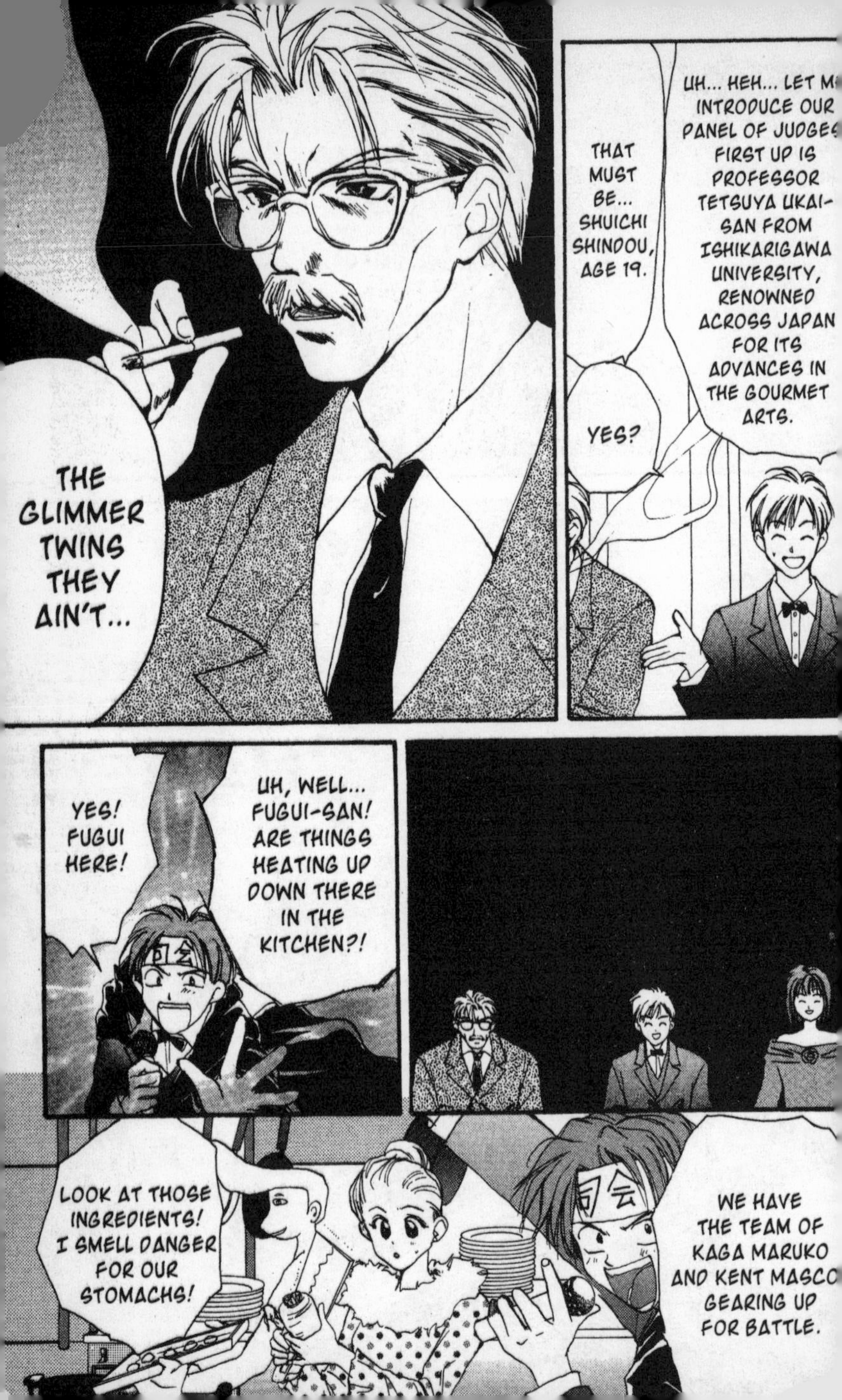

UH... HEH... LET M
INTRODUCE OUR PANEL OF JUDGE
FIRST UP IS PROFESSOR TETSUYA UKAI-SAN FROM ISHIKARIGAWA UNIVERSITY, RENOWNED ACROSS JAPAN FOR ITS ADVANCES IN THE GOURMET ARTS.
THAT MUST BE... SHUICHI SHINDOU, AGE 19.
YES?
THE GLIMMER TWINS THEY AIN'T...
UH, WELL... FUGUI-SAN! ARE THINGS HEATING UP DOWN THERE IN THE KITCHEN?!
YES! FUGUI HERE!
WE HAVE THE TEAM OF KAGA MARUKO AND KENT MASCO GEARING UP FOR BATTLE.
LOOK AT THOSE INGREDIENTS! I SMELL DANGER FOR OUR STOMACHS!

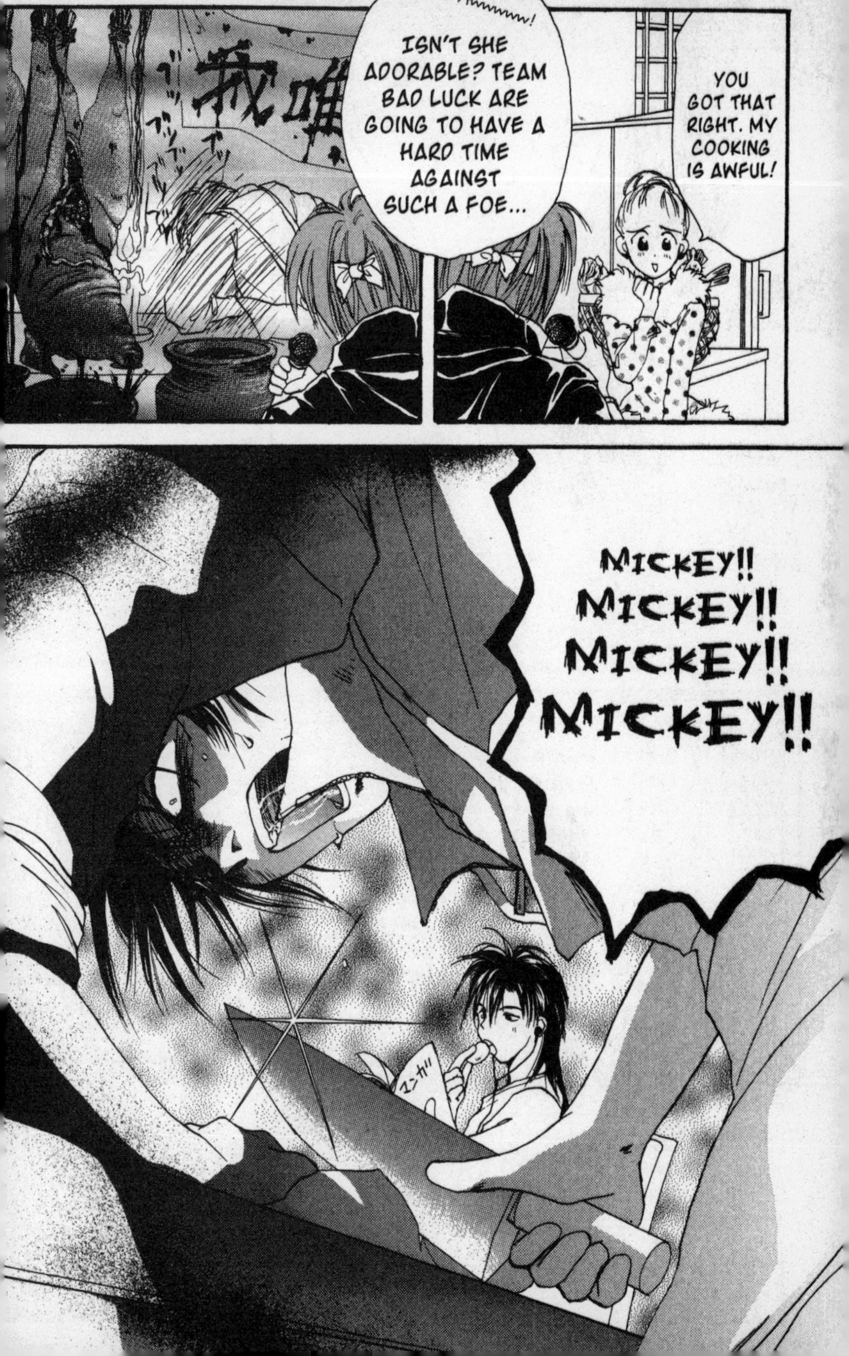
Awwwww!
ISN'T SHE ADORABLE? TEAM BAD LUCK ARE GOING TO HAVE A HARD TIME AGAINST SUCH A FOE...
YOU GOT THAT RIGHT. MY COOKING IS AWFUL!
MICKEY!! MICKEY!! MICKEY!! MICKEY!!

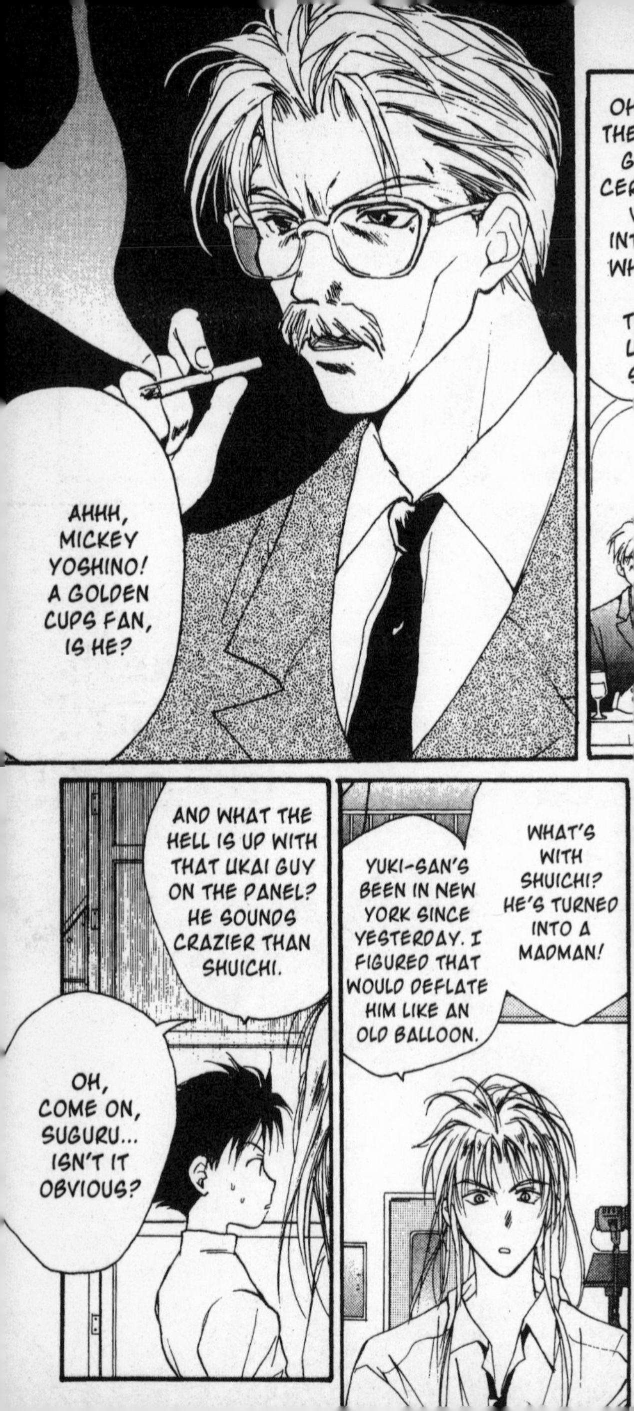
AHHH, MICKEY YOSHINO! A GOLDEN CUPS FAN, IS HE?
WHAT'S WITH SHUICHI? HE'S TURNED INTO A MADMAN!
YUKI-SAN'S BEEN IN NEW YORK SINCE YESTERDAY. I FIGURED THAT WOULD DEFLATE HIM LIKE AN OLD BALLOON.
AND WHAT THE HELL IS UP WITH THAT UKAI GUY ON THE PANEL? HE SOUNDS CRAZIER THAN SHUICHI.
OH, COME ON, SUGURU... ISN'T IT OBVIOUS?

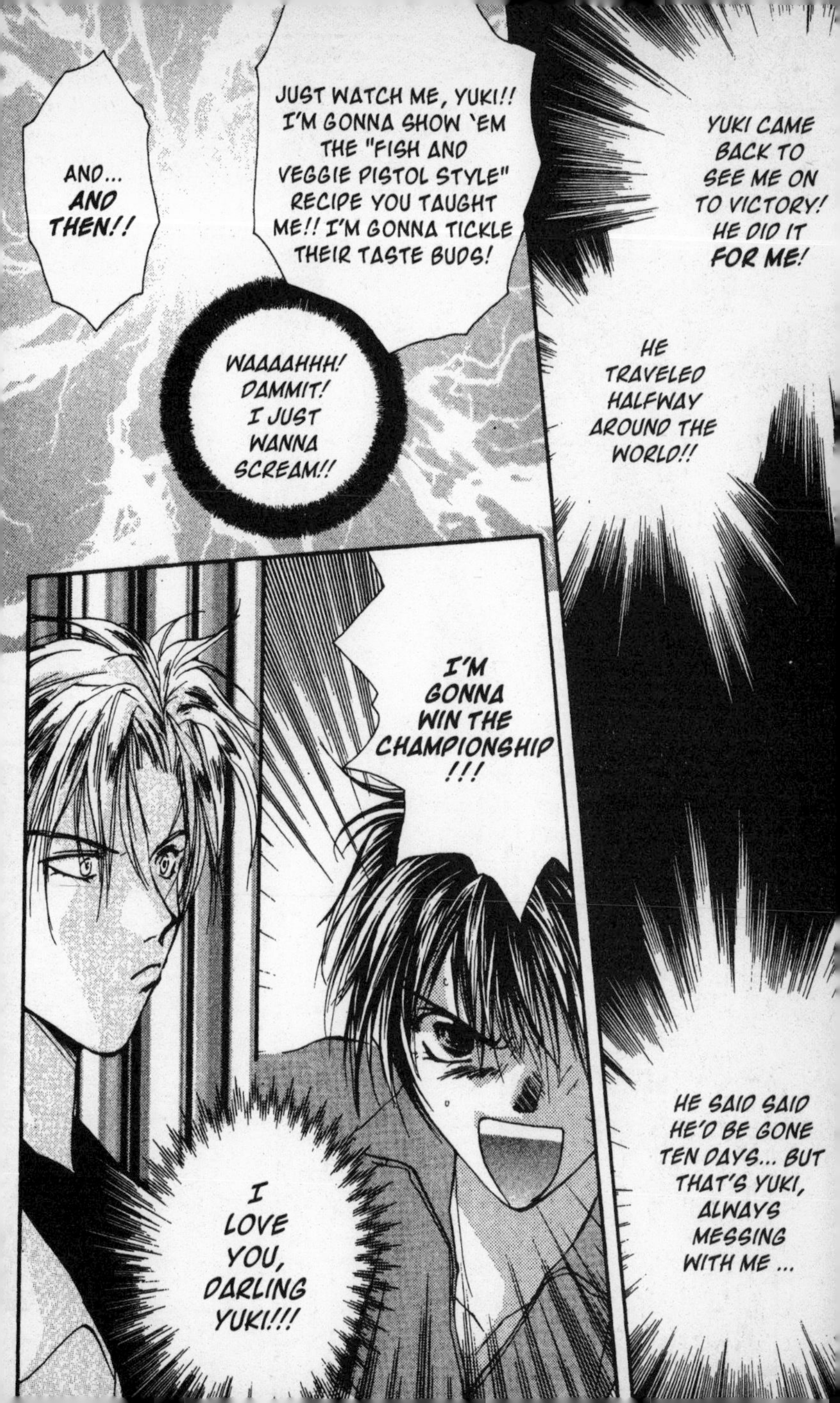
YUKI CAME BACK TO SEE ME ON TO VICTORY! HE DID IT FOR ME!
HE TRAVELED HALFWAY AROUND THE WORLD!!
HE SAID SAID HE'D BE GONE TEN DAYS... BUT THAT'S YUKI, ALWAYS MESSING WITH ME ...
JUST WATCH ME, YUKI!! I'M GONNA SHOW 'EM THE "FISH AND VEGGIE PISTOL STYLE" RECIPE YOU TAUGHT ME!! I'M GONNA TICKLE THEIR TASTE BUDS!
AND... AND THEN!!
WAAAAHHH! DAMMIT! I JUST WANNA SCREAM!!
I'M GONNA WIN THE CHAMPIONSHIP !!!
I LOVE YOU, DARLING YUKI!!!

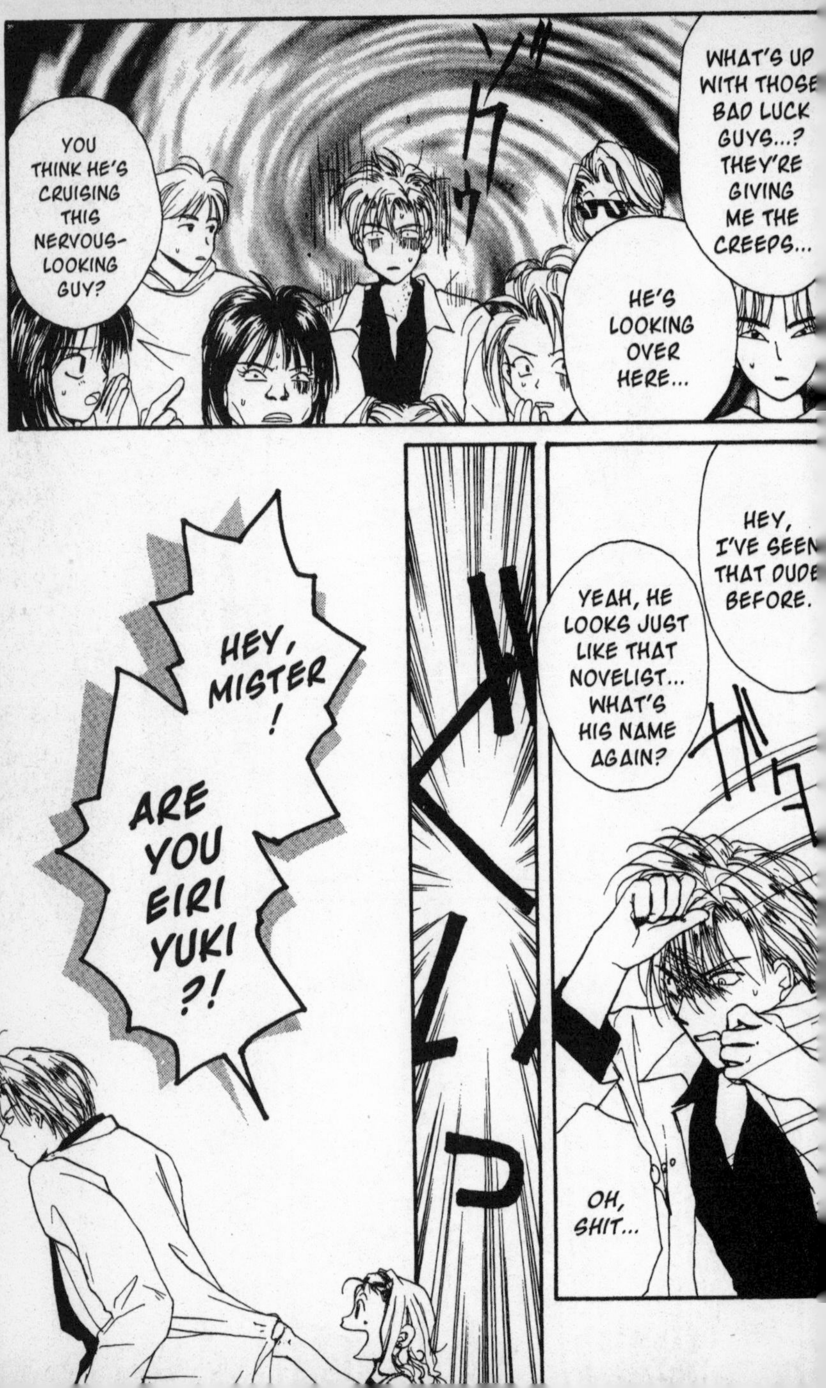
WHAT'S UP WITH THOSE BAD LUCK GUYS...? THEY'RE GIVING ME THE CREEPS...
HE'S LOOKING OVER HERE...
YOU THINK HE'S CRUISING THIS NERVOUS-LOOKING GUY?
HEY, I'VE SEEN THAT DUDE BEFORE.
YEAH, HE LOOKS JUST LIKE THAT NOVELIST... WHAT'S HIS NAME AGAIN?
OH, SHIT...
HEY, MISTER!
ARE YOU EIRI YUKI?!

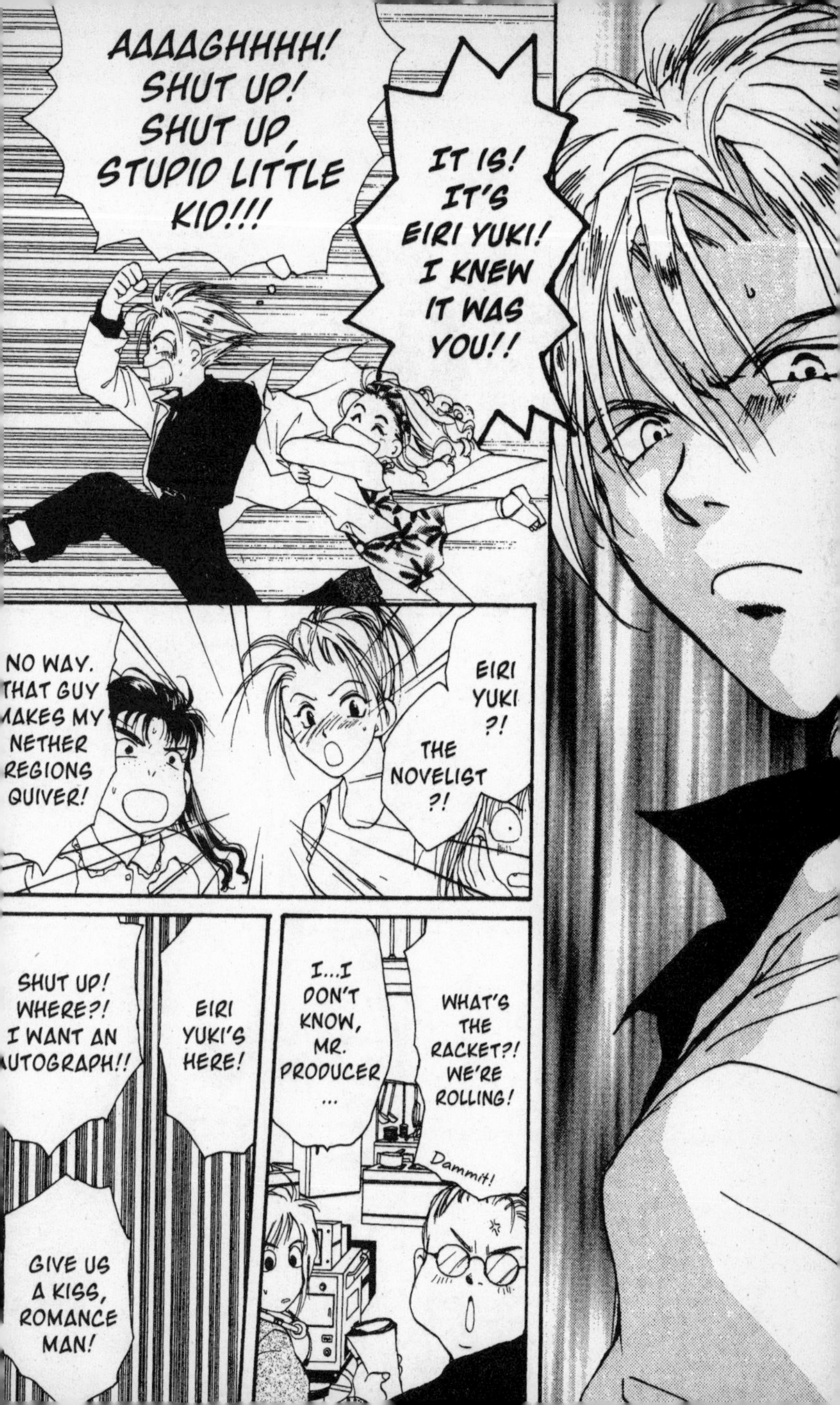
AAAAGHHHH! SHUT UP! SHUT UP, STUPID LITTLE KID!!!
IT IS! IT'S EIRI YUKI! I KNEW IT WAS YOU!!
EIRI YUKI ?!
THE NOVELIST ?!
NO WAY. THAT GUY AKES MY NETHER REGIONS QUIVER!
WHAT'S THE RACKET?! WE'RE ROLLING!
I...I DON'T KNOW, MR. PRODUCER ...
Dammit!
EIRI YUKI'S HERE!
SHUT UP! WHERE?! I WANT AN UTOGRAPH!!
GIVE US A KISS, ROMANCE MAN!

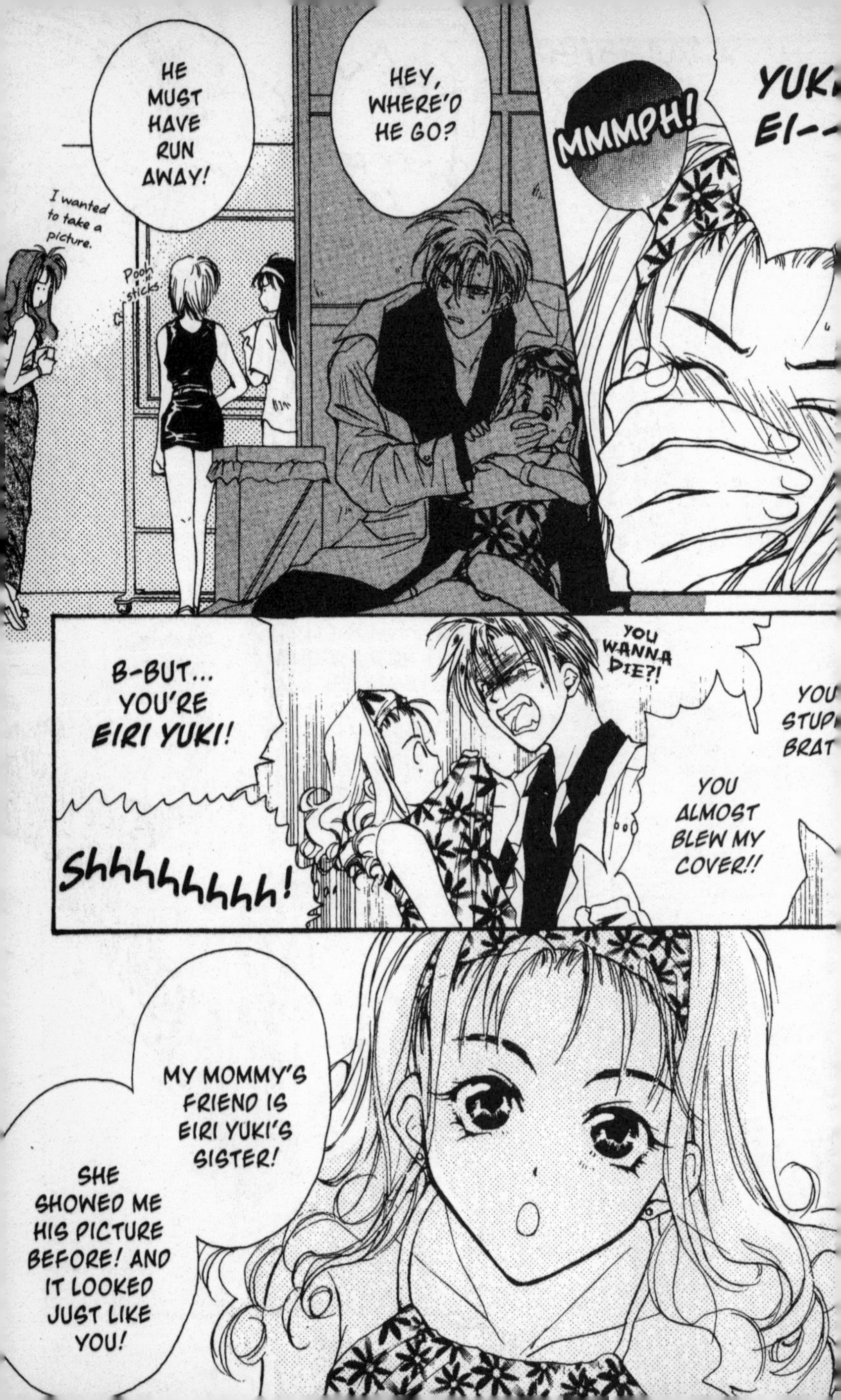
YUK EI--
MMMPH!
HEY, WHERE'D HE GO?
HE MUST HAVE RUN AWAY!
I wanted to take a picture.
Pooh sticks.
YOU STUP BRAT
YOU WANNA DIE?!
YOU ALMOST BLEW MY COVER!!
B-BUT... YOU'RE EIRI YUKI!
Shhhhhhhhh!
MY MOMMY'S FRIEND IS EIRI YUKI'S SISTER!
SHE SHOWED ME HIS PICTURE BEFORE! AND IT LOOKED JUST LIKE YOU!

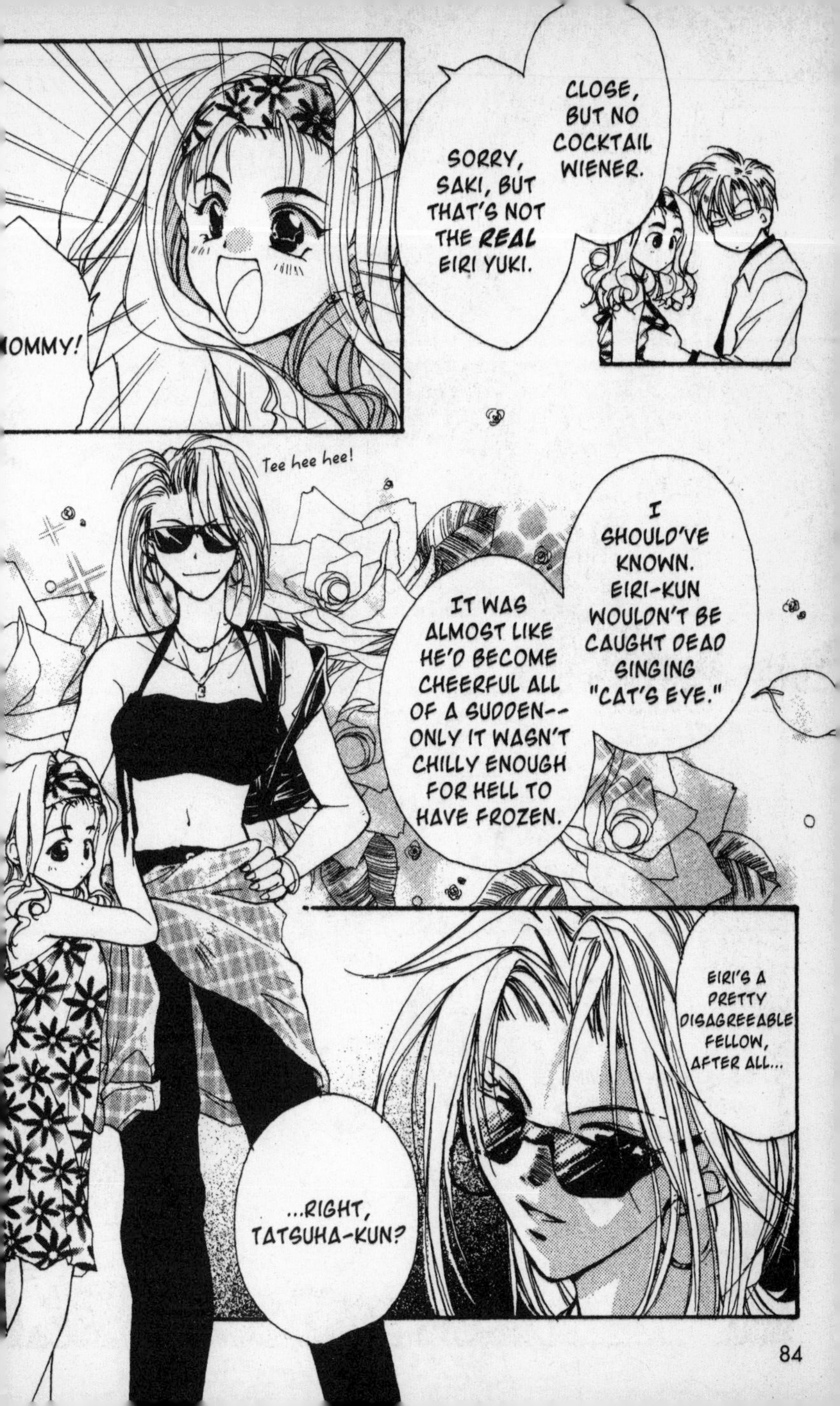
CLOSE, BUT NO COCKTAIL WIENER.
SORRY, SAKI, BUT THAT'S NOT THE *REAL* EIRI YUKI.
OMMY!
Tee hee hee!
I SHOULD'VE KNOWN. EIRI-KUN WOULDN'T BE CAUGHT DEAD SINGING "CAT'S EYE."
IT WAS ALMOST LIKE HE'D BECOME CHEERFUL ALL OF A SUDDEN--ONLY IT WASN'T CHILLY ENOUGH FOR HELL TO HAVE FROZEN.
EIRI'S A PRETTY DISAGREEABLE FELLOW, AFTER ALL...
...RIGHT, TATSUHA-KUN?

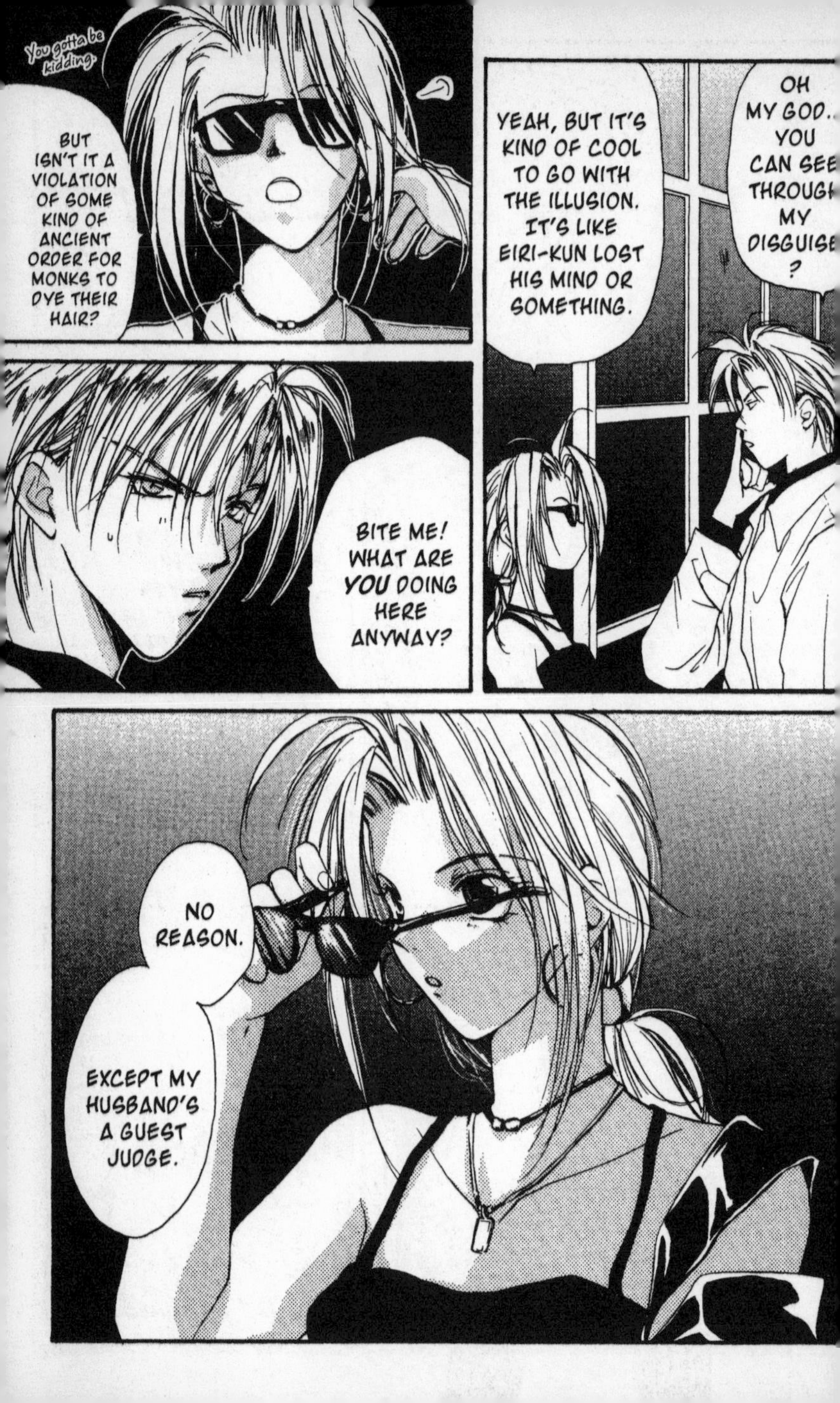

OH MY GOD... YOU CAN SEE THROUGH MY DISGUISE?
YEAH, BUT IT'S KIND OF COOL TO GO WITH THE ILLUSION. IT'S LIKE EIRI-KUN LOST HIS MIND OR SOMETHING.
You gotta be kidding.
BUT ISN'T IT A VIOLATION OF SOME KIND OF ANCIENT ORDER FOR MONKS TO DYE THEIR HAIR?
BITE ME! WHAT ARE *YOU* DOING HERE ANYWAY?
NO REASON.
EXCEPT MY HUSBAND'S A GUEST JUDGE.

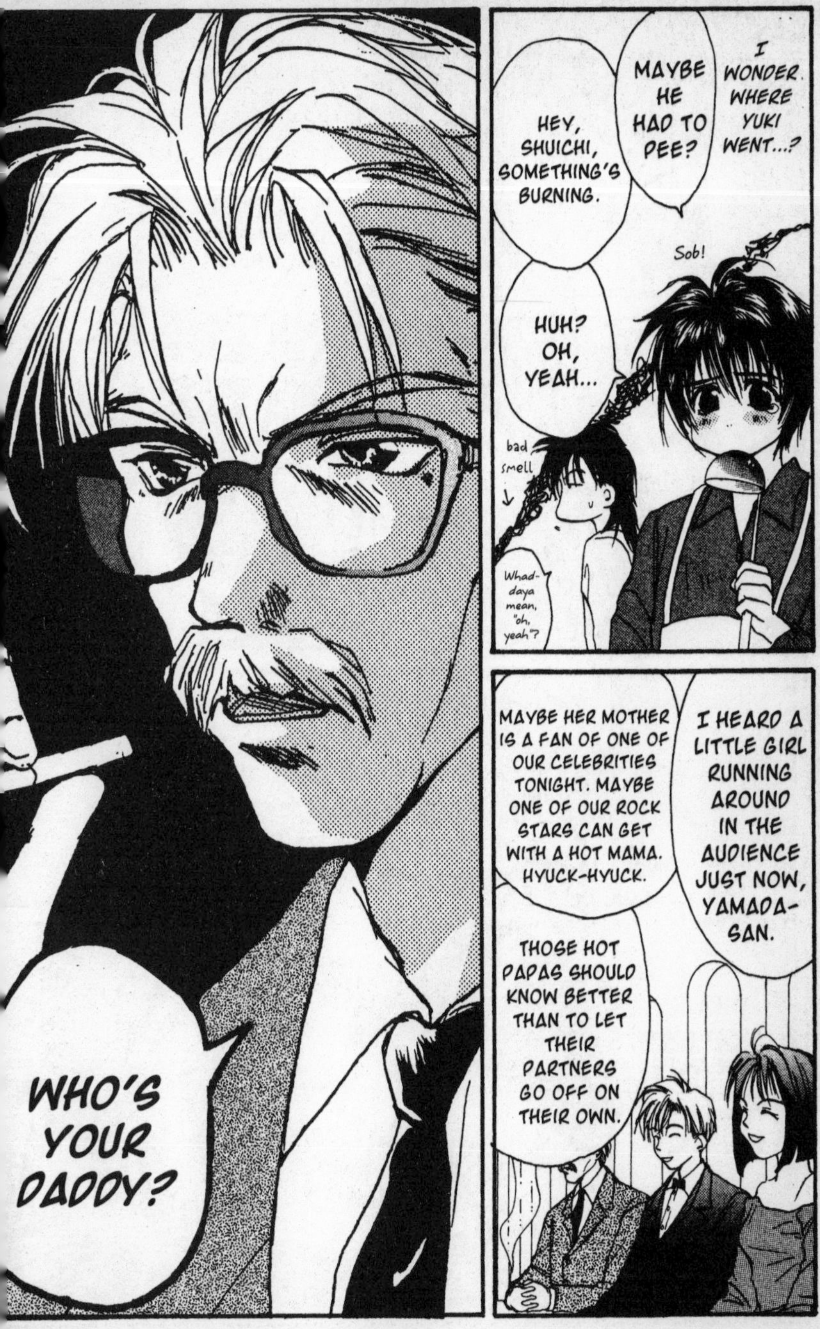

I WONDER WHERE YUKI WENT...?
MAYBE HE HAD TO PEE?
HEY, SHUICHI, SOMETHING'S BURNING.
Sob!
HUH? OH, YEAH...
bad smell
Whad-daya mean, "oh, yeah"?
I HEARD A LITTLE GIRL RUNNING AROUND IN THE AUDIENCE JUST NOW, YAMADA-SAN.
MAYBE HER MOTHER IS A FAN OF ONE OF OUR CELEBRITIES TONIGHT. MAYBE ONE OF OUR ROCK STARS CAN GET WITH A HOT MAMA. HYUCK-HYUCK.
THOSE HOT PAPAS SHOULD KNOW BETTER THAN TO LET THEIR PARTNERS GO OFF ON THEIR OWN.
WHO'S YOUR DADDY?

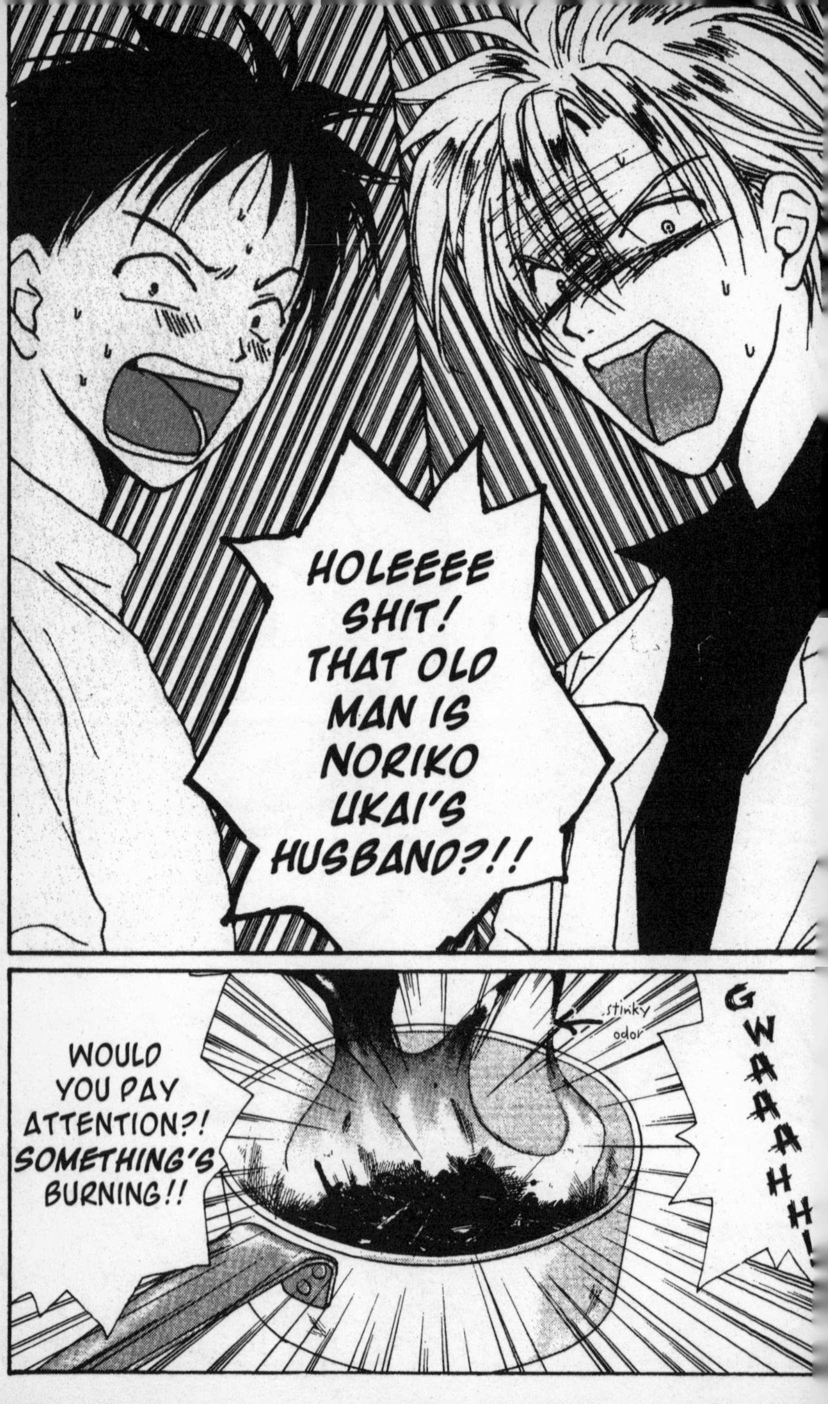
HOLEEEE SHIT! THAT OLD MAN IS NORIKO UKAI'S HUSBAND?!!
GWAAAHH!
stinky odor
WOULD YOU PAY ATTENTION?! SOMETHING'S BURNING!!

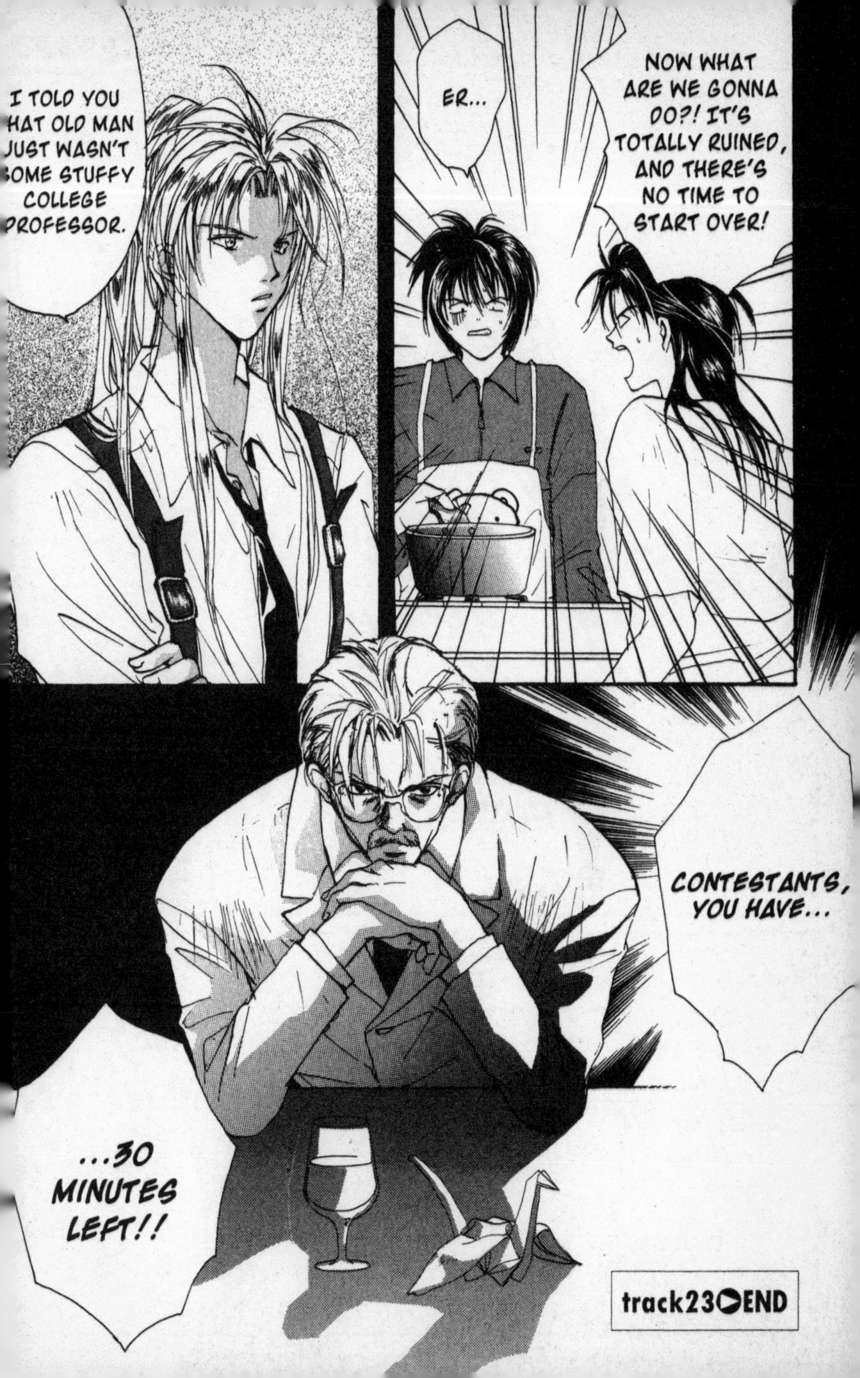
NOW WHAT ARE WE GONNA DO?! IT'S TOTALLY RUINED, AND THERE'S NO TIME TO START OVER!
ER...
I TOLD YOU HAT OLD MAN JUST WASN'T SOME STUFFY COLLEGE PROFESSOR.
CONTESTANTS, YOU HAVE...
...30 MINUTES LEFT!!
track23 END

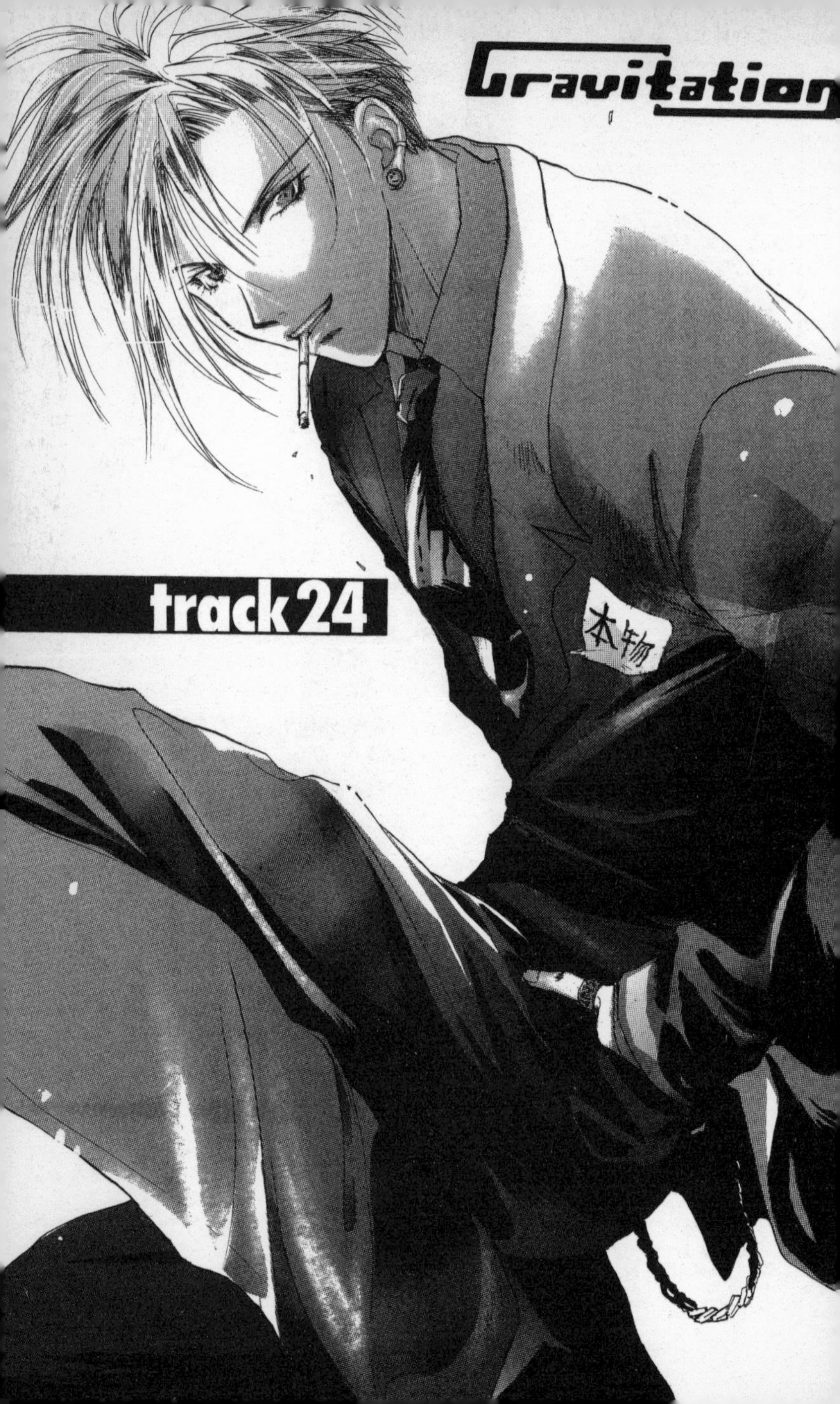
Gravitation
track 24
本物

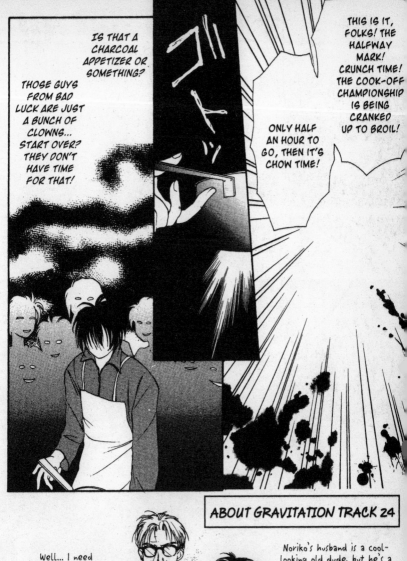

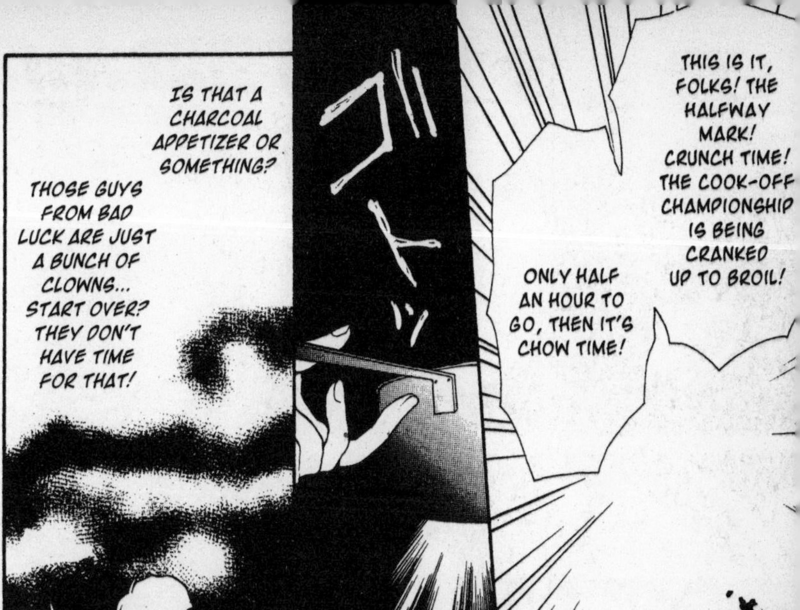
THIS IS IT, FOLKS! THE HALFWAY MARK! CRUNCH TIME! THE COOK-OFF CHAMPIONSHIP IS BEING CRANKED UP TO BROIL!
ONLY HALF AN HOUR TO GO, THEN IT'S CHOW TIME!
ゴトッ
IS THAT A CHARCOAL APPETIZER OR SOMETHING?
THOSE GUYS FROM BAD LUCK ARE JUST A BUNCH OF CLOWNS... START OVER? THEY DON'T HAVE TIME FOR THAT!

ABOUT GRAVITATION TRACK 24

Noriko's husband is a cool-looking old dude, but he's a little strange. Just for the hell of it, I decided to draw Hiro next to him. Totally pointless, isn't it? I guess...but you **did** ask for drawings.

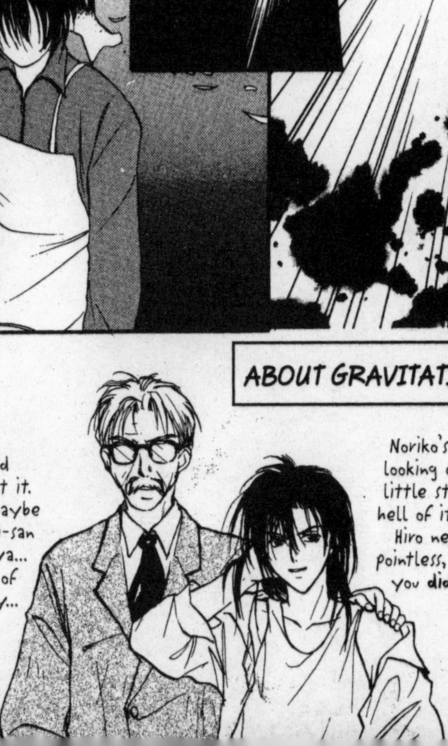

Well... I need another shot at it. So next time, maybe I'll draw in Eiri-san next to Tetsuya... Oops. I'm out of space already...

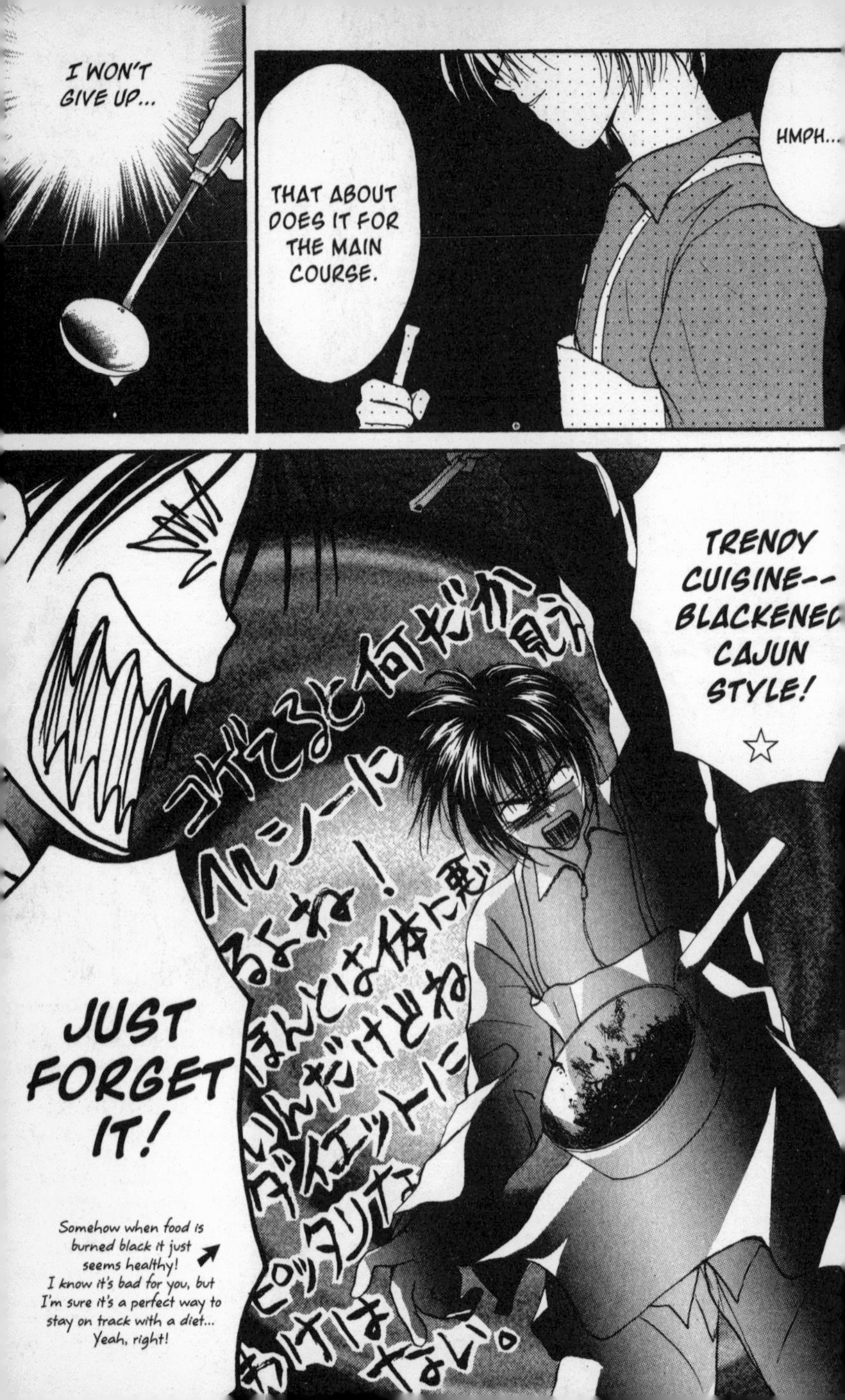
HMPH...
THAT ABOUT DOES IT FOR THE MAIN COURSE.
I WON'T GIVE UP...
TRENDY CUISINE--BLACKENED CAJUN STYLE! ☆
JUST FORGET IT!
Somehow when food is burned black it just seems healthy! I know it's bad for you, but I'm sure it's a perfect way to stay on track with a diet... Yeah, right!

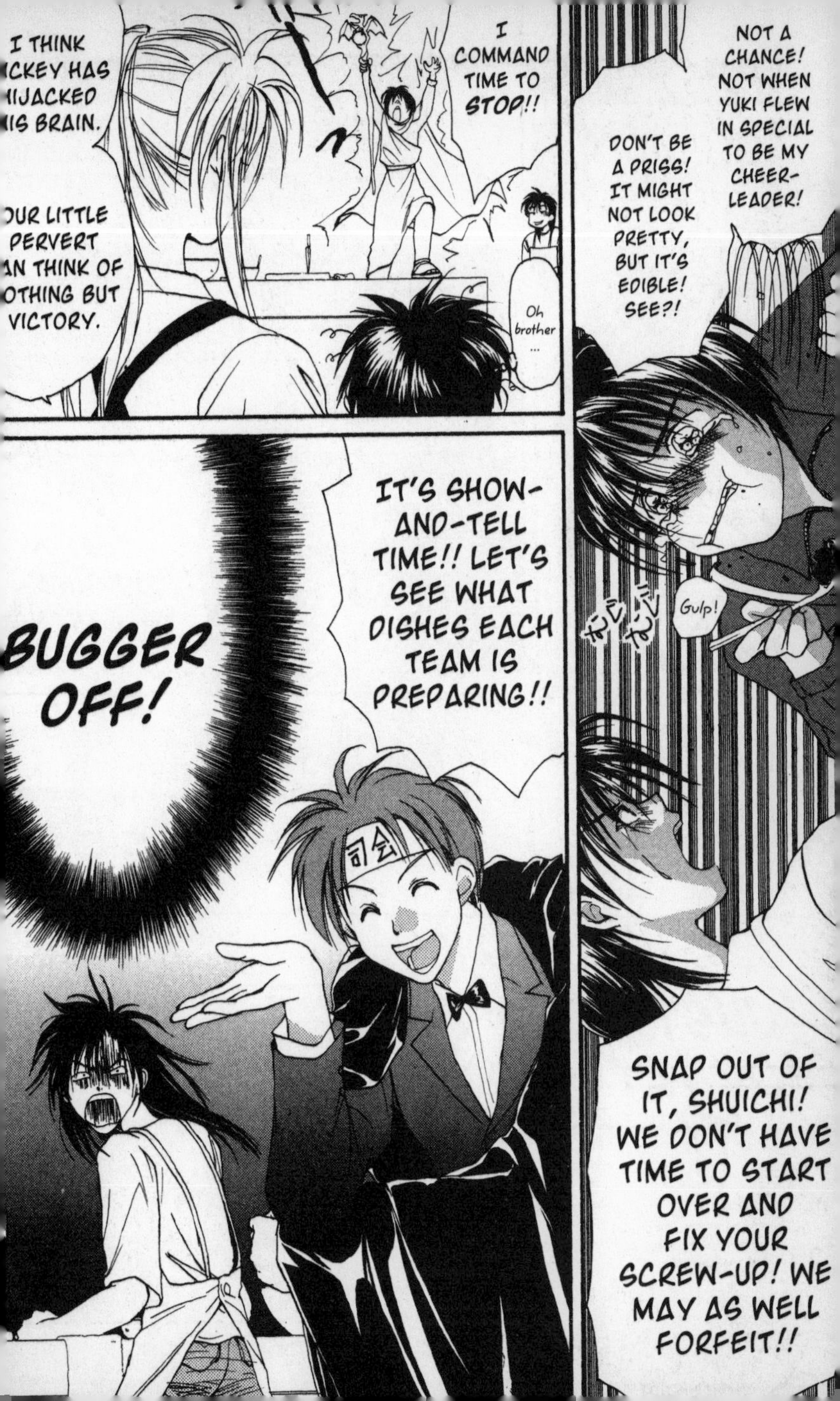
NOT A CHANCE! NOT WHEN YUKI FLEW IN SPECIAL TO BE MY CHEER-LEADER!
DON'T BE A PRISS! IT MIGHT NOT LOOK PRETTY, BUT IT'S EDIBLE! SEE?!
Gulp!
SNAP OUT OF IT, SHUICHI! WE DON'T HAVE TIME TO START OVER AND FIX YOUR SCREW-UP! WE MAY AS WELL FORFEIT!!
I COMMAND TIME TO STOP!!
Oh brother...
I THINK ICKEY HAS IIJACKED IIS BRAIN.
OUR LITTLE PERVERT AN THINK OF OTHING BUT VICTORY.
IT'S SHOW-AND-TELL TIME!! LET'S SEE WHAT DISHES EACH TEAM IS PREPARING!!
司会
BUGGER OFF!

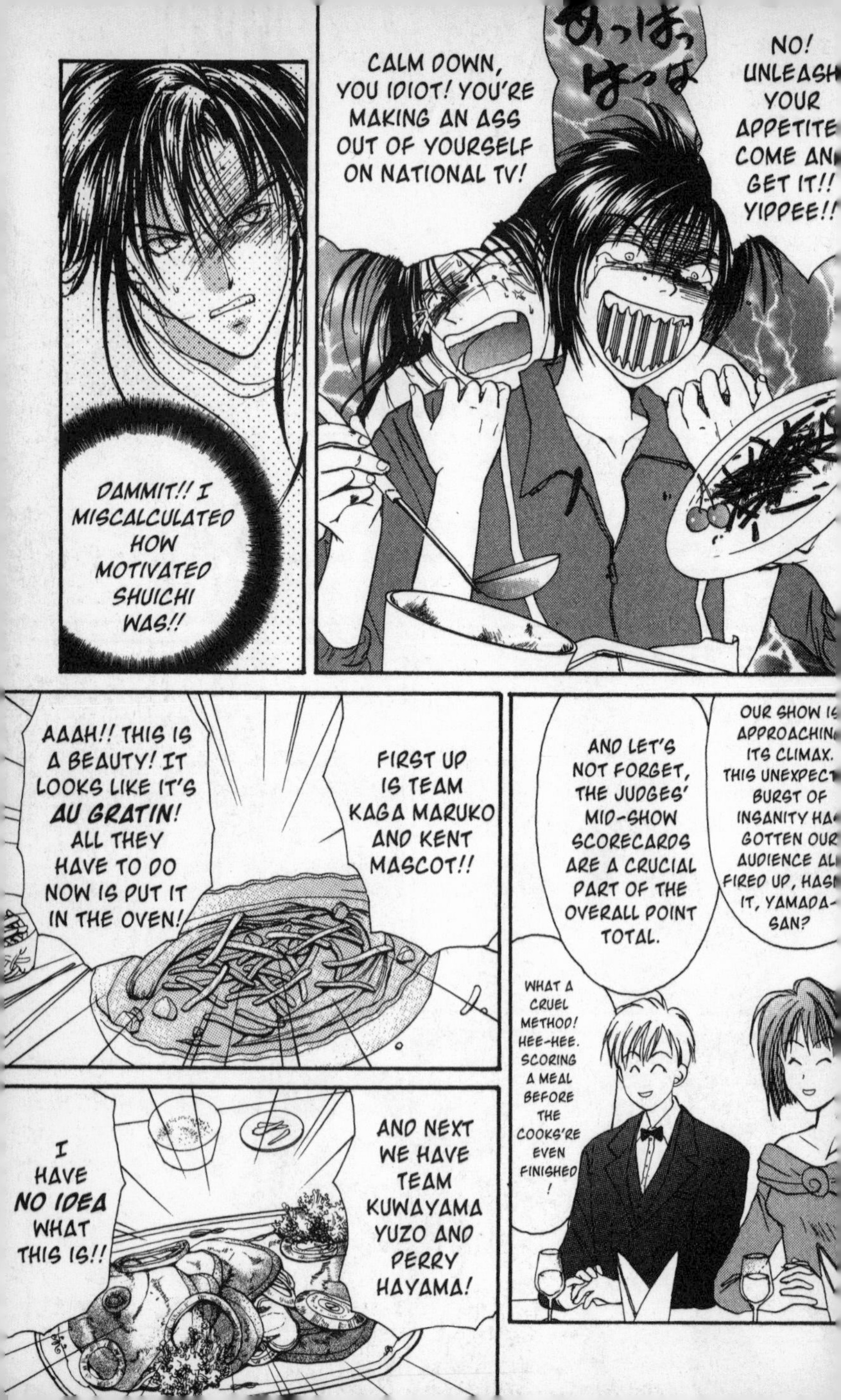
あっはっ はっは
NO! UNLEASH YOUR APPETITE COME AN GET IT!! YIPPEE!!
CALM DOWN, YOU IDIOT! YOU'RE MAKING AN ASS OUT OF YOURSELF ON NATIONAL TV!
DAMMIT!! I MISCALCULATED HOW MOTIVATED SHUICHI WAS!!
OUR SHOW IS APPROACHIN ITS CLIMAX. THIS UNEXPECT BURST OF INSANITY HA GOTTEN OUR AUDIENCE AL FIRED UP, HASN IT, YAMADA-SAN?
AND LET'S NOT FORGET, THE JUDGES' MID-SHOW SCORECARDS ARE A CRUCIAL PART OF THE OVERALL POINT TOTAL.
WHAT A CRUEL METHOD! HEE-HEE. SCORING A MEAL BEFORE THE COOKS'RE EVEN FINISHED!
FIRST UP IS TEAM KAGA MARUKO AND KENT MASCOT!!
AAAH!! THIS IS A BEAUTY! IT LOOKS LIKE IT'S AU GRATIN! ALL THEY HAVE TO DO NOW IS PUT IT IN THE OVEN!
AND NEXT WE HAVE TEAM KUWAYAMA YUZO AND PERRY HAYAMA!
I HAVE NO IDEA WHAT THIS IS!!

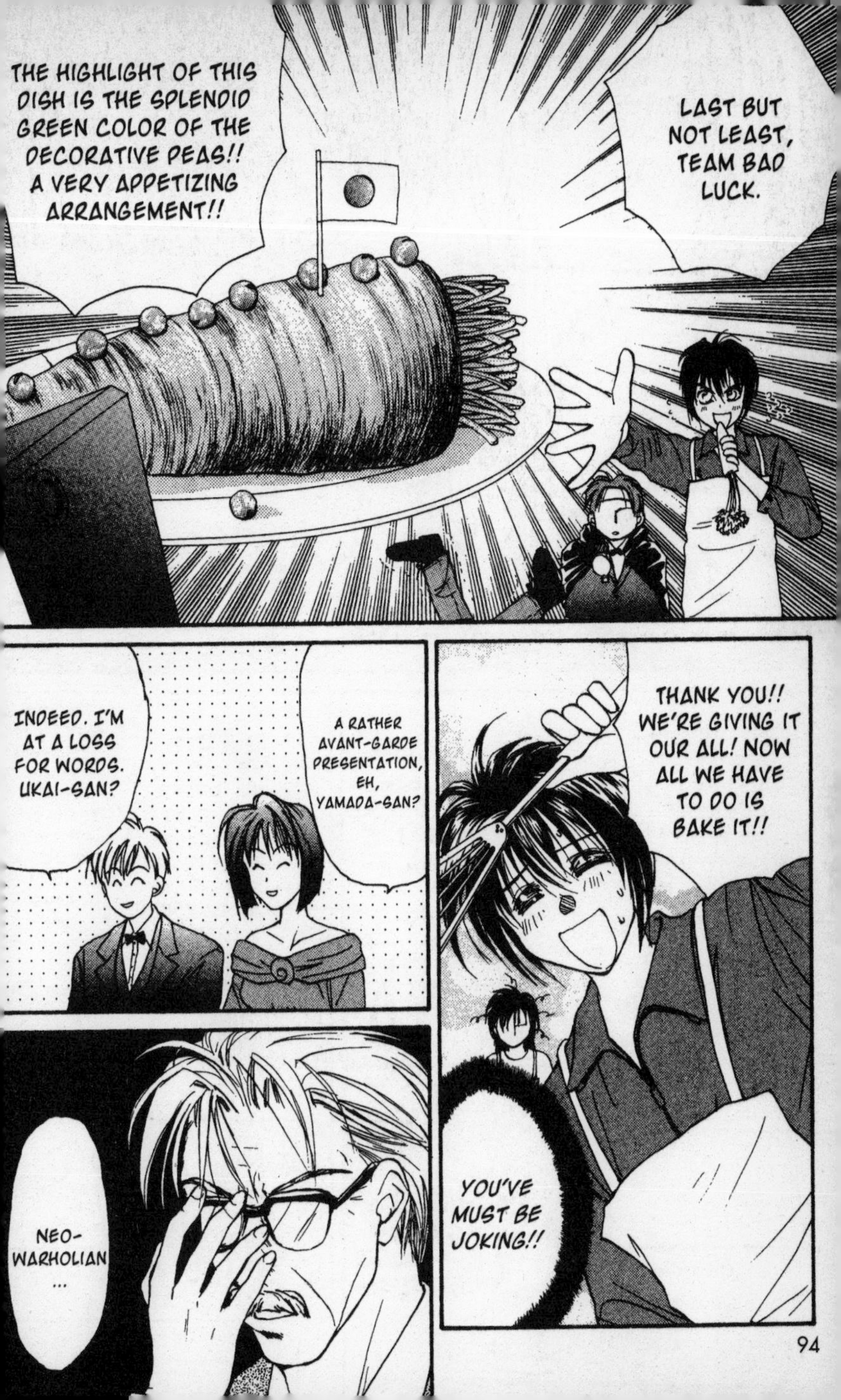
LAST BUT NOT LEAST, TEAM BAD LUCK.
THE HIGHLIGHT OF THIS DISH IS THE SPLENDID GREEN COLOR OF THE DECORATIVE PEAS!! A VERY APPETIZING ARRANGEMENT!!
THANK YOU!! WE'RE GIVING IT OUR ALL! NOW ALL WE HAVE TO DO IS BAKE IT!!
YOU'VE MUST BE JOKING!!
A RATHER AVANT-GARDE PRESENTATION, EH, YAMADA-SAN?
INDEED. I'M AT A LOSS FOR WORDS. UKAI-SAN?
NEO-WARHOLIAN ...

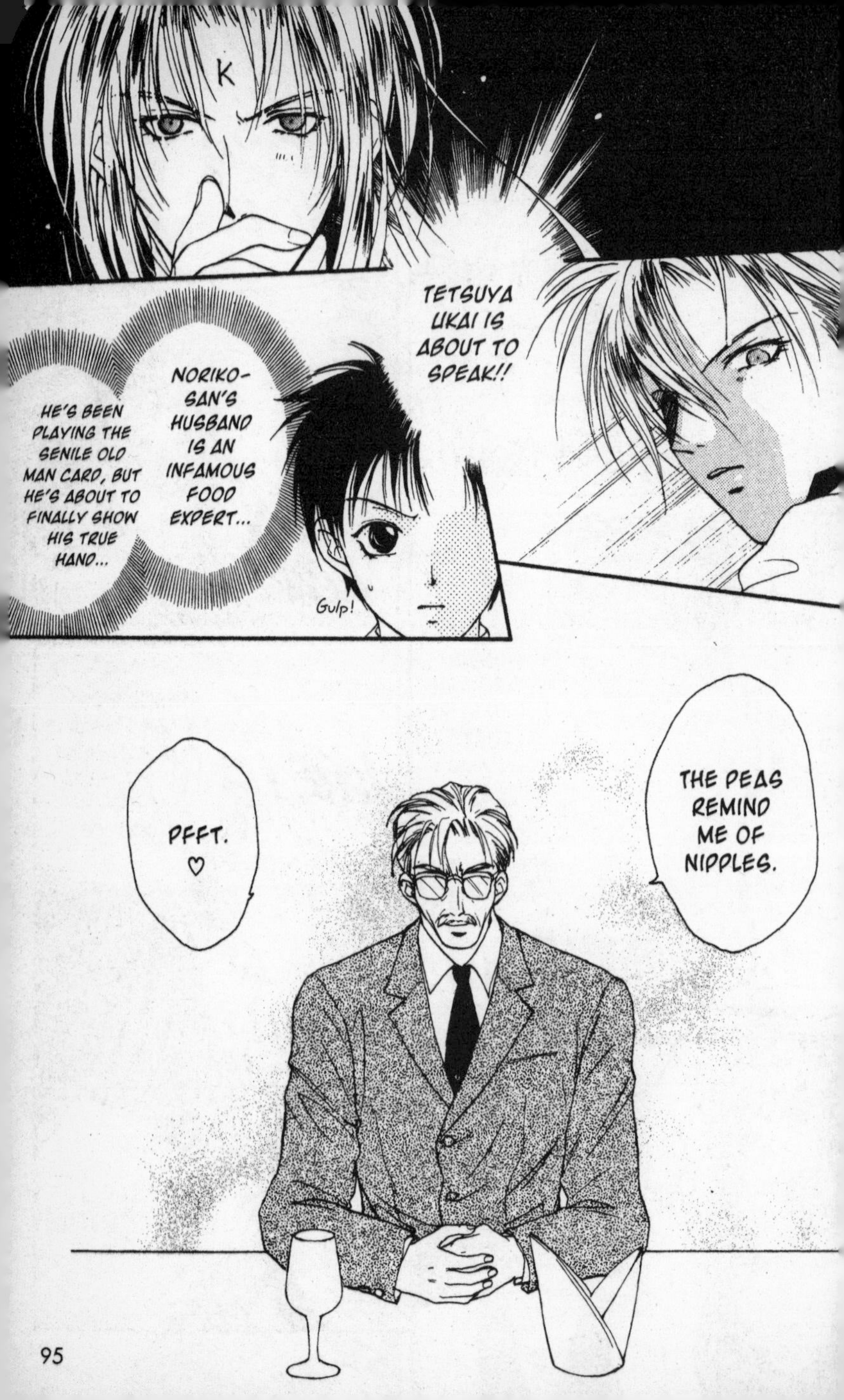
K
TETSUYA UKAI IS ABOUT TO SPEAK!!
NORIKO-SAN'S HUSBAND IS AN INFAMOUS FOOD EXPERT...
HE'S BEEN PLAYING THE SENILE OLD MAN CARD, BUT HE'S ABOUT TO FINALLY SHOW HIS TRUE HAND...
Gulp!
THE PEAS REMIND ME OF NIPPLES.
PFFT. ♡

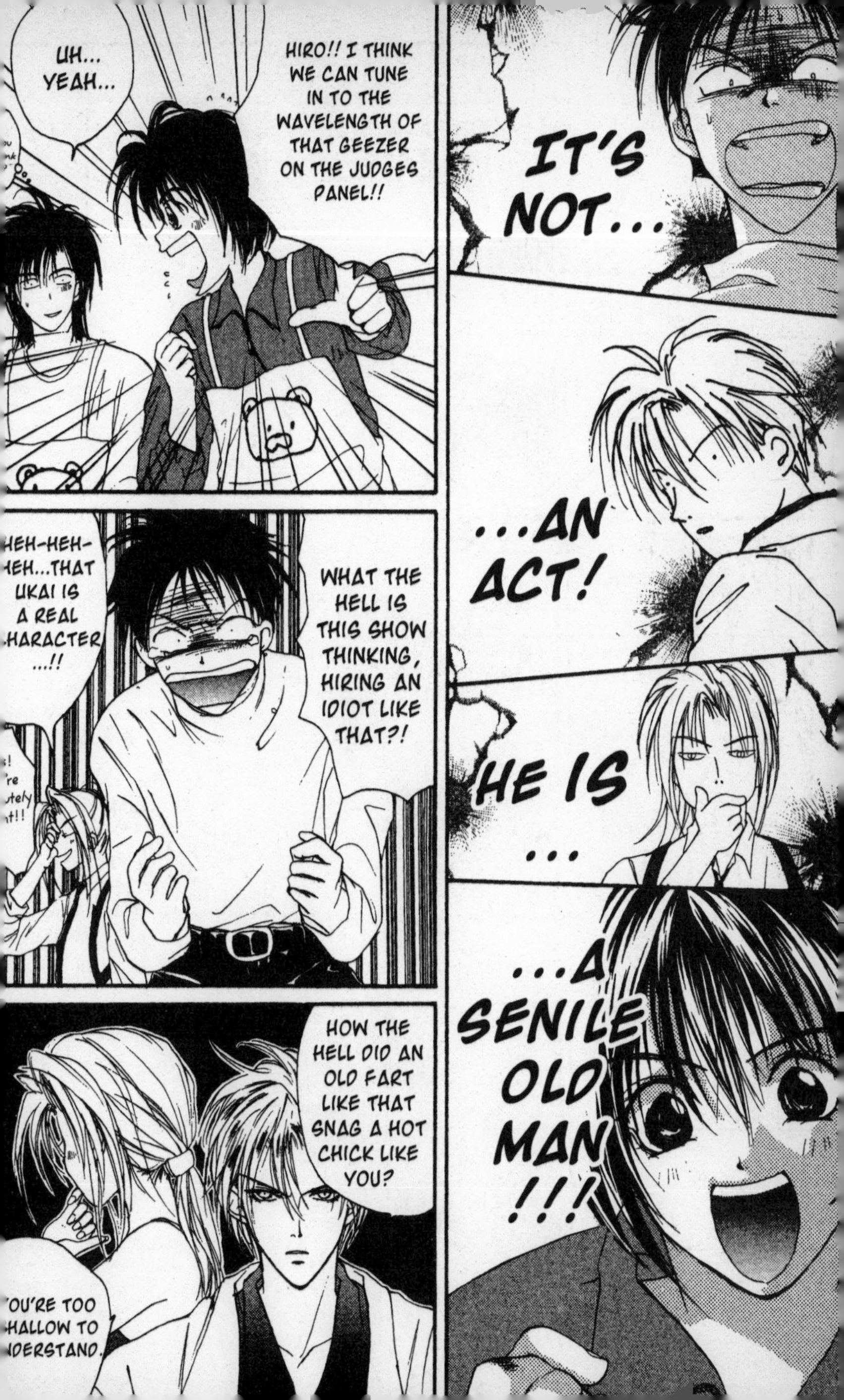
IT'S NOT...
...AN ACT!
HE IS ...
...A SENILE OLD MAN !!!
HIRO!! I THINK WE CAN TUNE IN TO THE WAVELENGTH OF THAT GEEZER ON THE JUDGES PANEL!!
UH... YEAH...
WHAT THE HELL IS THIS SHOW THINKING, HIRING AN IDIOT LIKE THAT?!
HEH-HEH-HEH...THAT UKAI IS A REAL CHARACTER ...!!
HOW THE HELL DID AN OLD FART LIKE THAT SNAG A HOT CHICK LIKE YOU?
YOU'RE TOO SHALLOW TO UNDERSTAND.

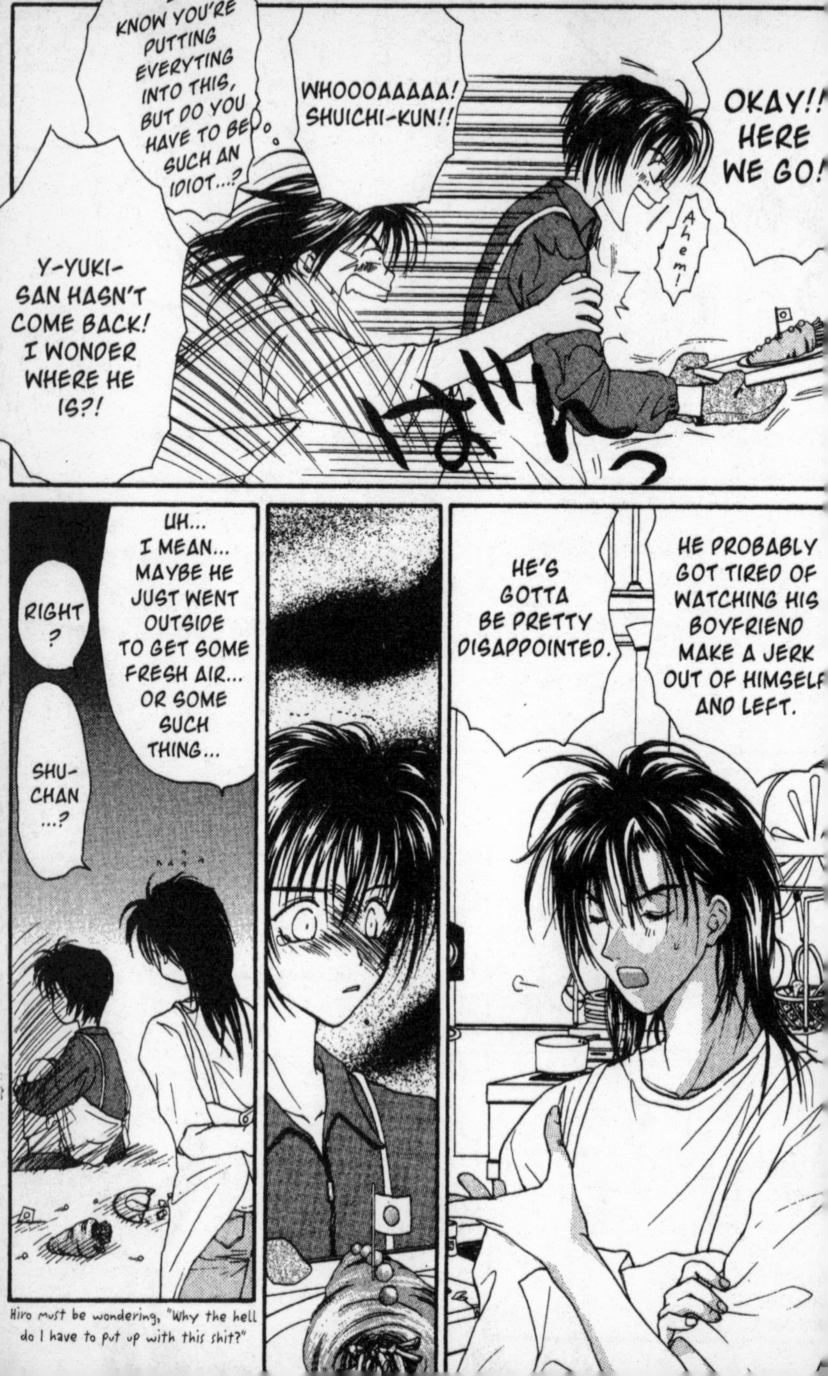
OKAY!! HERE WE GO!
Ahem!
WHOOOAAAAA! SHUICHI-KUN!!
I KNOW YOU'RE PUTTING EVERYTING INTO THIS, BUT DO YOU HAVE TO BE SUCH AN IDIOT...?
Y-YUKI-SAN HASN'T COME BACK! I WONDER WHERE HE IS?!
HE PROBABLY GOT TIRED OF WATCHING HIS BOYFRIEND MAKE A JERK OUT OF HIMSELF AND LEFT.
HE'S GOTTA BE PRETTY DISAPPOINTED.
UH... I MEAN... MAYBE HE JUST WENT OUTSIDE TO GET SOME FRESH AIR... OR SOME SUCH THING...
RIGHT?
SHU-CHAN...?

Hiro must be wondering, "Why the hell do I have to put up with this shit?"

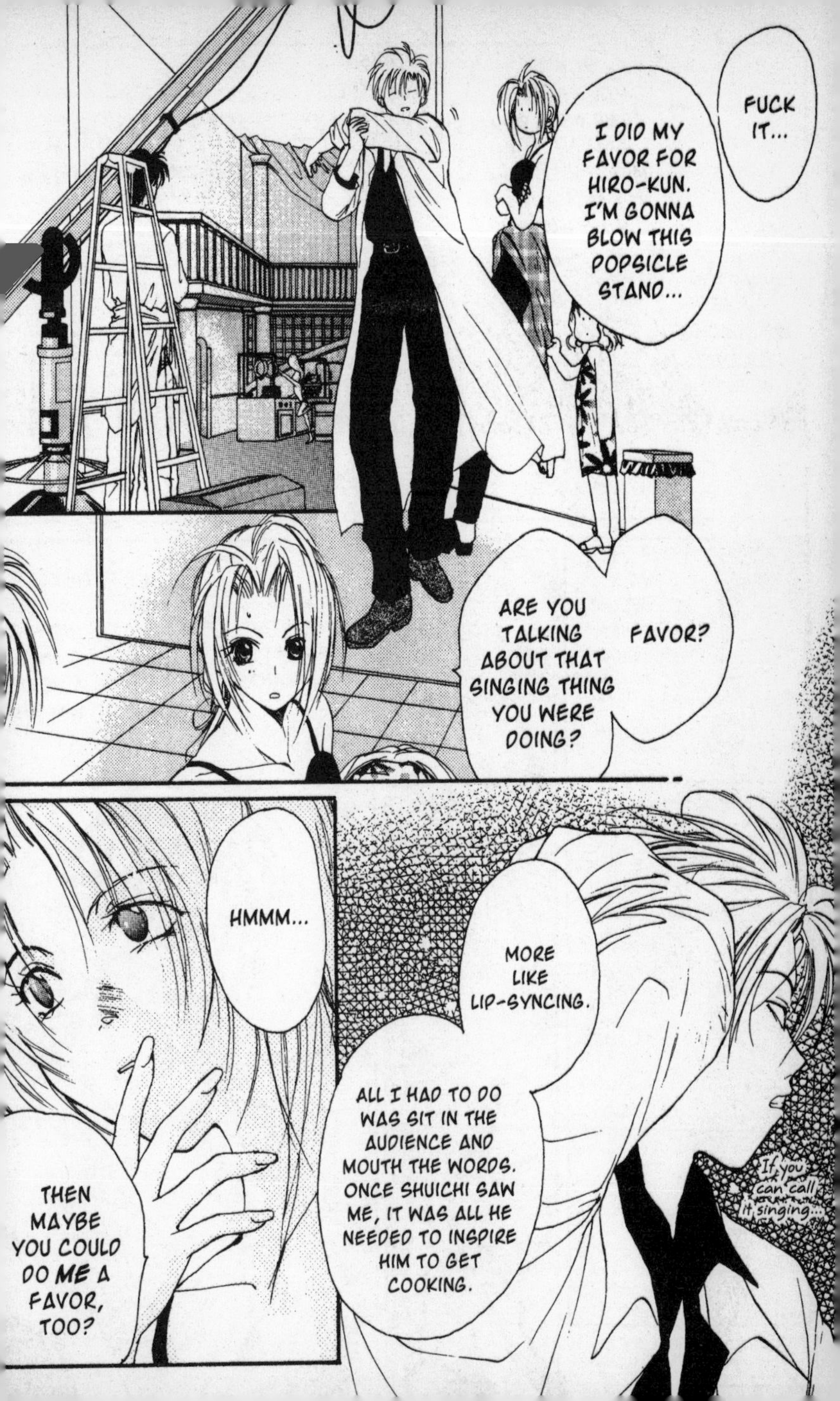
FUCK IT...
I DID MY FAVOR FOR HIRO-KUN. I'M GONNA BLOW THIS POPSICLE STAND...
FAVOR?
ARE YOU TALKING ABOUT THAT SINGING THING YOU WERE DOING?
MORE LIKE LIP-SYNCING.
ALL I HAD TO DO WAS SIT IN THE AUDIENCE AND MOUTH THE WORDS. ONCE SHUICHI SAW ME, IT WAS ALL HE NEEDED TO INSPIRE HIM TO GET COOKING.
If you can call it singing...
HMMM...
THEN MAYBE YOU COULD DO **ME** A FAVOR, TOO?

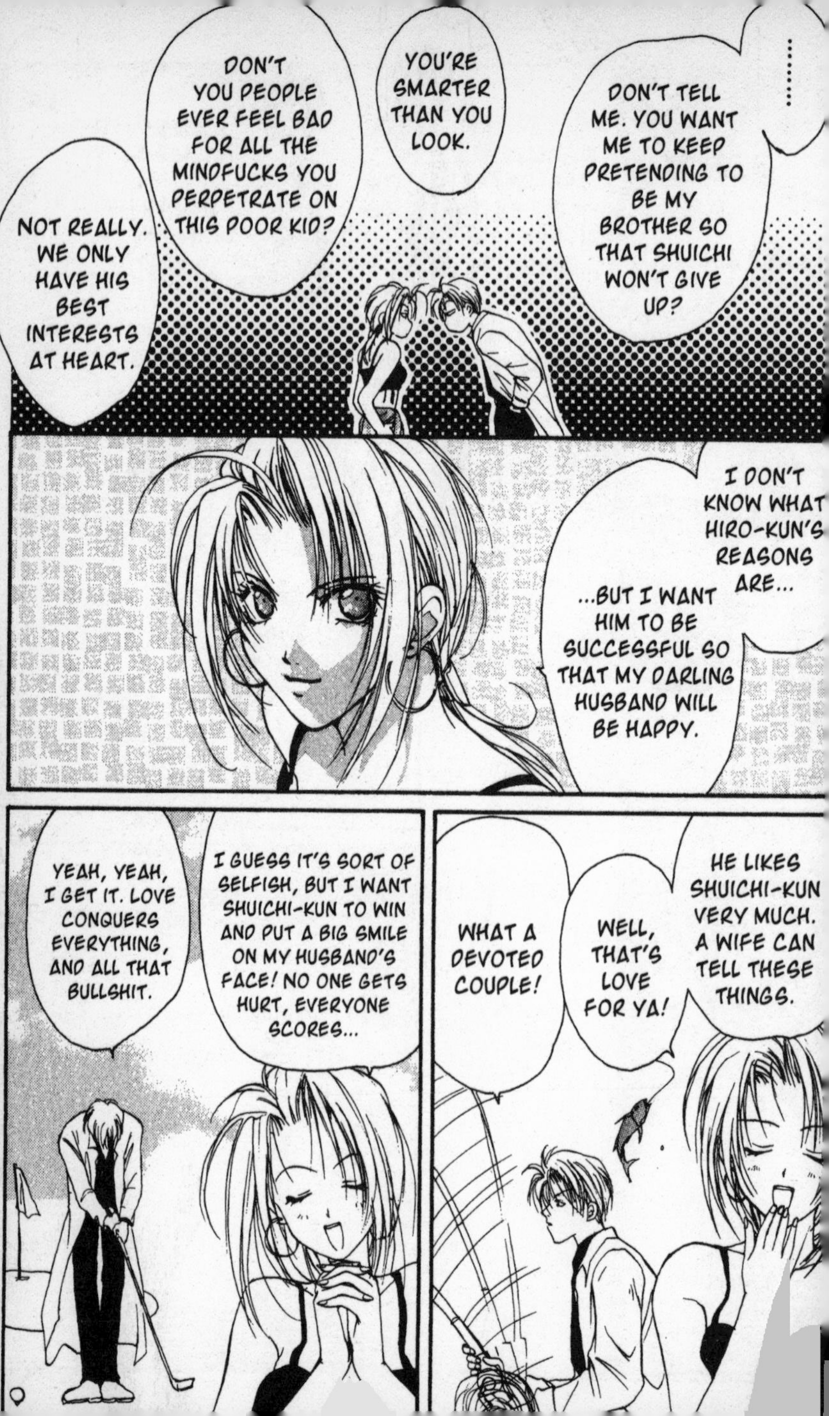
......
DON'T TELL ME. YOU WANT ME TO KEEP PRETENDING TO BE MY BROTHER SO THAT SHUICHI WON'T GIVE UP?
YOU'RE SMARTER THAN YOU LOOK.
DON'T YOU PEOPLE EVER FEEL BAD FOR ALL THE MINDFUCKS YOU PERPETRATE ON THIS POOR KID?
NOT REALLY. WE ONLY HAVE HIS BEST INTERESTS AT HEART.
I DON'T KNOW WHAT HIRO-KUN'S REASONS ARE...
...BUT I WANT HIM TO BE SUCCESSFUL SO THAT MY DARLING HUSBAND WILL BE HAPPY.
HE LIKES SHUICHI-KUN VERY MUCH. A WIFE CAN TELL THESE THINGS.
WELL, THAT'S LOVE FOR YA!
WHAT A DEVOTED COUPLE!
I GUESS IT'S SORT OF SELFISH, BUT I WANT SHUICHI-KUN TO WIN AND PUT A BIG SMILE ON MY HUSBAND'S FACE! NO ONE GETS HURT, EVERYONE SCORES...
YEAH, YEAH, I GET IT. LOVE CONQUERS EVERYTHING, AND ALL THAT BULLSHIT.

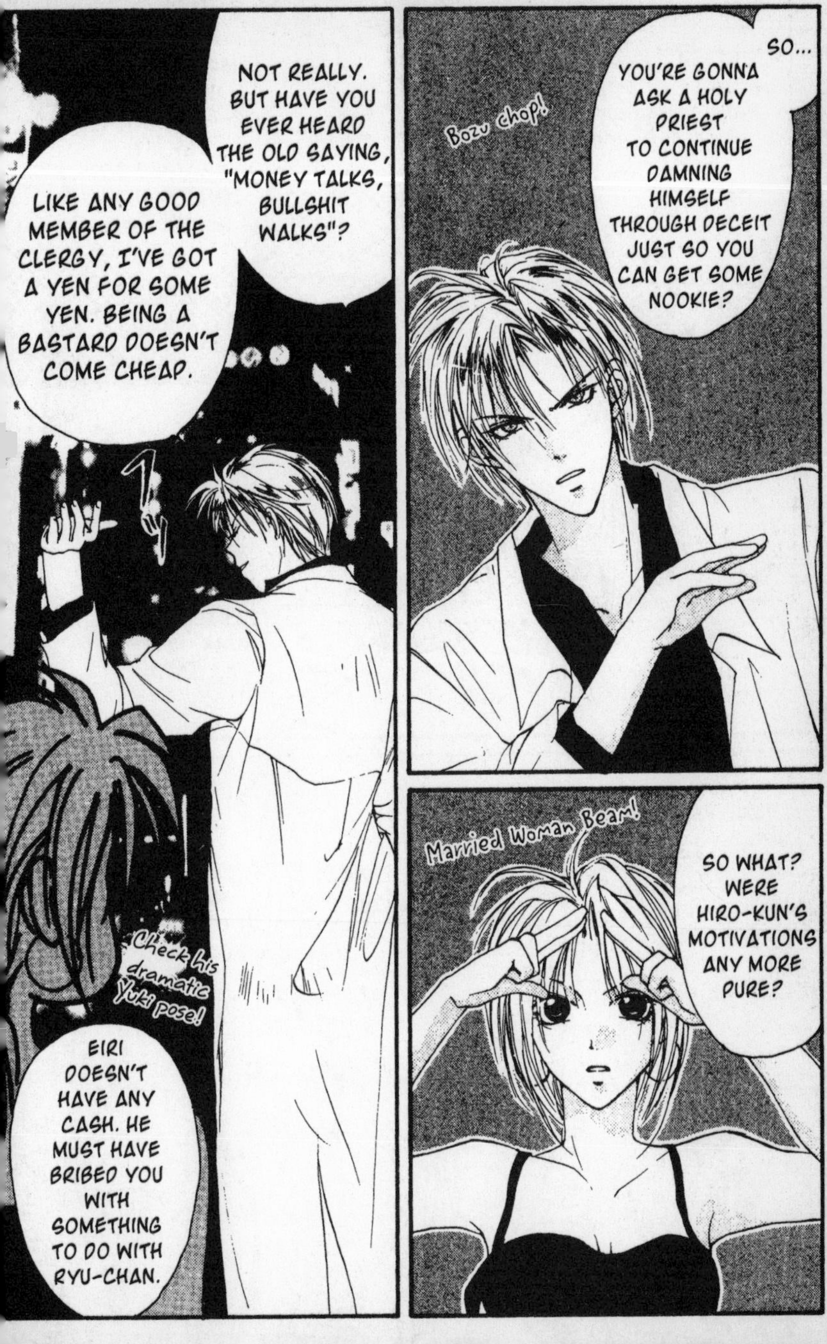
EIRI DOESN'T HAVE ANY CASH. HE MUST HAVE BRIBED YOU WITH SOMETHING TO DO WITH RYU-CHAN.
NOT REALLY. BUT HAVE YOU EVER HEARD THE OLD SAYING, "MONEY TALKS, BULLSHIT WALKS"?
LIKE ANY GOOD MEMBER OF THE CLERGY, I'VE GOT A YEN FOR SOME YEN. BEING A BASTARD DOESN'T COME CHEAP.
Check his dramatic Yuki pose!
SO...
YOU'RE GONNA ASK A HOLY PRIEST TO CONTINUE DAMNING HIMSELF THROUGH DECEIT JUST SO YOU CAN GET SOME NOOKIE?
Bozu chop!
Married Woman Beam!
SO WHAT? WERE HIRO-KUN'S MOTIVATIONS ANY MORE PURE?

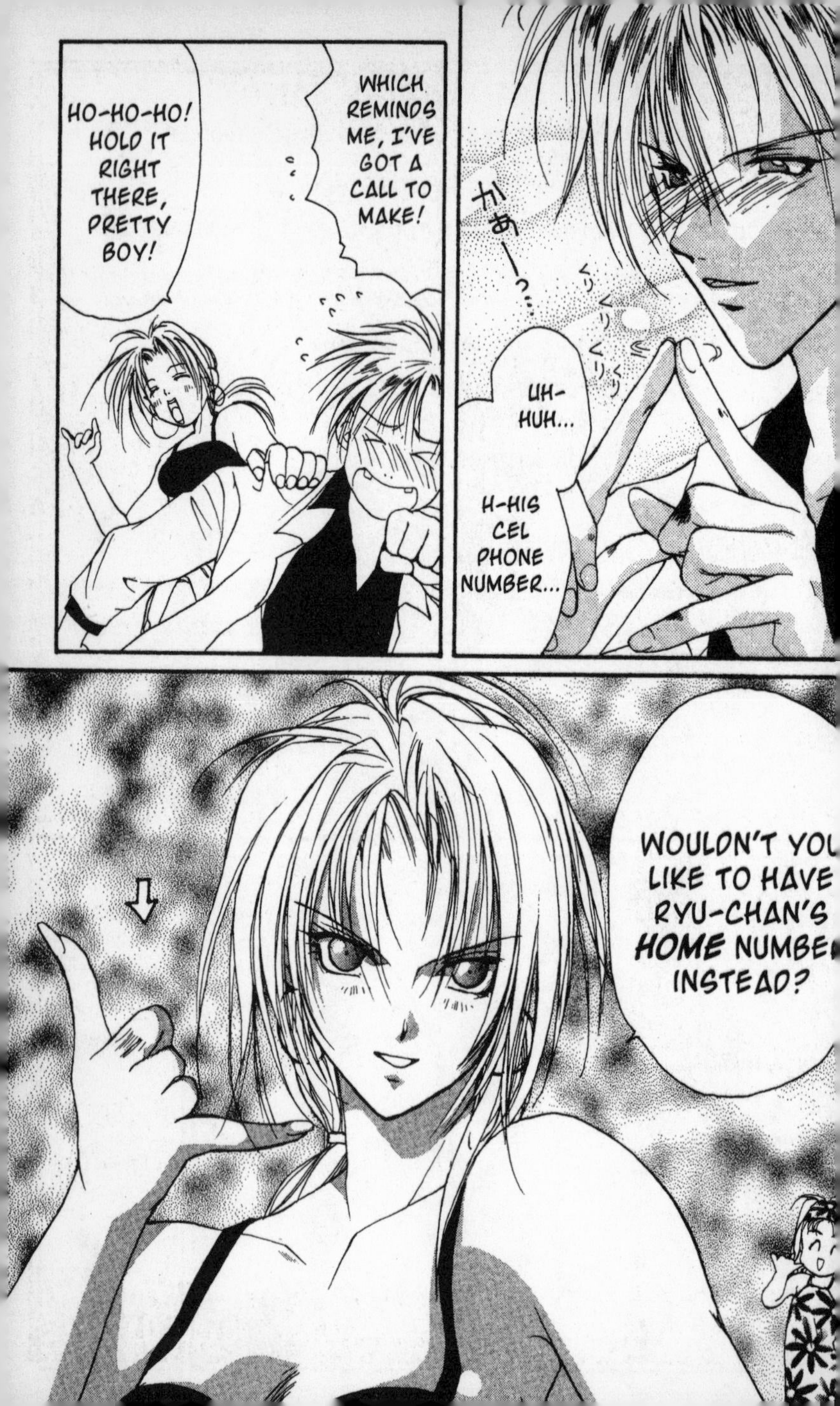
かぁーっ…
くりくりくり
UH-HUH...
H-HIS CEL PHONE NUMBER...
WHICH REMINDS ME, I'VE GOT A CALL TO MAKE!
HO-HO-HO! HOLD IT RIGHT THERE, PRETTY BOY!
WOULDN'T YOU LIKE TO HAVE RYU-CHAN'S *HOME* NUMBE INSTEAD?

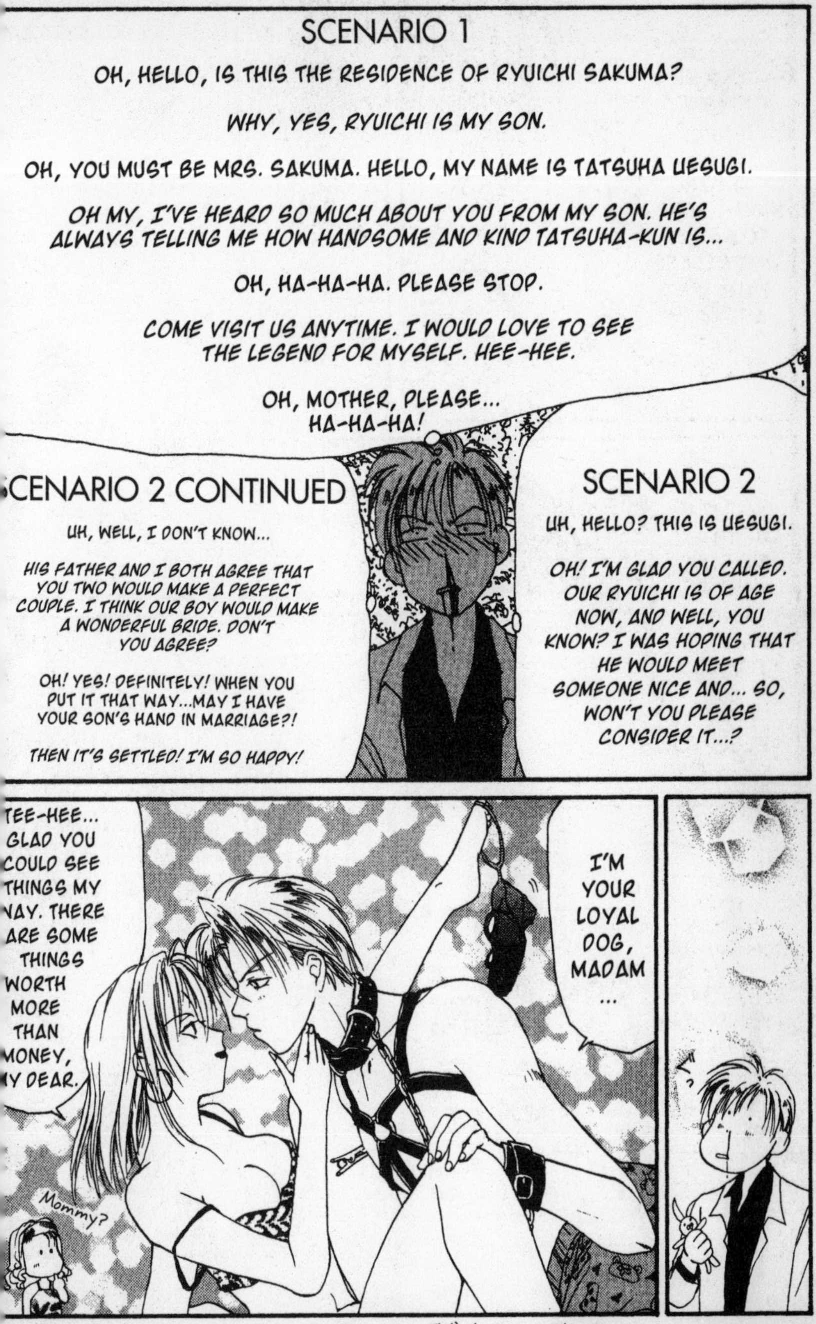
SCENARIO 1
OH, HELLO, IS THIS THE RESIDENCE OF RYUICHI SAKUMA?
WHY, YES, RYUICHI IS MY SON.
OH, YOU MUST BE MRS. SAKUMA. HELLO, MY NAME IS TATSUHA UESUGI.
OH MY, I'VE HEARD SO MUCH ABOUT YOU FROM MY SON. HE'S ALWAYS TELLING ME HOW HANDSOME AND KIND TATSUHA-KUN IS...
OH, HA-HA-HA. PLEASE STOP.
COME VISIT US ANYTIME. I WOULD LOVE TO SEE THE LEGEND FOR MYSELF. HEE-HEE.
OH, MOTHER, PLEASE... HA-HA-HA!
SCENARIO 2
UH, HELLO? THIS IS UESUGI.
OH! I'M GLAD YOU CALLED. OUR RYUICHI IS OF AGE NOW, AND WELL, YOU KNOW? I WAS HOPING THAT HE WOULD MEET SOMEONE NICE AND... SO, WON'T YOU PLEASE CONSIDER IT...?
SCENARIO 2 CONTINUED
UH, WELL, I DON'T KNOW...
HIS FATHER AND I BOTH AGREE THAT YOU TWO WOULD MAKE A PERFECT COUPLE. I THINK OUR BOY WOULD MAKE A WONDERFUL BRIDE. DON'T YOU AGREE?
OH! YES! DEFINITELY! WHEN YOU PUT IT THAT WAY...MAY I HAVE YOUR SON'S HAND IN MARRIAGE?!
THEN IT'S SETTLED! I'M SO HAPPY!
I'M YOUR LOYAL DOG, MADAM...
TEE-HEE... GLAD YOU COULD SEE THINGS MY WAY. THERE ARE SOME THINGS WORTH MORE THAN MONEY, MY DEAR.
Mommy?

Damage to Eiri's image: 4-1/2 stars

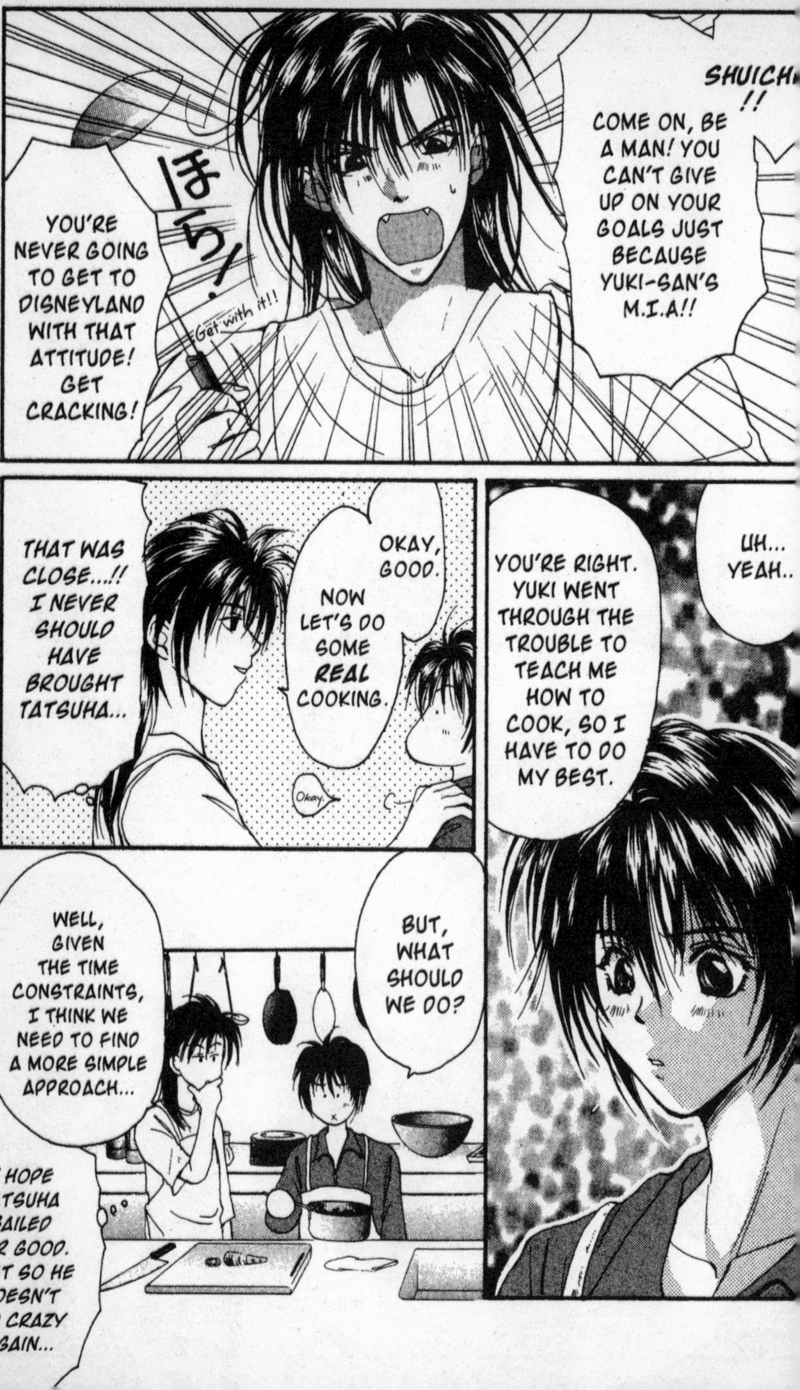
SHUICH !!
COME ON, BE A MAN! YOU CAN'T GIVE UP ON YOUR GOALS JUST BECAUSE YUKI-SAN'S M.I.A!!
ほら!
Get with it!!
YOU'RE NEVER GOING TO GET TO DISNEYLAND WITH THAT ATTITUDE! GET CRACKING!
UH... YEAH..
YOU'RE RIGHT. YUKI WENT THROUGH THE TROUBLE TO TEACH ME HOW TO COOK, SO I HAVE TO DO MY BEST.
OKAY, GOOD.
NOW LET'S DO SOME REAL COOKING.
THAT WAS CLOSE...!! I NEVER SHOULD HAVE BROUGHT TATSUHA...
Okay.
BUT, WHAT SHOULD WE DO?
WELL, GIVEN THE TIME CONSTRAINTS, I THINK WE NEED TO FIND A MORE SIMPLE APPROACH...
I HOPE TATSUHA BAILED FOR GOOD. JUST SO HE DOESN'T GO CRAZY AGAIN...

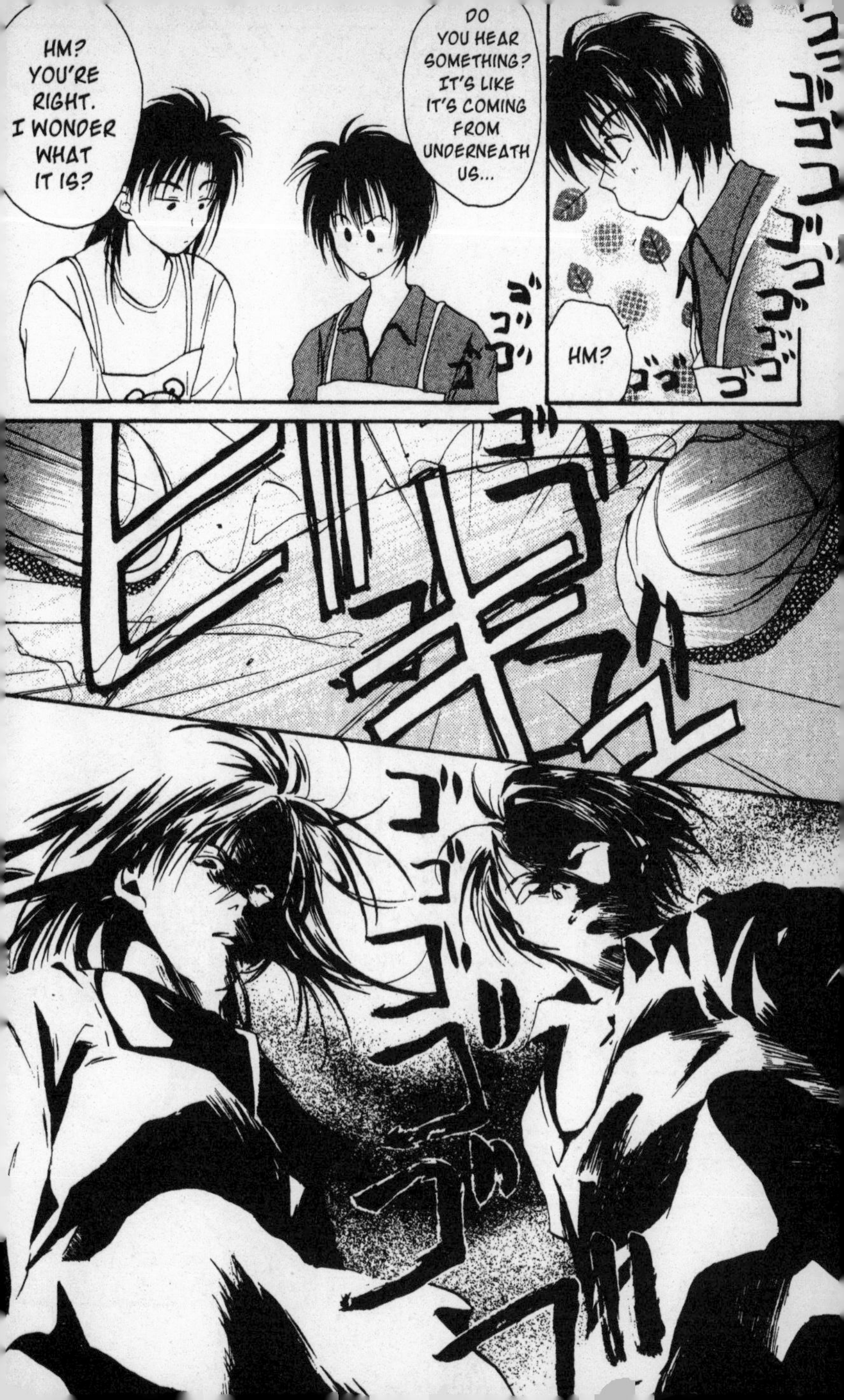
HM?
DO YOU HEAR SOMETHING? IT'S LIKE IT'S COMING FROM UNDERNEATH US...
HM? YOU'RE RIGHT. I WONDER WHAT IT IS?

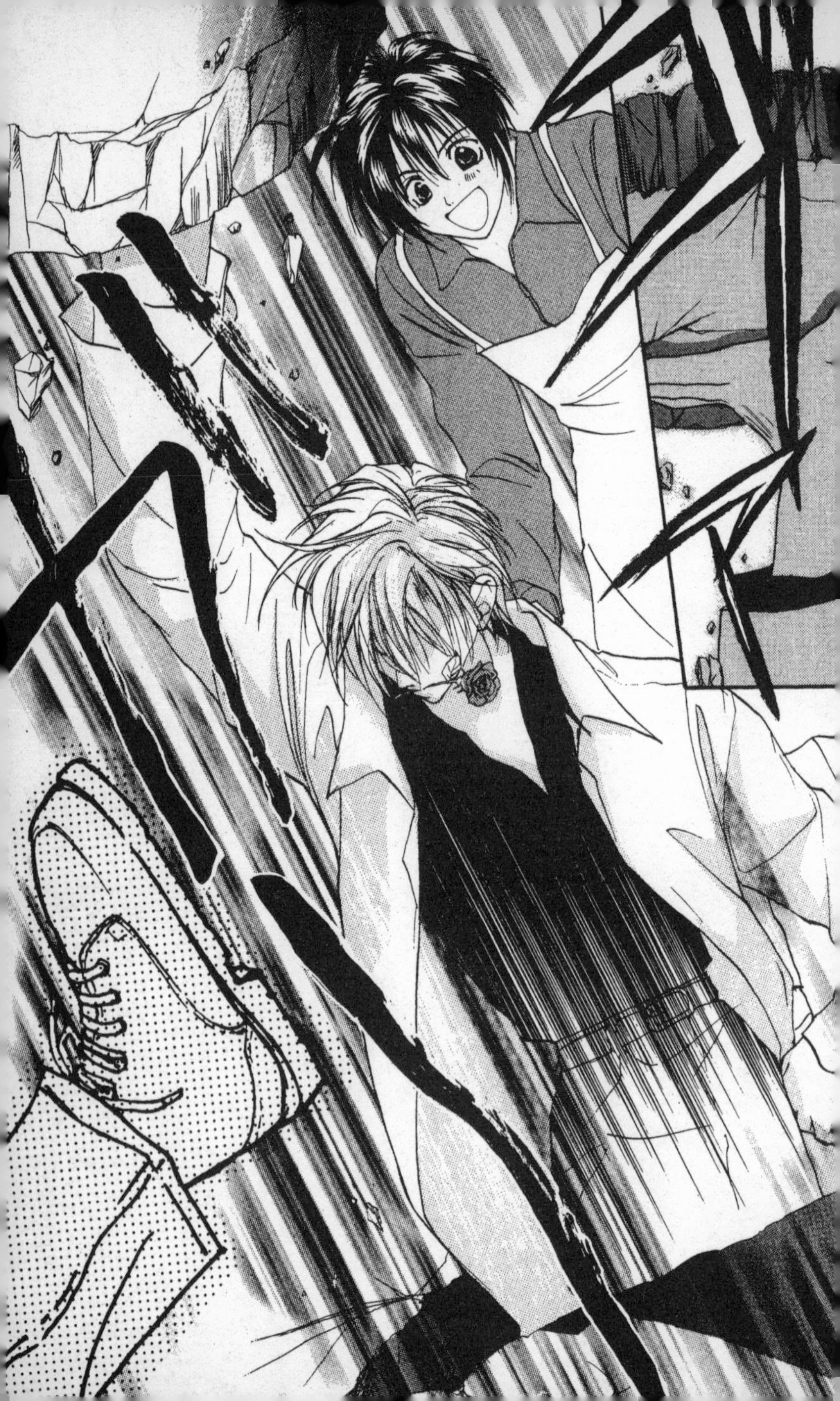

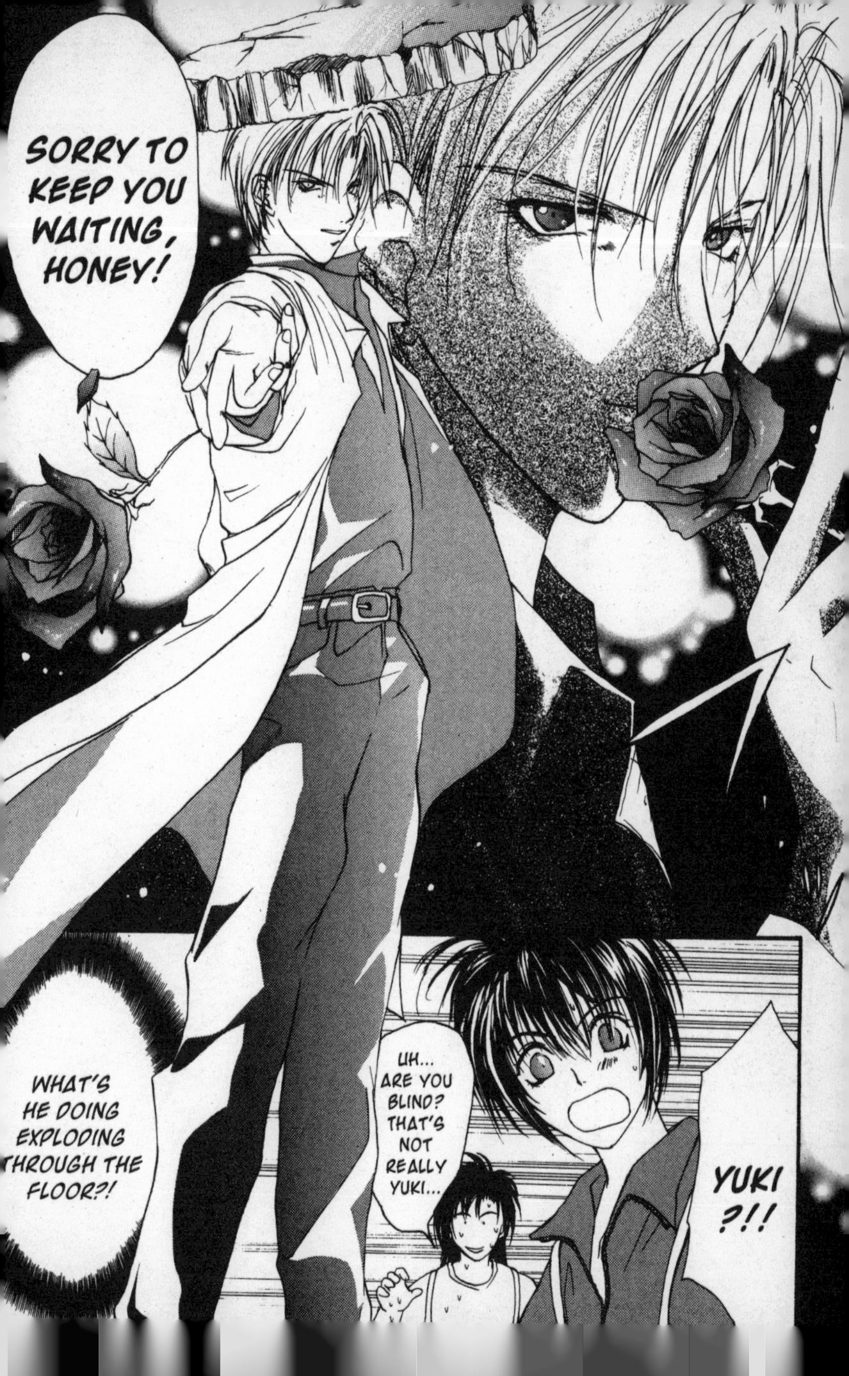
SORRY TO KEEP YOU WAITING, HONEY!
YUKI ?!!
UH... ARE YOU BLIND? THAT'S NOT REALLY YUKI...
WHAT'S HE DOING EXPLODING THROUGH THE FLOOR?!

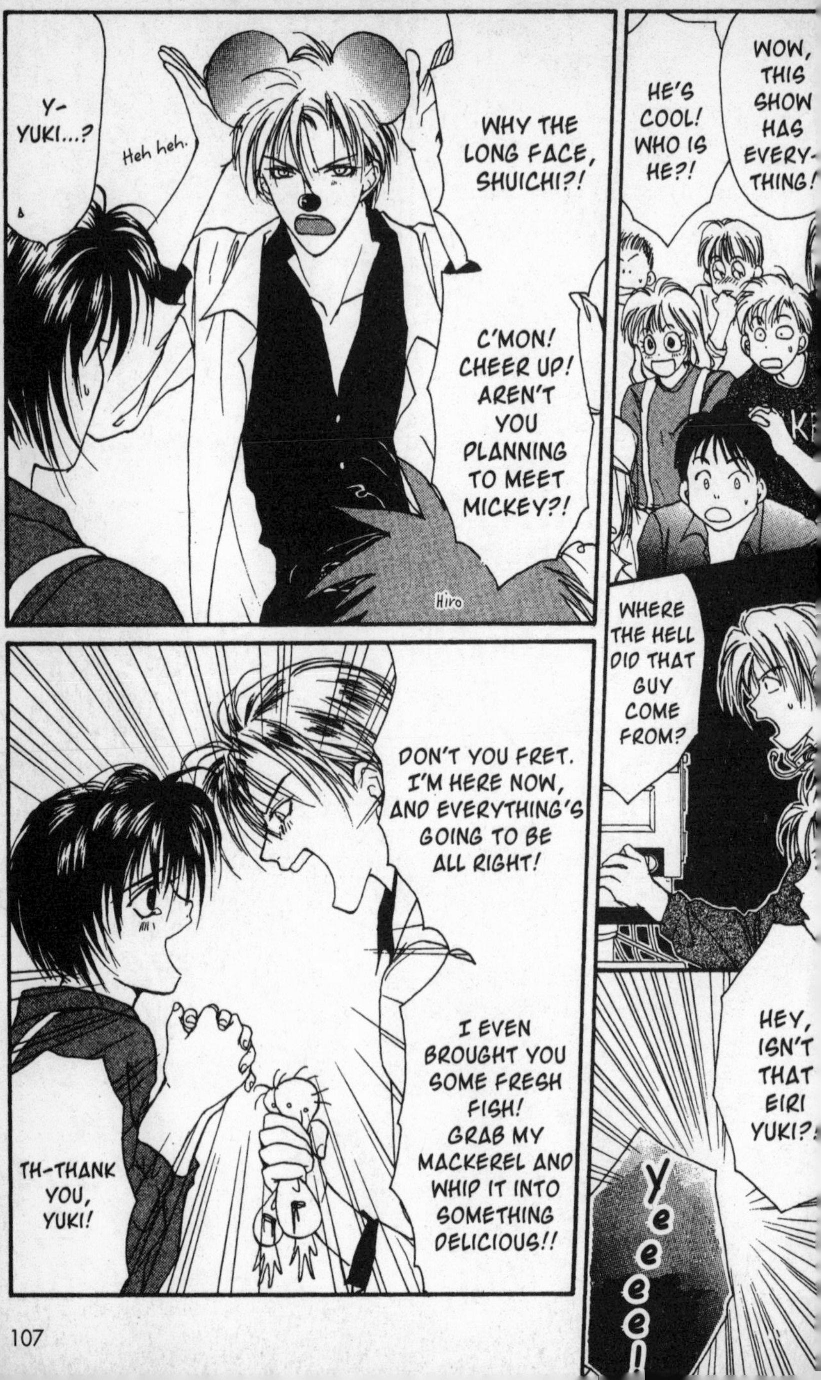
WOW, THIS SHOW HAS EVERY-THING!
HE'S COOL! WHO IS HE?!
Y-YUKI...?
Heh heh.
WHY THE LONG FACE, SHUICHI?!
C'MON! CHEER UP! AREN'T YOU PLANNING TO MEET MICKEY?!
Hiro
WHERE THE HELL DID THAT GUY COME FROM?
DON'T YOU FRET. I'M HERE NOW, AND EVERYTHING'S GOING TO BE ALL RIGHT!
I EVEN BROUGHT YOU SOME FRESH FISH! GRAB MY MACKEREL AND WHIP IT INTO SOMETHING DELICIOUS!!
TH-THANK YOU, YUKI!
HEY, ISN'T THAT EIRI YUKI?
Yeeeee!

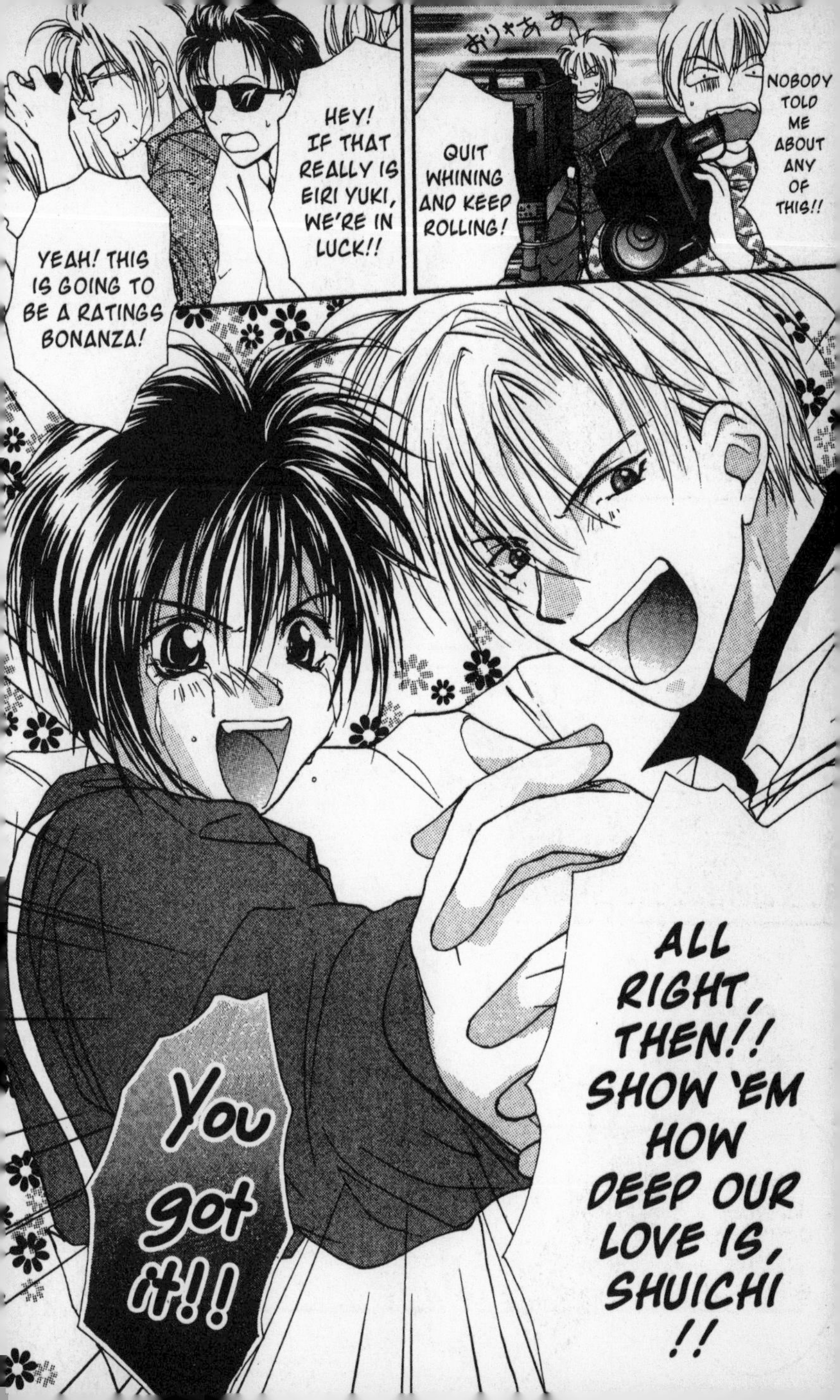
NOBODY TOLD ME ABOUT ANY OF THIS!!
QUIT WHINING AND KEEP ROLLING!
HEY! IF THAT REALLY IS EIRI YUKI, WE'RE IN LUCK!!
YEAH! THIS IS GOING TO BE A RATINGS BONANZA!
ALL RIGHT, THEN!! SHOW 'EM HOW DEEP OUR LOVE IS, SHUICHI!!
You got it!!

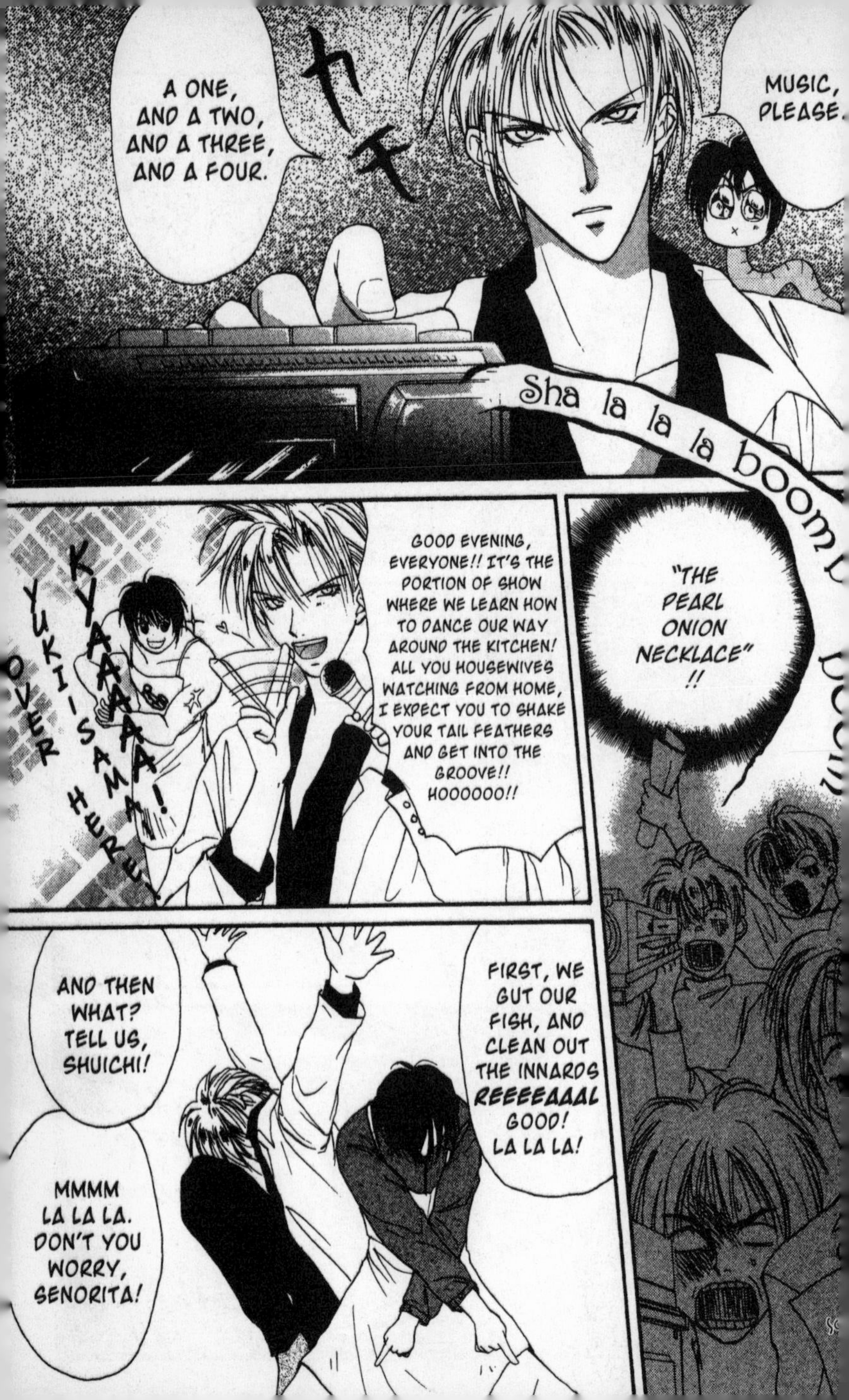
MUSIC, PLEASE.
カチ
A ONE, AND A TWO, AND A THREE, AND A FOUR.
Sha la la la boom
"THE PEARL ONION NECKLACE" !!
GOOD EVENING, EVERYONE!! IT'S THE PORTION OF SHOW WHERE WE LEARN HOW TO DANCE OUR WAY AROUND THE KITCHEN! ALL YOU HOUSEWIVES WATCHING FROM HOME, I EXPECT YOU TO SHAKE YOUR TAIL FEATHERS AND GET INTO THE GROOVE!! HOOOOOO!!
KYAAAAAAA!
YUKI-SAMA!
OVER HERE!
FIRST, WE GUT OUR FISH, AND CLEAN OUT THE INNARDS REEEEAAAL GOOD! LA LA LA!
AND THEN WHAT? TELL US, SHUICHI!
MMMM LA LA LA. DON'T YOU WORRY, SENORITA!

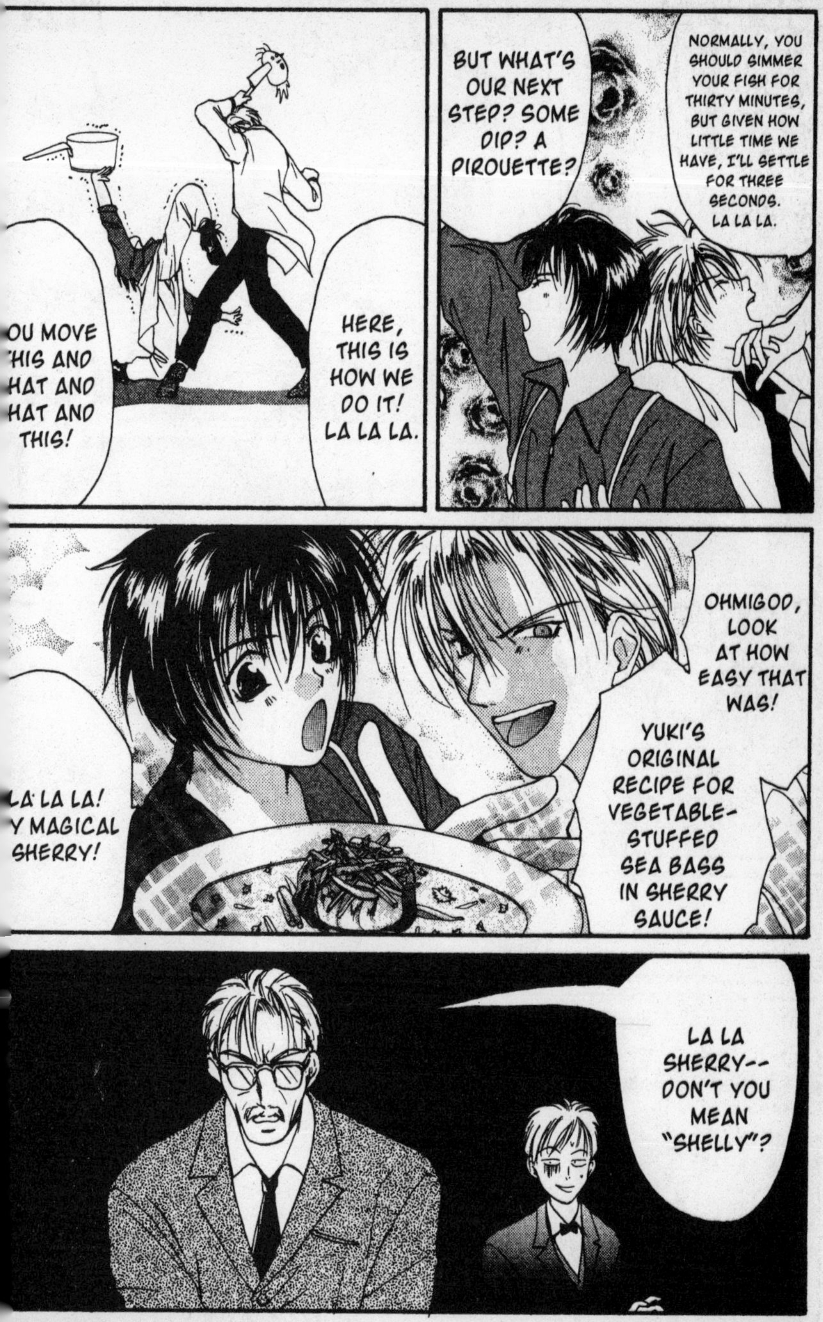

NORMALLY, YOU SHOULD SIMMER YOUR FISH FOR THIRTY MINUTES, BUT GIVEN HOW LITTLE TIME WE HAVE, I'LL SETTLE FOR THREE SECONDS. LA LA LA.
BUT WHAT'S OUR NEXT STEP? SOME DIP? A PIROUETTE?
HERE, THIS IS HOW WE DO IT! LA LA LA.
OU MOVE HIS AND HAT AND HAT AND THIS!
OHMIGOD, LOOK AT HOW EASY THAT WAS!
YUKI'S ORIGINAL RECIPE FOR VEGETABLE-STUFFED SEA BASS IN SHERRY SAUCE!
LA LA LA! Y MAGICAL SHERRY!
LA LA SHERRY-- DON'T YOU MEAN "SHELLY"?

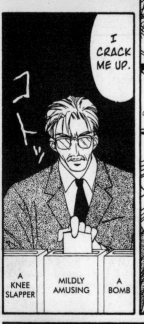

I CRACK ME UP.

コトッ

A KNEE SLAPPER	MILDLY AMUSING	A BOMB

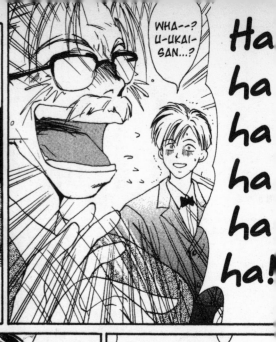

WHA--? U-UKAI-SAN...?

Ha ha ha ha ha!

EIRI-SAN... YOU...YOU DIDN'T HAVE TO POP OUT FROM THE FLOOR...

I'M SORRY... THAT'S THE ONLY THING I CAN THINK OF TO SAY RIGHT NOW...

NO ONE TOLD ME THAT YUKI-SAN WAS BACK IN JAPAN! GOOD JOB, SHUICHI! THAT WAS A RIOT!!

HA-HA-HA-HA-HA! I DIDN'T SEE THAT ONE COMING

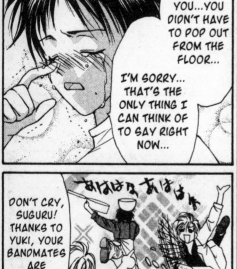

DON'T CRY, SUGURU! THANKS TO YUKI, YOUR BANDMATES ARE FINALLY BACK IN THE GAME!!

あはは あはは

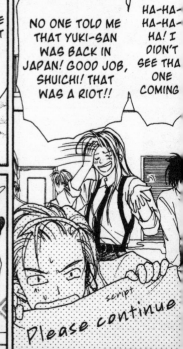

Please continue

script

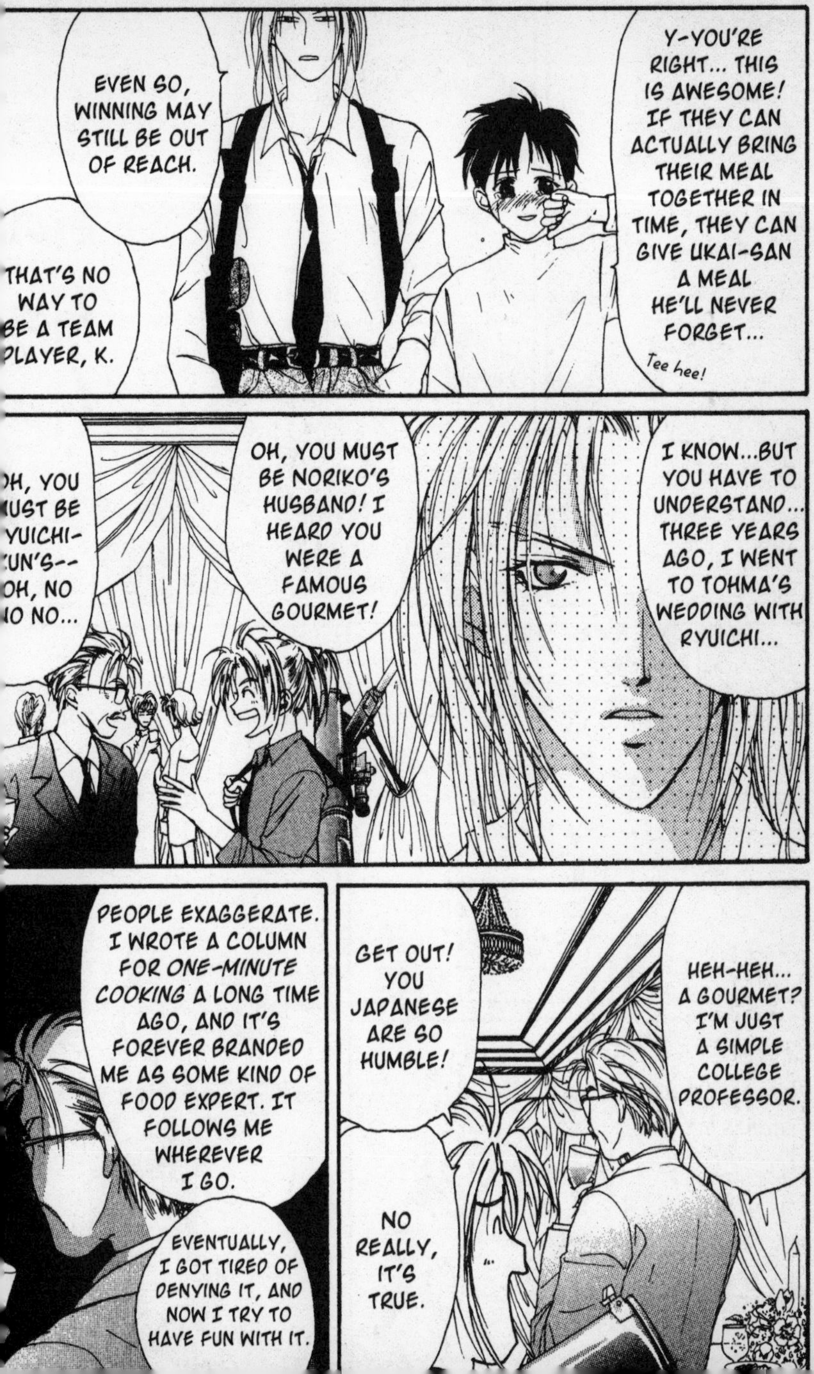

Y-YOU'RE RIGHT... THIS IS AWESOME! IF THEY CAN ACTUALLY BRING THEIR MEAL TOGETHER IN TIME, THEY CAN GIVE UKAI-SAN A MEAL HE'LL NEVER FORGET...
Tee hee!
EVEN SO, WINNING MAY STILL BE OUT OF REACH.
THAT'S NO WAY TO BE A TEAM PLAYER, K.
I KNOW...BUT YOU HAVE TO UNDERSTAND... THREE YEARS AGO, I WENT TO TOHMA'S WEDDING WITH RYUICHI...
OH, YOU MUST BE NORIKO'S HUSBAND! I HEARD YOU WERE A FAMOUS GOURMET!
H, YOU UST BE YUICHI-UN'S--OH, NO O NO...
HEH-HEH... A GOURMET? I'M JUST A SIMPLE COLLEGE PROFESSOR.
GET OUT! YOU JAPANESE ARE SO HUMBLE!
NO REALLY, IT'S TRUE.
...
PEOPLE EXAGGERATE. I WROTE A COLUMN FOR ONE-MINUTE COOKING A LONG TIME AGO, AND IT'S FOREVER BRANDED ME AS SOME KIND OF FOOD EXPERT. IT FOLLOWS ME WHEREVER I GO.
EVENTUALLY, I GOT TIRED OF DENYING IT, AND NOW I TRY TO HAVE FUN WITH IT.

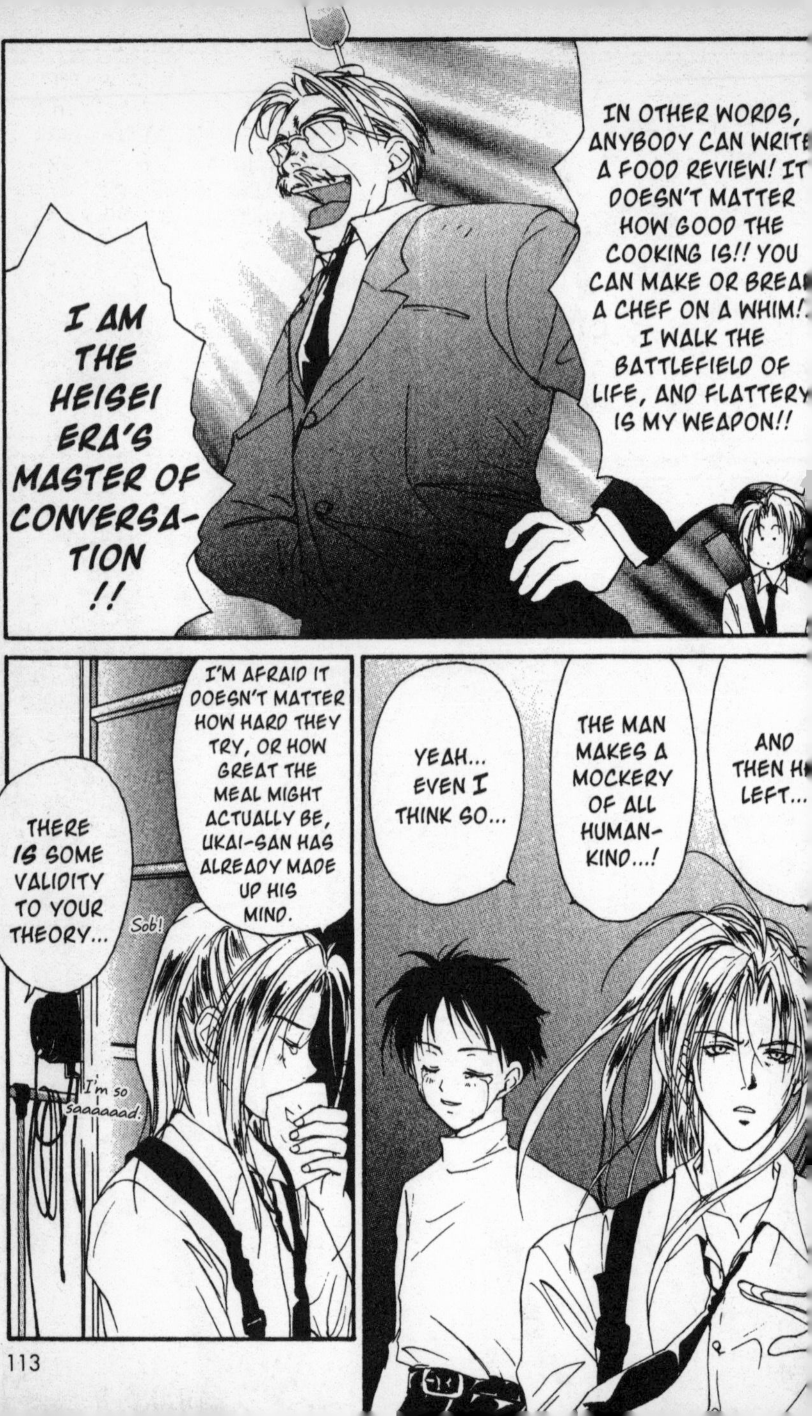
IN OTHER WORDS, ANYBODY CAN WRITE A FOOD REVIEW! IT DOESN'T MATTER HOW GOOD THE COOKING IS!! YOU CAN MAKE OR BREAK A CHEF ON A WHIM!. I WALK THE BATTLEFIELD OF LIFE, AND FLATTERY IS MY WEAPON!!
I AM THE HEISEI ERA'S MASTER OF CONVERSATION!!
AND THEN H LEFT...
THE MAN MAKES A MOCKERY OF ALL HUMANKIND...!
YEAH... EVEN I THINK SO...
I'M AFRAID IT DOESN'T MATTER HOW HARD THEY TRY, OR HOW GREAT THE MEAL MIGHT ACTUALLY BE, UKAI-SAN HAS ALREADY MADE UP HIS MIND.
Sob!
THERE *IS* SOME VALIDITY TO YOUR THEORY...
I'm so saaaaaad.

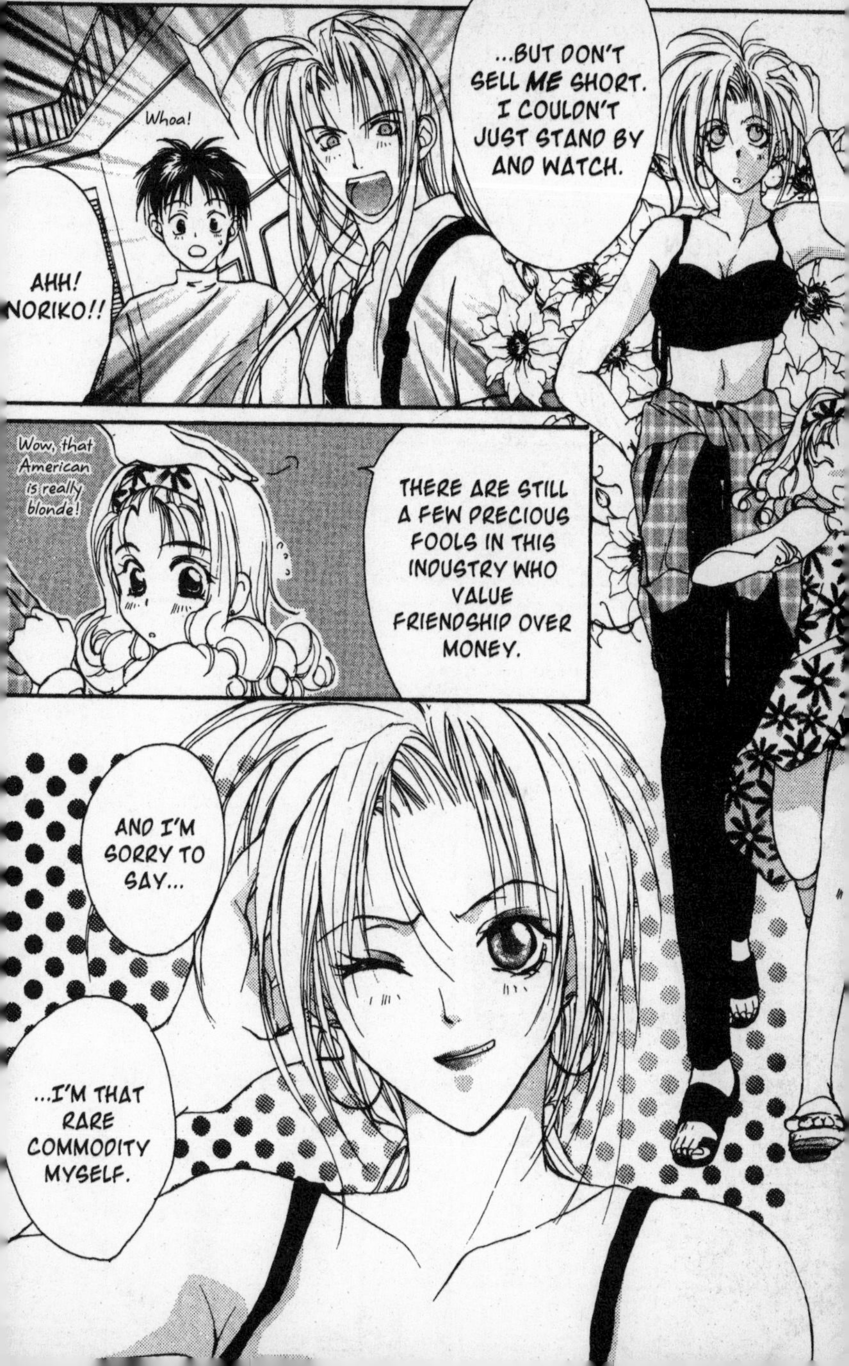
...BUT DON'T SELL *ME* SHORT. I COULDN'T JUST STAND BY AND WATCH.
Whoa!
AHH! NORIKO!!
THERE ARE STILL A FEW PRECIOUS FOOLS IN THIS INDUSTRY WHO VALUE FRIENDSHIP OVER MONEY.
Wow, that American is really blonde!
AND I'M SORRY TO SAY...
...I'M THAT RARE COMMODITY MYSELF.

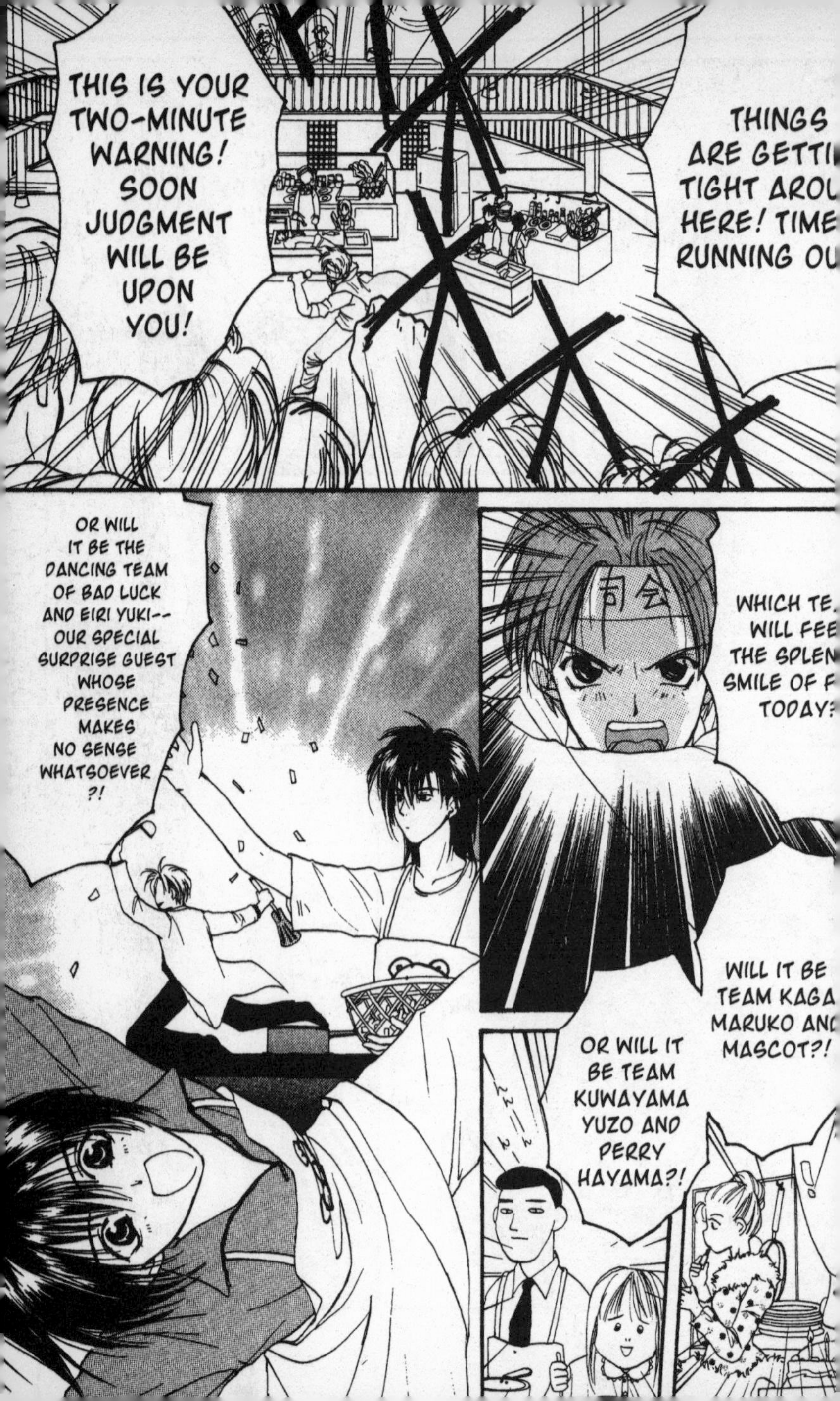
THINGS ARE GETTI TIGHT AROU HERE! TIME RUNNING OU
THIS IS YOUR TWO-MINUTE WARNING! SOON JUDGMENT WILL BE UPON YOU!
WHICH TE WILL FEE THE SPLEN SMILE OF F TODAY?
WILL IT BE TEAM KAGA MARUKO AN MASCOT?!
OR WILL IT BE TEAM KUWAYAMA YUZO AND PERRY HAYAMA?!
OR WILL IT BE THE DANCING TEAM OF BAD LUCK AND EIRI YUKI-- OUR SPECIAL SURPRISE GUEST WHOSE PRESENCE MAKES NO SENSE WHATSOEVER ?!

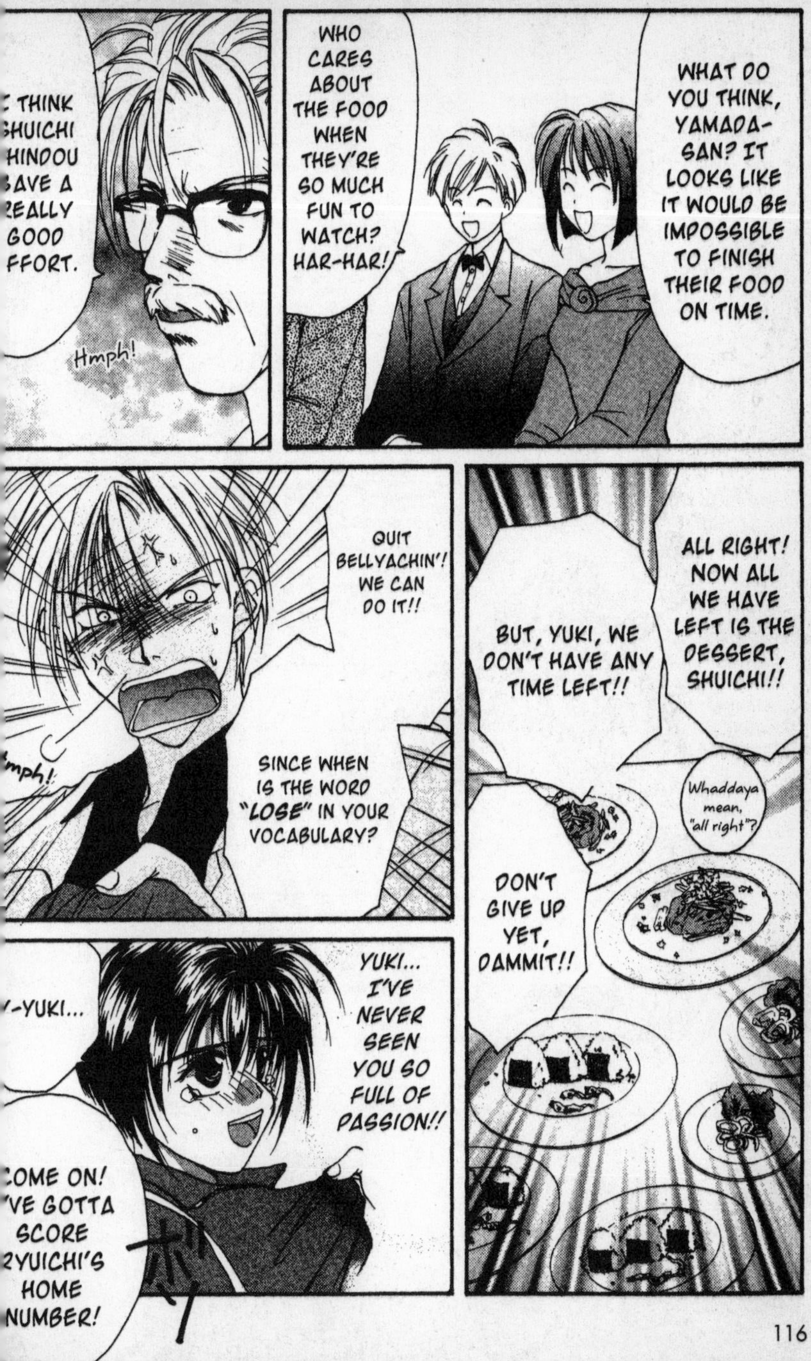
WHAT DO YOU THINK, YAMADA-SAN? IT LOOKS LIKE IT WOULD BE IMPOSSIBLE TO FINISH THEIR FOOD ON TIME.
WHO CARES ABOUT THE FOOD WHEN THEY'RE SO MUCH FUN TO WATCH? HAR-HAR!
THINK SHUICHI HINDOU AVE A REALLY GOOD FFORT.
Hmph!
ALL RIGHT! NOW ALL WE HAVE LEFT IS THE DESSERT, SHUICHI!!
BUT, YUKI, WE DON'T HAVE ANY TIME LEFT!!
Whaddaya mean, "all right"?
DON'T GIVE UP YET, DAMMIT!!
QUIT BELLYACHIN'! WE CAN DO IT!!
SINCE WHEN IS THE WORD "LOSE" IN YOUR VOCABULARY?
mph!
YUKI... I'VE NEVER SEEN YOU SO FULL OF PASSION!!
-YUKI...
OME ON! VE GOTTA SCORE YUICHI'S HOME NUMBER!

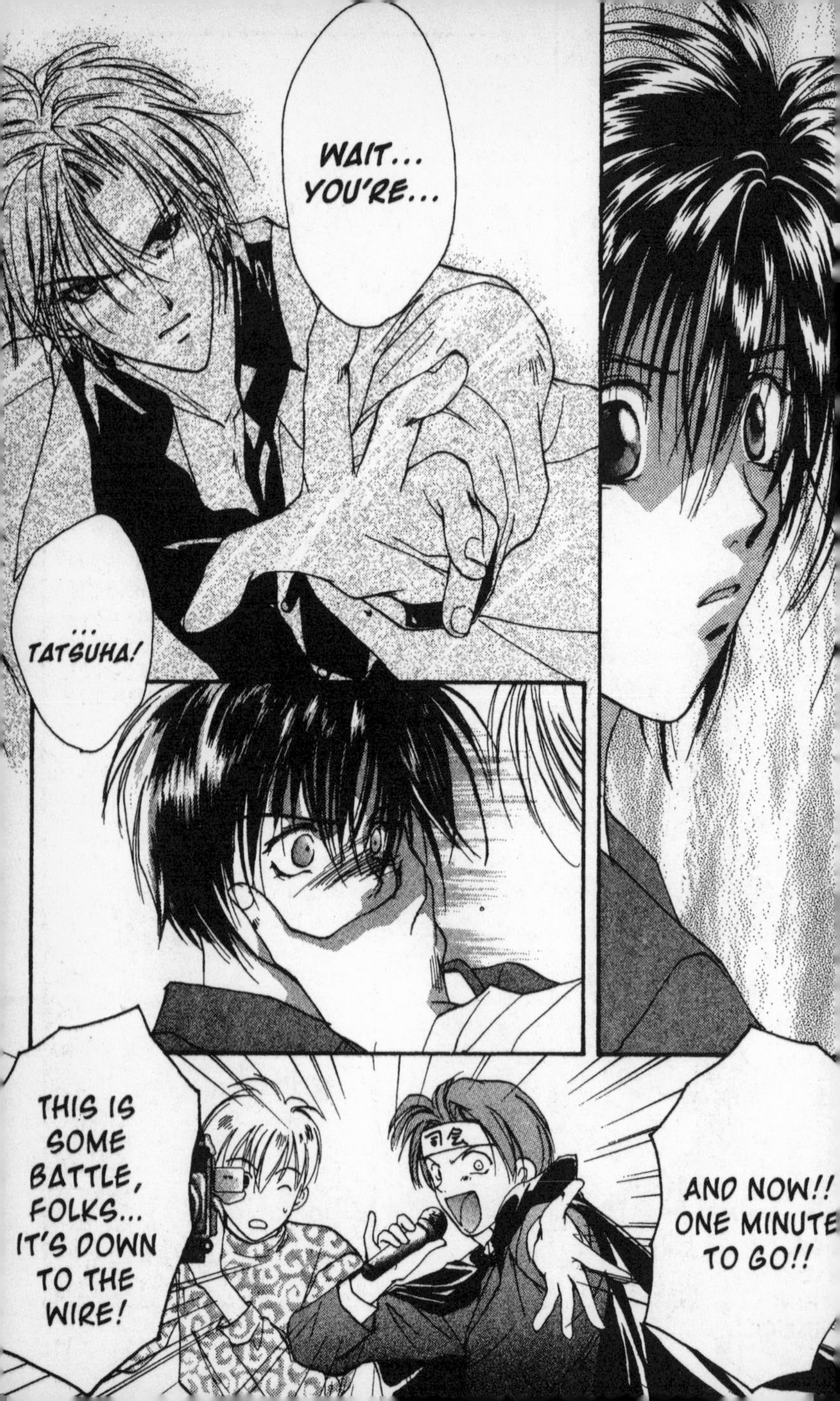
WAIT... YOU'RE...
... TATSUHA!
AND NOW!! ONE MINUTE TO GO!!
THIS IS SOME BATTLE, FOLKS... IT'S DOWN TO THE WIRE!

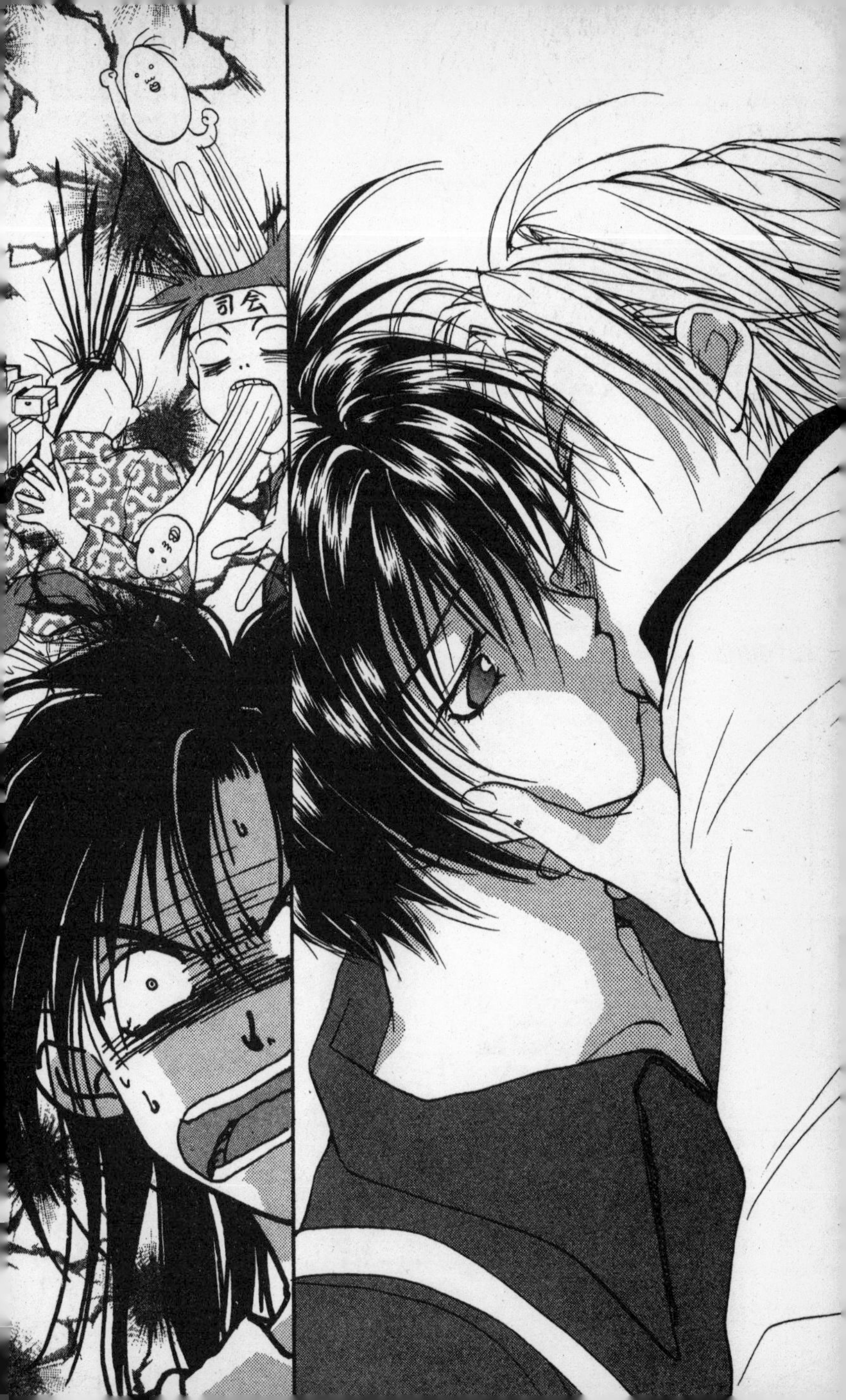
司会

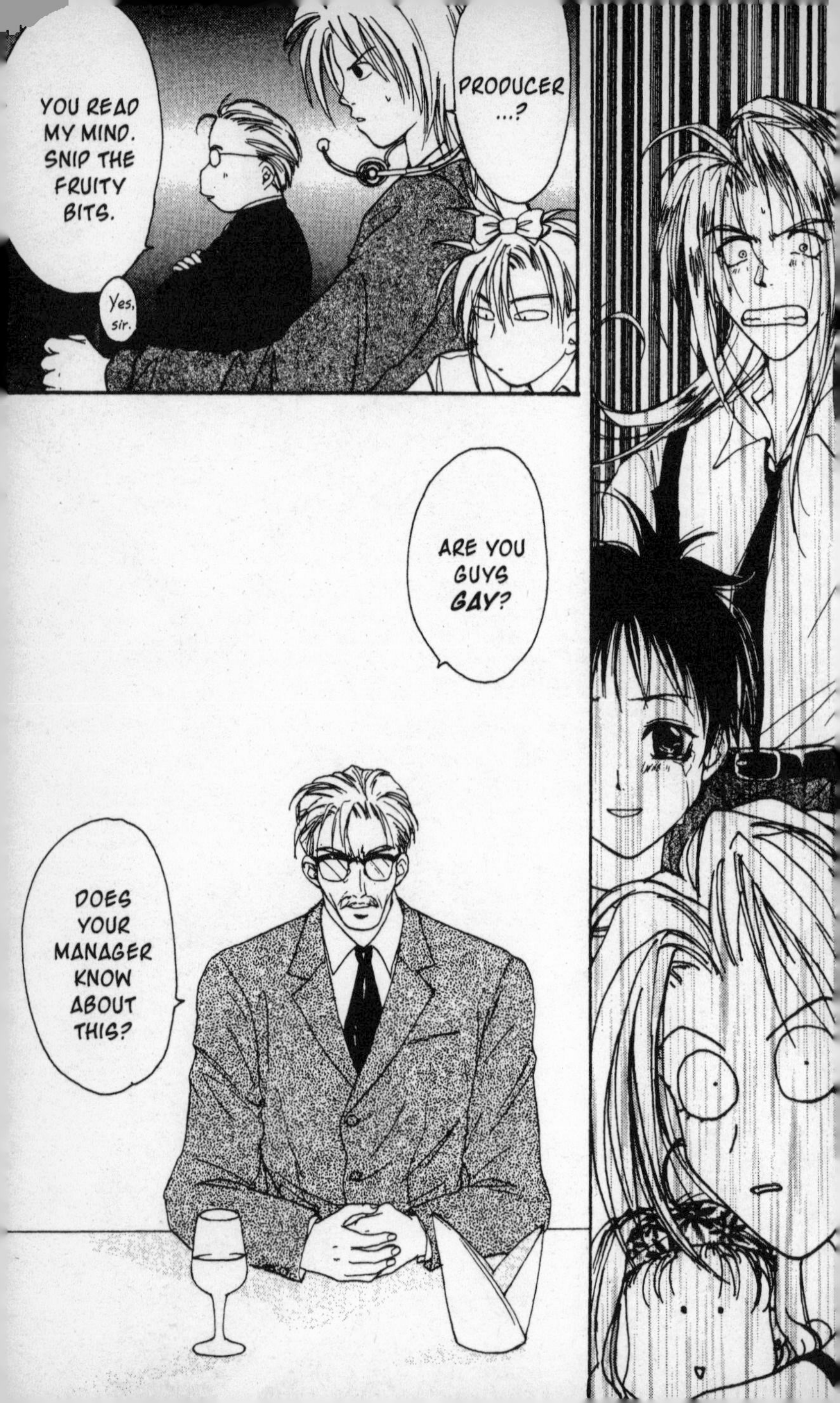
PRODUCER ...?
YOU READ MY MIND. SNIP THE FRUITY BITS.
Yes, sir.
ARE YOU GUYS GAY?
DOES YOUR MANAGER KNOW ABOUT THIS?

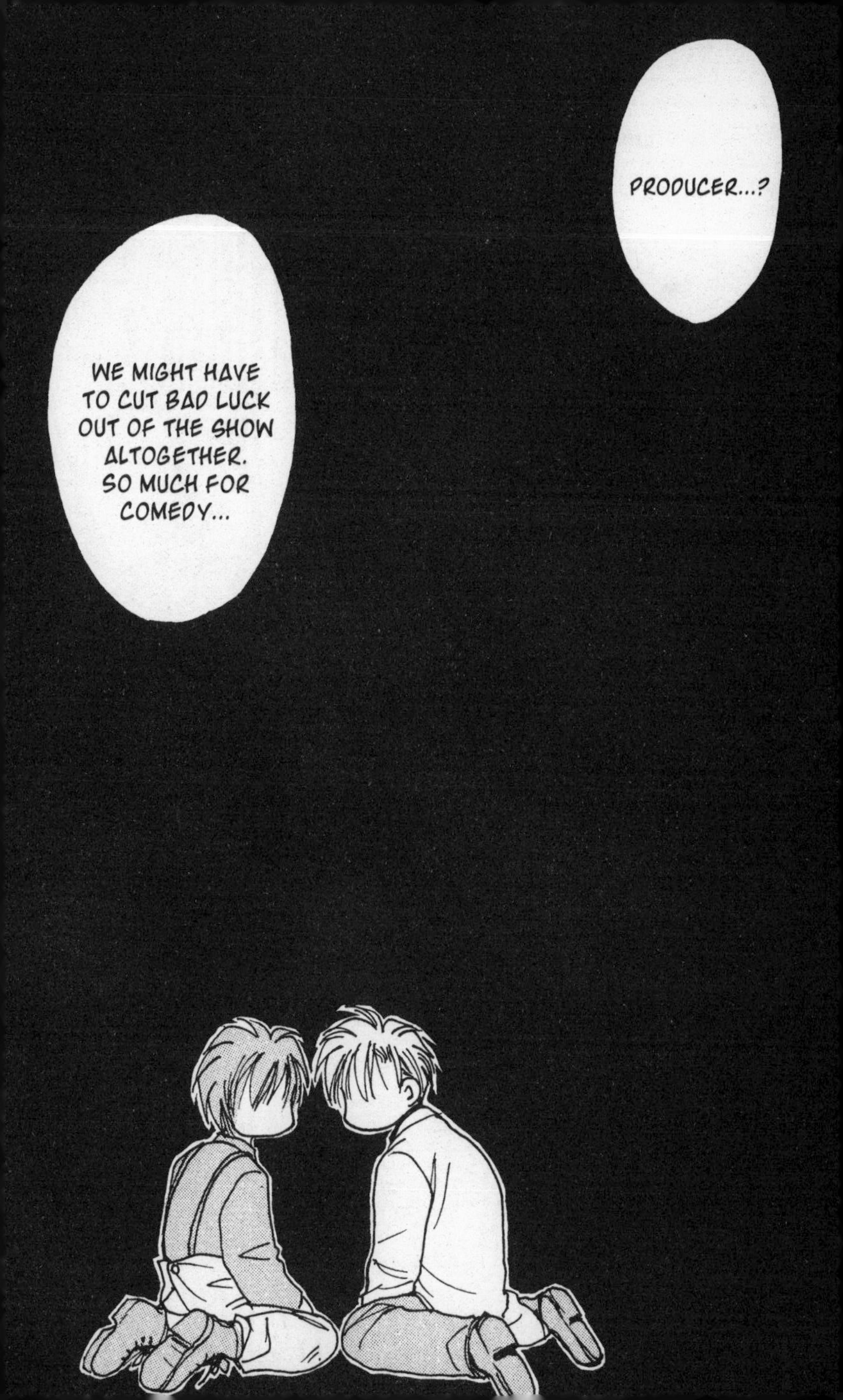
PRODUCER...?
WE MIGHT HAVE TO CUT BAD LUCK OUT OF THE SHOW ALTOGETHER. SO MUCH FOR COMEDY...

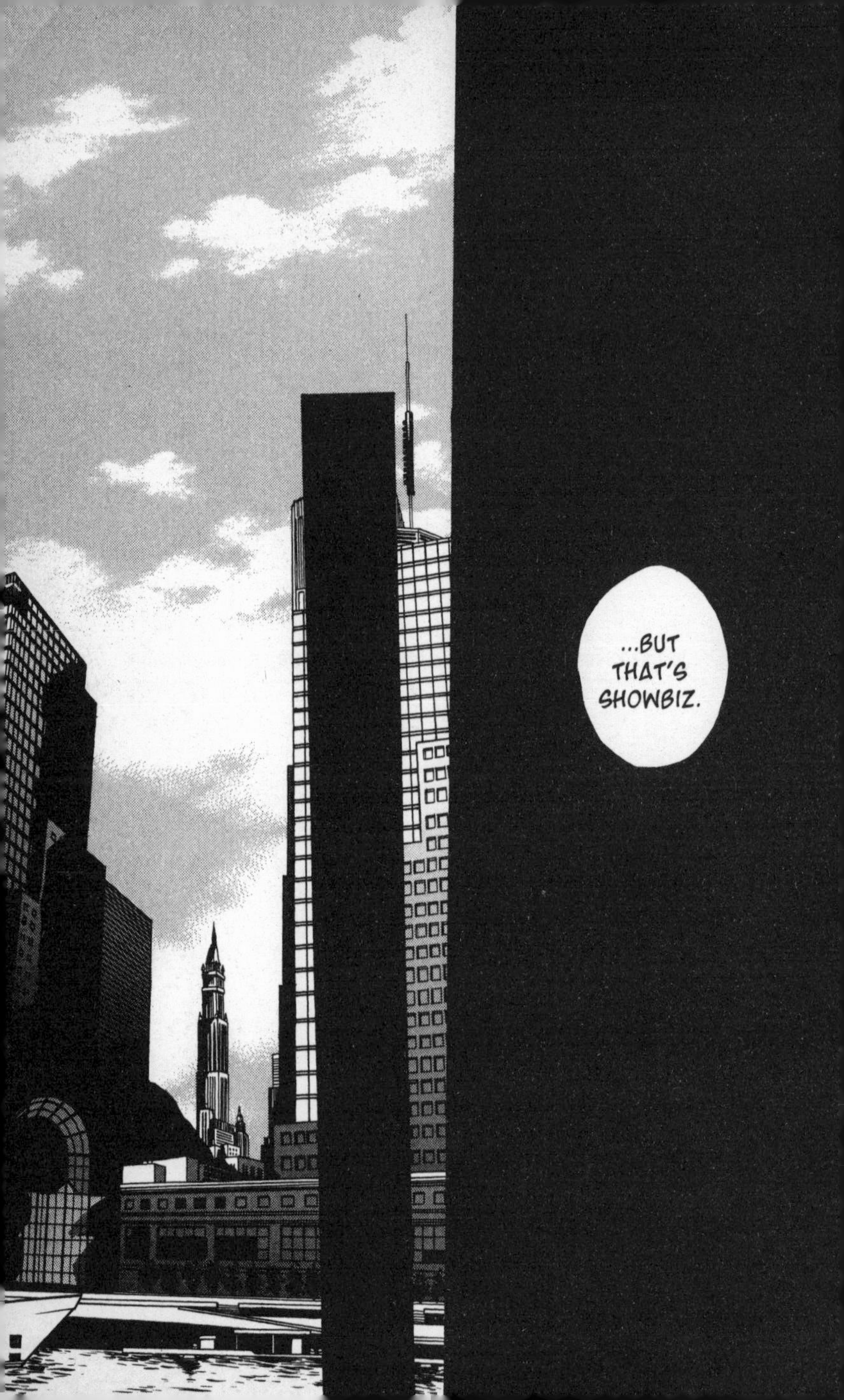
...BUT THAT'S SHOWBIZ.

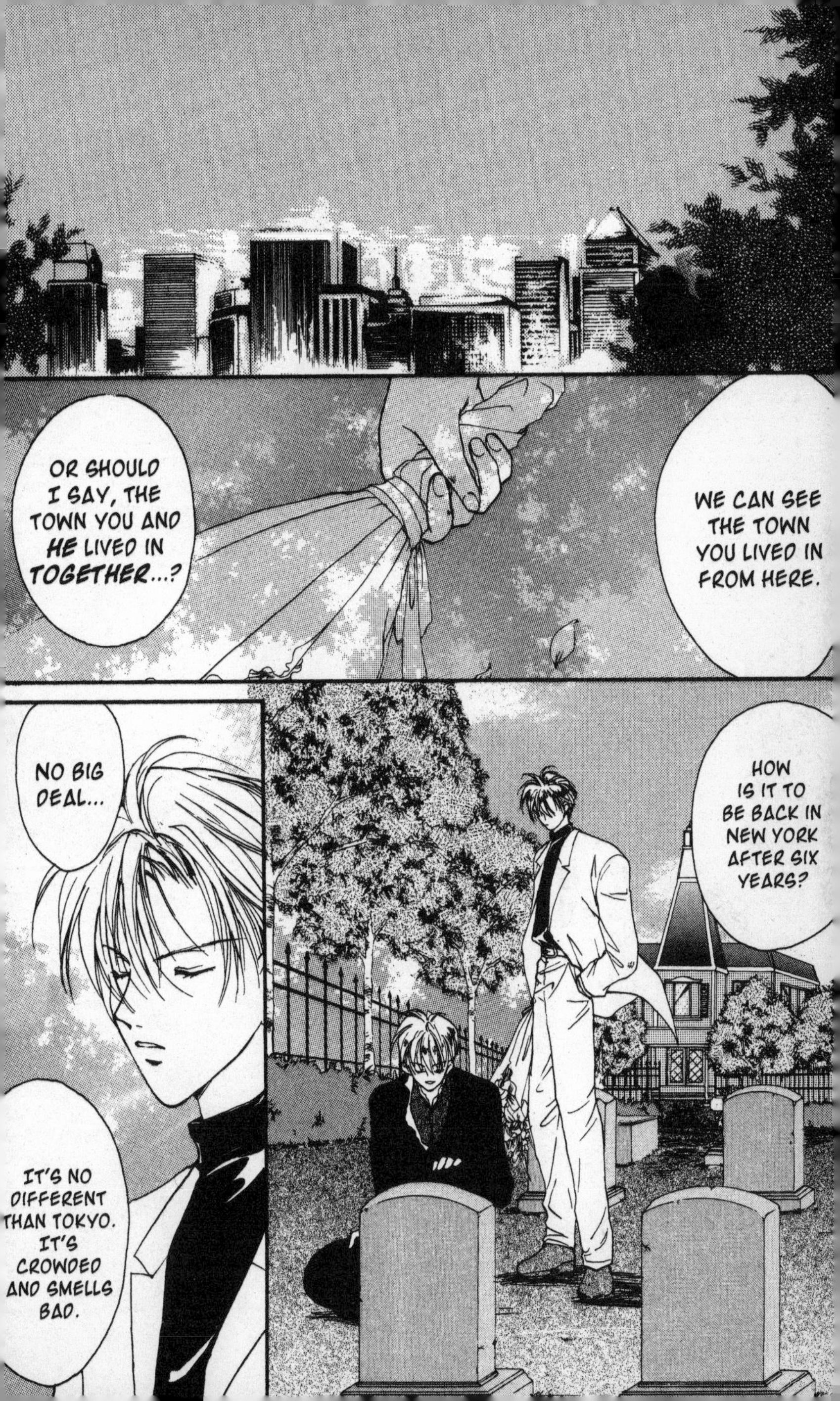
WE CAN SEE THE TOWN YOU LIVED IN FROM HERE.
OR SHOULD I SAY, THE TOWN YOU AND HE LIVED IN TOGETHER...?
HOW IS IT TO BE BACK IN NEW YORK AFTER SIX YEARS?
NO BIG DEAL...
IT'S NO DIFFERENT THAN TOKYO. IT'S CROWDED AND SMELLS BAD.

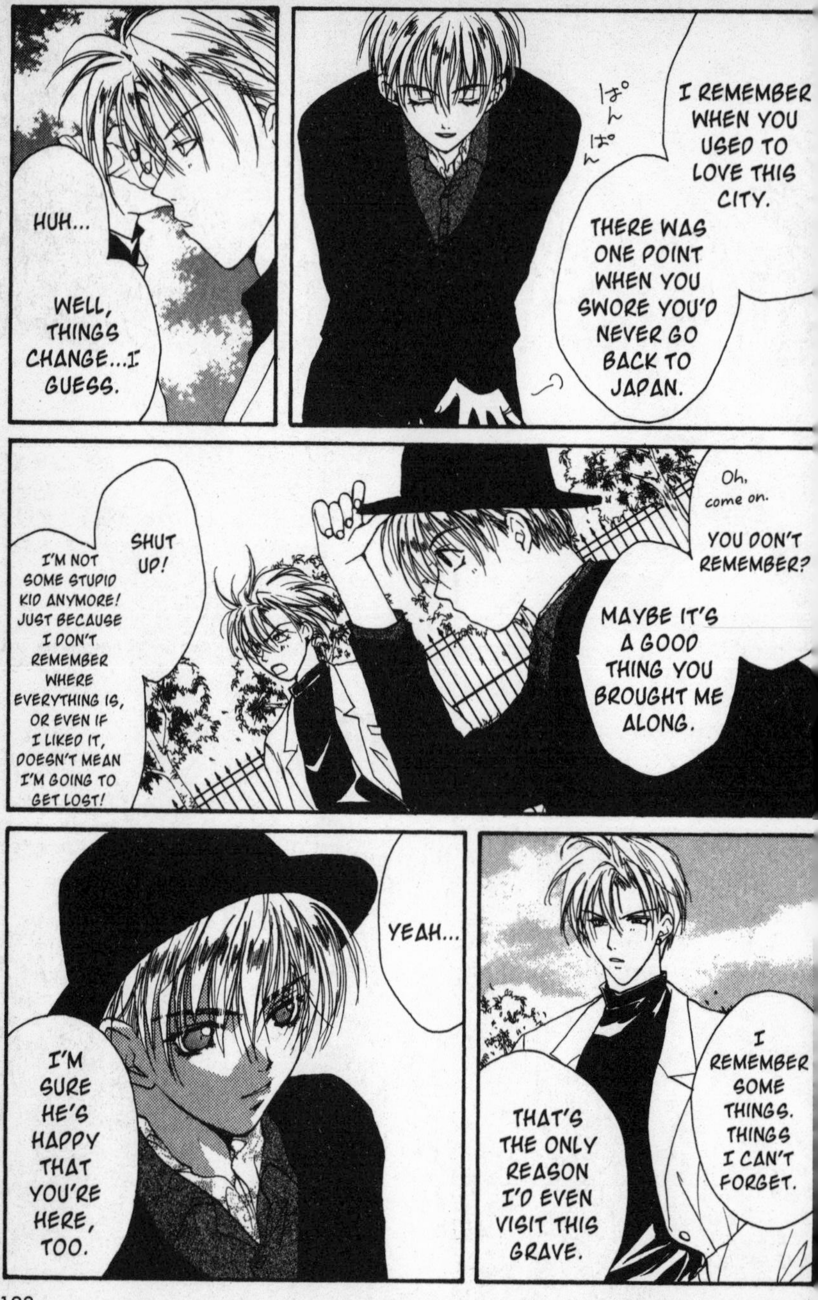

I REMEMBER WHEN YOU USED TO LOVE THIS CITY.
ぱんぱん
THERE WAS ONE POINT WHEN YOU SWORE YOU'D NEVER GO BACK TO JAPAN.
HUH...
WELL, THINGS CHANGE...I GUESS.
Oh, come on.
YOU DON'T REMEMBER?
MAYBE IT'S A GOOD THING YOU BROUGHT ME ALONG.
SHUT UP!
I'M NOT SOME STUPID KID ANYMORE! JUST BECAUSE I DON'T REMEMBER WHERE EVERYTHING IS, OR EVEN IF I LIKED IT, DOESN'T MEAN I'M GOING TO GET LOST!
I REMEMBER SOME THINGS. THINGS I CAN'T FORGET.
THAT'S THE ONLY REASON I'D EVEN VISIT THIS GRAVE.
YEAH...
I'M SURE HE'S HAPPY THAT YOU'RE HERE, TOO.

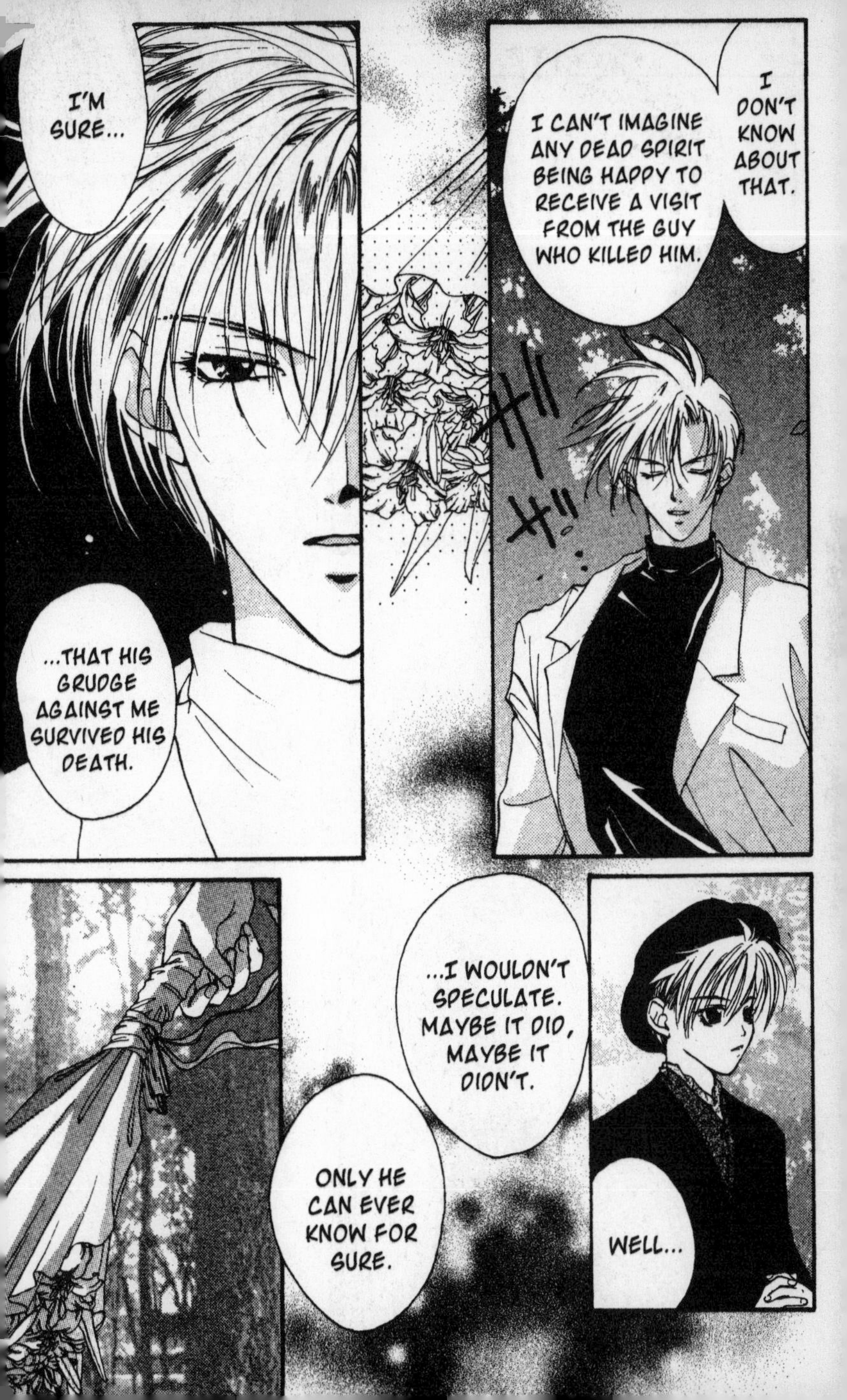
I DON'T KNOW ABOUT THAT.
I CAN'T IMAGINE ANY DEAD SPIRIT BEING HAPPY TO RECEIVE A VISIT FROM THE GUY WHO KILLED HIM.
I'M SURE...
...THAT HIS GRUDGE AGAINST ME SURVIVED HIS DEATH.
WELL...
...I WOULDN'T SPECULATE. MAYBE IT DID, MAYBE IT DIDN'T.
ONLY HE CAN EVER KNOW FOR SURE.

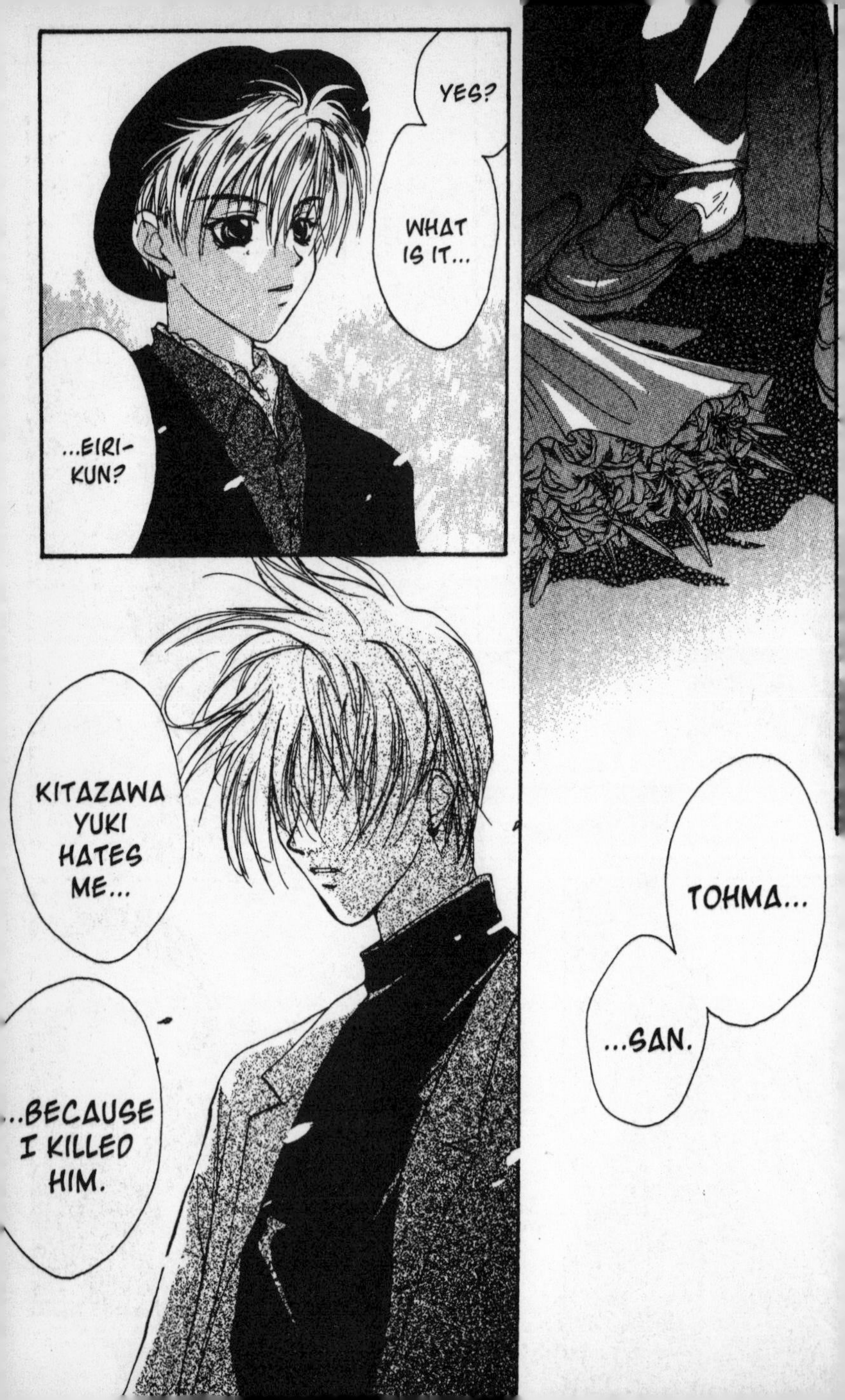
TOHMA...
...SAN.
YES?
WHAT IS IT...
...EIRI-KUN?
KITAZAWA YUKI HATES ME...
...BECAUSE I KILLED HIM.

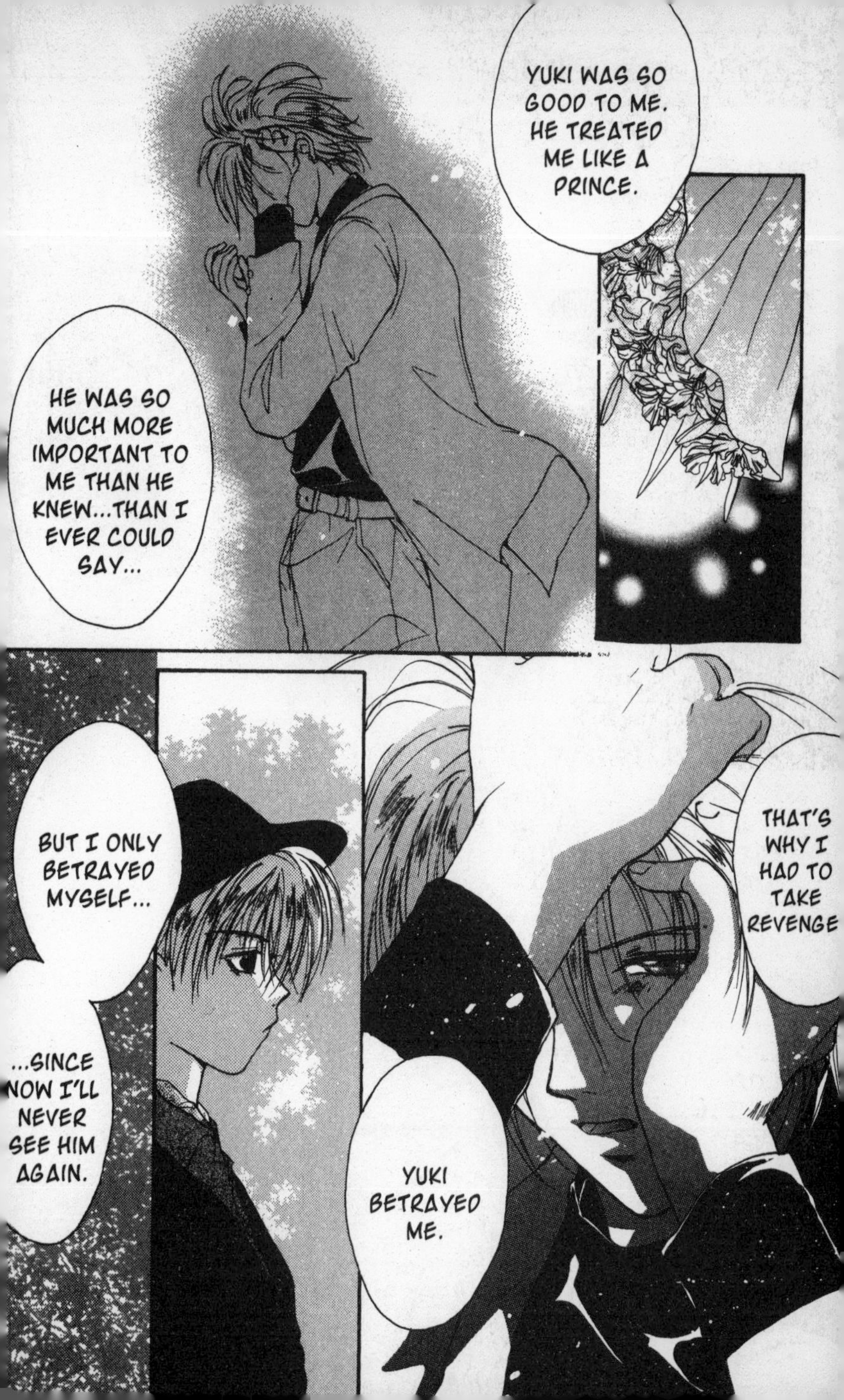
YUKI WAS SO GOOD TO ME. HE TREATED ME LIKE A PRINCE.
HE WAS SO MUCH MORE IMPORTANT TO ME THAN HE KNEW...THAN I EVER COULD SAY...
THAT'S WHY I HAD TO TAKE REVENGE
YUKI BETRAYED ME.
BUT I ONLY BETRAYED MYSELF...
...SINCE NOW I'LL NEVER SEE HIM AGAIN.

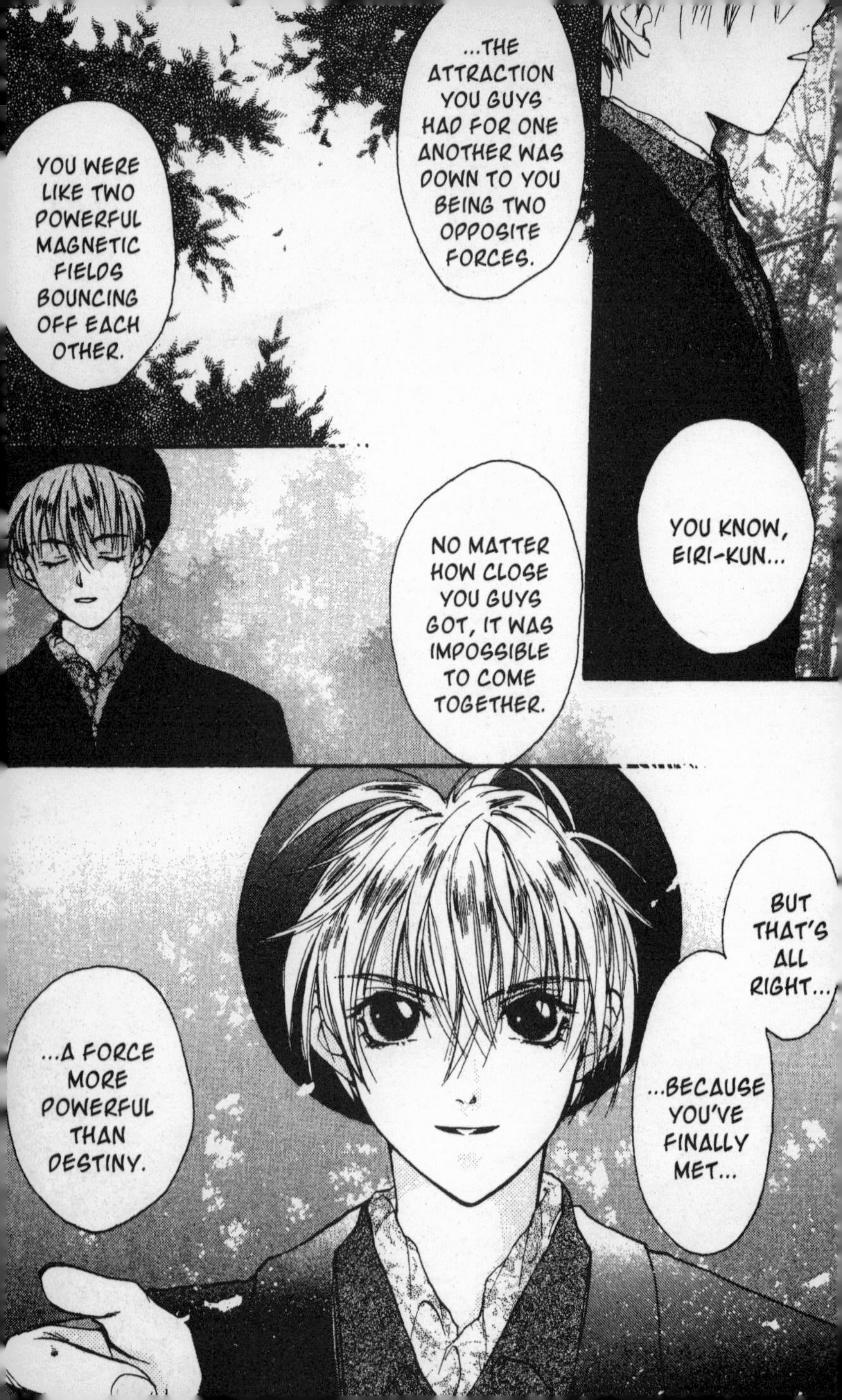
YOU KNOW, EIRI-KUN...
...THE ATTRACTION YOU GUYS HAD FOR ONE ANOTHER WAS DOWN TO YOU BEING TWO OPPOSITE FORCES.
YOU WERE LIKE TWO POWERFUL MAGNETIC FIELDS BOUNCING OFF EACH OTHER.
NO MATTER HOW CLOSE YOU GUYS GOT, IT WAS IMPOSSIBLE TO COME TOGETHER.
BUT THAT'S ALL RIGHT...
...BECAUSE YOU'VE FINALLY MET...
...A FORCE MORE POWERFUL THAN DESTINY.

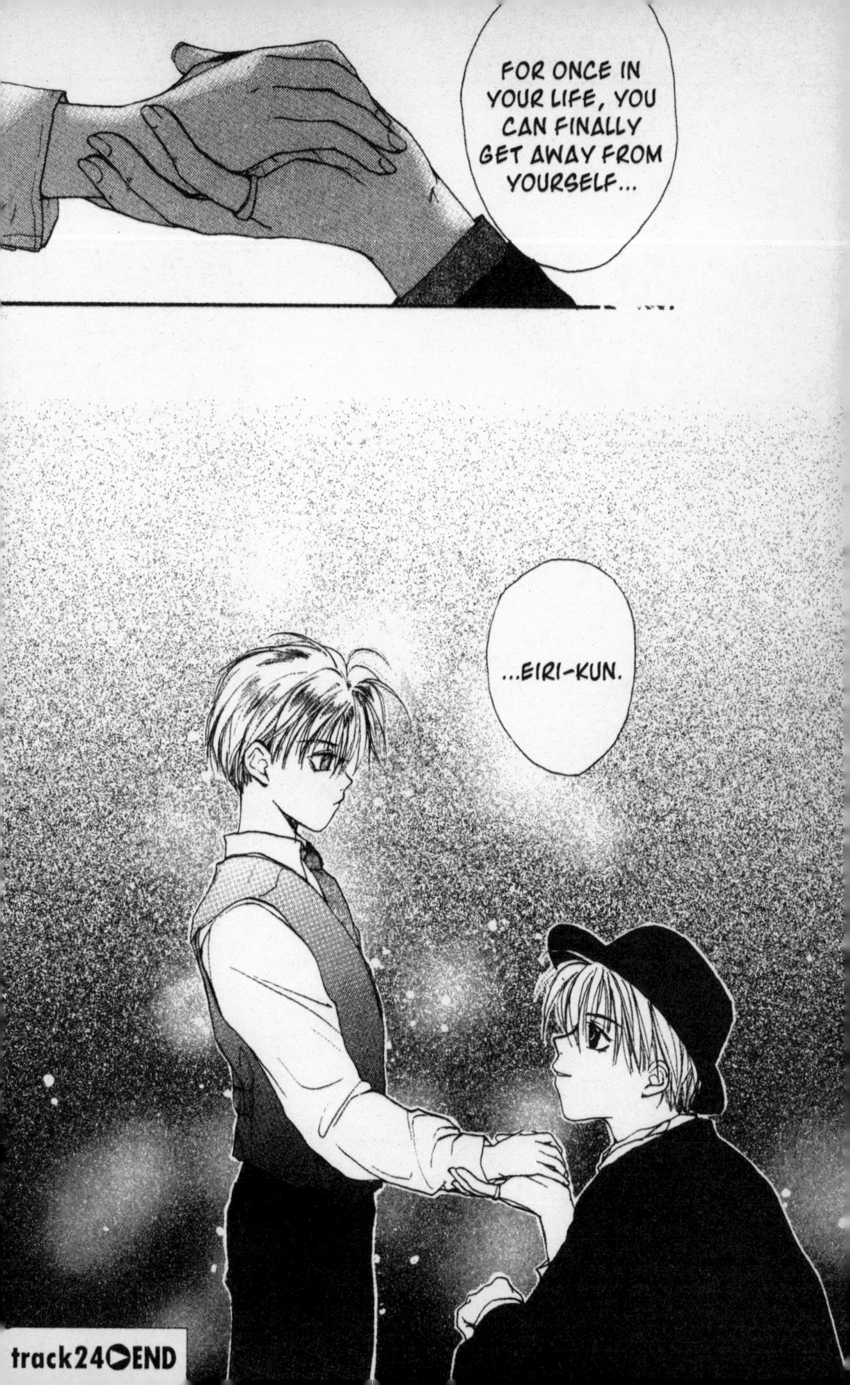
FOR ONCE IN YOUR LIFE, YOU CAN FINALLY GET AWAY FROM YOURSELF...
...EIRI-KUN.
track24▶END

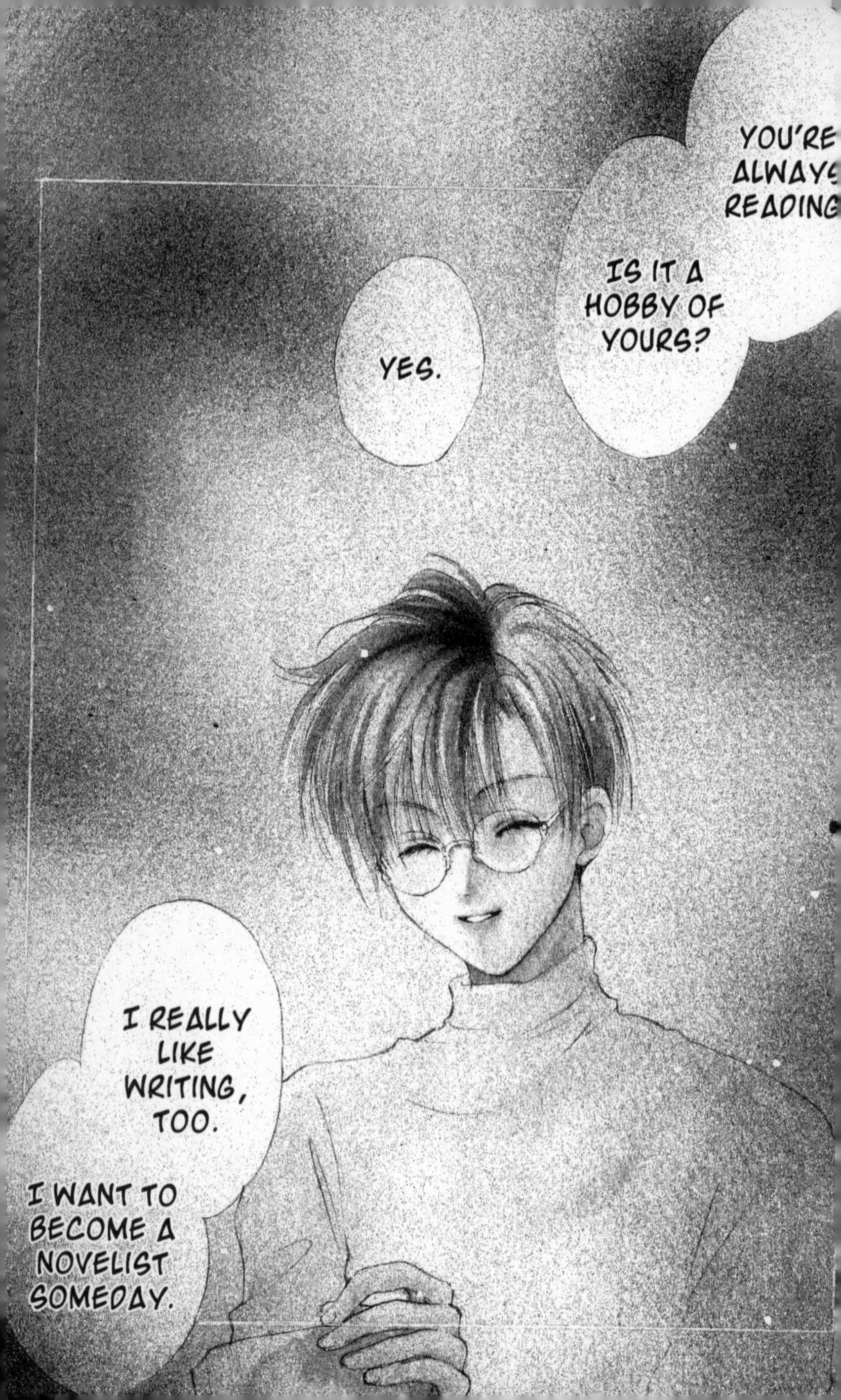

YOU'RE ALWAYS READING
IS IT A HOBBY OF YOURS?
YES.
I REALLY LIKE WRITING, TOO.
I WANT TO BECOME A NOVELIST SOMEDAY.

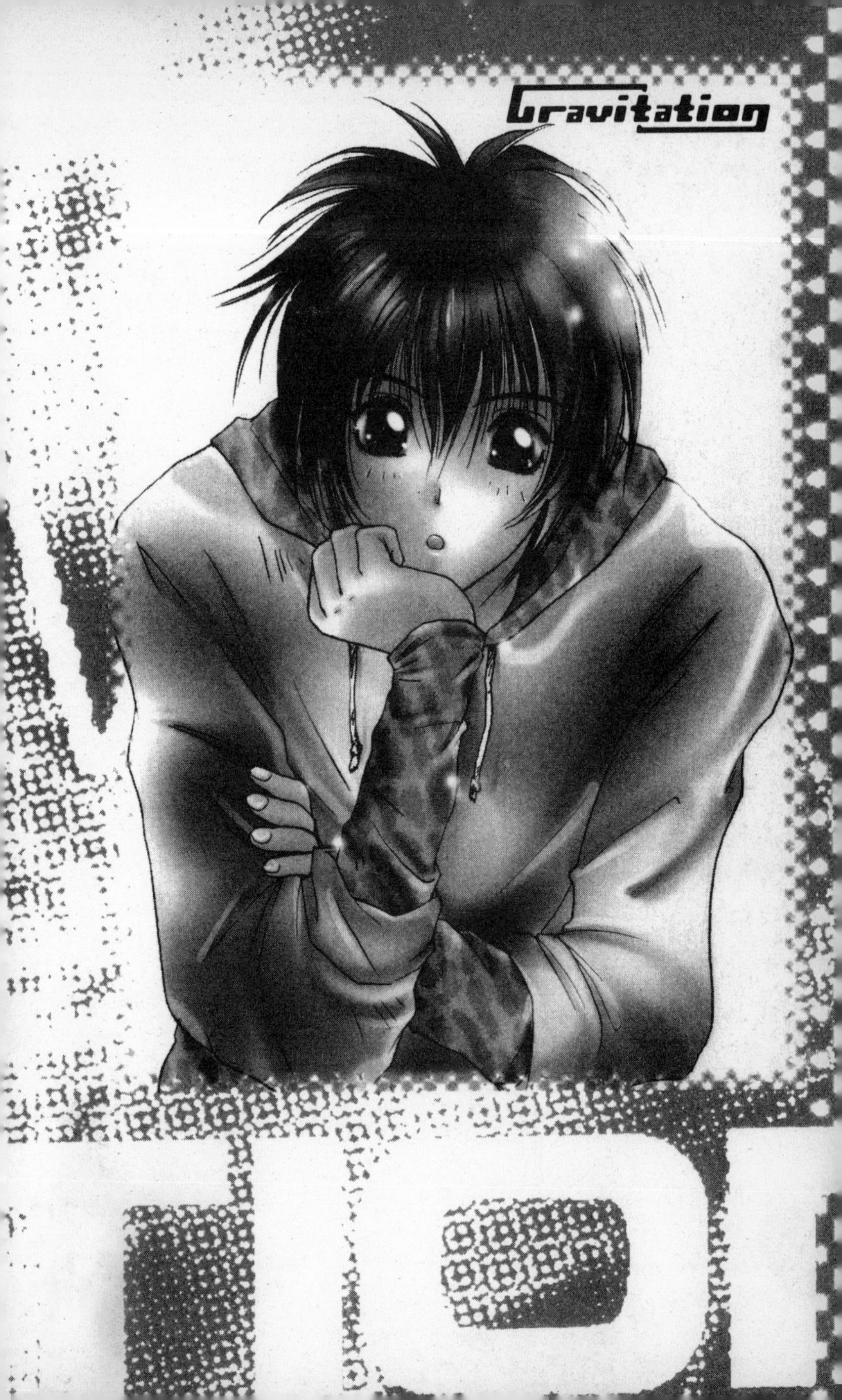
Gravitation

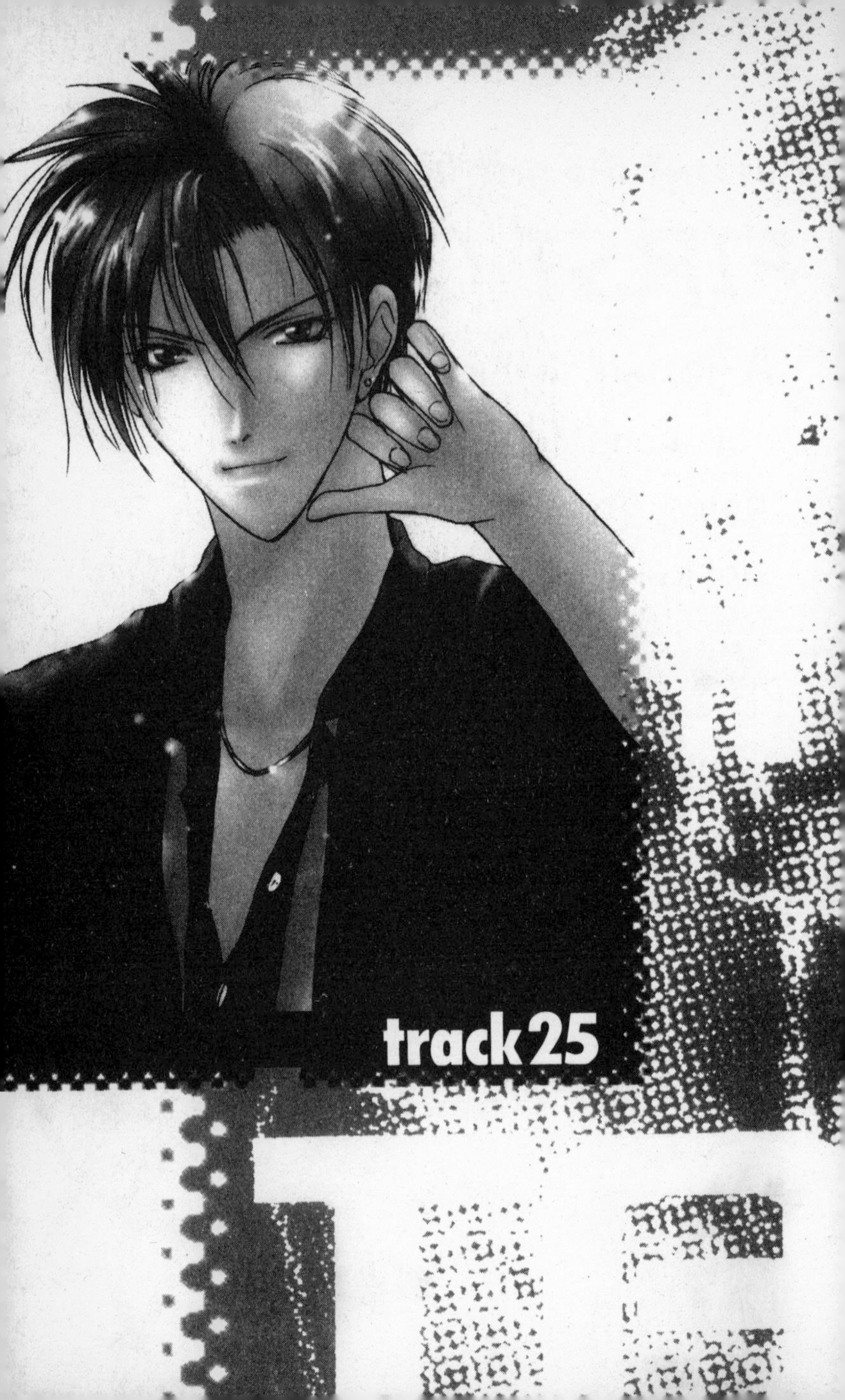
track 25

This isn't the first time, but...

FIRST OF ALL...

Amazing! We're in them middle of Book 6!! Is this story ever going to end?! I, Murakami, am working hard!! The ever-absurd Gravitation Book 6!! Please enjoy...with your family, with your lovers, with your friends!!

President of
N-G Records Ltd.

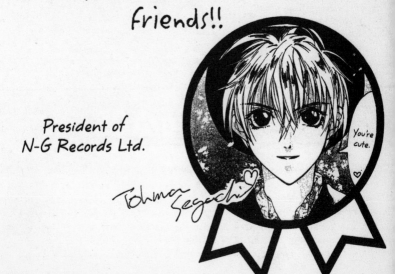

You're cute.

Tohma Seguchi

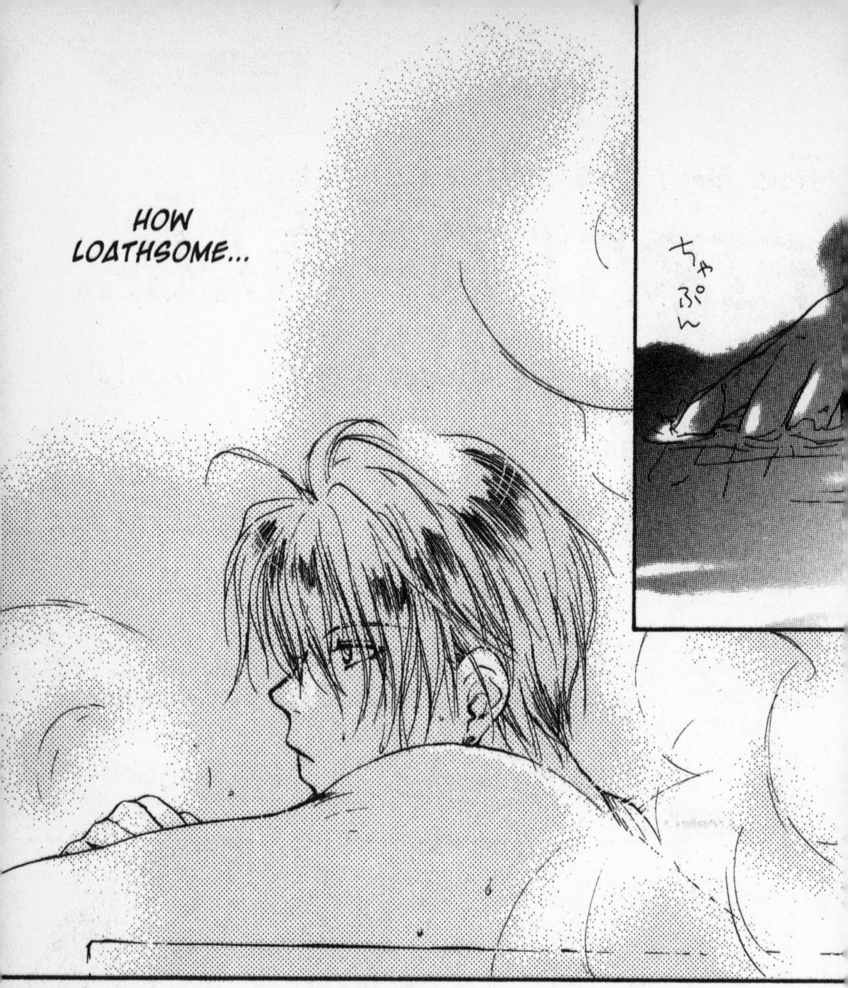
ちゃぷん
HOW LOATHSOME...

ABOUT GRAVITATION TRACK 25

What was I thinking? Don't you think this book has been going in some pretty crazy directions, especially in the second half of the last episode? This is turning into a serious problem. Tohma-san is saying some pretty sexually charged things to Eiri-san. I have to be honest, that whole graveyard scene is doing my head in. There are plenty of things that are still nagging at me, and I'm not sure I pulled it off as best as I could. Hiroshi's hair is getting long, too. And I don't really like the lines I drew after not getting enough sleep.

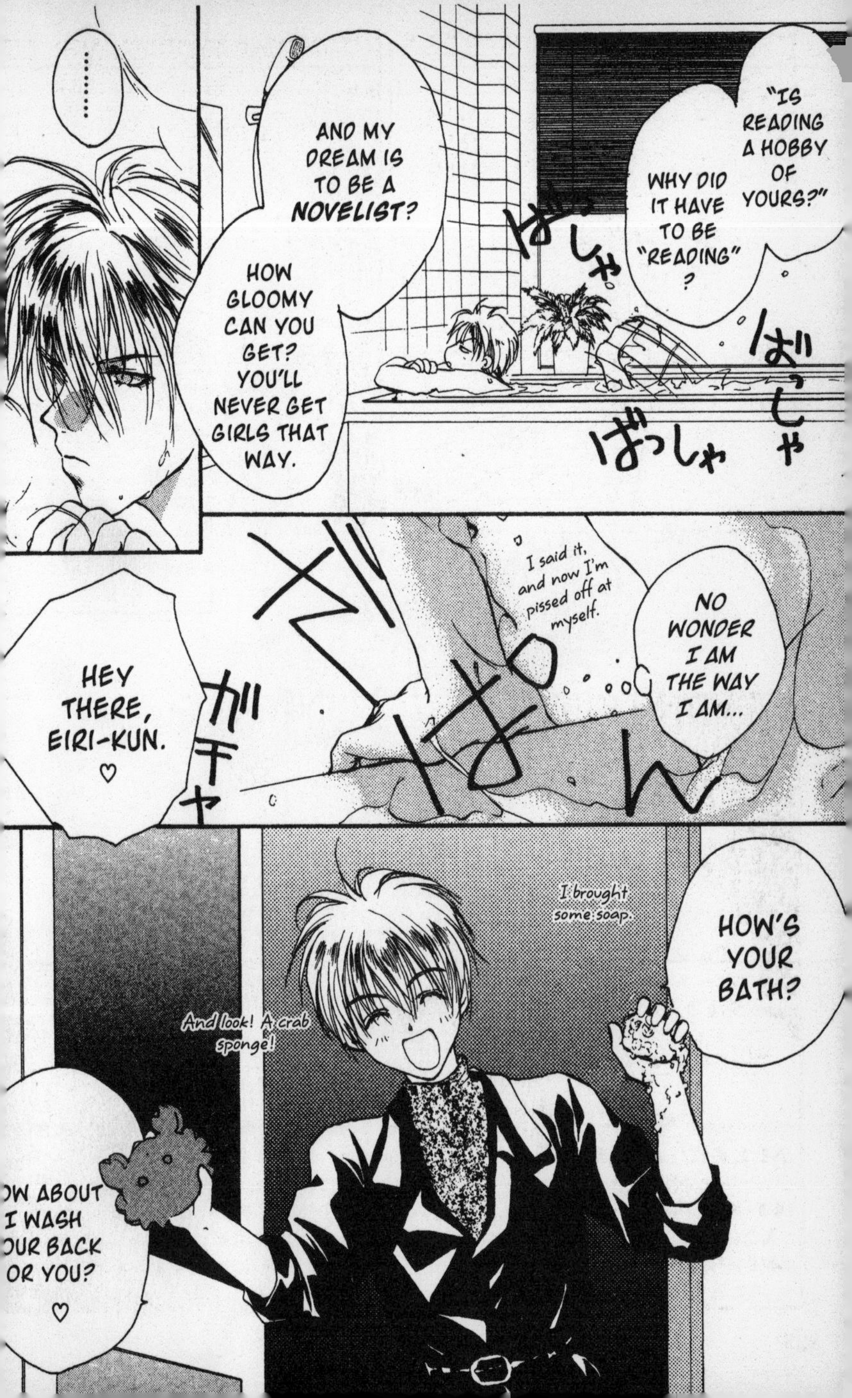

"IS READING A HOBBY OF YOURS?"
WHY DID IT HAVE TO BE "READING"?
ばっしゃ
ばっしゃ
ばしゃ
AND MY DREAM IS TO BE A NOVELIST?
HOW GLOOMY CAN YOU GET? YOU'LL NEVER GET GIRLS THAT WAY.
……
NO WONDER I AM THE WAY I AM...
I said it, and now I'm pissed off at myself.
ガチャ
HEY THERE, EIRI-KUN. ♡
HOW'S YOUR BATH?
I brought some soap.
And look! A crab sponge!
OW ABOUT I WASH OUR BACK OR YOU? ♡

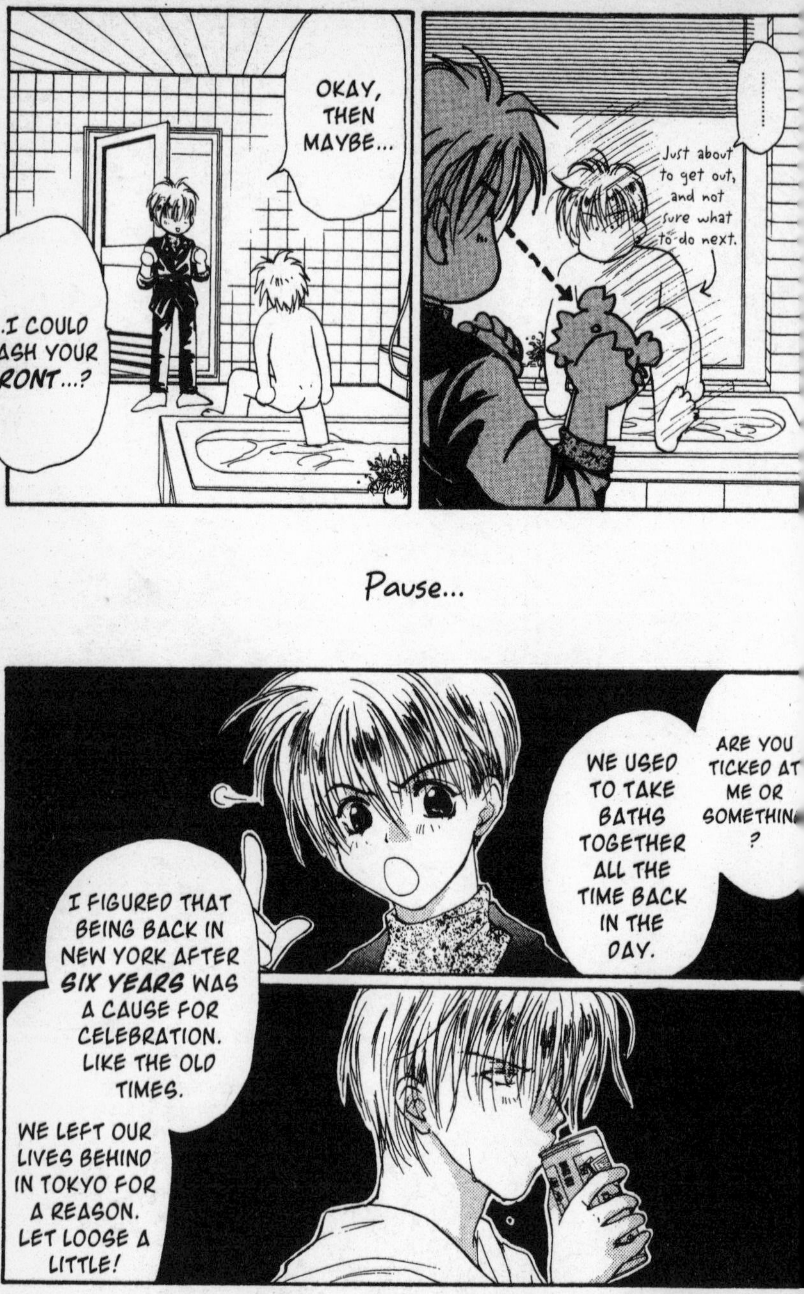

......
Just about to get out, and not sure what to do next.
OKAY, THEN MAYBE...
...I COULD WASH YOUR FRONT...?
Pause...
ARE YOU TICKED AT ME OR SOMETHIN ?
WE USED TO TAKE BATHS TOGETHER ALL THE TIME BACK IN THE DAY.
I FIGURED THAT BEING BACK IN NEW YORK AFTER SIX YEARS WAS A CAUSE FOR CELEBRATION. LIKE THE OLD TIMES.
WE LEFT OUR LIVES BEHIND IN TOKYO FOR A REASON. LET LOOSE A LITTLE!

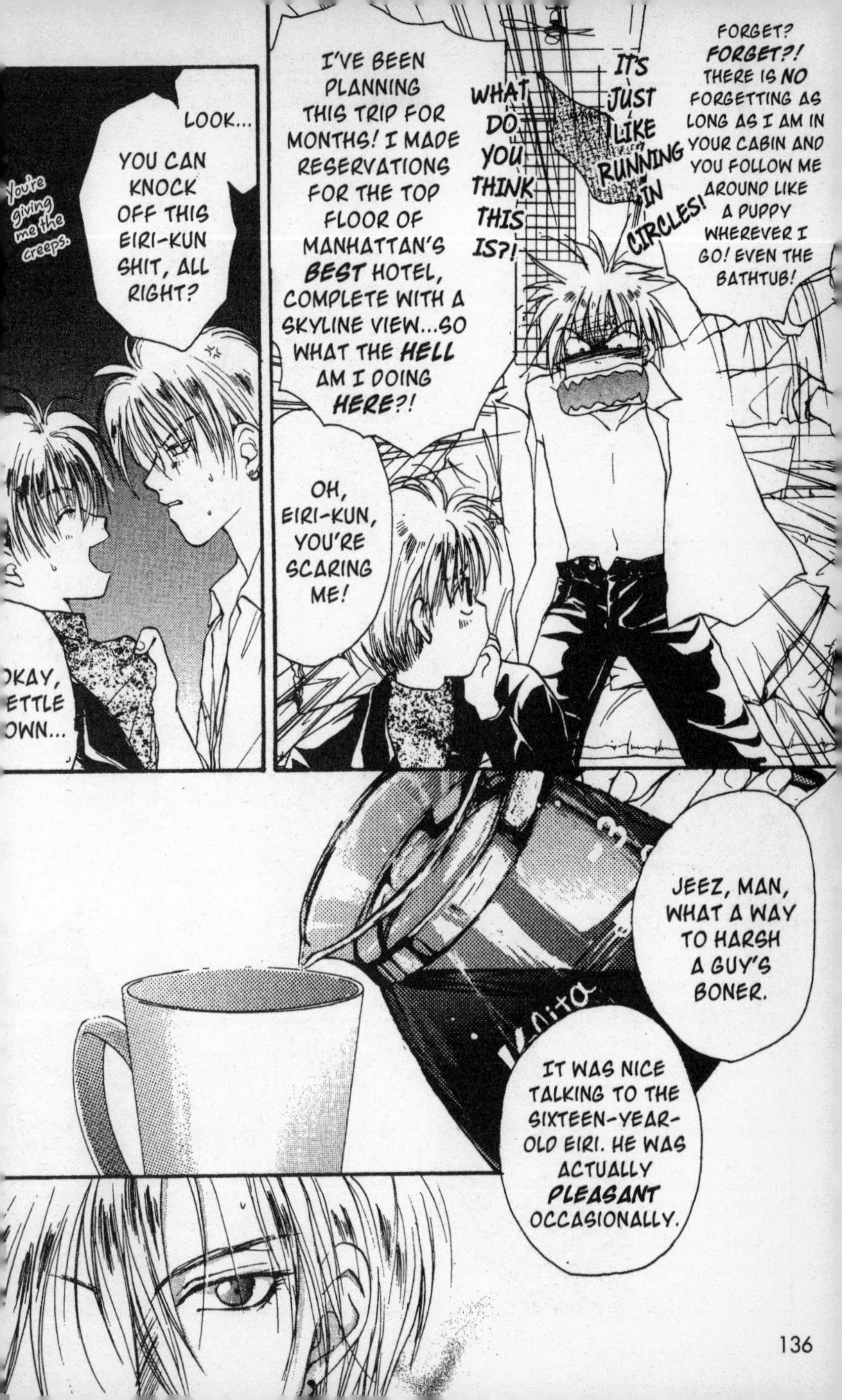
FORGET? FORGET?! THERE IS NO FORGETTING AS LONG AS I AM IN YOUR CABIN AND YOU FOLLOW ME AROUND LIKE A PUPPY WHEREVER I GO! EVEN THE BATHTUB!
IT'S JUST LIKE RUNNING IN CIRCLES!
WHAT DO YOU THINK THIS IS?!
I'VE BEEN PLANNING THIS TRIP FOR MONTHS! I MADE RESERVATIONS FOR THE TOP FLOOR OF MANHATTAN'S BEST HOTEL, COMPLETE WITH A SKYLINE VIEW...SO WHAT THE HELL AM I DOING HERE?!
OH, EIRI-KUN, YOU'RE SCARING ME!
LOOK...
YOU CAN KNOCK OFF THIS EIRI-KUN SHIT, ALL RIGHT?
You're giving me the creeps.
OKAY, ETTLE OWN...
JEEZ, MAN, WHAT A WAY TO HARSH A GUY'S BONER.
IT WAS NICE TALKING TO THE SIXTEEN-YEAR-OLD EIRI. HE WAS ACTUALLY PLEASANT OCCASIONALLY.

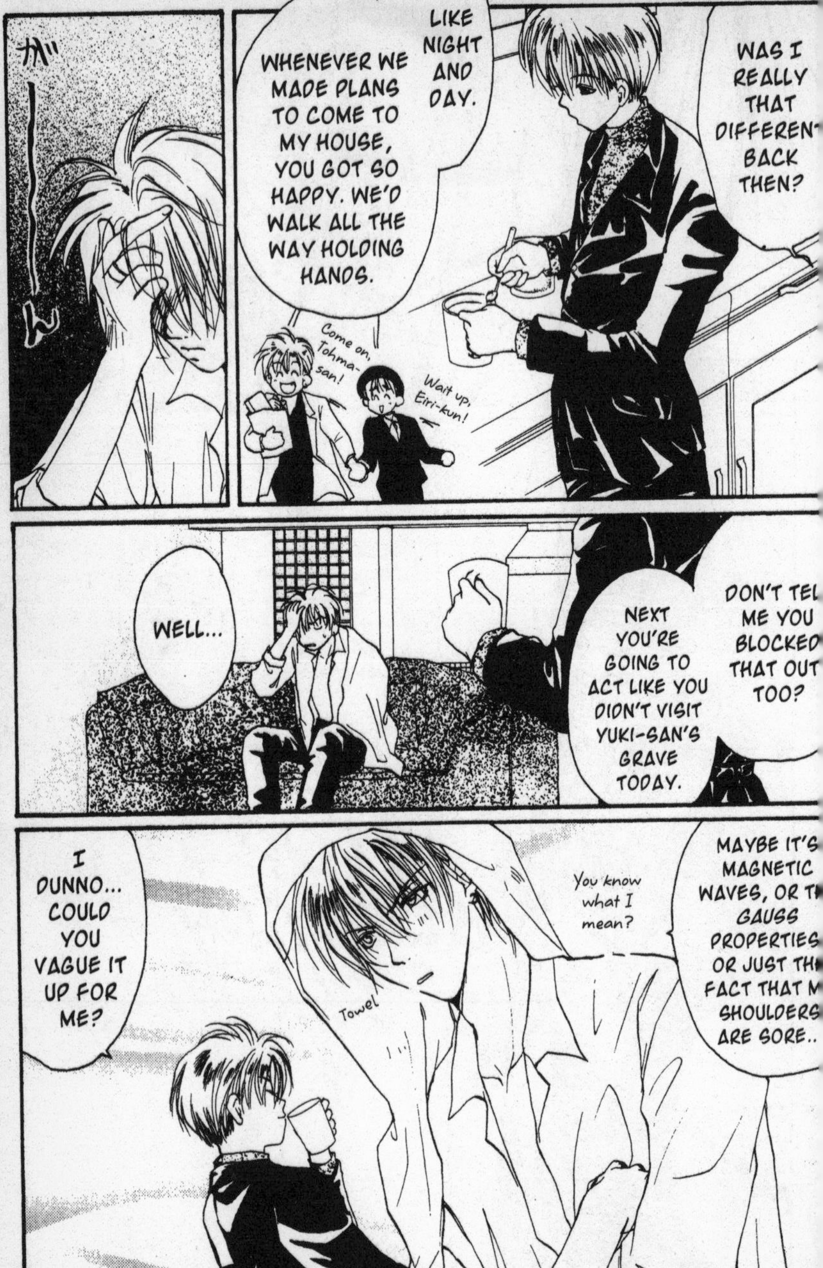
WAS I REALLY THAT DIFFEREN- BACK THEN?
LIKE NIGHT AND DAY.
WHENEVER WE MADE PLANS TO COME TO MY HOUSE, YOU GOT SO HAPPY. WE'D WALK ALL THE WAY HOLDING HANDS.
Come on, Tohma-san!
Wait up, Eiri-kun!
ガバ
DON'T TEL ME YOU BLOCKED THAT OUT TOO?
NEXT YOU'RE GOING TO ACT LIKE YOU DIDN'T VISIT YUKI-SAN'S GRAVE TODAY.
WELL...
MAYBE IT'S MAGNETIC WAVES, OR TH GAUSS PROPERTIES OR JUST TH FACT THAT M SHOULDERS ARE SORE...
You know what I mean?
Towel
I DUNNO... COULD YOU VAGUE IT UP FOR ME?

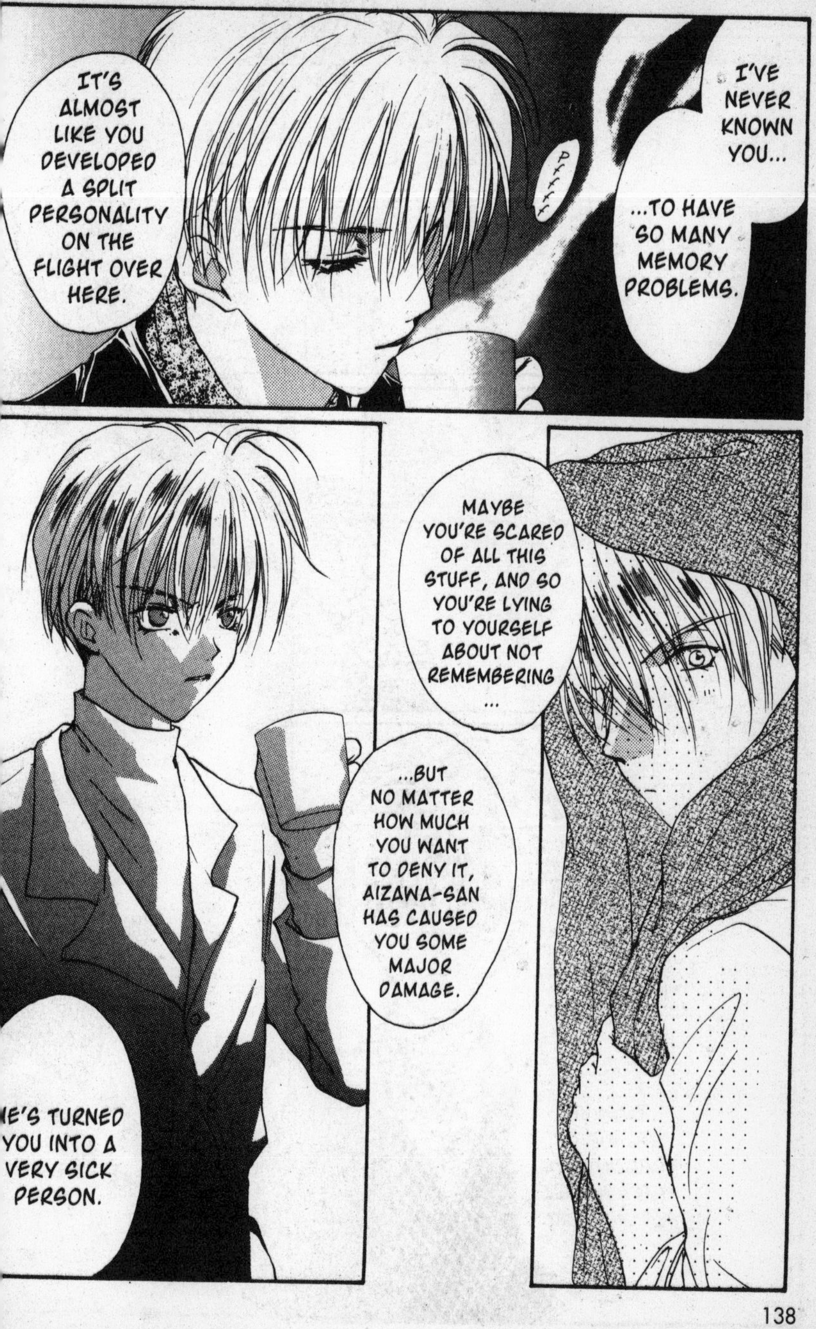
I'VE NEVER KNOWN YOU...
...TO HAVE SO MANY MEMORY PROBLEMS.
IT'S ALMOST LIKE YOU DEVELOPED A SPLIT PERSONALITY ON THE FLIGHT OVER HERE.
MAYBE YOU'RE SCARED OF ALL THIS STUFF, AND SO YOU'RE LYING TO YOURSELF ABOUT NOT REMEMBERING...
...BUT NO MATTER HOW MUCH YOU WANT TO DENY IT, AIZAWA-SAN HAS CAUSED YOU SOME MAJOR DAMAGE.
E'S TURNED YOU INTO A VERY SICK PERSON.

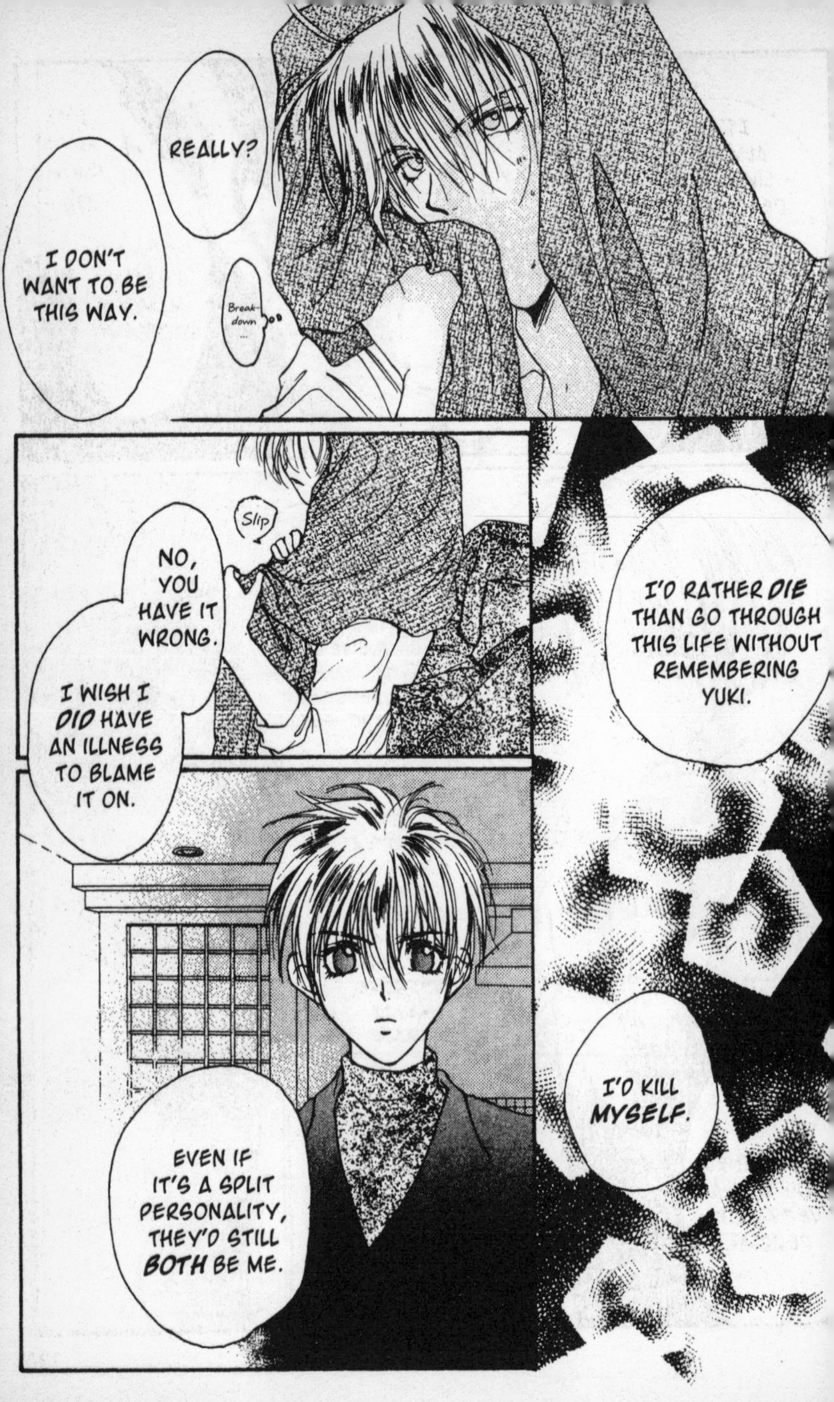
REALLY?
Break-down...
I DON'T WANT TO BE THIS WAY.
I'D RATHER DIE THAN GO THROUGH THIS LIFE WITHOUT REMEMBERING YUKI.
I'D KILL MYSELF.
Slip
NO, YOU HAVE IT WRONG.
I WISH I DID HAVE AN ILLNESS TO BLAME IT ON.
EVEN IF IT'S A SPLIT PERSONALITY, THEY'D STILL BOTH BE ME.

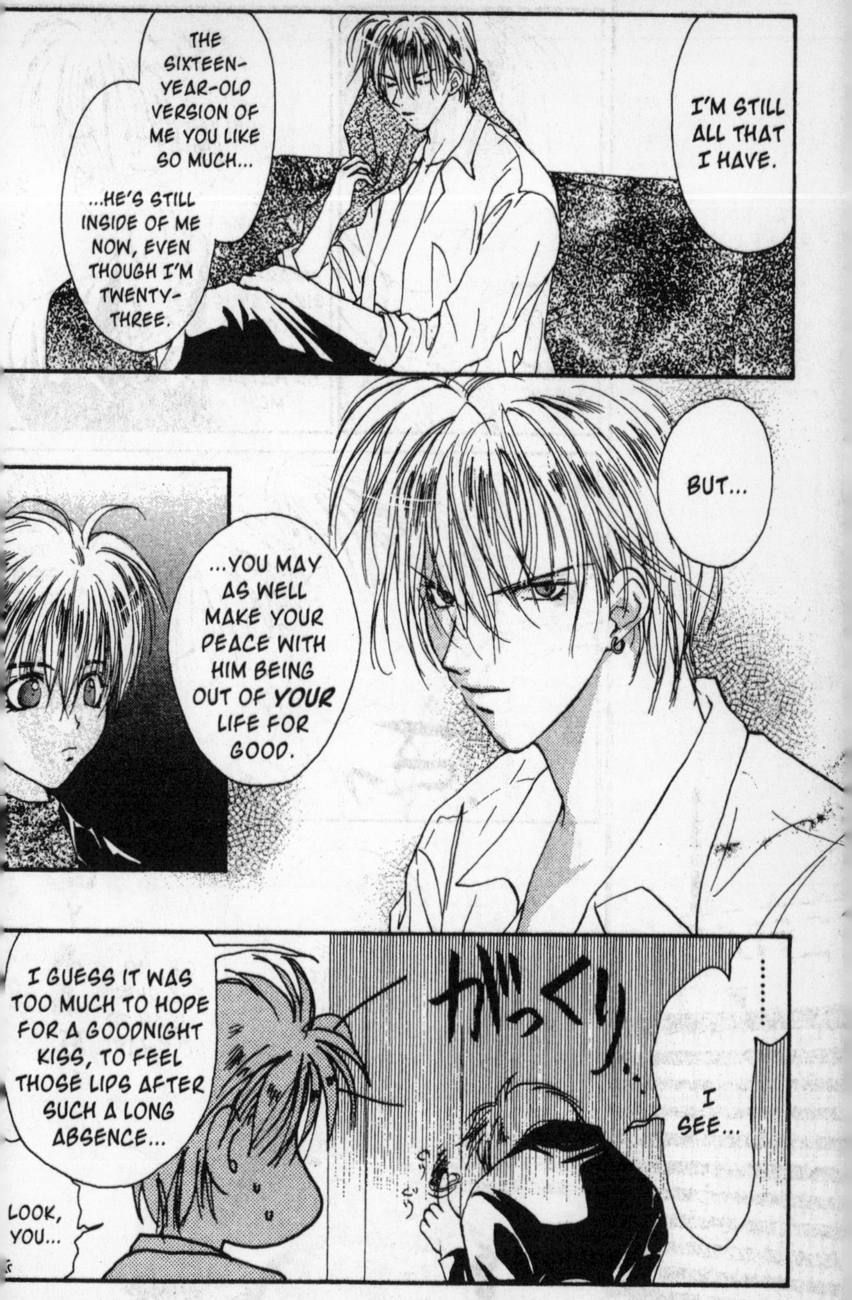
I'M STILL ALL THAT I HAVE.
THE SIXTEEN-YEAR-OLD VERSION OF ME YOU LIKE SO MUCH...
...HE'S STILL INSIDE OF ME NOW, EVEN THOUGH I'M TWENTY-THREE.
BUT...
...YOU MAY AS WELL MAKE YOUR PEACE WITH HIM BEING OUT OF *YOUR* LIFE FOR GOOD.
......
I SEE...
がっくり
I GUESS IT WAS TOO MUCH TO HOPE FOR A GOODNIGHT KISS, TO FEEL THOSE LIPS AFTER SUCH A LONG ABSENCE...
LOOK, YOU...

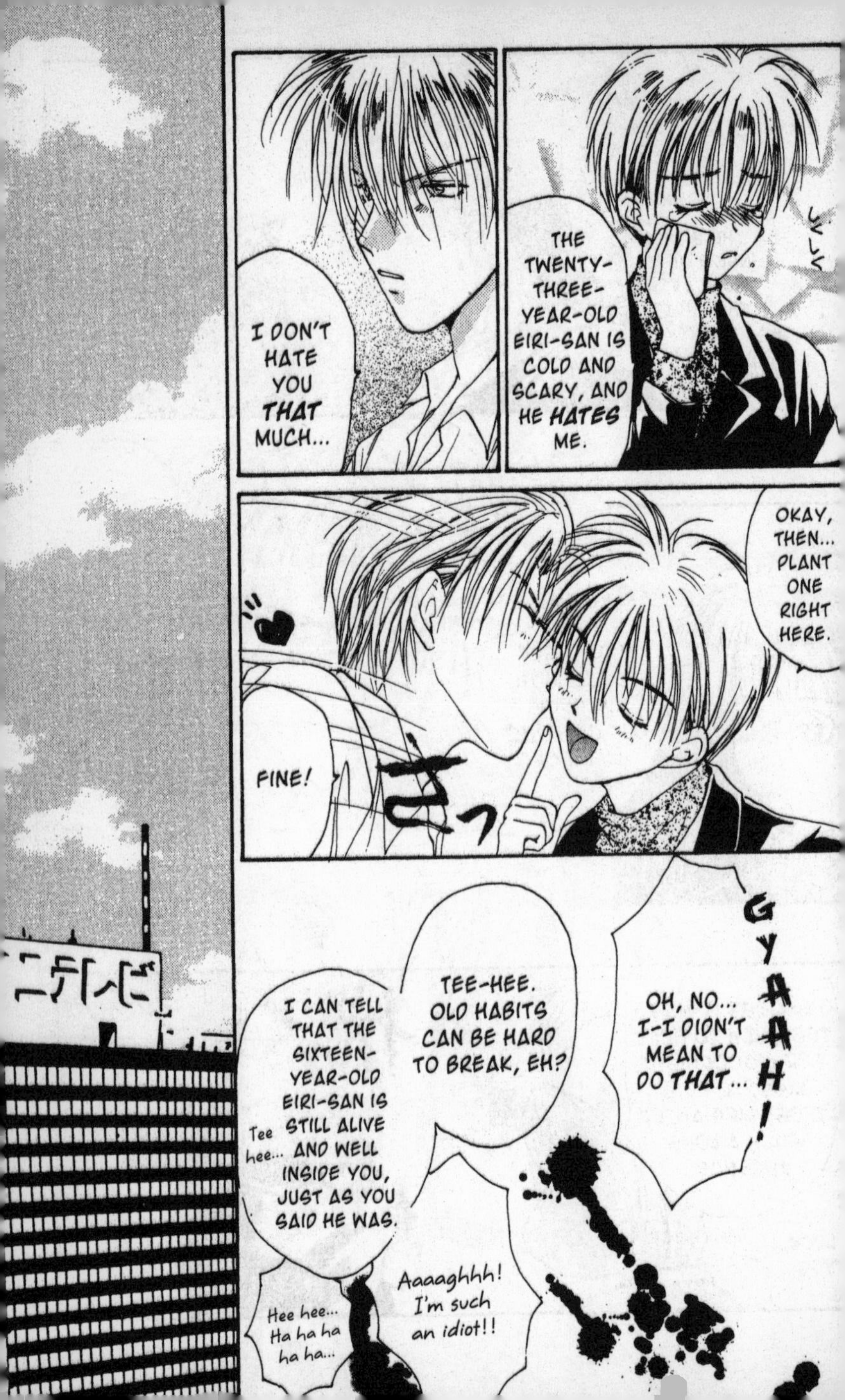
THE TWENTY-THREE-YEAR-OLD EIRI-SAN IS COLD AND SCARY, AND HE HATES ME.
I DON'T HATE YOU THAT MUCH...
OKAY, THEN... PLANT ONE RIGHT HERE.
FINE!
GYAAH!
OH, NO... I-I DIDN'T MEAN TO DO THAT...
TEE-HEE. OLD HABITS CAN BE HARD TO BREAK, EH?
I CAN TELL THAT THE SIXTEEN-YEAR-OLD EIRI-SAN IS STILL ALIVE AND WELL INSIDE YOU, JUST AS YOU SAID HE WAS.
Tee hee...
Aaaaghhh! I'm such an idiot!!
Hee hee... Ha ha ha ha ha...

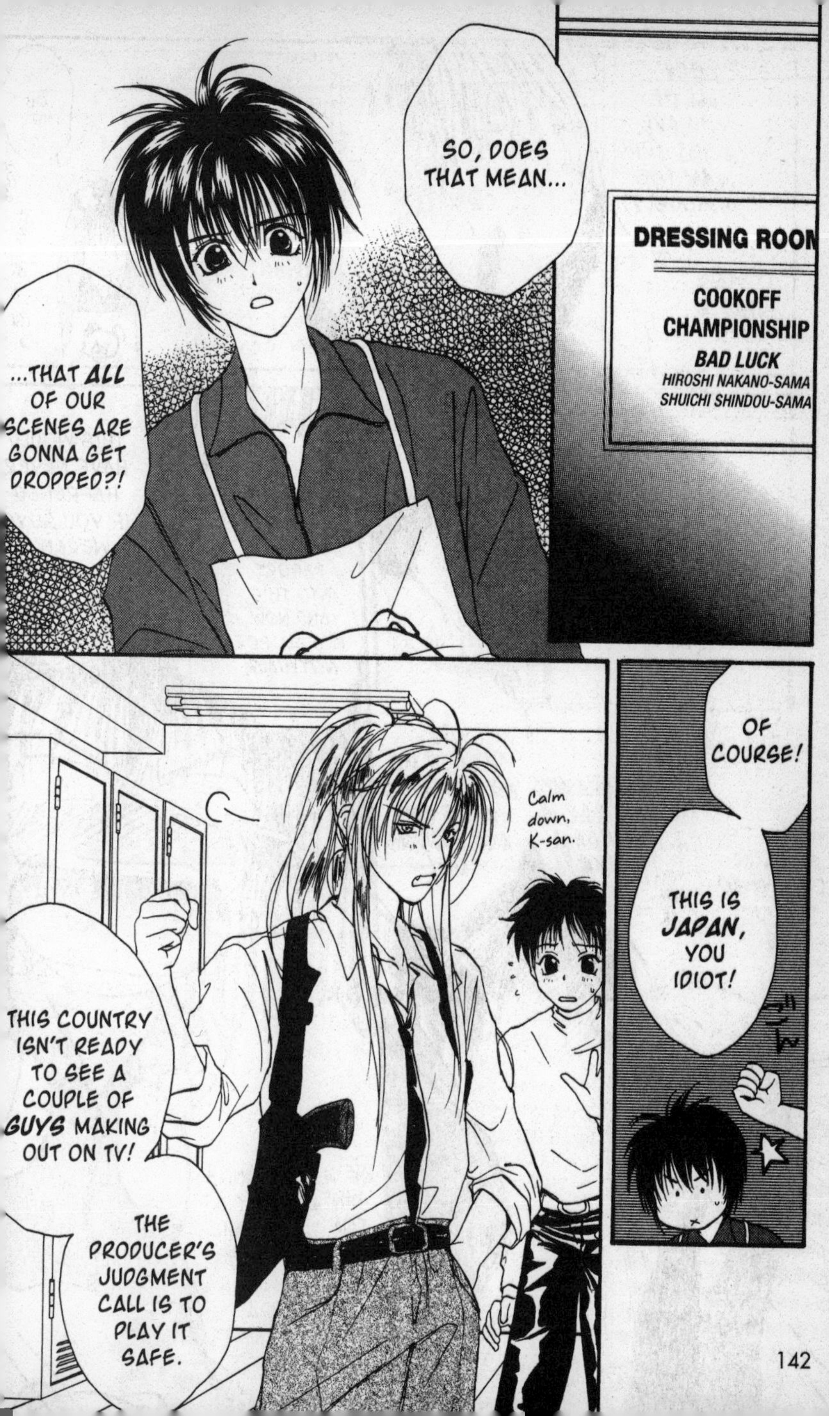
SO, DOES THAT MEAN...
...THAT **ALL** OF OUR SCENES ARE GONNA GET DROPPED?!
DRESSING ROOM
COOKOFF CHAMPIONSHIP
BAD LUCK
HIROSHI NAKANO-SAMA
SHUICHI SHINDOU-SAMA
OF COURSE!
THIS IS **JAPAN**, YOU IDIOT!
Calm down, K-san.
THIS COUNTRY ISN'T READY TO SEE A COUPLE OF **GUYS** MAKING OUT ON TV!
THE PRODUCER'S JUDGMENT CALL IS TO PLAY IT SAFE.

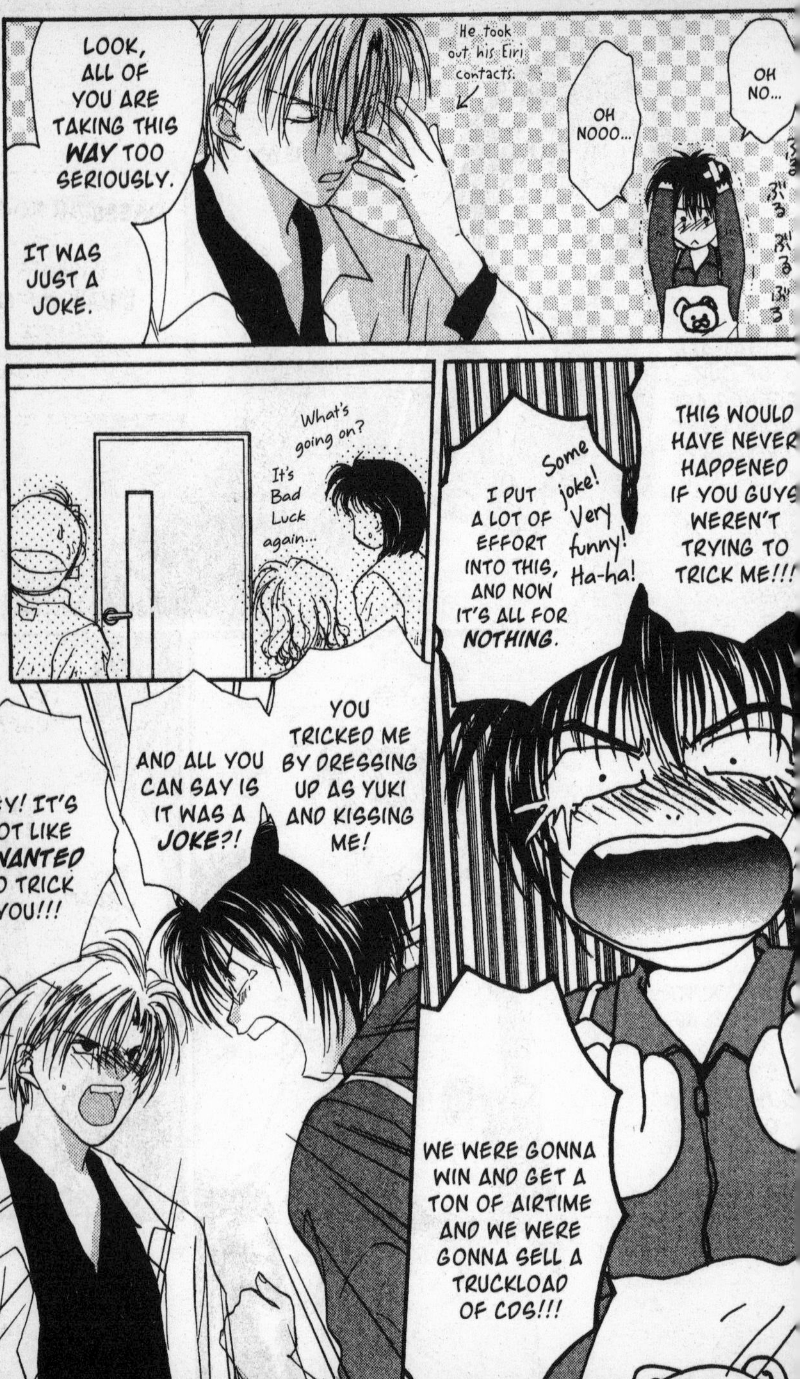

OH NO...
OH NOOO...
He took out his Eiri contacts.
LOOK, ALL OF YOU ARE TAKING THIS WAY TOO SERIOUSLY.
IT WAS JUST A JOKE.
THIS WOULD HAVE NEVER HAPPENED IF YOU GUYS WEREN'T TRYING TO TRICK ME!!!
Some joke! Very funny! Ha-ha!
I PUT A LOT OF EFFORT INTO THIS, AND NOW IT'S ALL FOR NOTHING.
WE WERE GONNA WIN AND GET A TON OF AIRTIME AND WE WERE GONNA SELL A TRUCKLOAD OF CDS!!!
What's going on?
It's Bad Luck again...
YOU TRICKED ME BY DRESSING UP AS YUKI AND KISSING ME!
AND ALL YOU CAN SAY IS IT WAS A JOKE?!
HEY! IT'S NOT LIKE I WANTED TO TRICK YOU!!!

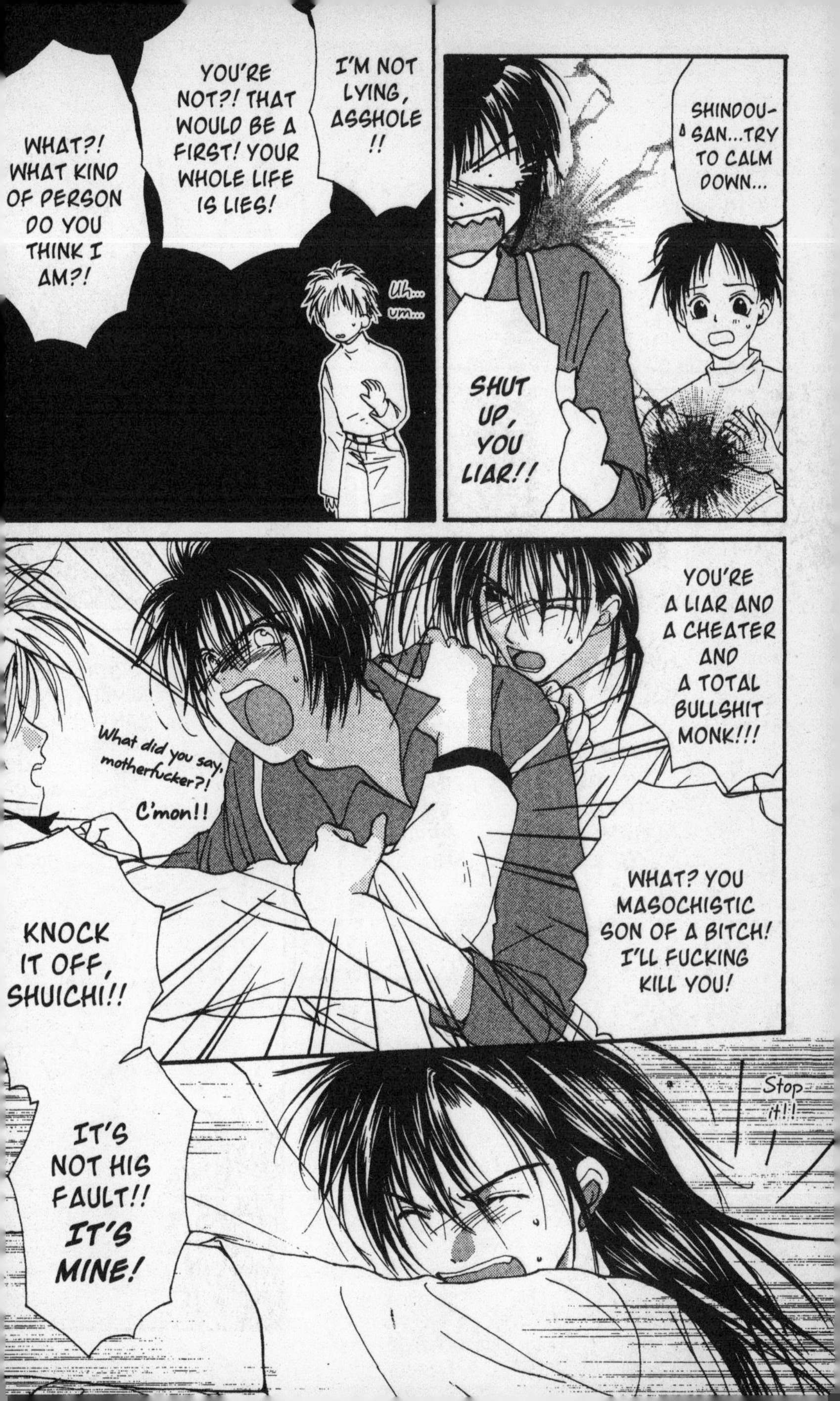
SHINDOU-SAN...TRY TO CALM DOWN...
SHUT UP, YOU LIAR!!
I'M NOT LYING, ASSHOLE!!
YOU'RE NOT?! THAT WOULD BE A FIRST! YOUR WHOLE LIFE IS LIES!
Uh... um...
WHAT?! WHAT KIND OF PERSON DO YOU THINK I AM?!
YOU'RE A LIAR AND A CHEATER AND A TOTAL BULLSHIT MONK!!!
What did you say, motherfucker?!
C'mon!!
WHAT? YOU MASOCHISTIC SON OF A BITCH! I'LL FUCKING KILL YOU!
KNOCK IT OFF, SHUICHI!!
Stop it!!
IT'S NOT HIS FAULT!! IT'S MINE!

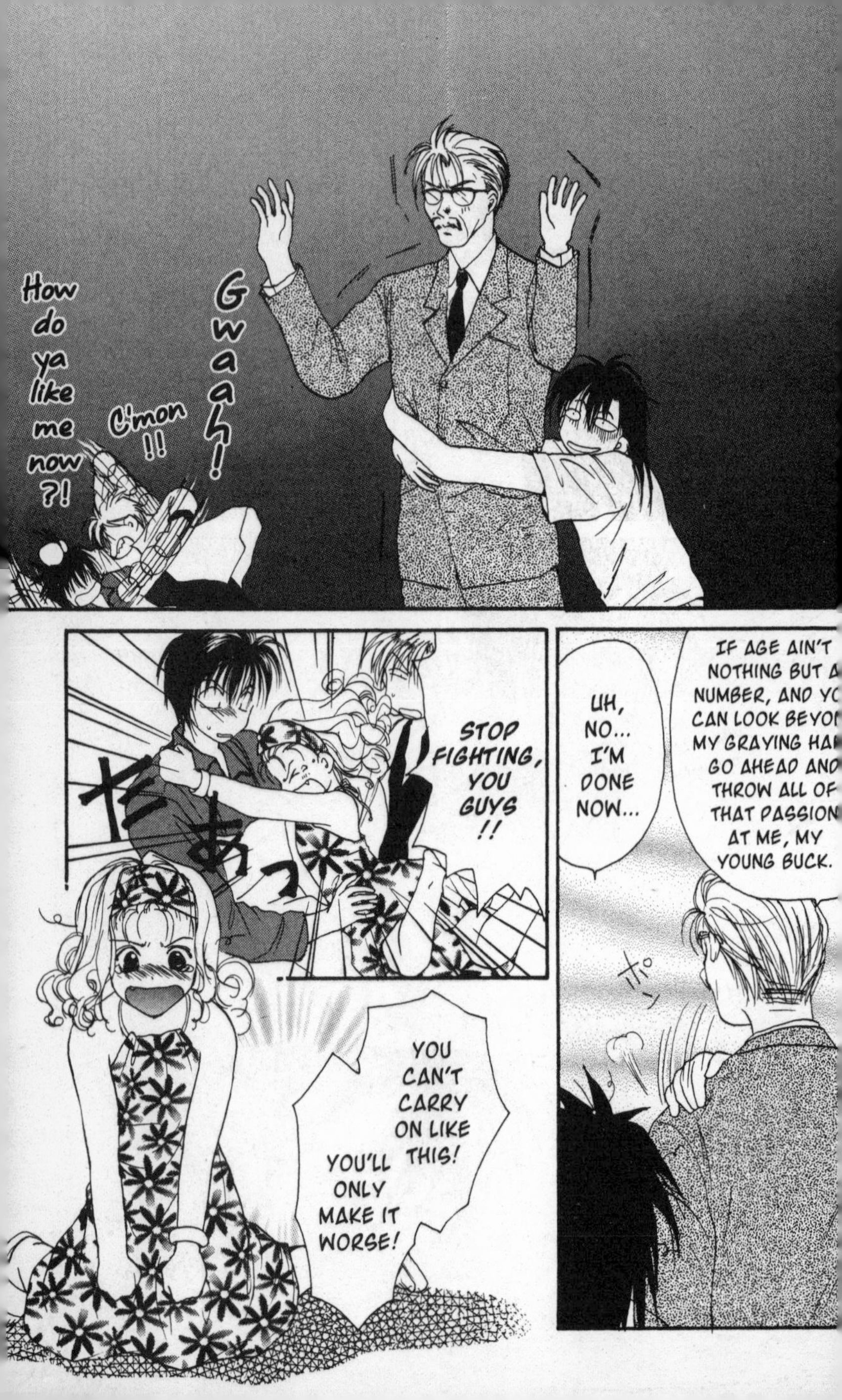
Gwaah!
C'mon!!
How do ya like me now?!
IF AGE AIN'T NOTHING BUT A NUMBER, AND YO CAN LOOK BEYON MY GRAYING HA GO AHEAD AND THROW ALL OF THAT PASSION AT ME, MY YOUNG BUCK.
UH, NO... I'M DONE NOW...
STOP FIGHTING, YOU GUYS!!
YOU CAN'T CARRY ON LIKE THIS!
YOU'LL ONLY MAKE IT WORSE!

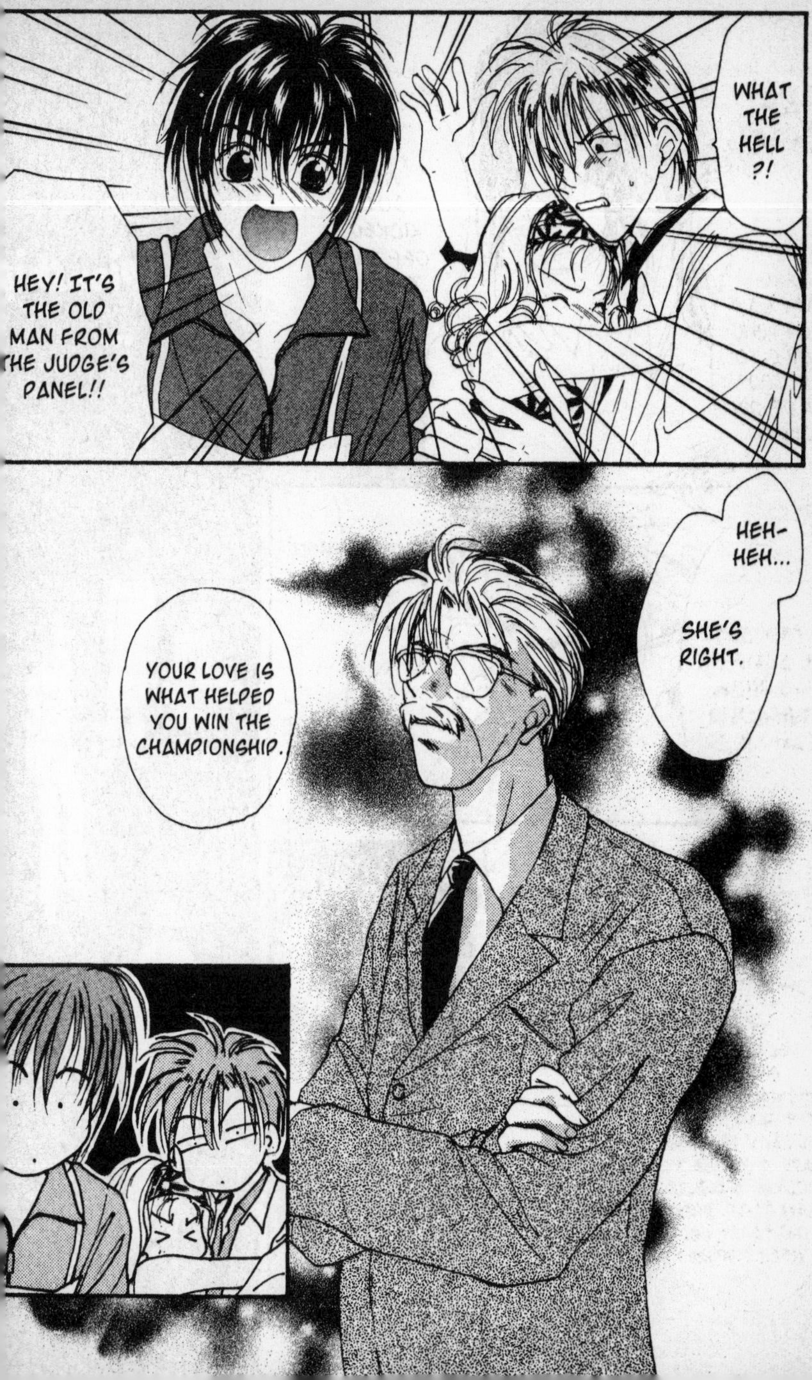
WHAT THE HELL?!
HEY! IT'S THE OLD MAN FROM THE JUDGE'S PANEL!!
HEH-HEH...
SHE'S RIGHT.
YOUR LOVE IS WHAT HELPED YOU WIN THE CHAMPIONSHIP.

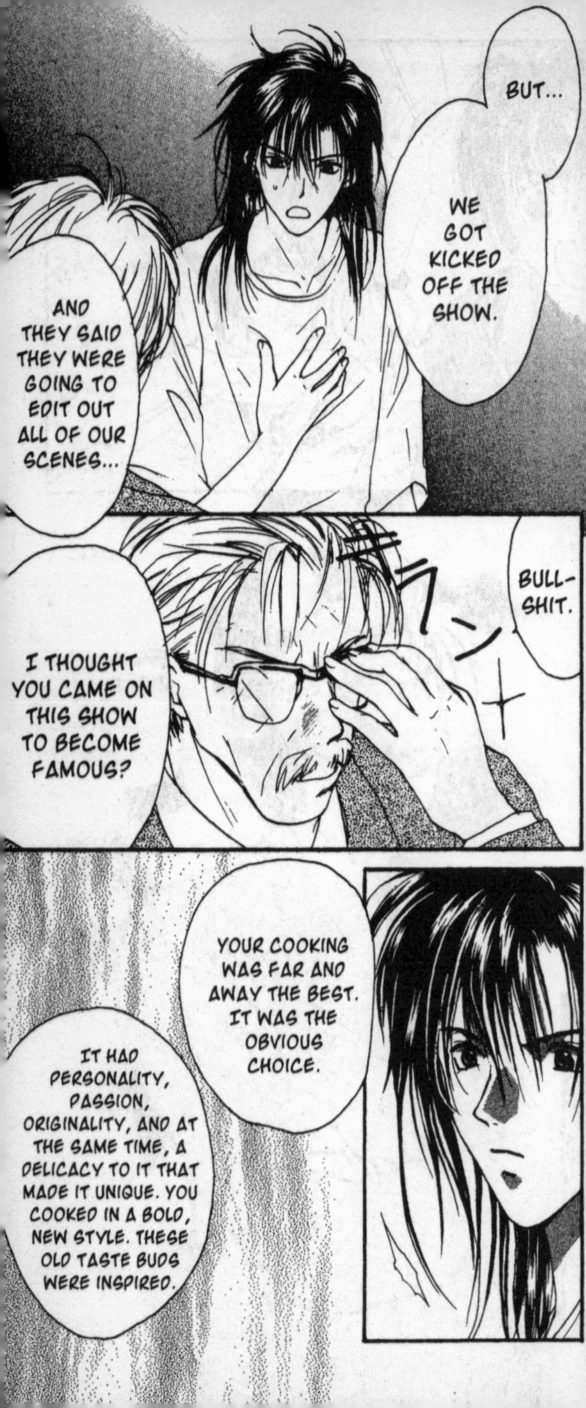
BUT...
WE GOT KICKED OFF THE SHOW.
AND THEY SAID THEY WERE GOING TO EDIT OUT ALL OF OUR SCENES...
BULL-SHIT.
I THOUGHT YOU CAME ON THIS SHOW TO BECOME FAMOUS?
YOUR COOKING WAS FAR AND AWAY THE BEST. IT WAS THE OBVIOUS CHOICE.
IT HAD PERSONALITY, PASSION, ORIGINALITY, AND AT THE SAME TIME, A DELICACY TO IT THAT MADE IT UNIQUE. YOU COOKED IN A BOLD, NEW STYLE. THESE OLD TASTE BUDS WERE INSPIRED.

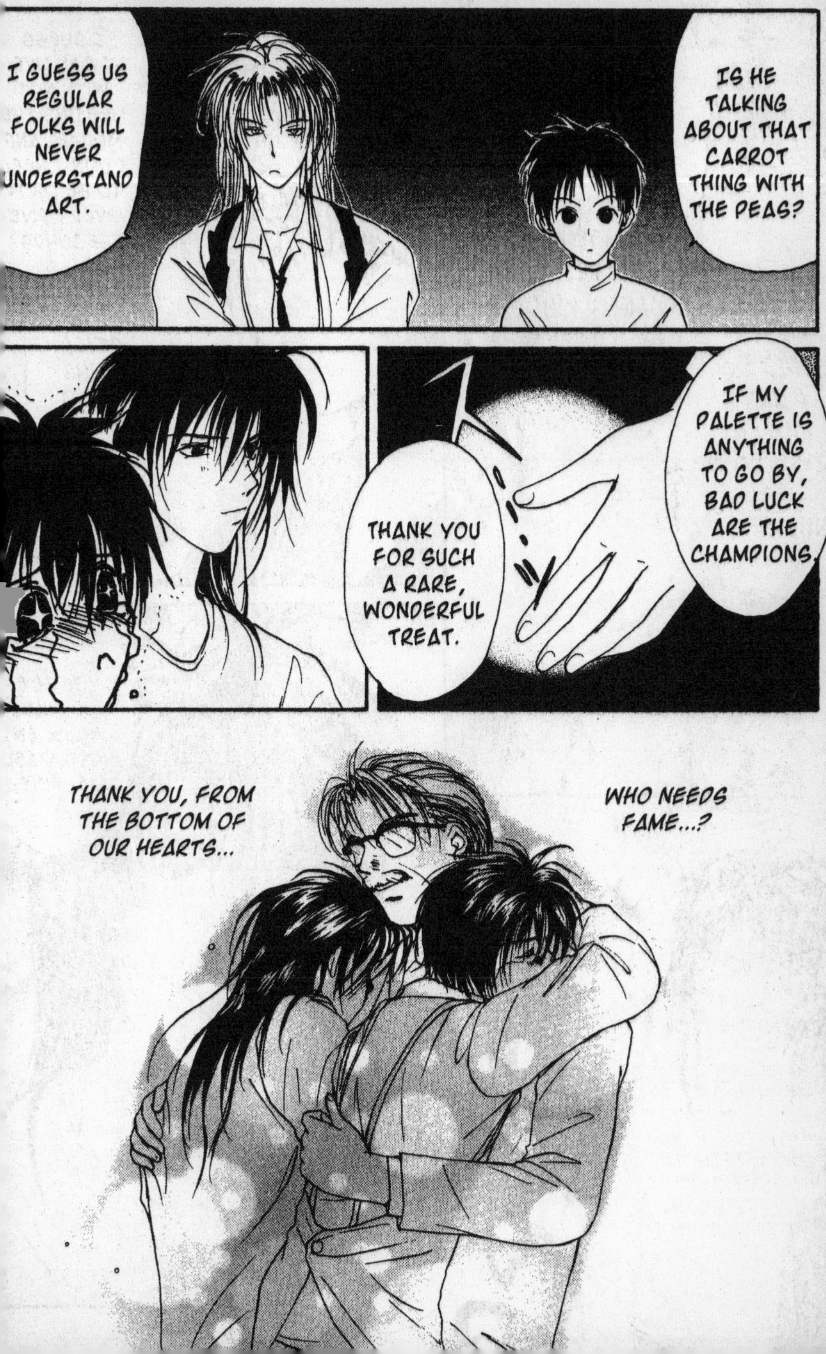
IS HE TALKING ABOUT THAT CARROT THING WITH THE PEAS?
I GUESS US REGULAR FOLKS WILL NEVER UNDERSTAND ART.
IF MY PALETTE IS ANYTHING TO GO BY, BAD LUCK ARE THE CHAMPIONS.
THANK YOU FOR SUCH A RARE, WONDERFUL TREAT.
WHO NEEDS FAME...?
THANK YOU, FROM THE BOTTOM OF OUR HEARTS...

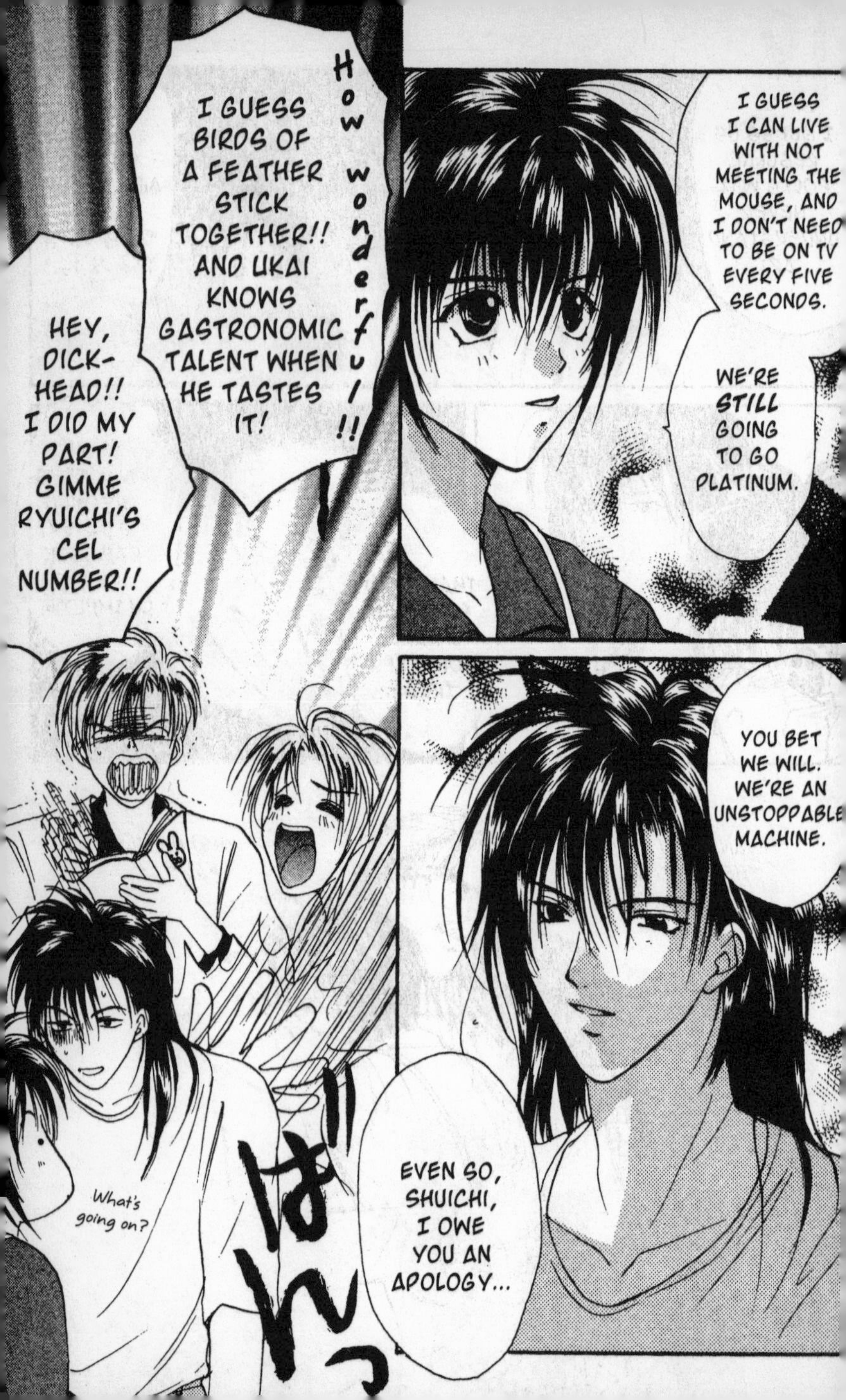
I GUESS I CAN LIVE WITH NOT MEETING THE MOUSE, AND I DON'T NEED TO BE ON TV EVERY FIVE SECONDS.
WE'RE **STILL** GOING TO GO PLATINUM.
YOU BET WE WILL. WE'RE AN UNSTOPPABLE MACHINE.
EVEN SO, SHUICHI, I OWE YOU AN APOLOGY...
I GUESS BIRDS OF A FEATHER STICK TOGETHER!! AND UKAI KNOWS GASTRONOMIC TALENT WHEN HE TASTES IT!
How wonderful!!
HEY, DICK-HEAD!! I DID MY PART! GIMME RYUICHI'S CEL NUMBER!!
What's going on?
はっ

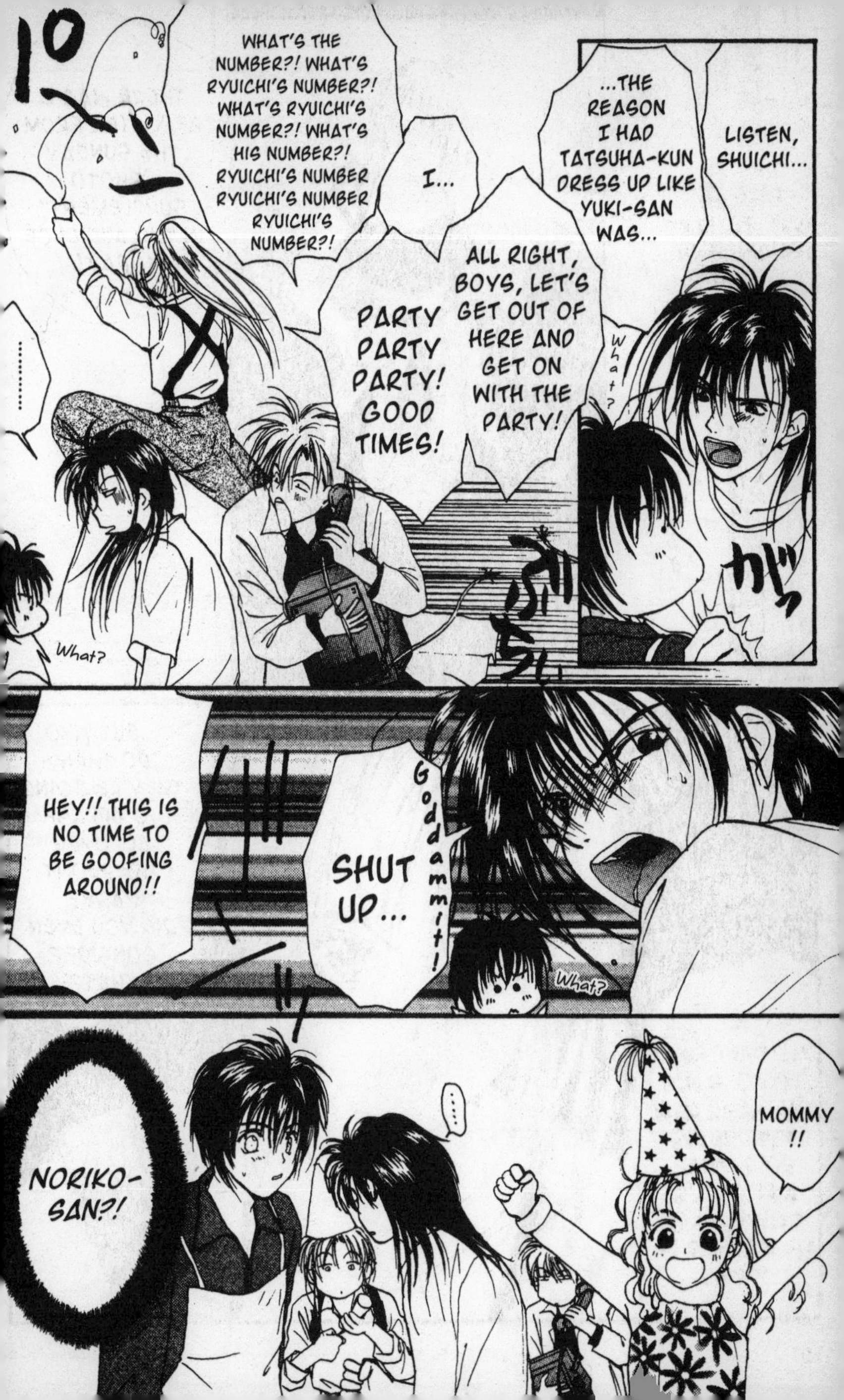
LISTEN, SHUICHI...
...THE REASON I HAD TATSUHA-KUN DRESS UP LIKE YUKI-SAN WAS...
What?
I...
WHAT'S THE NUMBER?! WHAT'S RYUICHI'S NUMBER?! WHAT'S RYUICHI'S NUMBER?! WHAT'S HIS NUMBER?! RYUICHI'S NUMBER RYUICHI'S NUMBER RYUICHI'S NUMBER?!
ALL RIGHT, BOYS, LET'S GET OUT OF HERE AND GET ON WITH THE PARTY!
PARTY PARTY PARTY! GOOD TIMES!
....
What?
SHUT UP...
Goddammit!
What?
HEY!! THIS IS NO TIME TO BE GOOFING AROUND!!
MOMMY !!
.....
NORIKO-SAN?!

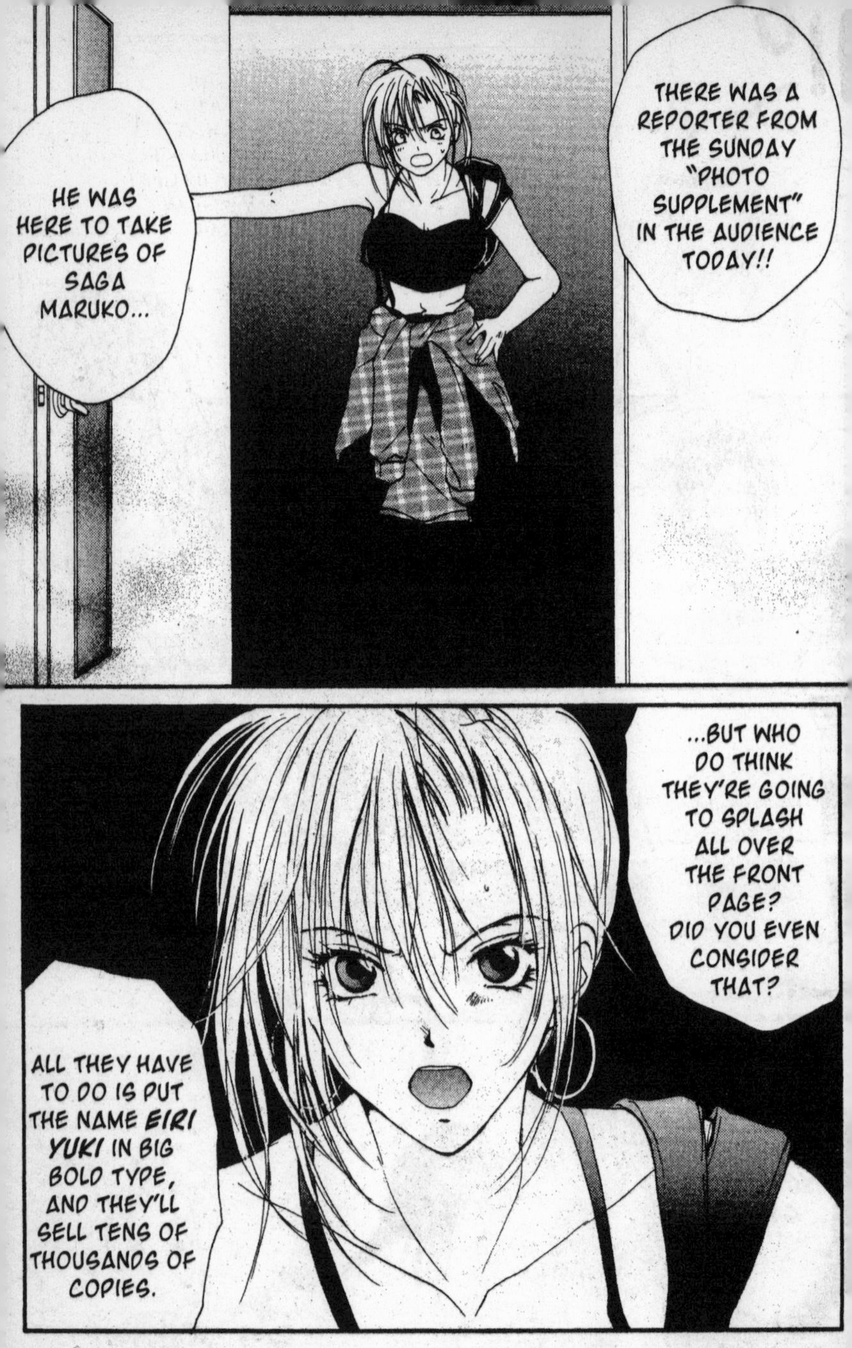
THERE WAS A REPORTER FROM THE SUNDAY "PHOTO SUPPLEMENT" IN THE AUDIENCE TODAY!!
HE WAS HERE TO TAKE PICTURES OF SAGA MARUKO...
...BUT WHO DO THINK THEY'RE GOING TO SPLASH ALL OVER THE FRONT PAGE? DID YOU EVEN CONSIDER THAT?
ALL THEY HAVE TO DO IS PUT THE NAME *EIRI YUKI* IN BIG BOLD TYPE, AND THEY'LL SELL TENS OF THOUSANDS OF COPIES.

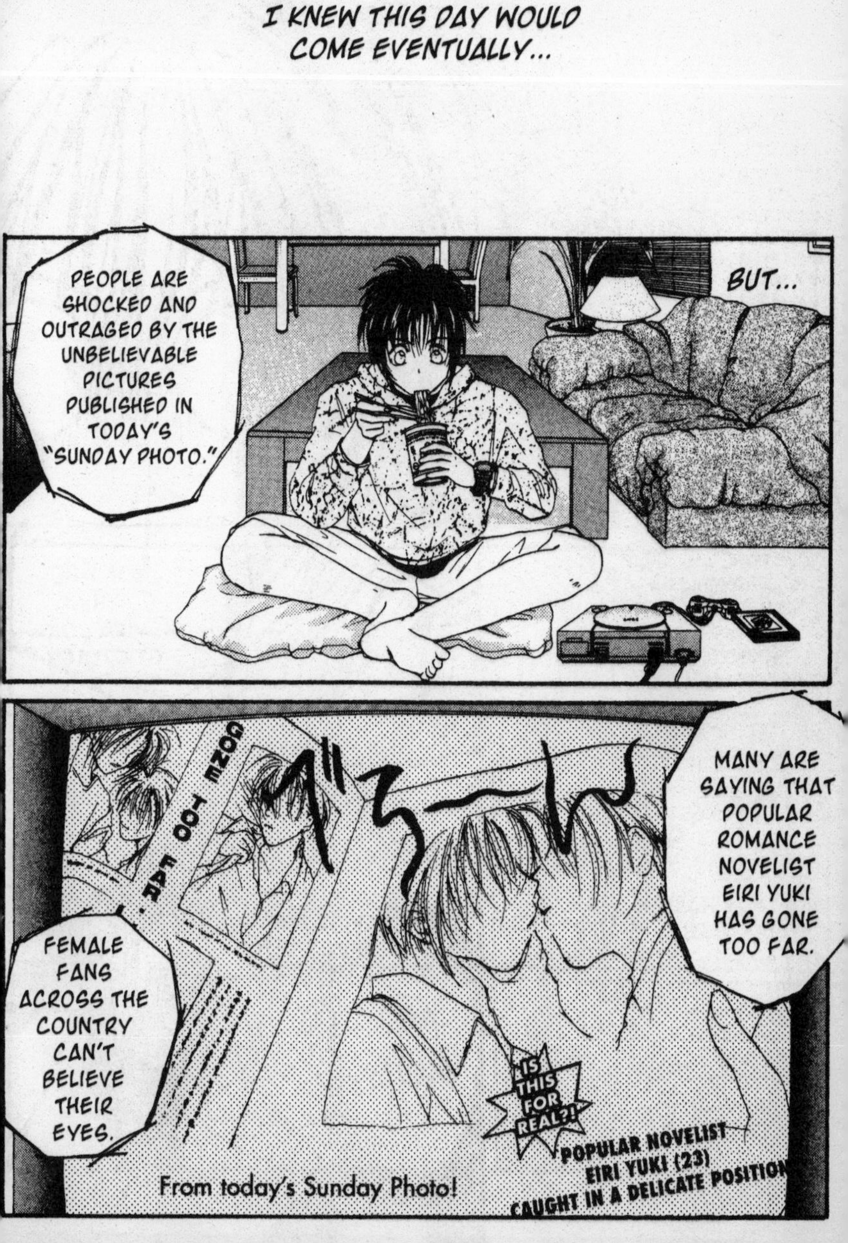
I KNEW THIS DAY WOULD COME EVENTUALLY...
BUT...
PEOPLE ARE SHOCKED AND OUTRAGED BY THE UNBELIEVABLE PICTURES PUBLISHED IN TODAY'S "SUNDAY PHOTO."
MANY ARE SAYING THAT POPULAR ROMANCE NOVELIST EIRI YUKI HAS GONE TOO FAR.
GONE TOO FAR.
IS THIS FOR REAL?!
POPULAR NOVELIST EIRI YUKI (23) CAUGHT IN A DELICATE POSITION
FEMALE FANS ACROSS THE COUNTRY CAN'T BELIEVE THEIR EYES.
From today's Sunday Photo!

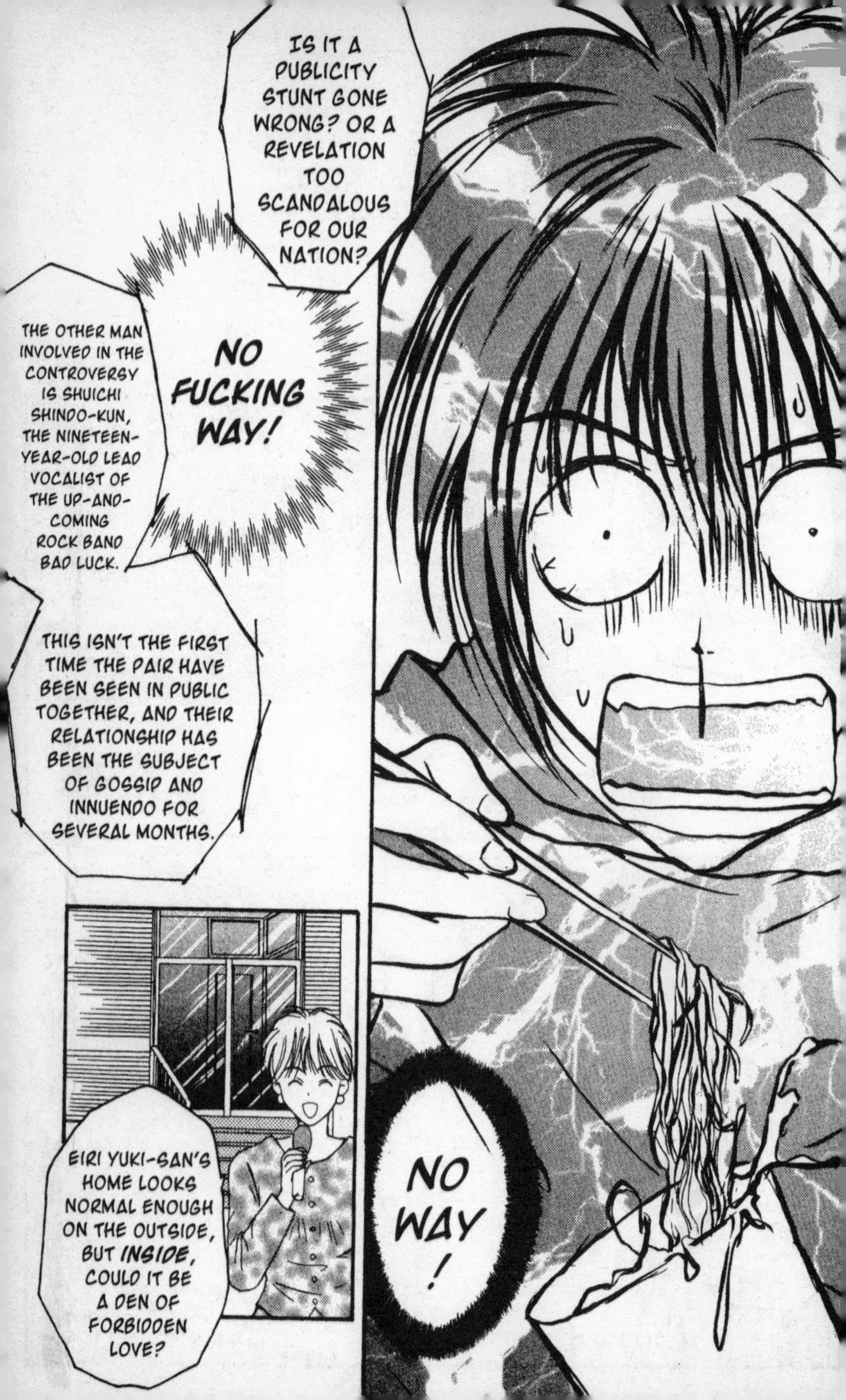
IS IT A PUBLICITY STUNT GONE WRONG? OR A REVELATION TOO SCANDALOUS FOR OUR NATION?
NO FUCKING WAY!
THE OTHER MAN INVOLVED IN THE CONTROVERSY IS SHUICHI SHINDO-KUN, THE NINETEEN-YEAR-OLD LEAD VOCALIST OF THE UP-AND-COMING ROCK BAND BAD LUCK.
THIS ISN'T THE FIRST TIME THE PAIR HAVE BEEN SEEN IN PUBLIC TOGETHER, AND THEIR RELATIONSHIP HAS BEEN THE SUBJECT OF GOSSIP AND INNUENDO FOR SEVERAL MONTHS.
NO WAY!
EIRI YUKI-SAN'S HOME LOOKS NORMAL ENOUGH ON THE OUTSIDE, BUT *INSIDE*, COULD IT BE A DEN OF FORBIDDEN LOVE?

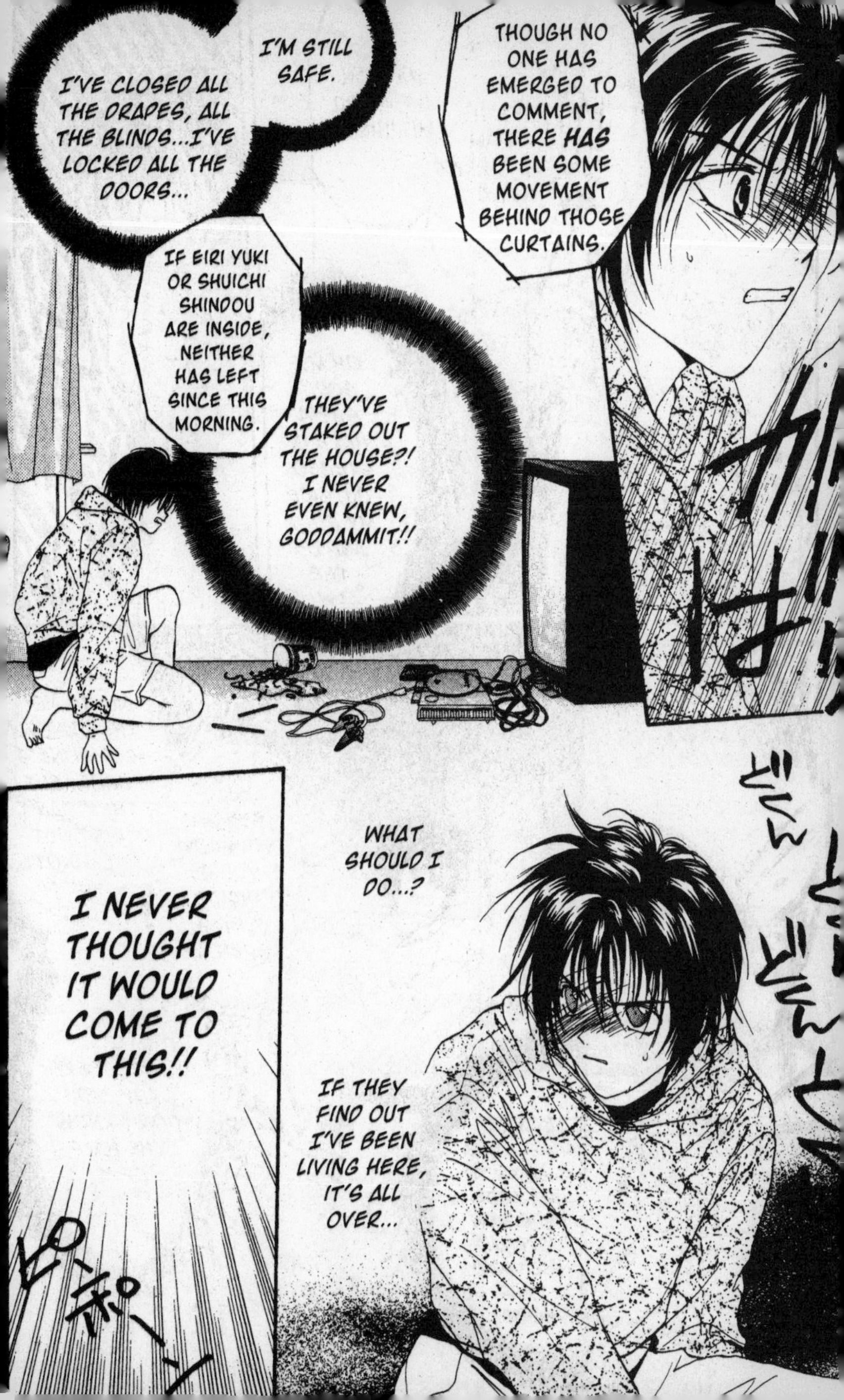
THOUGH NO ONE HAS EMERGED TO COMMENT, THERE HAS BEEN SOME MOVEMENT BEHIND THOSE CURTAINS.
IF EIRI YUKI OR SHUICHI SHINDOU ARE INSIDE, NEITHER HAS LEFT SINCE THIS MORNING.
THEY'VE STAKED OUT THE HOUSE?! I NEVER EVEN KNEW, GODDAMMIT!!
I'VE CLOSED ALL THE DRAPES, ALL THE BLINDS...I'VE LOCKED ALL THE DOORS...
I'M STILL SAFE.
WHAT SHOULD I DO...?
IF THEY FIND OUT I'VE BEEN LIVING HERE, IT'S ALL OVER...
I NEVER THOUGHT IT WOULD COME TO THIS!!

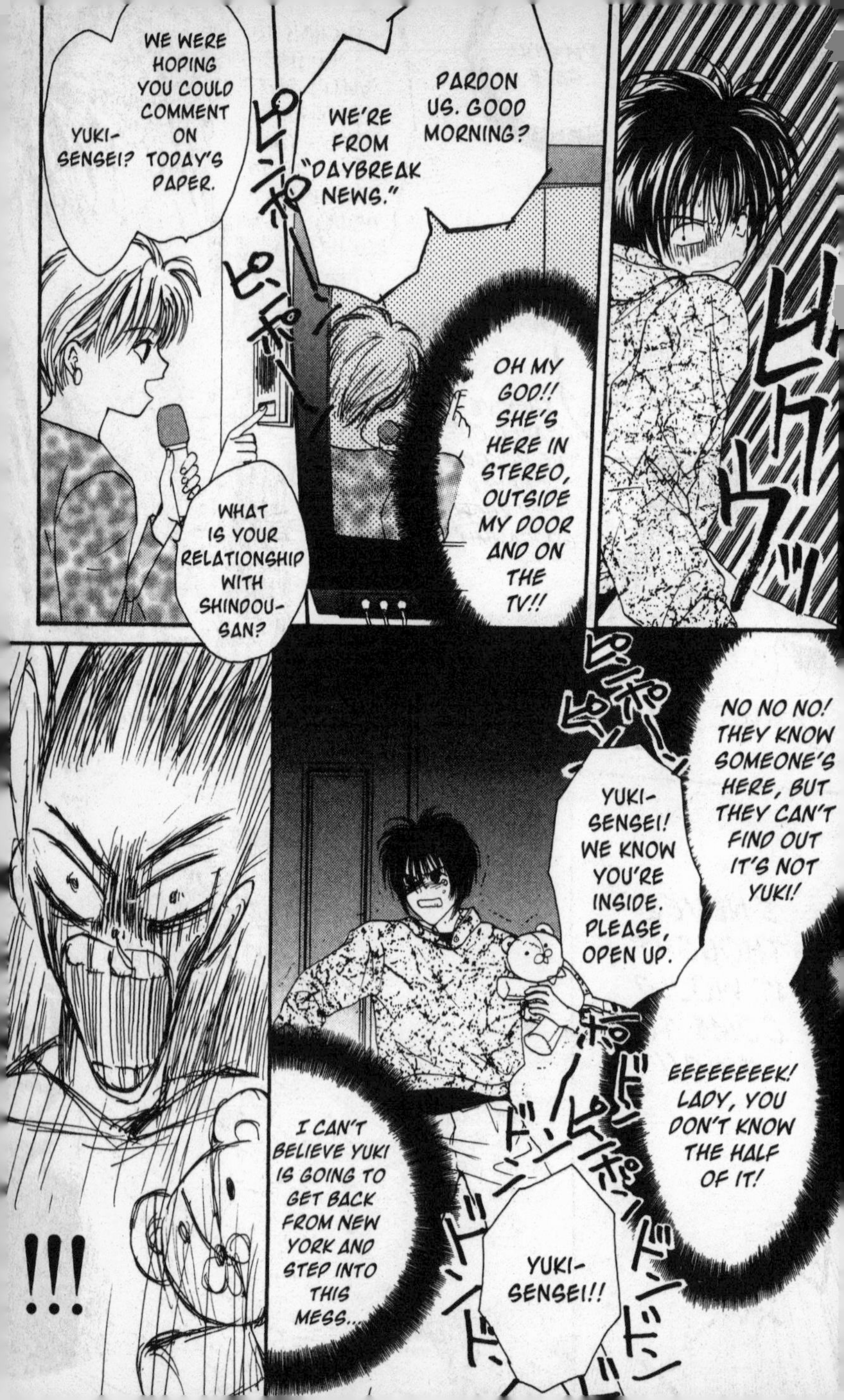
PARDON US. GOOD MORNING?
WE'RE FROM "DAYBREAK NEWS."
OH MY GOD!! SHE'S HERE IN STEREO, OUTSIDE MY DOOR AND ON THE TV!!
YUKI-SENSEI? WE WERE HOPING YOU COULD COMMENT ON TODAY'S PAPER.
WHAT IS YOUR RELATIONSHIP WITH SHINDOU-SAN?
NO NO NO! THEY KNOW SOMEONE'S HERE, BUT THEY CAN'T FIND OUT IT'S NOT YUKI!
YUKI-SENSEI! WE KNOW YOU'RE INSIDE. PLEASE, OPEN UP.
EEEEEEEEK! LADY, YOU DON'T KNOW THE HALF OF IT!
YUKI-SENSEI!!
I CAN'T BELIEVE YUKI IS GOING TO GET BACK FROM NEW YORK AND STEP INTO THIS MESS...
!!!

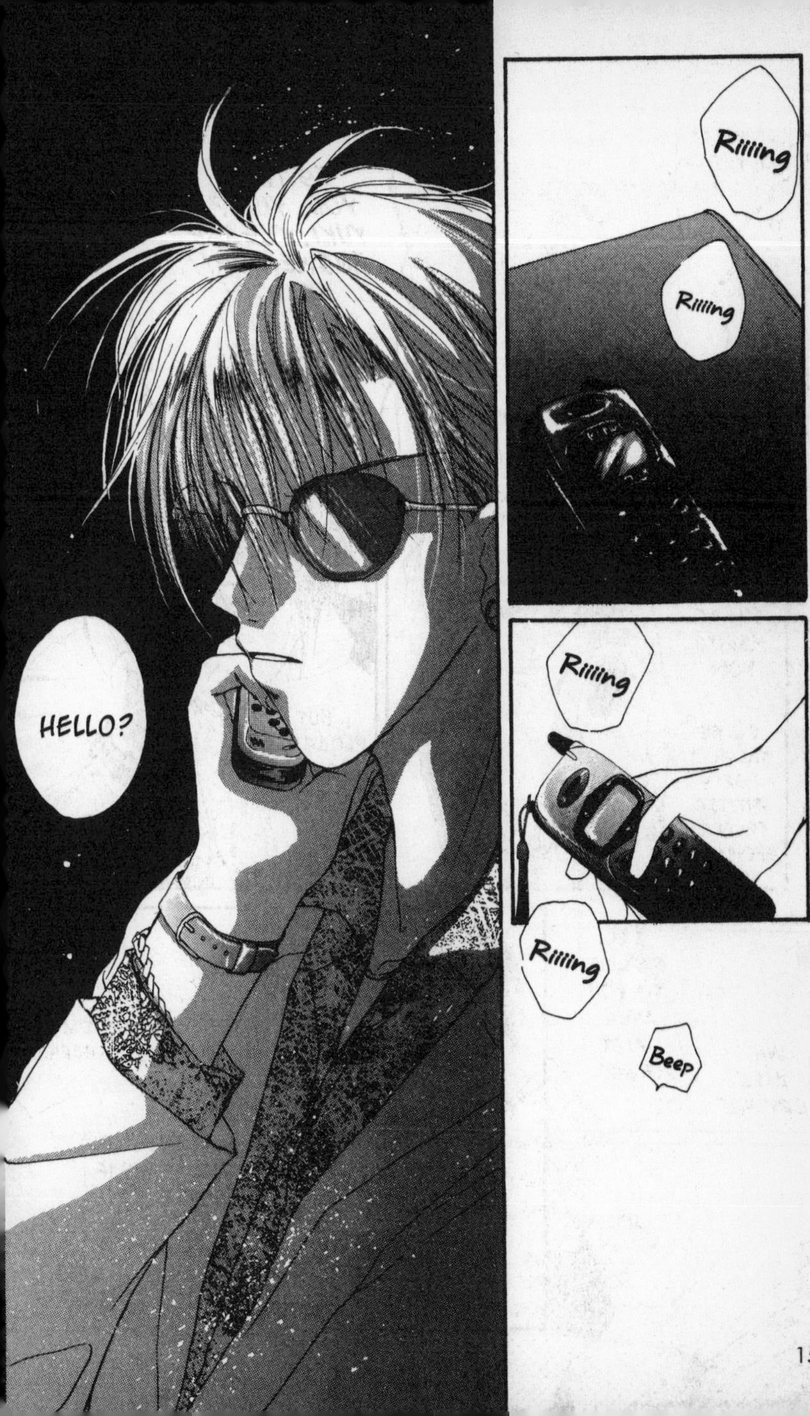
Riiiing
Riiiing
Riiiing
Riiiing
Beep
HELLO?

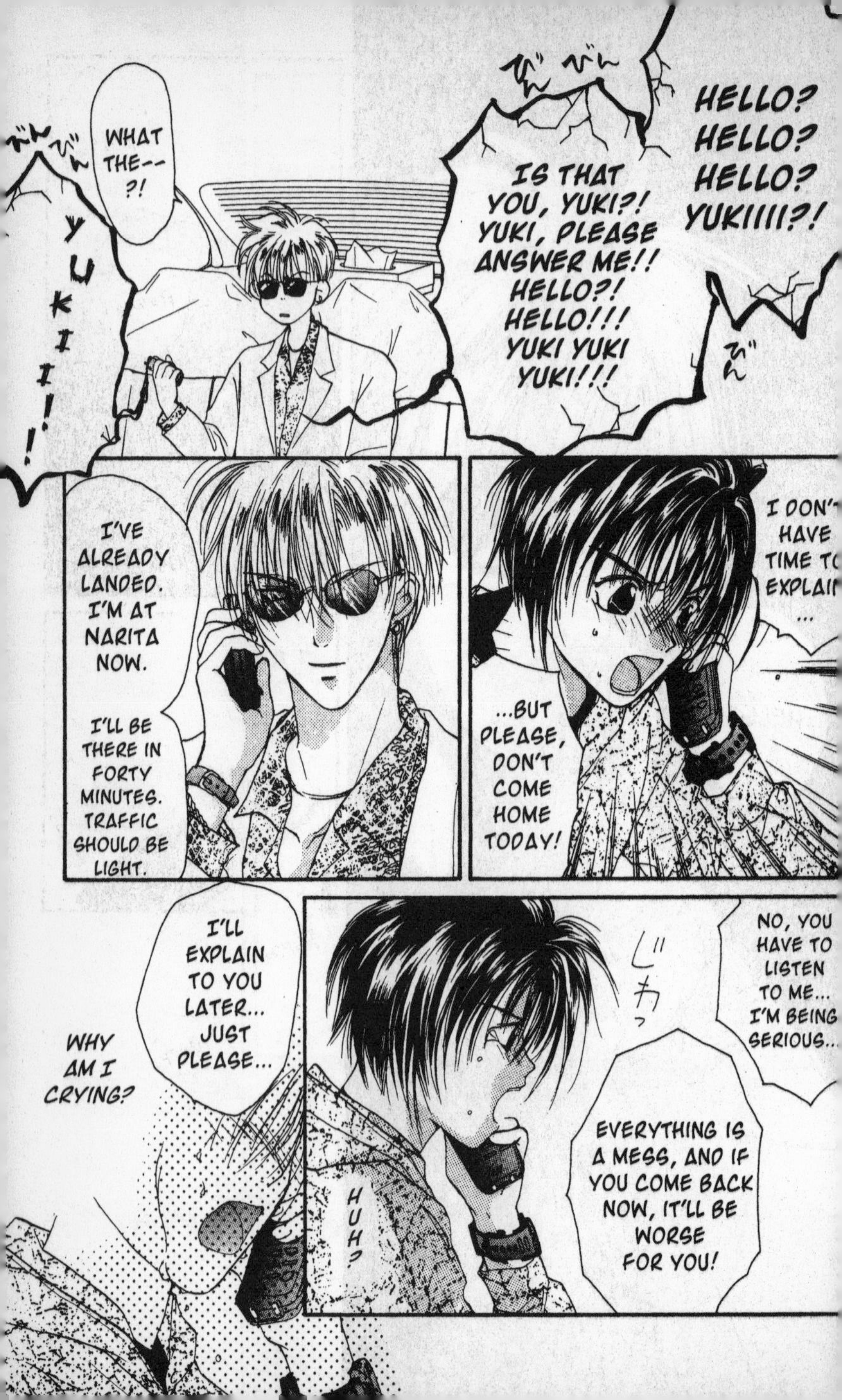
HELLO? HELLO? HELLO? YUKIIII?!
IS THAT YOU, YUKI?! YUKI, PLEASE ANSWER ME!! HELLO?! HELLO!!! YUKI YUKI YUKI!!!
WHAT THE--?!
YUKII!!
I DON’ HAVE TIME T EXPLAI ...
...BUT PLEASE, DON’T COME HOME TODAY!
I’VE ALREADY LANDED. I’M AT NARITA NOW.
I’LL BE THERE IN FORTY MINUTES. TRAFFIC SHOULD BE LIGHT.
NO, YOU HAVE TO LISTEN TO ME... I’M BEING SERIOUS...
EVERYTHING IS A MESS, AND IF YOU COME BACK NOW, IT’LL BE WORSE FOR YOU!
HUH?
I’LL EXPLAIN TO YOU LATER... JUST PLEASE...
WHY AM I CRYING?

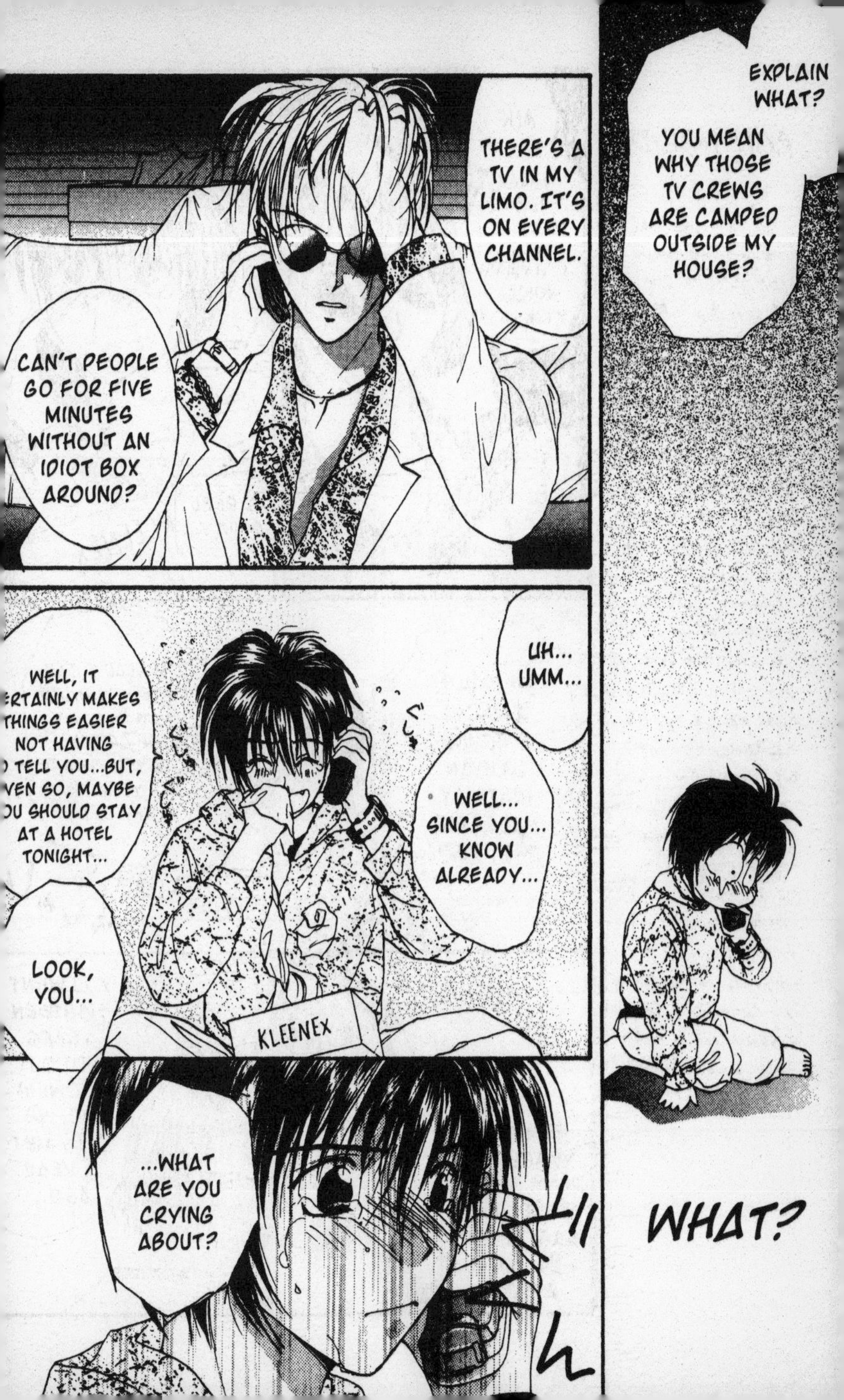
EXPLAIN WHAT?
YOU MEAN WHY THOSE TV CREWS ARE CAMPED OUTSIDE MY HOUSE?
WHAT?
THERE'S A TV IN MY LIMO. IT'S ON EVERY CHANNEL.
CAN'T PEOPLE GO FOR FIVE MINUTES WITHOUT AN IDIOT BOX AROUND?
UH... UMM...
WELL... SINCE YOU... KNOW ALREADY...
WELL, IT ERTAINLY MAKES THINGS EASIER NOT HAVING TELL YOU...BUT, VEN SO, MAYBE OU SHOULD STAY AT A HOTEL TONIGHT...
LOOK, YOU...
KLEENEX
...WHAT ARE YOU CRYING ABOUT?

CONTINUED...

This episode was completed under the absolute worst of conditions. Right now, it's a madhouse around here. Ughh... Help me... I've been pasting tone sheets and pasting and pasting and pasting and pasting for over 200,000 panels now, but look at them! They're still too white! And now, at the end, I've finally run out of gas...and Hiro's face is getting too long... I'm sorry. But I think I'm gonna go die now. All of my assistants have gone comatose on me. Forgive me, I just needed to vent my frustration. By the way, no matter how you look at it, Eiri's dressed like a mafia thug. How did that happen?

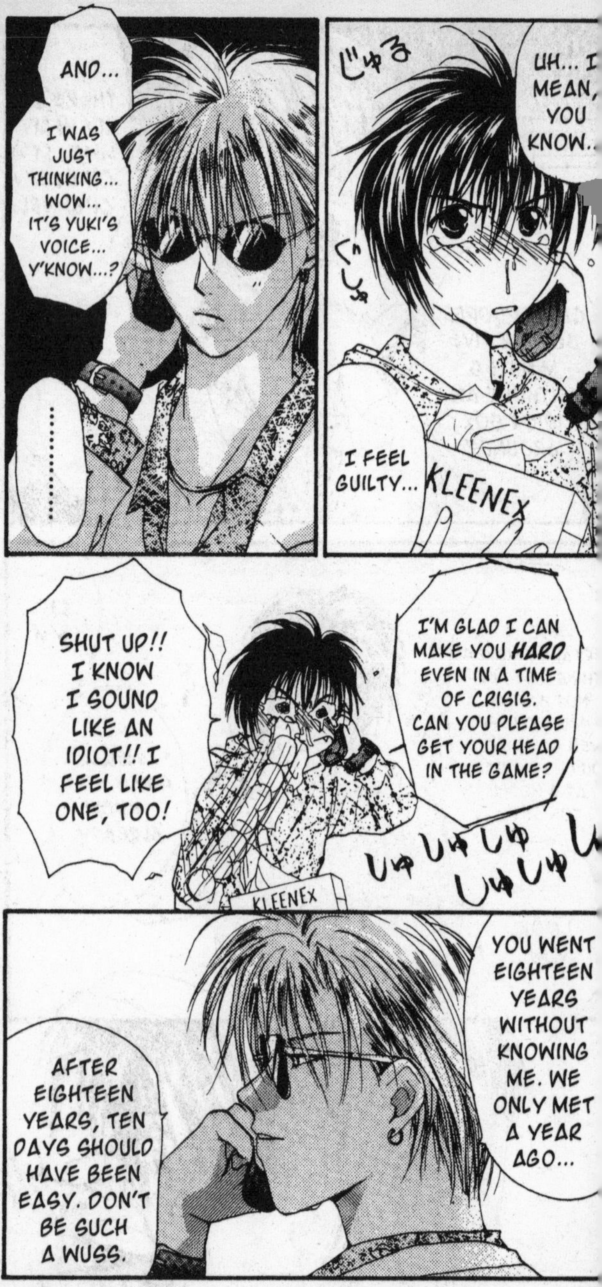

じゅる
UH... I MEAN, YOU KNOW...
ぐしゅ
I FEEL GUILTY...
KLEENEX
AND...
I WAS JUST THINKING... WOW... IT'S YUKI'S VOICE... Y'KNOW...?
....
I'M GLAD I CAN MAKE YOU **HARD** EVEN IN A TIME OF CRISIS. CAN YOU PLEASE GET YOUR HEAD IN THE GAME?
SHUT UP!! I KNOW I SOUND LIKE AN IDIOT!! I FEEL LIKE ONE, TOO!
KLEENEX
YOU WENT EIGHTEEN YEARS WITHOUT KNOWING ME. WE ONLY MET A YEAR AGO...
AFTER EIGHTEEN YEARS, TEN DAYS SHOULD HAVE BEEN EASY. DON'T BE SUCH A WUSS.

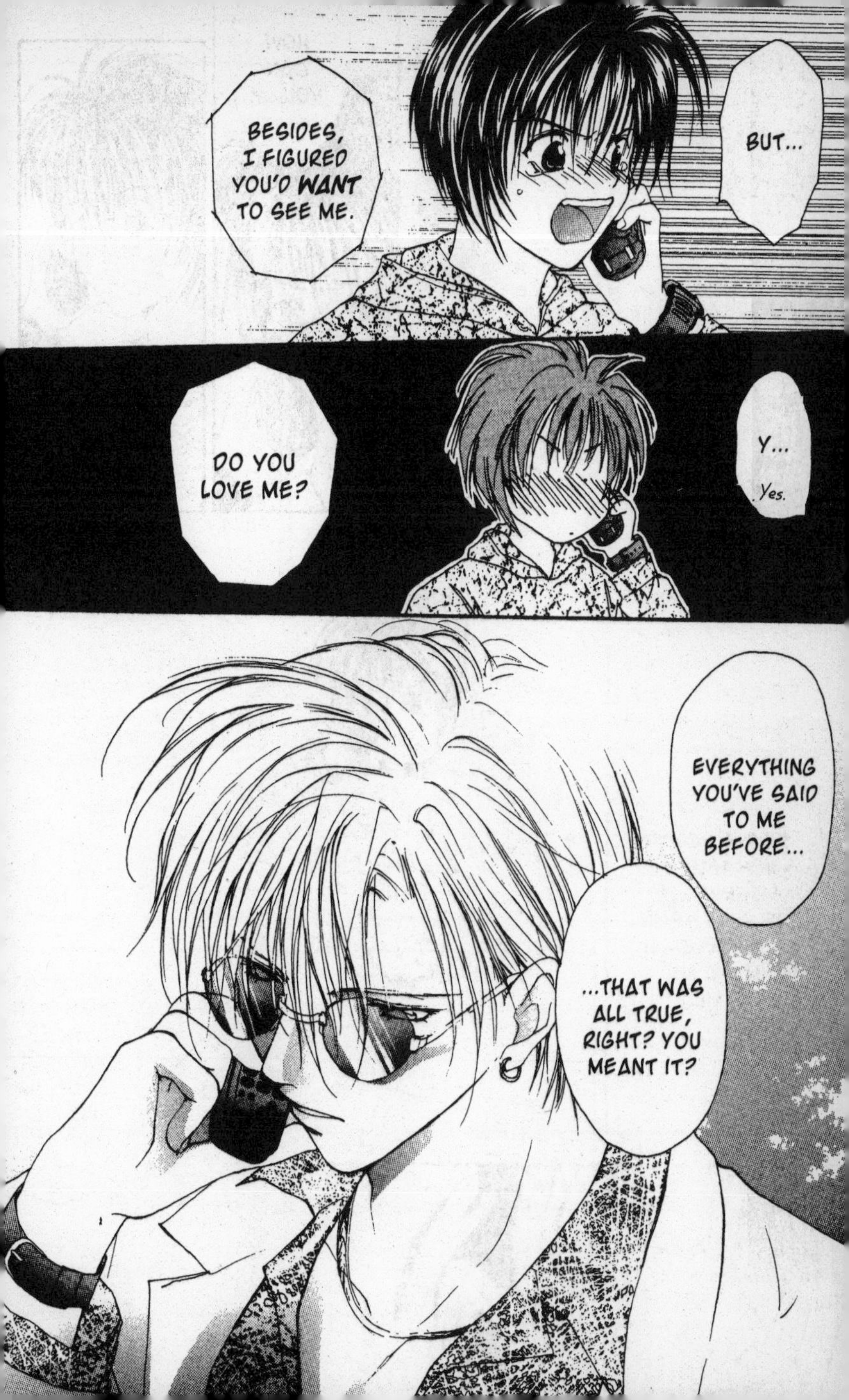
BUT...
BESIDES, I FIGURED YOU'D **WANT** TO SEE ME.
Y... Yes.
DO YOU LOVE ME?
EVERYTHING YOU'VE SAID TO ME BEFORE...
...THAT WAS ALL TRUE, RIGHT? YOU MEANT IT?

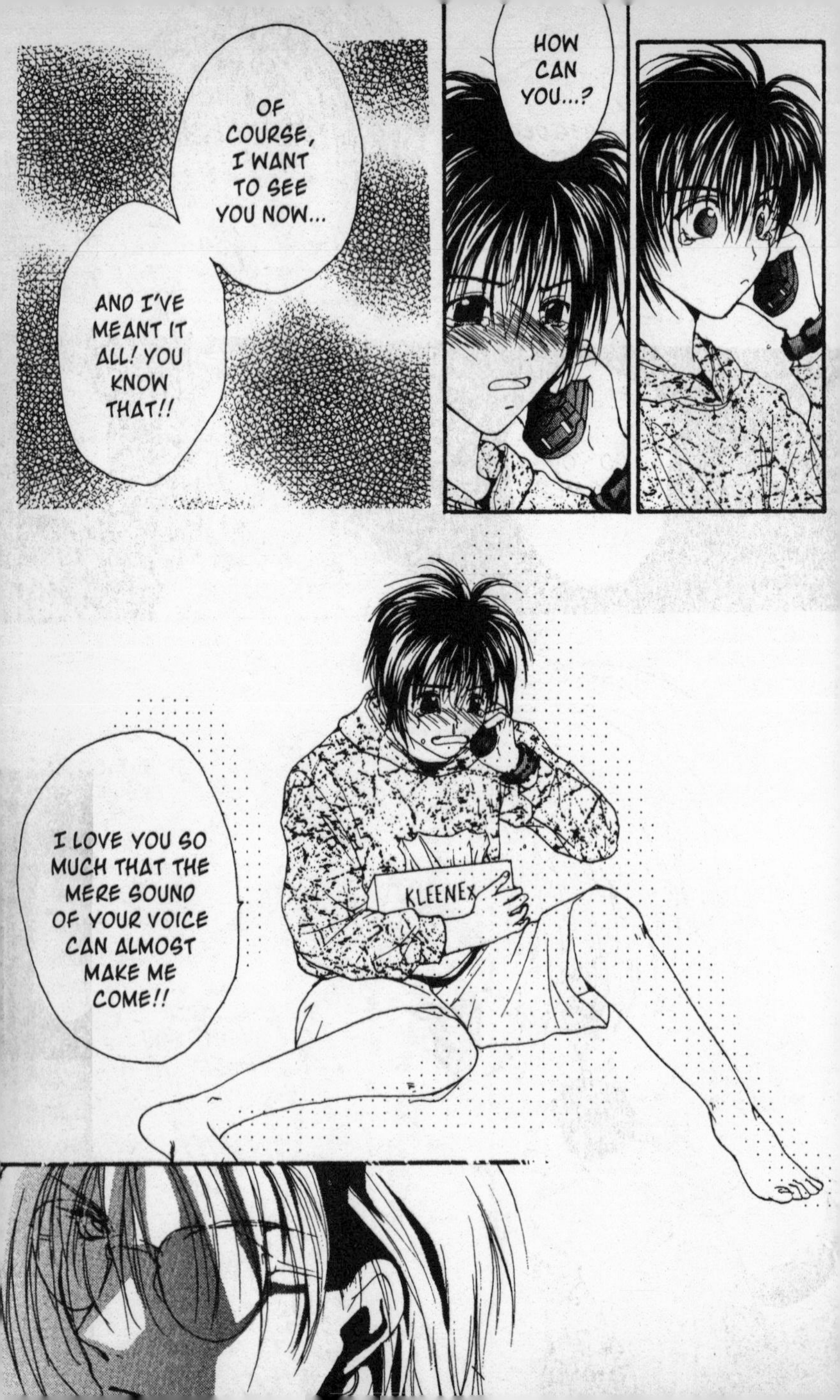
HOW CAN YOU...?
OF COURSE, I WANT TO SEE YOU NOW...
AND I'VE MEANT IT ALL! YOU KNOW THAT!!
KLEENEX
I LOVE YOU SO MUCH THAT THE MERE SOUND OF YOUR VOICE CAN ALMOST MAKE ME COME!!

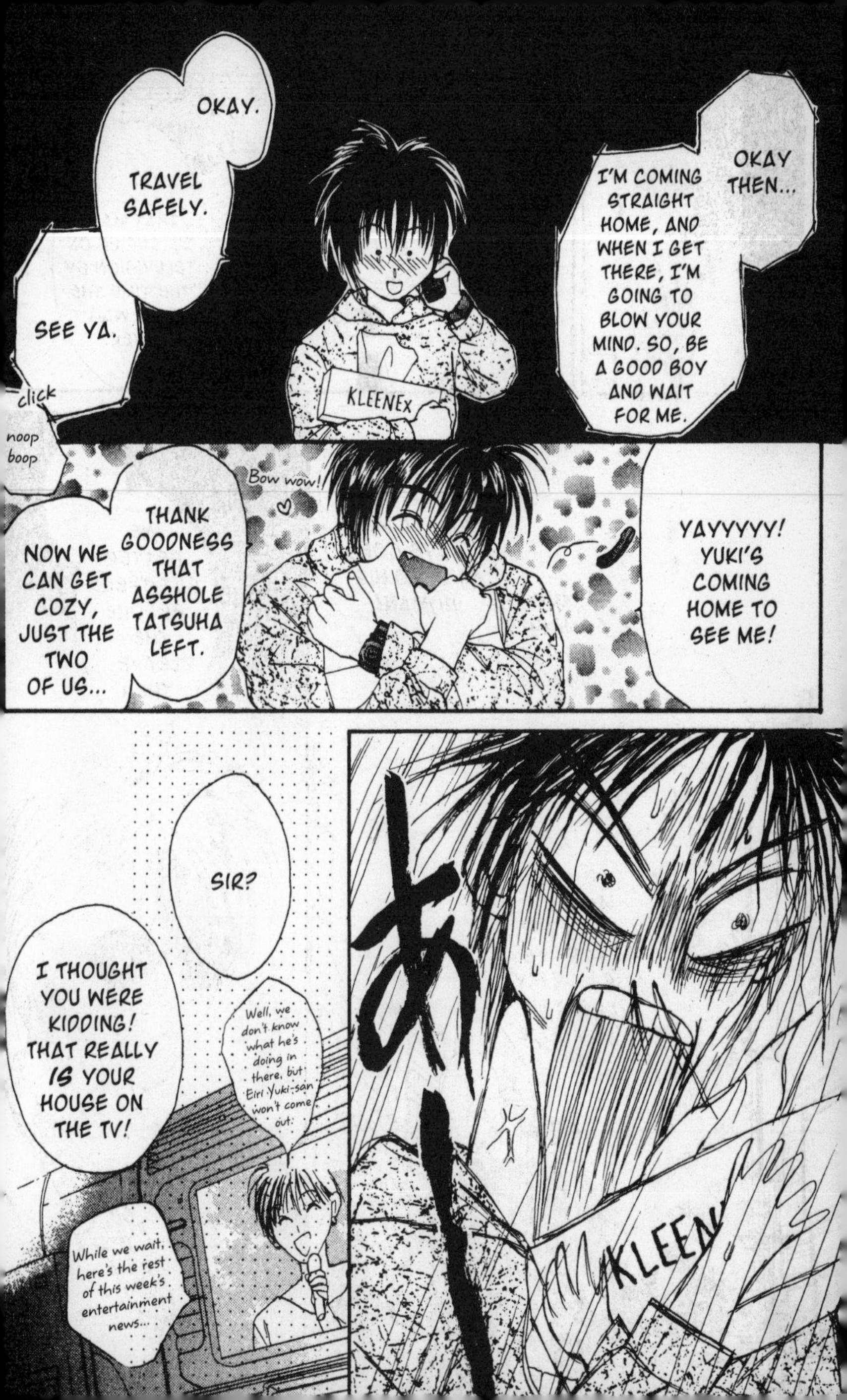
OKAY THEN...
I'M COMING STRAIGHT HOME, AND WHEN I GET THERE, I'M GOING TO BLOW YOUR MIND. SO, BE A GOOD BOY AND WAIT FOR ME.
OKAY.
TRAVEL SAFELY.
KLEENEX
SEE YA.
click
noop boop
YAYYYYY! YUKI'S COMING HOME TO SEE ME!
Bow wow!
THANK GOODNESS THAT ASSHOLE TATSUHA LEFT.
NOW WE CAN GET COZY, JUST THE TWO OF US...
あ
SIR?
I THOUGHT YOU WERE KIDDING! THAT REALLY *IS* YOUR HOUSE ON THE TV!
Well, we don't know what he's doing in there, but Eiri Yuki-san won't come out.
While we wait, here's the rest of this week's entertainment news...

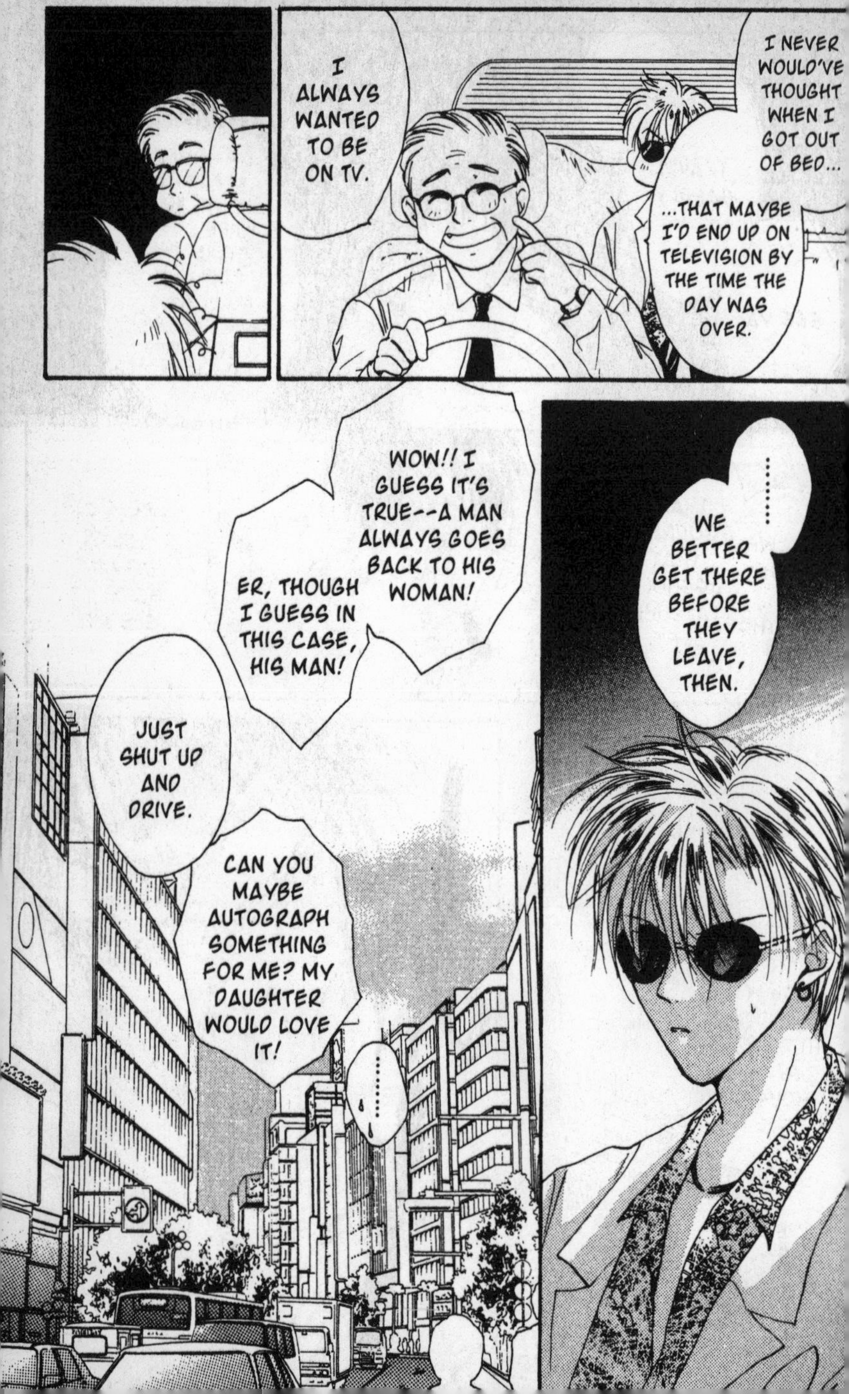
I NEVER WOULD'VE THOUGHT WHEN I GOT OUT OF BED...
...THAT MAYBE I'D END UP ON TELEVISION BY THE TIME THE DAY WAS OVER.
I ALWAYS WANTED TO BE ON TV.
......
WE BETTER GET THERE BEFORE THEY LEAVE, THEN.
WOW!! I GUESS IT'S TRUE--A MAN ALWAYS GOES BACK TO HIS WOMAN!
ER, THOUGH I GUESS IN THIS CASE, HIS MAN!
JUST SHUT UP AND DRIVE.
CAN YOU MAYBE AUTOGRAPH SOMETHING FOR ME? MY DAUGHTER WOULD LOVE IT!
......

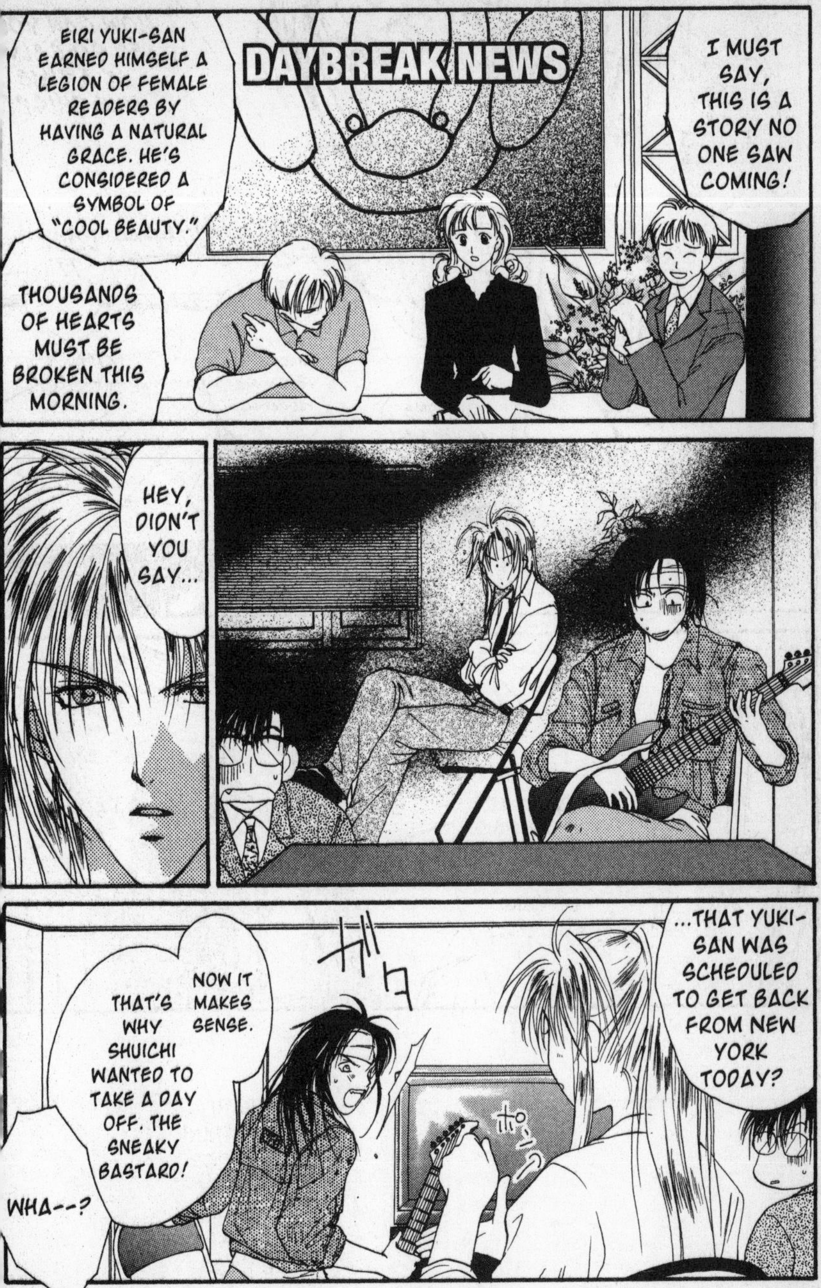

I MUST SAY, THIS IS A STORY NO ONE SAW COMING!
DAYBREAK NEWS
EIRI YUKI-SAN EARNED HIMSELF A LEGION OF FEMALE READERS BY HAVING A NATURAL GRACE. HE'S CONSIDERED A SYMBOL OF "COOL BEAUTY."
THOUSANDS OF HEARTS MUST BE BROKEN THIS MORNING.
HEY, DIDN'T YOU SAY...
...THAT YUKI-SAN WAS SCHEDULED TO GET BACK FROM NEW YORK TODAY?
NOW IT MAKES SENSE.
THAT'S WHY SHUICHI WANTED TO TAKE A DAY OFF. THE SNEAKY BASTARD!
WHA--?

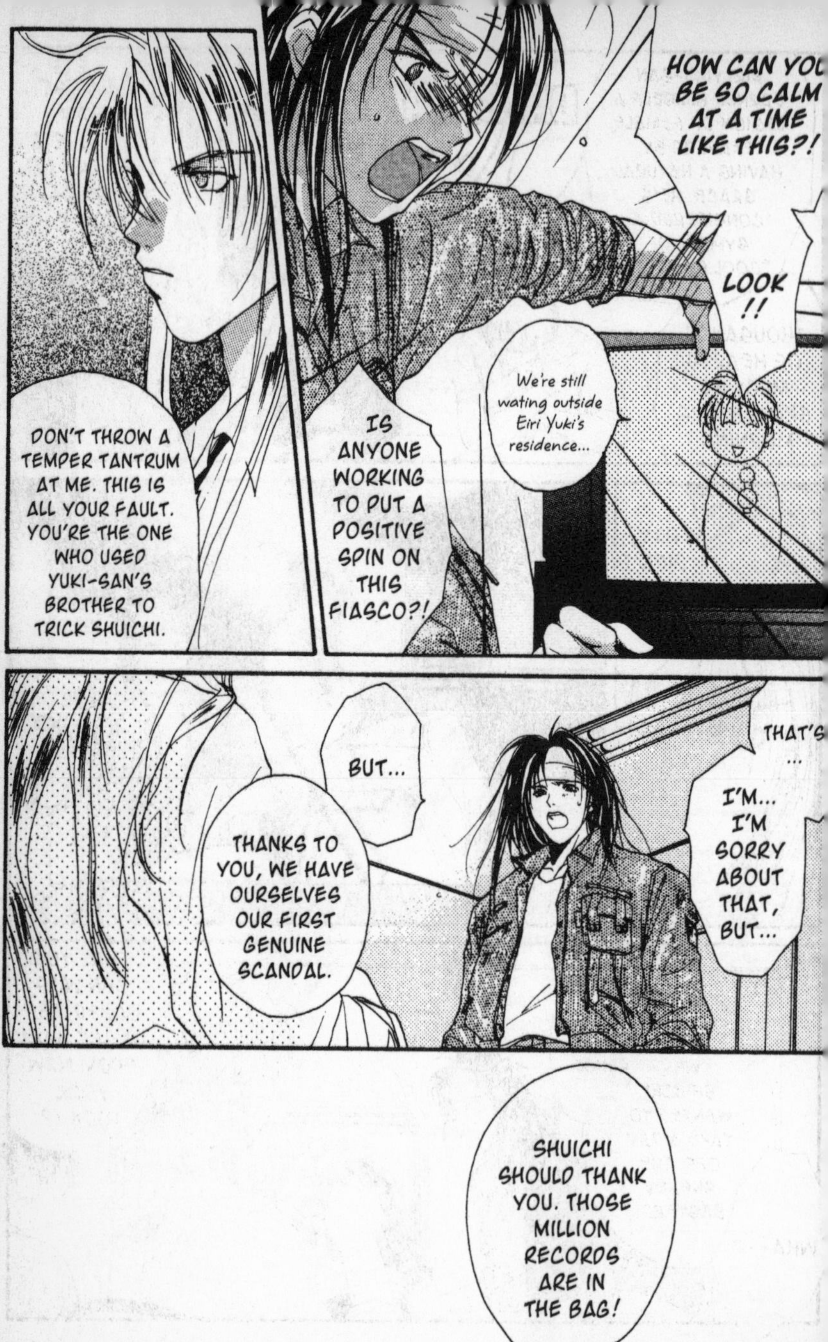
HOW CAN YOU BE SO CALM AT A TIME LIKE THIS?!
LOOK!!
We're still wating outside Eiri Yuki's residence...
IS ANYONE WORKING TO PUT A POSITIVE SPIN ON THIS FIASCO?!
DON'T THROW A TEMPER TANTRUM AT ME. THIS IS ALL YOUR FAULT. YOU'RE THE ONE WHO USED YUKI-SAN'S BROTHER TO TRICK SHUICHI.
THAT'S...
I'M... I'M SORRY ABOUT THAT, BUT...
BUT...
THANKS TO YOU, WE HAVE OURSELVES OUR FIRST GENUINE SCANDAL.
SHUICHI SHOULD THANK YOU. THOSE MILLION RECORDS ARE IN THE BAG!

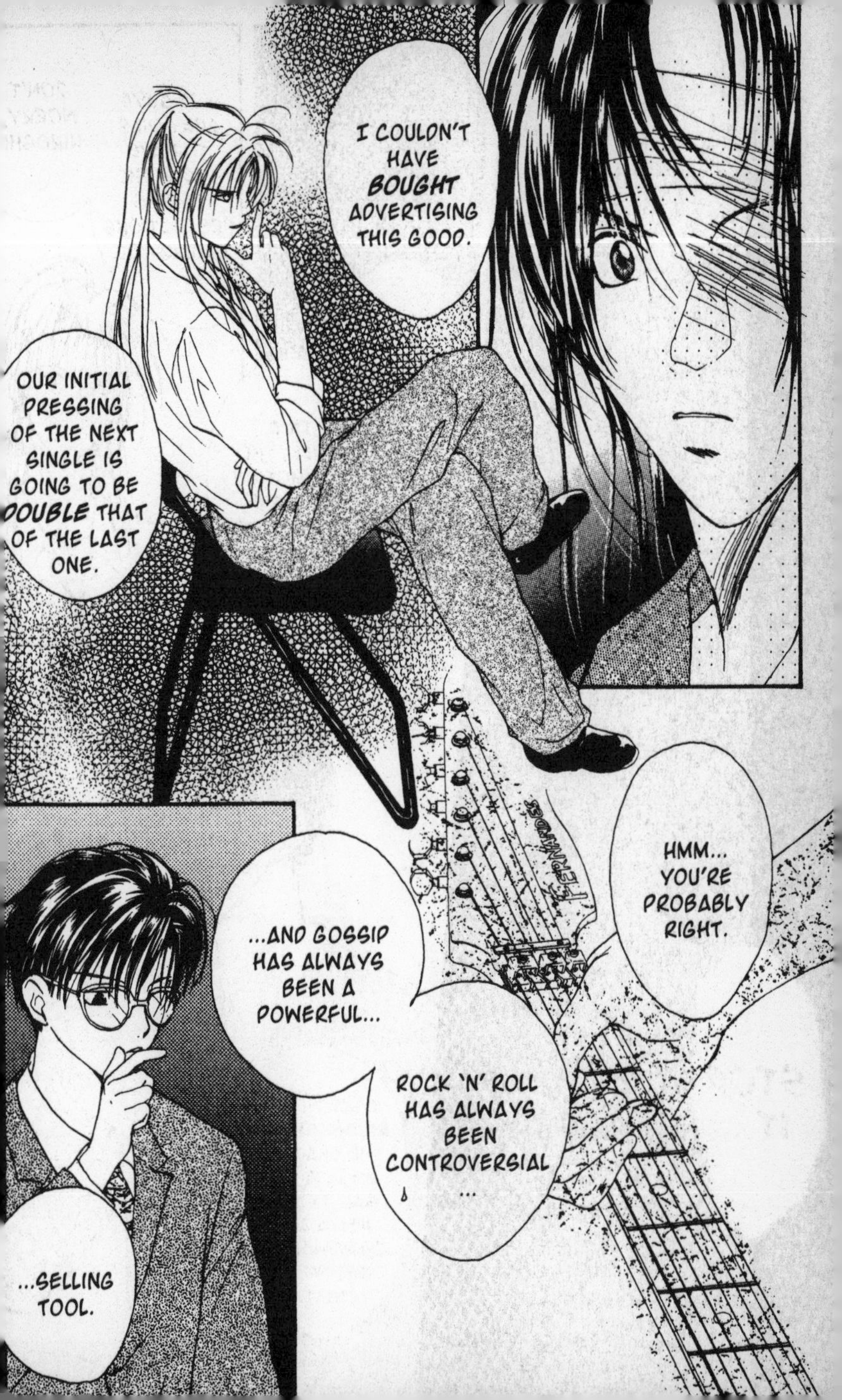
I COULDN'T HAVE **BOUGHT** ADVERTISING THIS GOOD.
OUR INITIAL PRESSING OF THE NEXT SINGLE IS GOING TO BE **DOUBLE** THAT OF THE LAST ONE.
HMM... YOU'RE PROBABLY RIGHT.
ROCK 'N' ROLL HAS ALWAYS BEEN CONTROVERSIAL ...
...AND GOSSIP HAS ALWAYS BEEN A POWERFUL...
...SELLING TOOL.

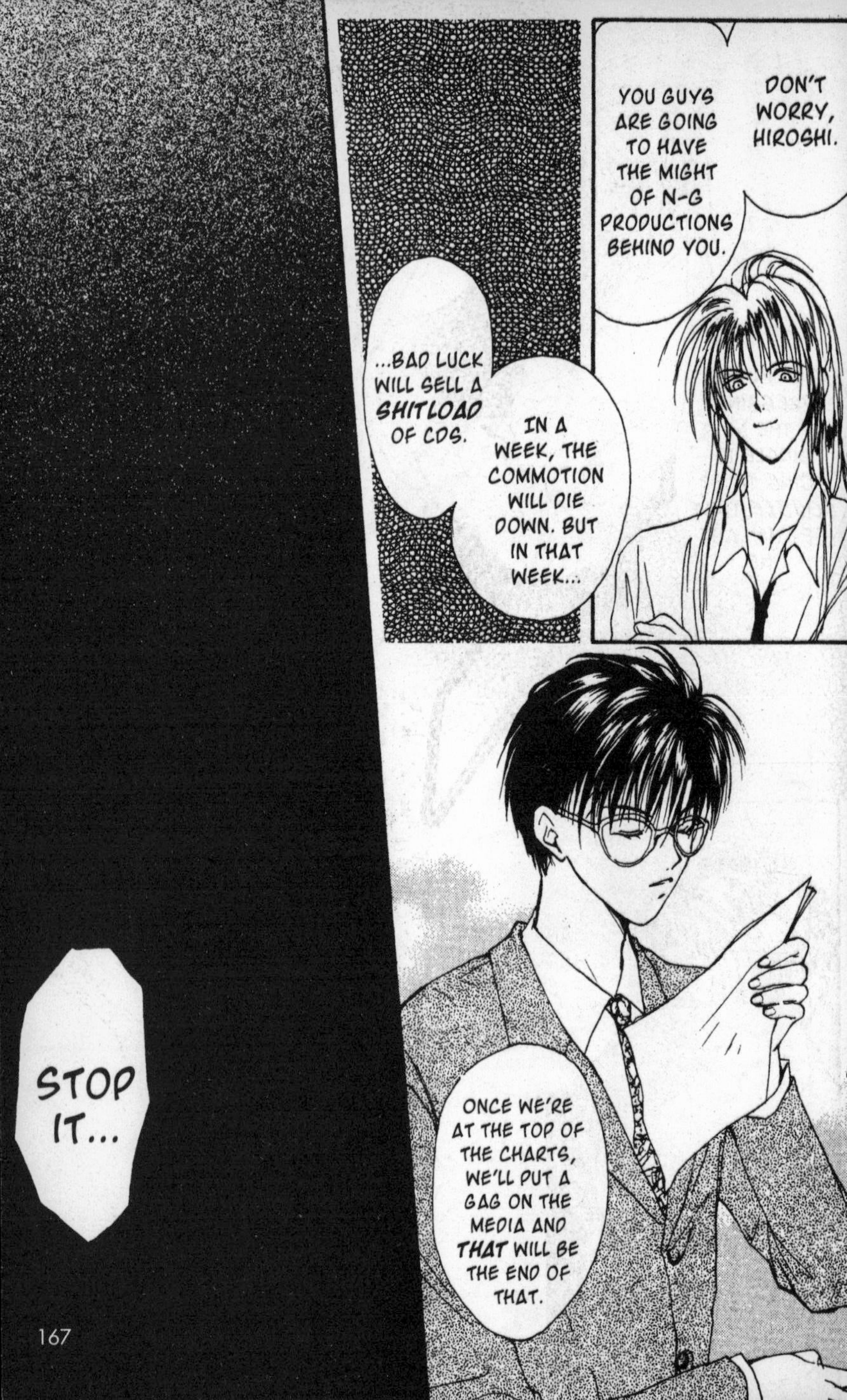
DON'T WORRY, HIROSHI.
YOU GUYS ARE GOING TO HAVE THE MIGHT OF N-G PRODUCTIONS BEHIND YOU.
IN A WEEK, THE COMMOTION WILL DIE DOWN. BUT IN THAT WEEK...
...BAD LUCK WILL SELL A **SHITLOAD** OF CDS.
ONCE WE'RE AT THE TOP OF THE CHARTS, WE'LL PUT A GAG ON THE MEDIA AND **THAT** WILL BE THE END OF THAT.
STOP IT...

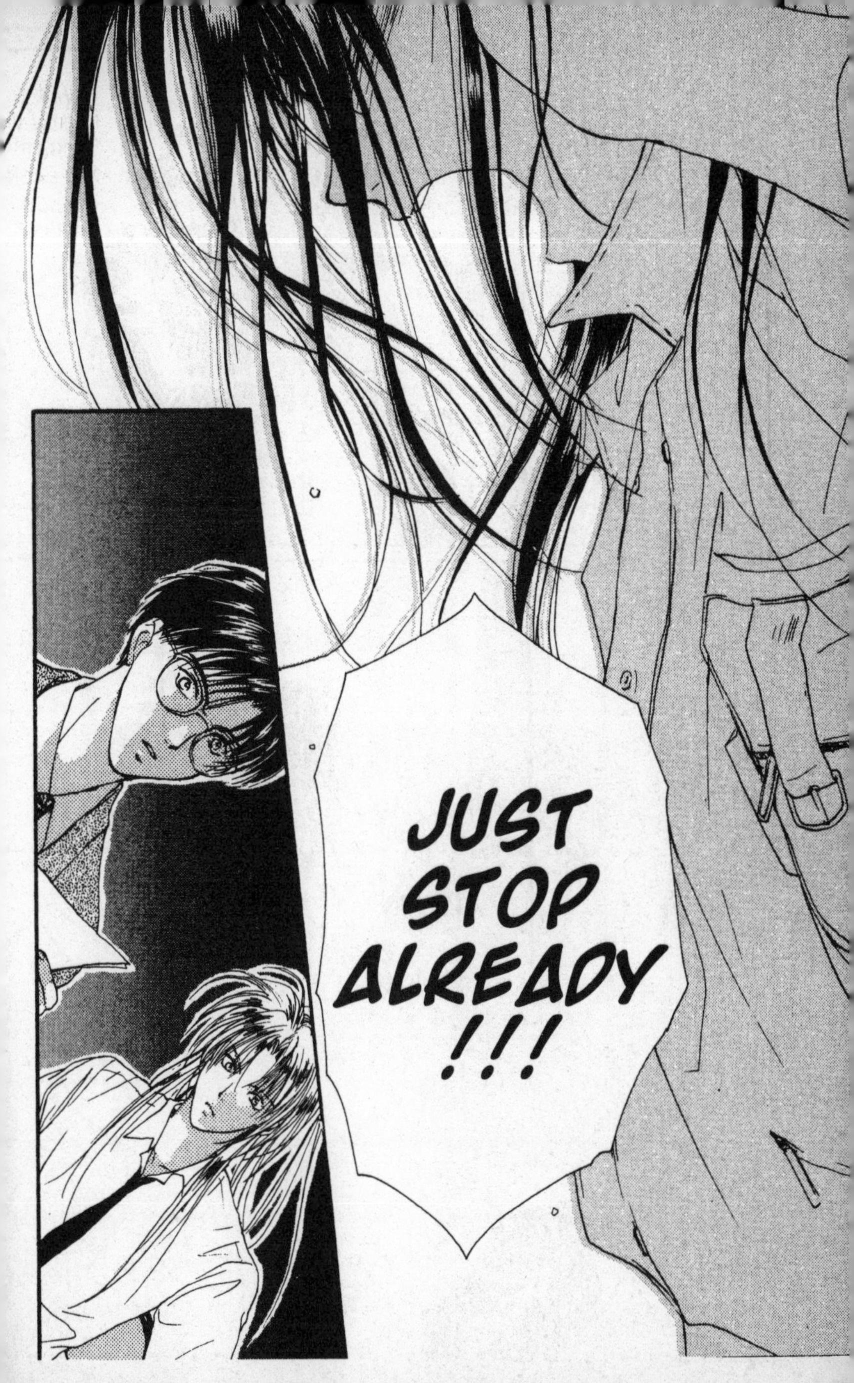
JUST STOP ALREADY !!!

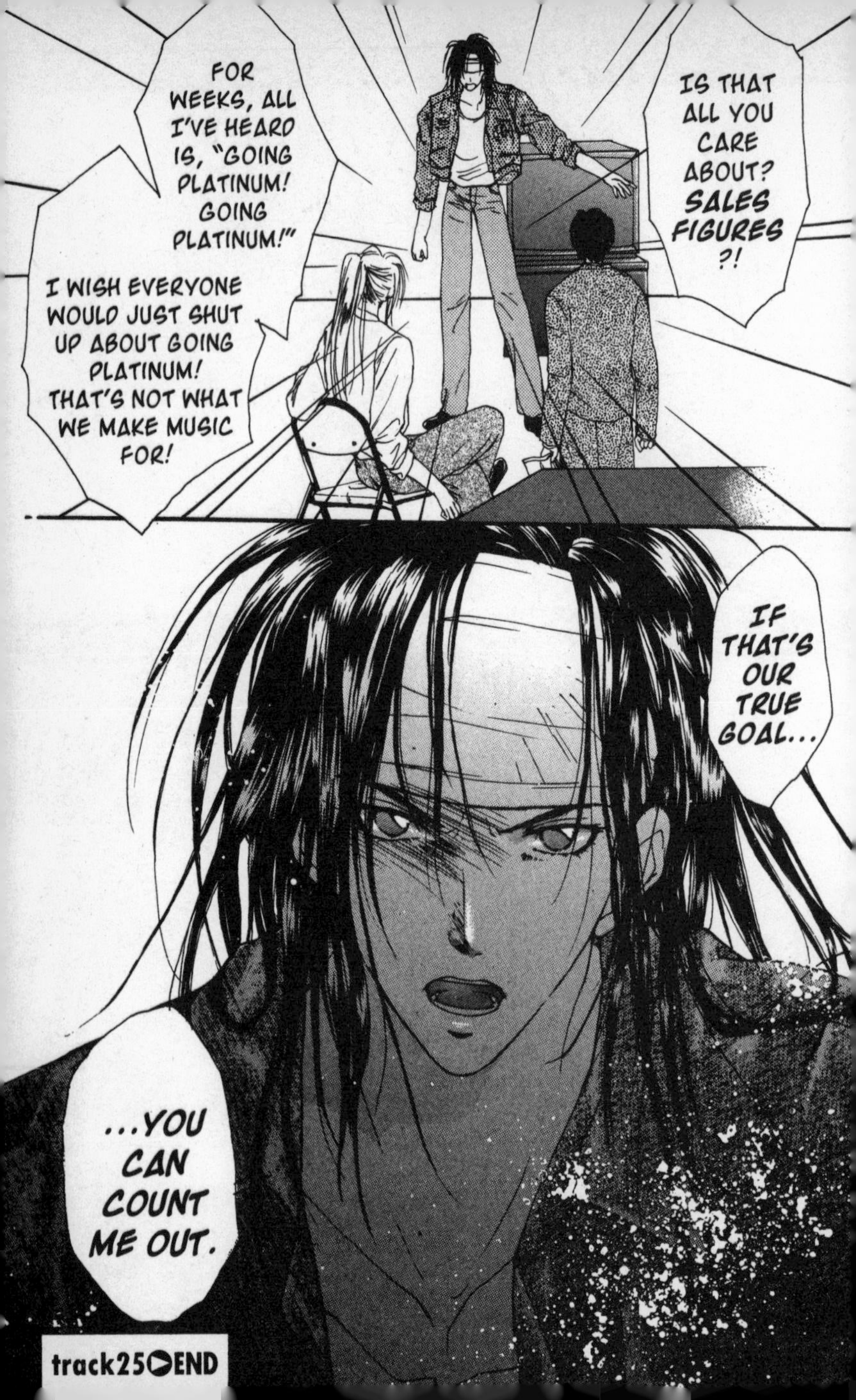
IS THAT ALL YOU CARE ABOUT? SALES FIGURES?!
FOR WEEKS, ALL I'VE HEARD IS, "GOING PLATINUM! GOING PLATINUM!"
I WISH EVERYONE WOULD JUST SHUT UP ABOUT GOING PLATINUM! THAT'S NOT WHAT WE MAKE MUSIC FOR!
IF THAT'S OUR TRUE GOAL...
...YOU CAN COUNT ME OUT.
track25▶END

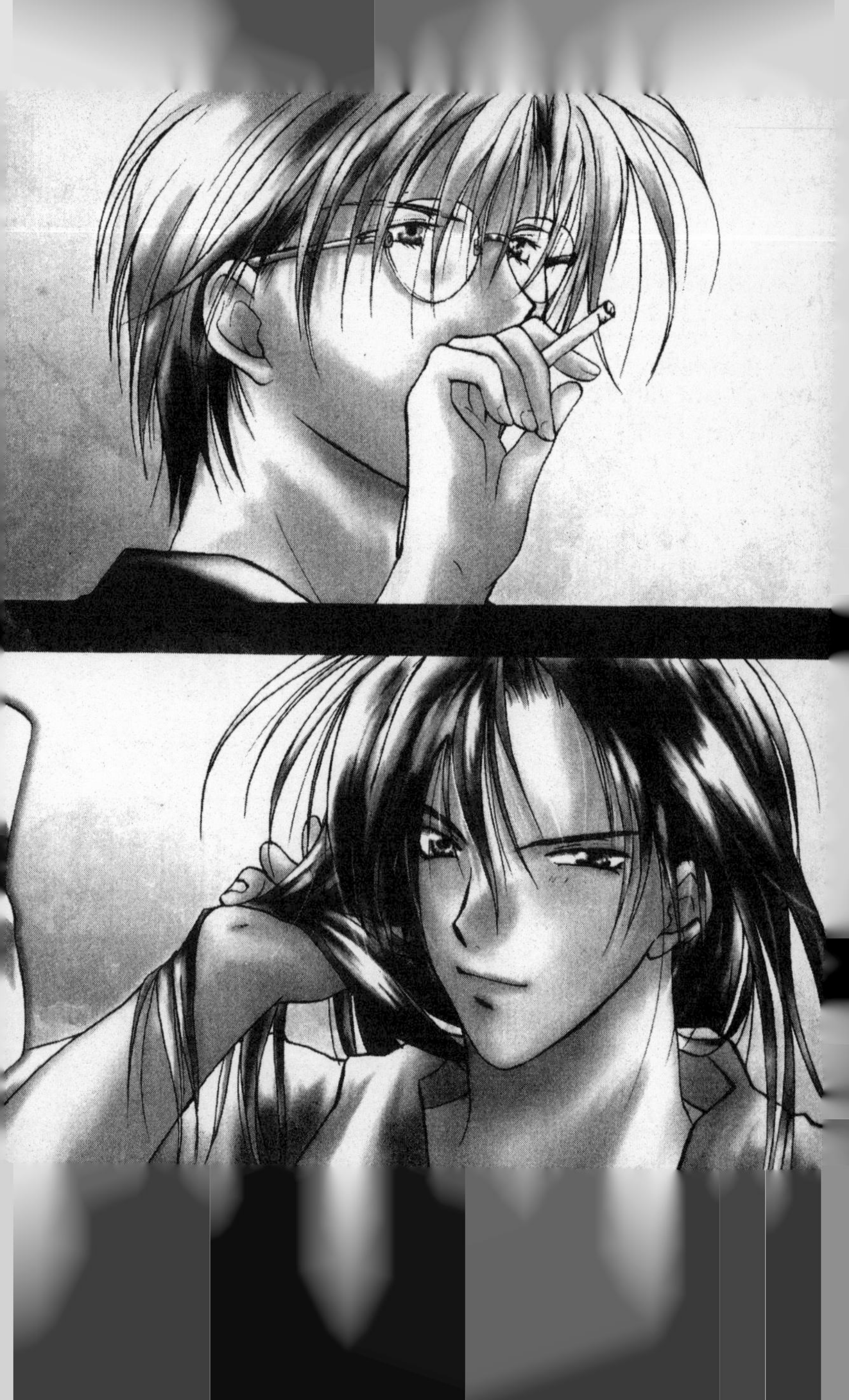

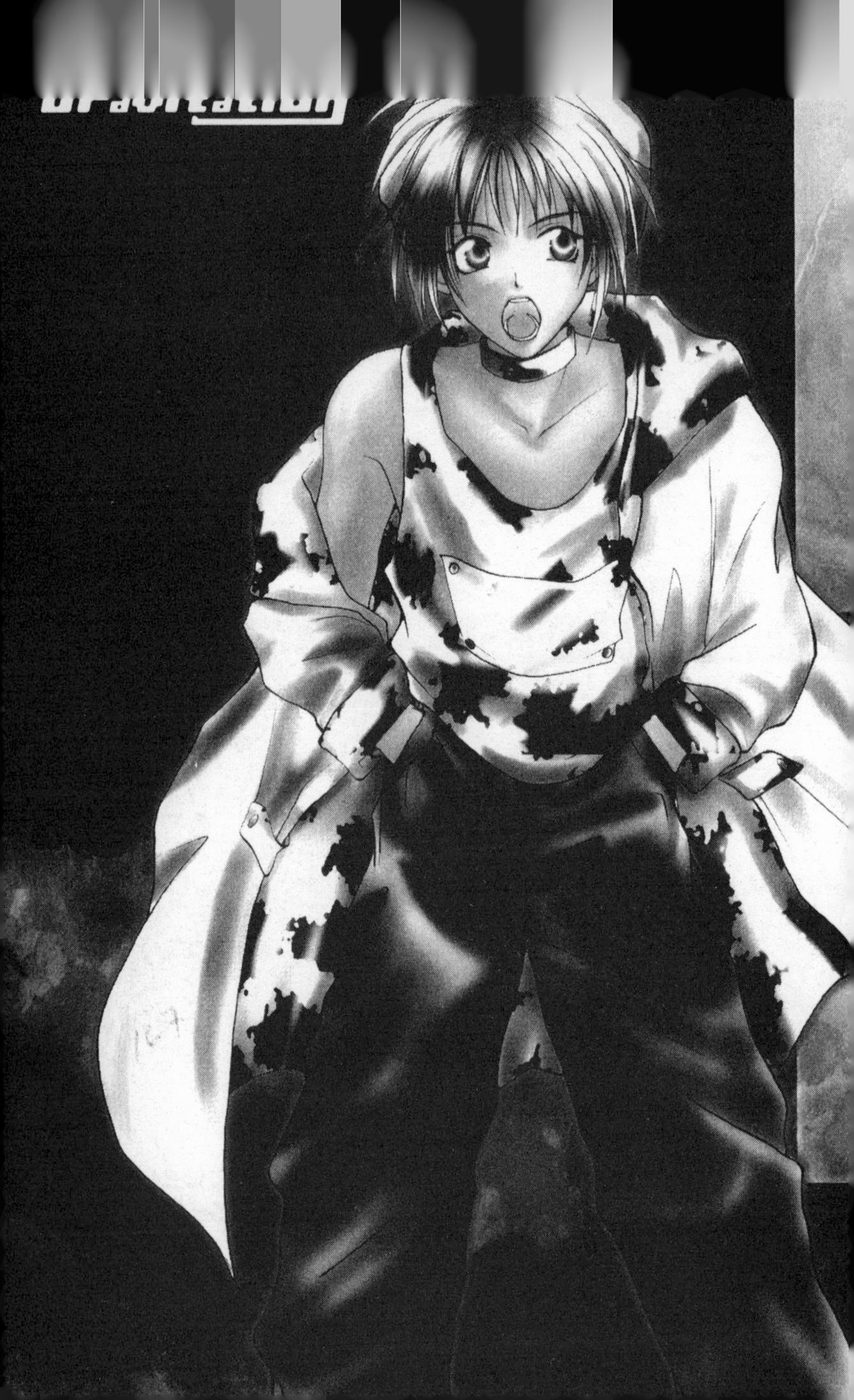

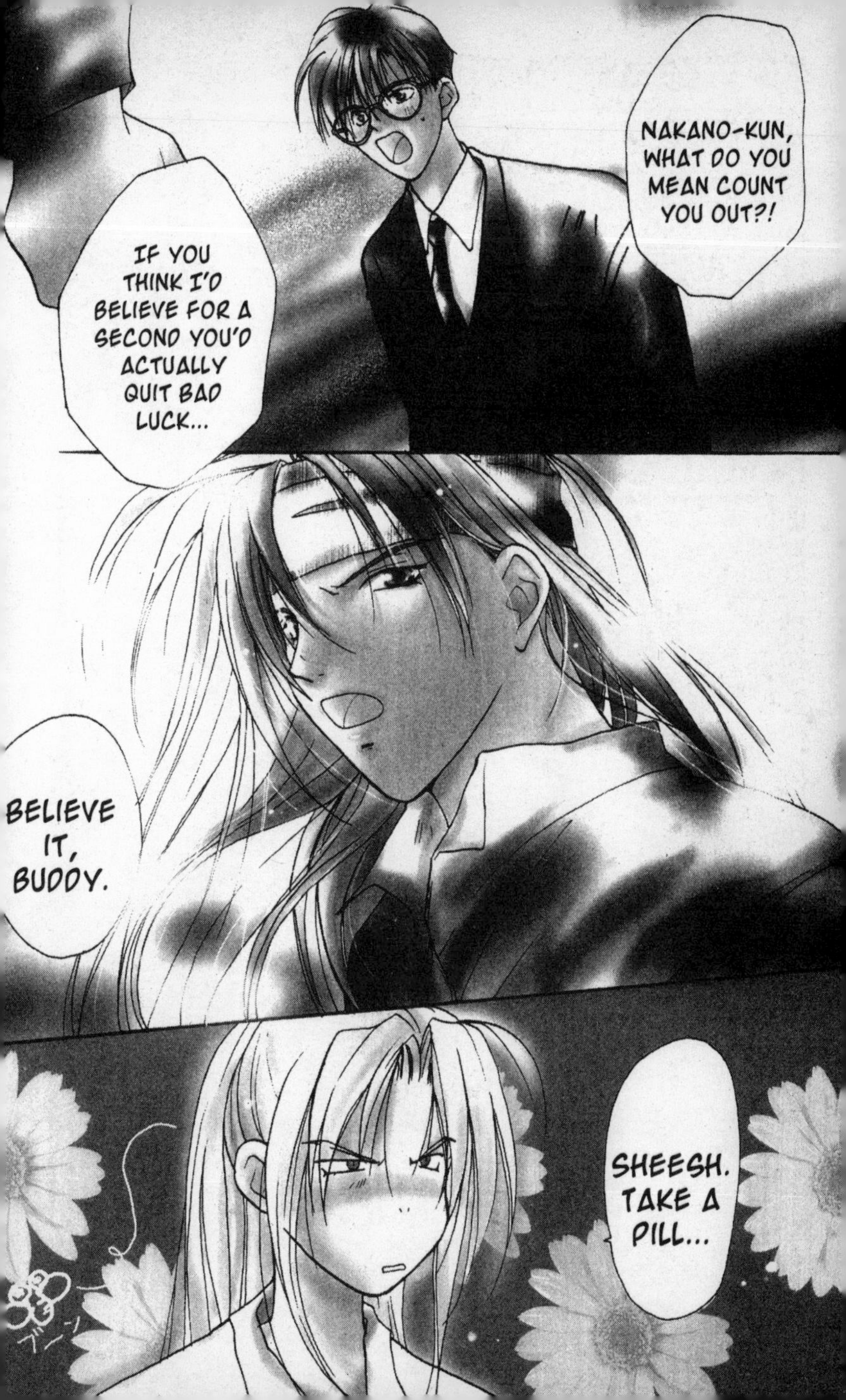
NAKANO-KUN, WHAT DO YOU MEAN COUNT YOU OUT?!
IF YOU THINK I'D BELIEVE FOR A SECOND YOU'D ACTUALLY QUIT BAD LUCK...
BELIEVE IT, BUDDY.
SHEESH. TAKE A PILL...

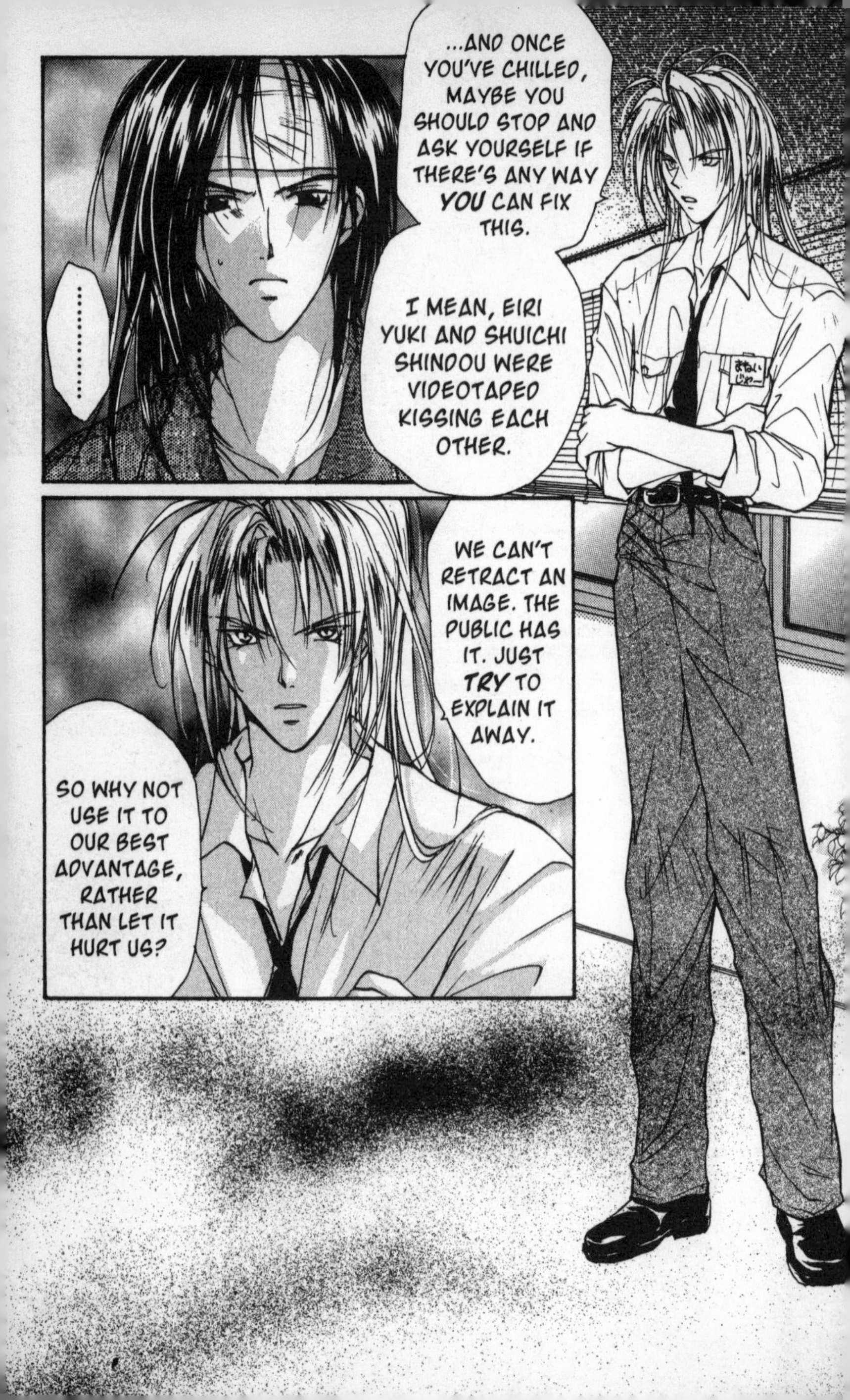
...AND ONCE YOU'VE CHILLED, MAYBE YOU SHOULD STOP AND ASK YOURSELF IF THERE'S ANY WAY YOU CAN FIX THIS.
I MEAN, EIRI YUKI AND SHUICHI SHINDOU WERE VIDEOTAPED KISSING EACH OTHER.
......
WE CAN'T RETRACT AN IMAGE. THE PUBLIC HAS IT. JUST TRY TO EXPLAIN IT AWAY.
SO WHY NOT USE IT TO OUR BEST ADVANTAGE, RATHER THAN LET IT HURT US?

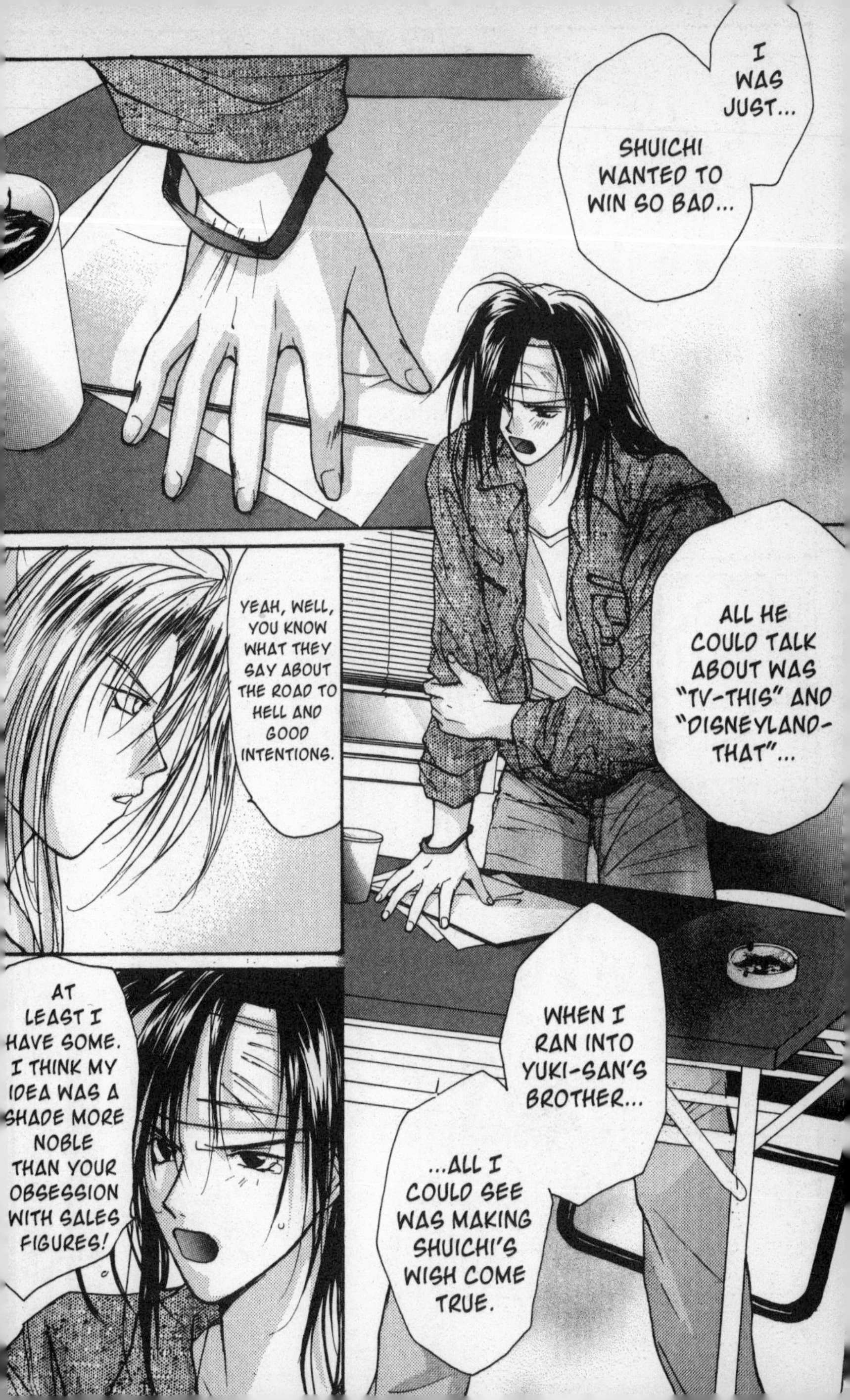
I WAS JUST...
SHUICHI WANTED TO WIN SO BAD...
ALL HE COULD TALK ABOUT WAS "TV-THIS" AND "DISNEYLAND-THAT"...
WHEN I RAN INTO YUKI-SAN'S BROTHER...
...ALL I COULD SEE WAS MAKING SHUICHI'S WISH COME TRUE.
YEAH, WELL, YOU KNOW WHAT THEY SAY ABOUT THE ROAD TO HELL AND GOOD INTENTIONS.
AT LEAST I HAVE SOME. I THINK MY IDEA WAS A SHADE MORE NOBLE THAN YOUR OBSESSION WITH SALES FIGURES!

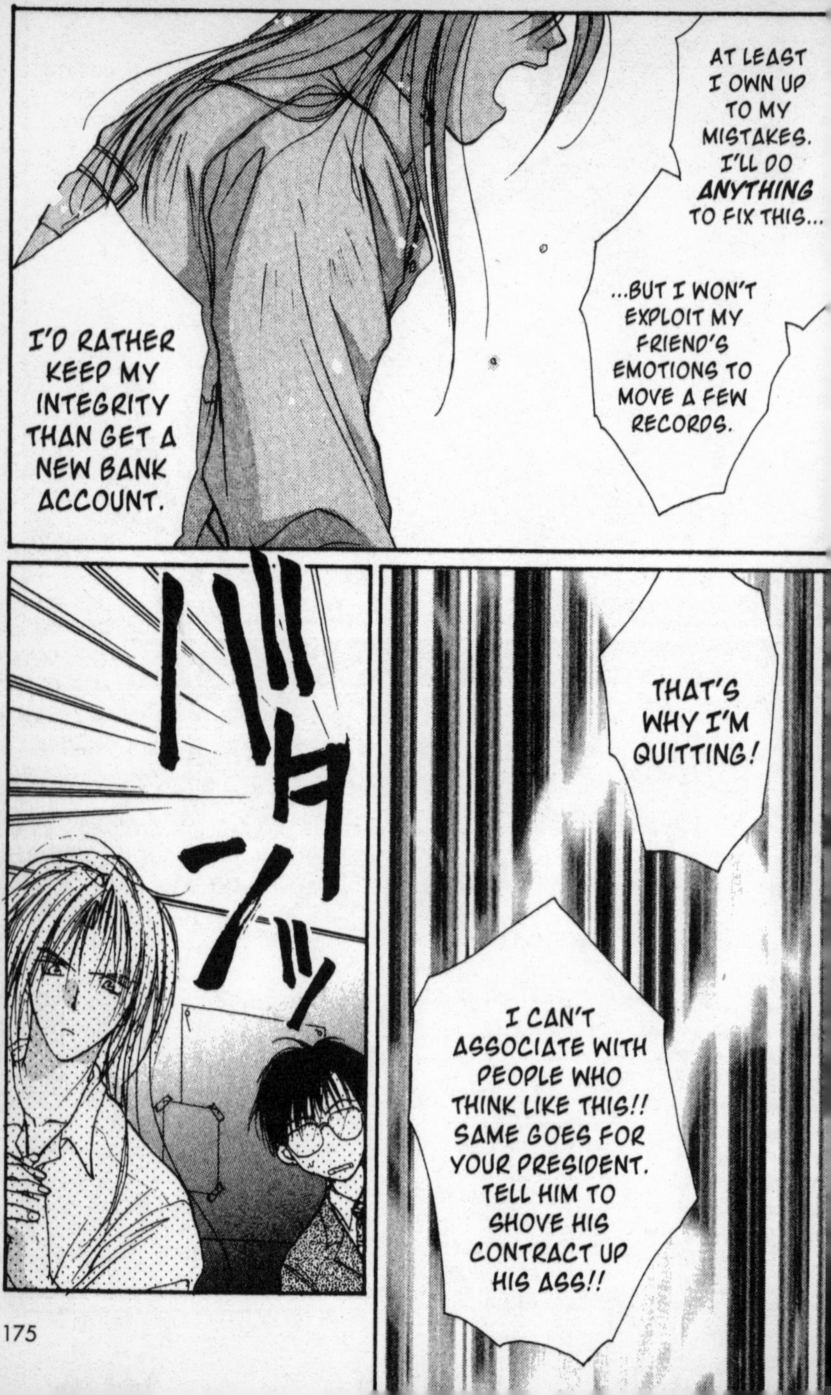
AT LEAST I OWN UP TO MY MISTAKES. I'LL DO **ANYTHING** TO FIX THIS...
...BUT I WON'T EXPLOIT MY FRIEND'S EMOTIONS TO MOVE A FEW RECORDS.
I'D RATHER KEEP MY INTEGRITY THAN GET A NEW BANK ACCOUNT.
THAT'S WHY I'M QUITTING!
I CAN'T ASSOCIATE WITH PEOPLE WHO THINK LIKE THIS!! SAME GOES FOR YOUR PRESIDENT. TELL HIM TO SHOVE HIS CONTRACT UP HIS ASS!!
バターンッ

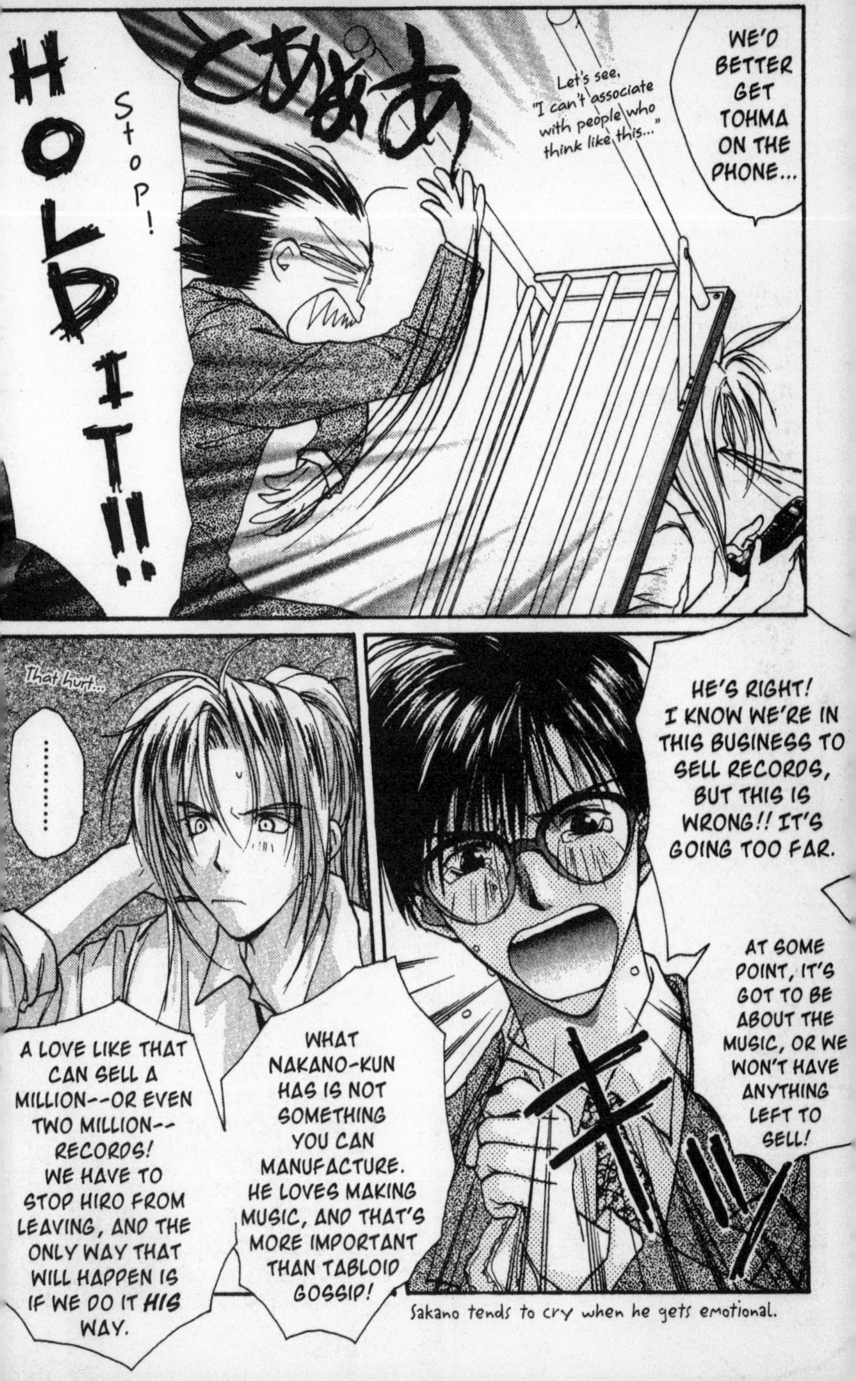
WE'D BETTER GET TOHMA ON THE PHONE...
Let's see, "I can't associate with people who think like this..."
Stop!
HOLD IT!!
HE'S RIGHT! I KNOW WE'RE IN THIS BUSINESS TO SELL RECORDS, BUT THIS IS WRONG!! IT'S GOING TOO FAR.
AT SOME POINT, IT'S GOT TO BE ABOUT THE MUSIC, OR WE WON'T HAVE ANYTHING LEFT TO SELL!
Sakano tends to cry when he gets emotional.
That hurt...
......
WHAT NAKANO-KUN HAS IS NOT SOMETHING YOU CAN MANUFACTURE. HE LOVES MAKING MUSIC, AND THAT'S MORE IMPORTANT THAN TABLOID GOSSIP!
A LOVE LIKE THAT CAN SELL A MILLION--OR EVEN TWO MILLION--RECORDS! WE HAVE TO STOP HIRO FROM LEAVING, AND THE ONLY WAY THAT WILL HAPPEN IS IF WE DO IT HIS WAY.

"Let's go after him!" thought Sakano.

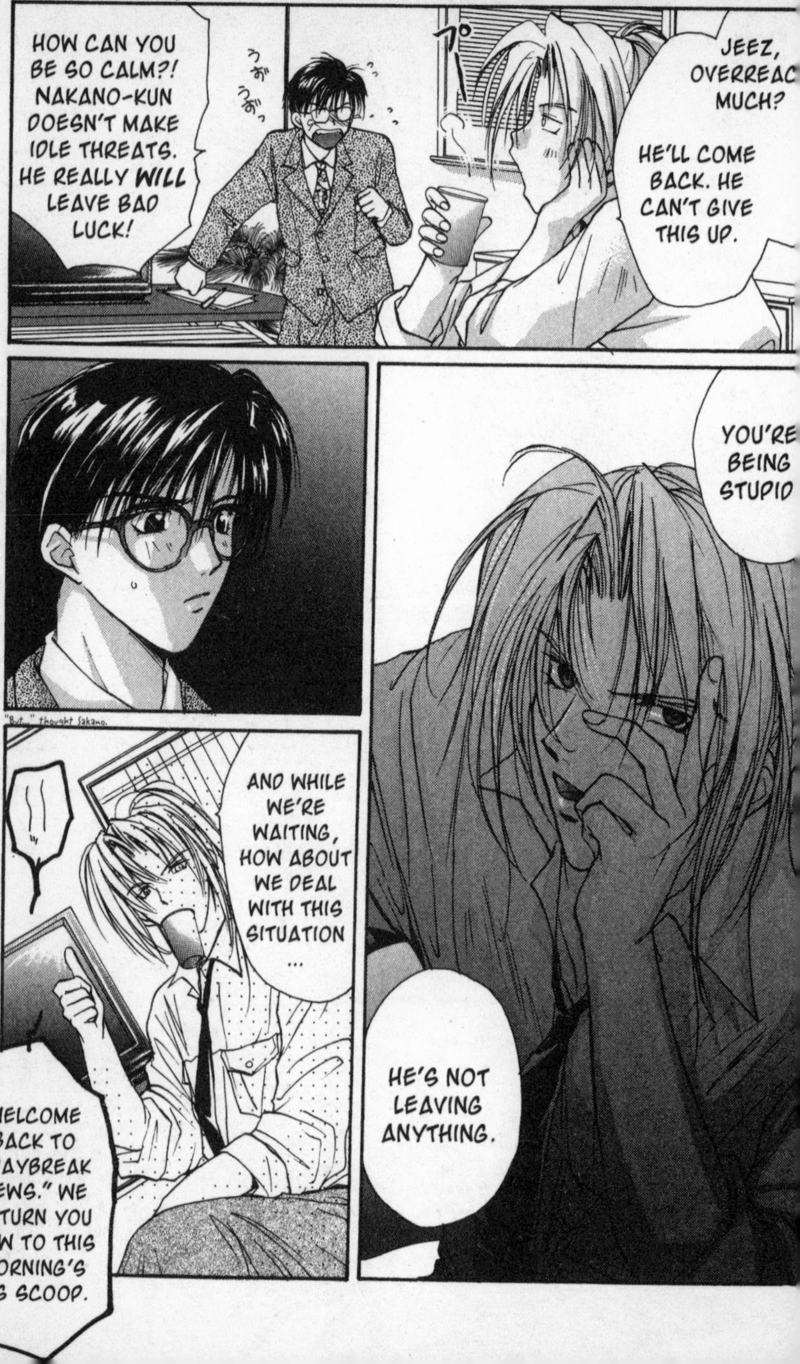
プ
JEEZ, OVERREAC MUCH?
HE'LL COME BACK. HE CAN'T GIVE THIS UP.
HOW CAN YOU BE SO CALM?! NAKANO-KUN DOESN'T MAKE IDLE THREATS. HE REALLY WILL LEAVE BAD LUCK!
うぉ うぉっ
YOU'RE BEING STUPID
HE'S NOT LEAVING ANYTHING.
AND WHILE WE'RE WAITING, HOW ABOUT WE DEAL WITH THIS SITUATION ...
WELCOME BACK TO "DAYBREAK NEWS." WE RETURN YOU NOW TO THIS MORNING'S BIG SCOOP.

"But..." thought Sakano.

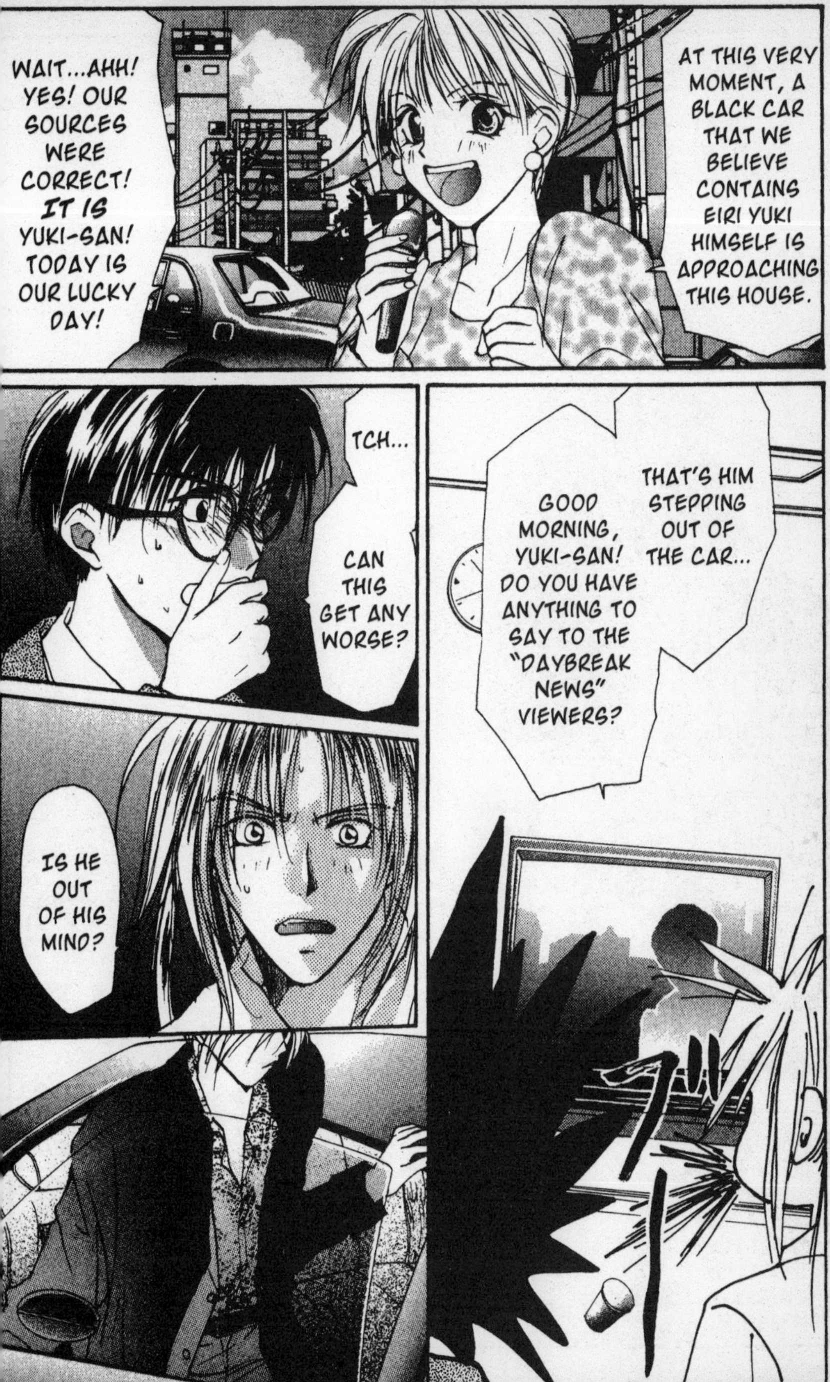
AT THIS VERY MOMENT, A BLACK CAR THAT WE BELIEVE CONTAINS EIRI YUKI HIMSELF IS APPROACHING THIS HOUSE.
WAIT...AHH! YES! OUR SOURCES WERE CORRECT! IT IS YUKI-SAN! TODAY IS OUR LUCKY DAY!
THAT'S HIM STEPPING OUT OF THE CAR...
GOOD MORNING, YUKI-SAN! DO YOU HAVE ANYTHING TO SAY TO THE "DAYBREAK NEWS" VIEWERS?
TCH...
CAN THIS GET ANY WORSE?
IS HE OUT OF HIS MIND?

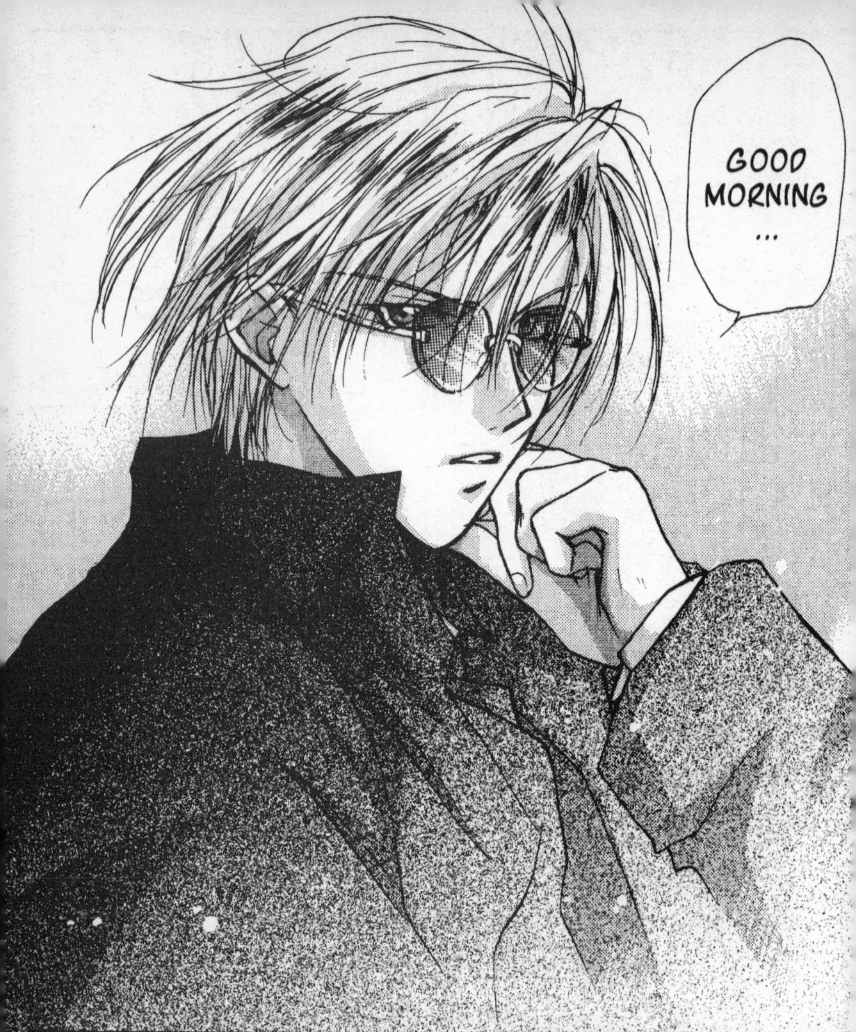
GOOD MORNING ...

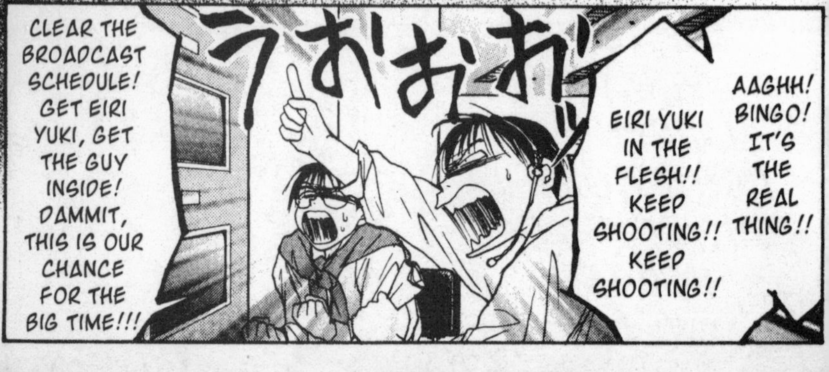
AAGHH! BINGO! IT'S THE REAL THING!!
うおおおッ
EIRI YUKI IN THE FLESH!! KEEP SHOOTING!! KEEP SHOOTING!!
CLEAR THE BROADCAST SCHEDULE! GET EIRI YUKI, GET THE GUY INSIDE! DAMMIT, THIS IS OUR CHANCE FOR THE BIG TIME!!!

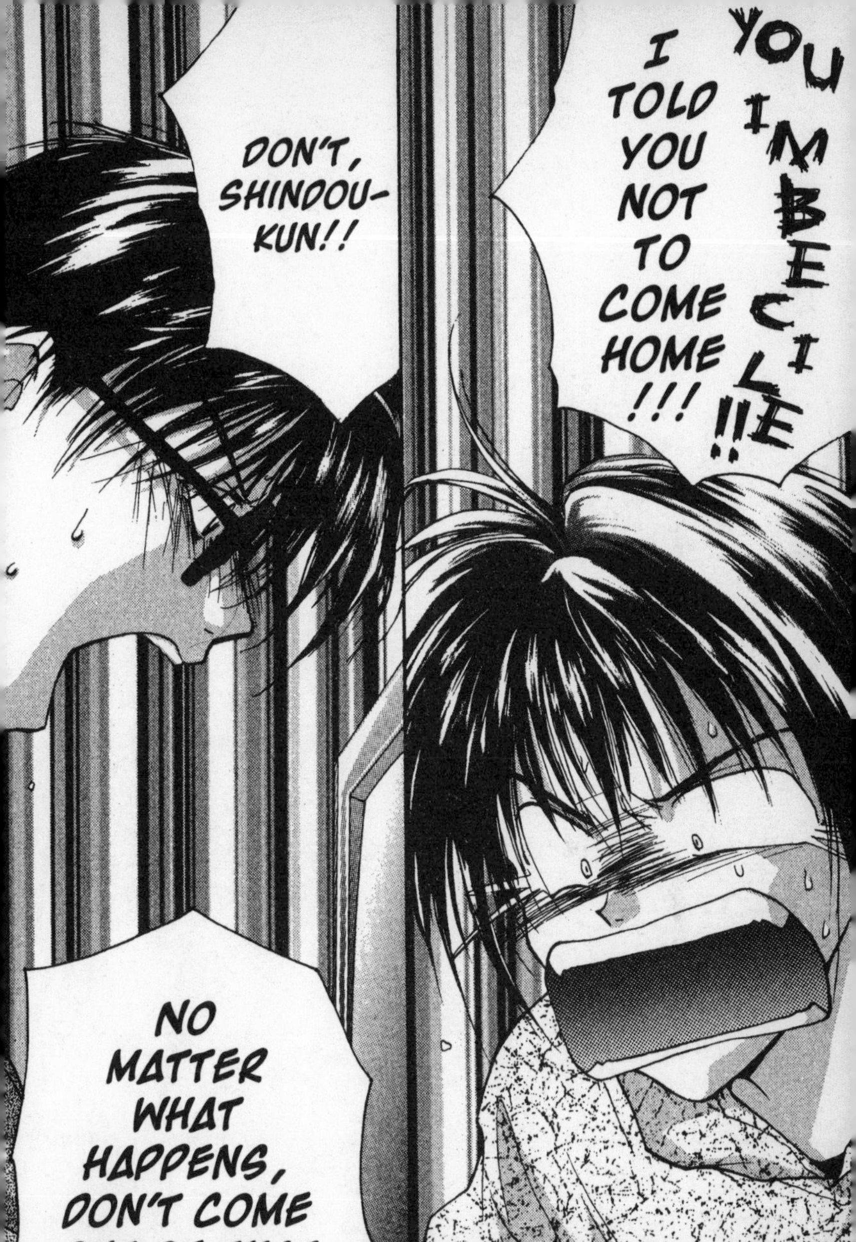
YOU IMBECILE!!
I TOLD YOU NOT TO COME HOME!!!
DON'T, SHINDOU-KUN!!
NO MATTER WHAT HAPPENS, DON'T COME OUT OF THAT

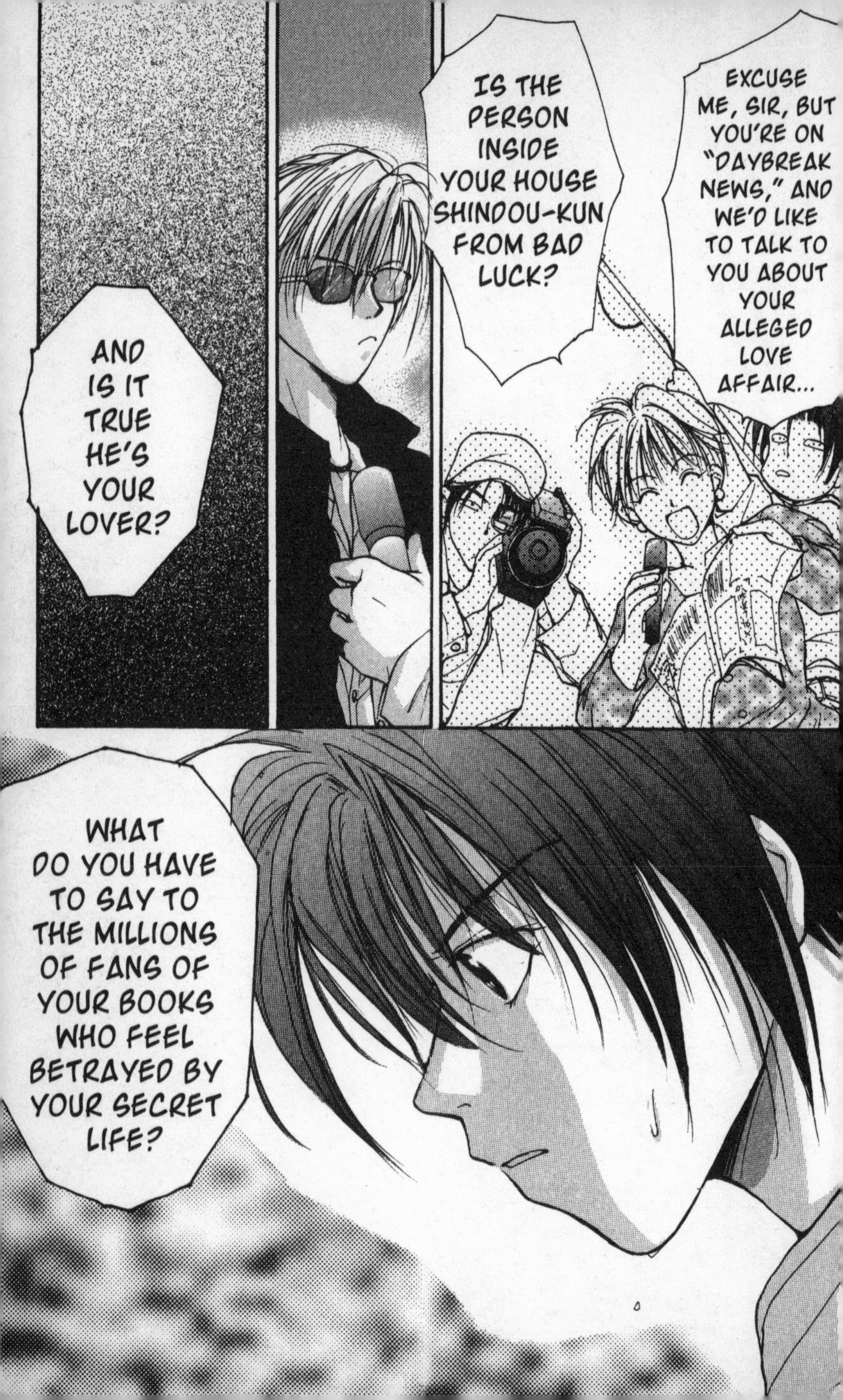
EXCUSE ME, SIR, BUT YOU'RE ON "DAYBREAK NEWS," AND WE'D LIKE TO TALK TO YOU ABOUT YOUR ALLEGED LOVE AFFAIR...
IS THE PERSON INSIDE YOUR HOUSE SHINDOU-KUN FROM BAD LUCK?
AND IS IT TRUE HE'S YOUR LOVER?
WHAT DO YOU HAVE TO SAY TO THE MILLIONS OF FANS OF YOUR BOOKS WHO FEEL BETRAYED BY YOUR SECRET LIFE?

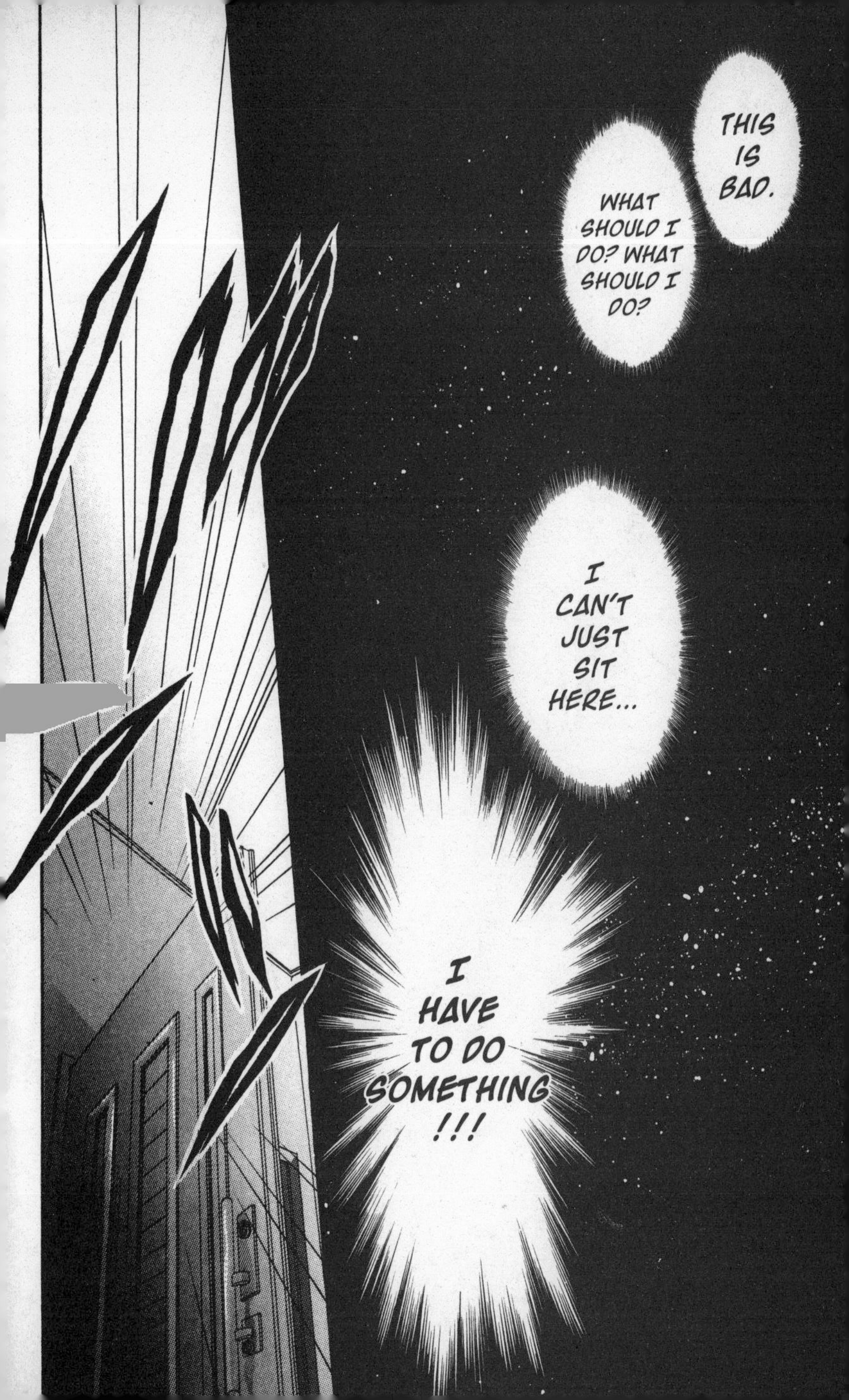
THIS IS BAD.
WHAT SHOULD I DO? WHAT SHOULD I DO?
I CAN'T JUST SIT HERE...
I HAVE TO DO SOMETHING!!!

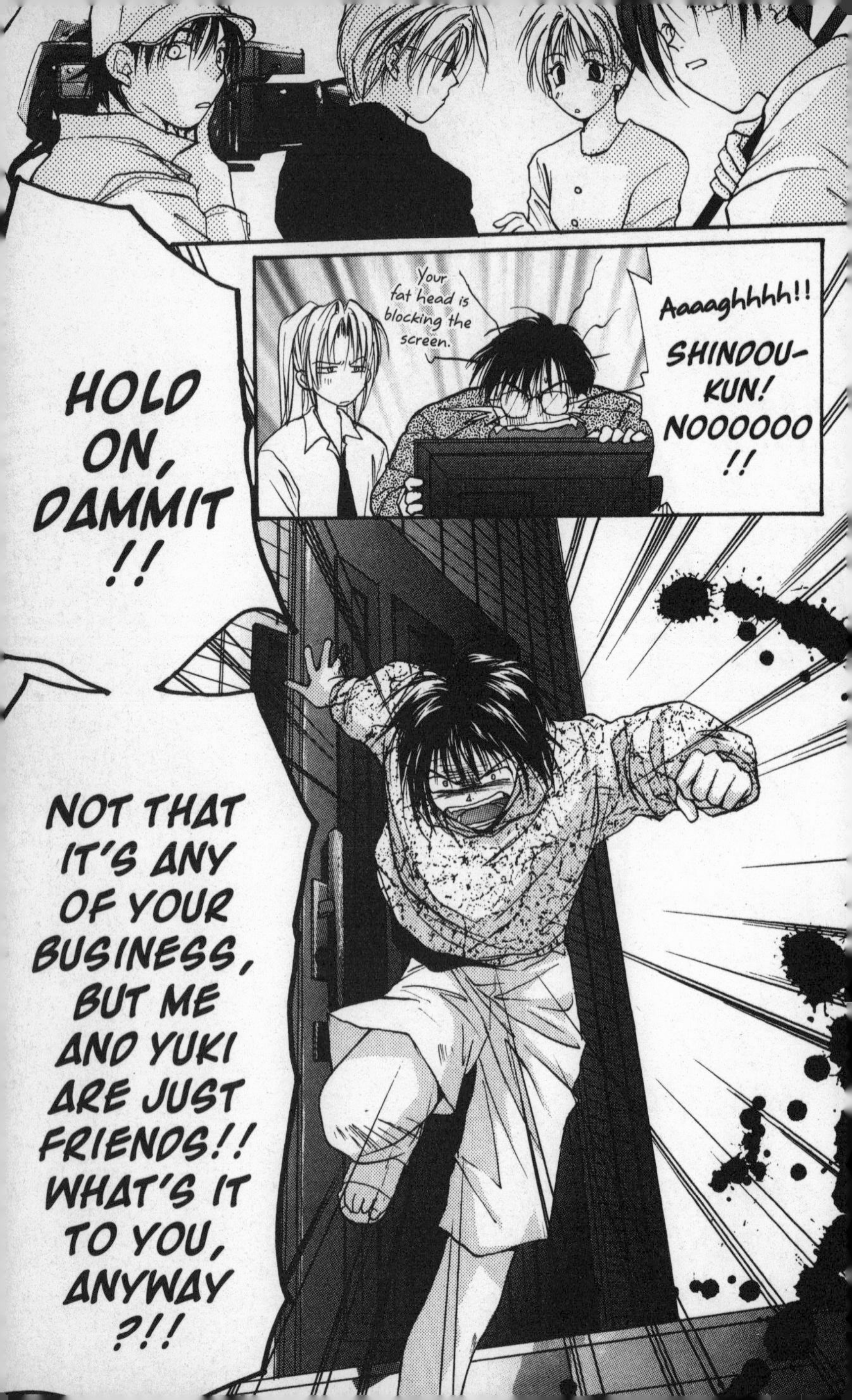
Aaaaghhhh!!
SHINDOU-KUN! NOOOOOO!!
Your fat head is blocking the screen.
HOLD ON, DAMMIT!!
NOT THAT IT'S ANY OF YOUR BUSINESS, BUT ME AND YUKI ARE JUST FRIENDS!! WHAT'S IT TO YOU, ANYWAY?!!

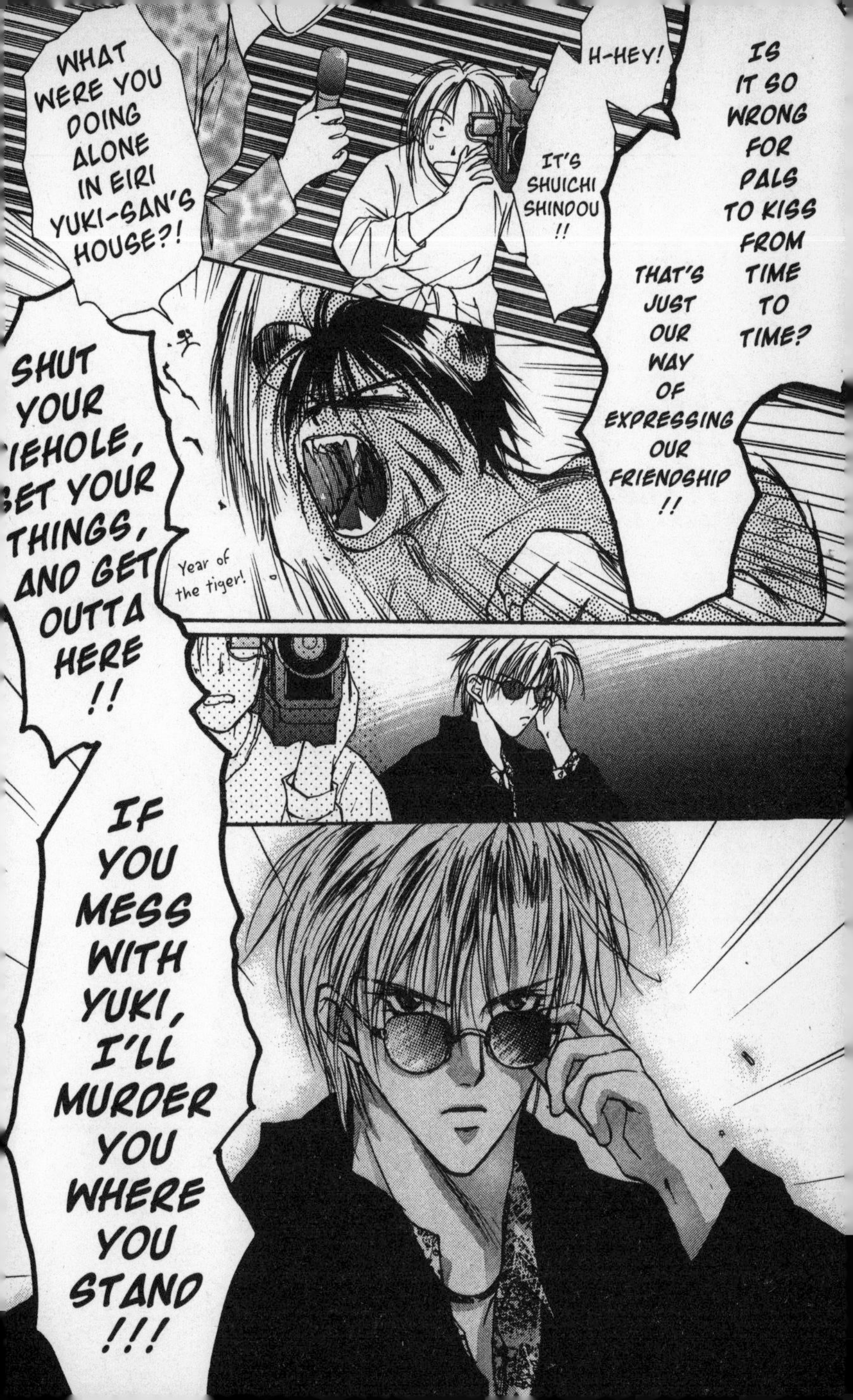
IS IT SO WRONG FOR PALS TO KISS FROM TIME TO TIME?
THAT'S JUST OUR WAY OF EXPRESSING OUR FRIENDSHIP!!
H-HEY!
IT'S SHUICHI SHINDOU!!
WHAT WERE YOU DOING ALONE IN EIRI YUKI-SAN'S HOUSE?!
SHUT YOUR IEHOLE, ET YOUR THINGS, AND GET OUTTA HERE!!
Year of the tiger!
IF YOU MESS WITH YUKI, I'LL MURDER YOU WHERE YOU STAND!!!

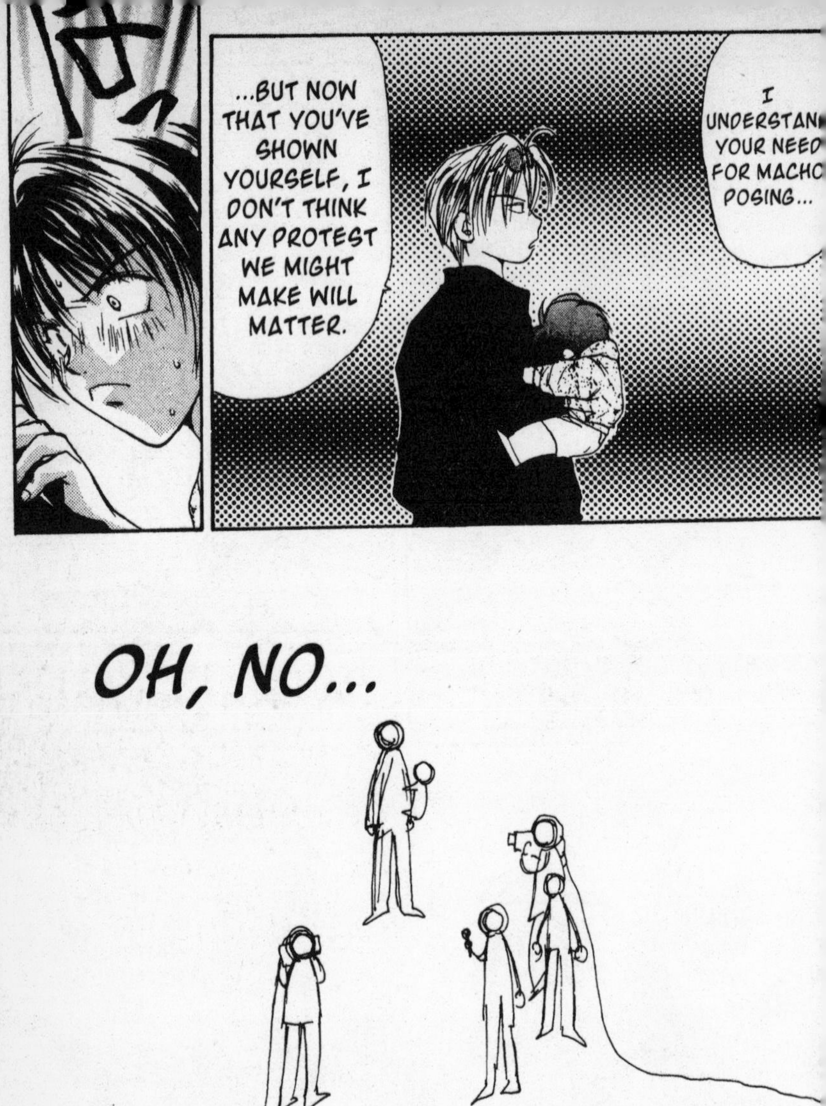
I UNDERSTAN YOUR NEED FOR MACHO POSING...
...BUT NOW THAT YOU'VE SHOWN YOURSELF, I DON'T THINK ANY PROTEST WE MIGHT MAKE WILL MATTER.
OH, NO...

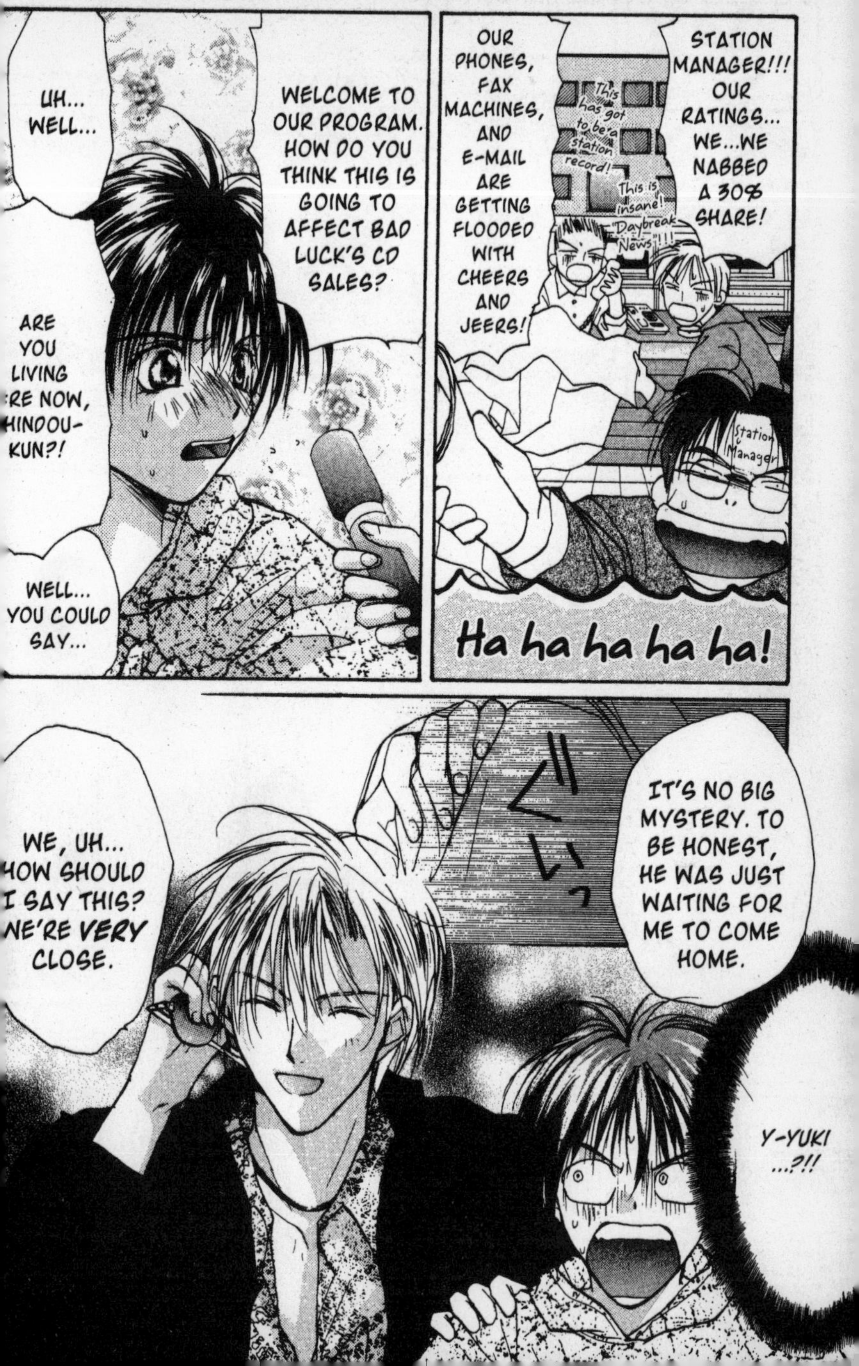
STATION MANAGER!!! OUR RATINGS... WE...WE NABBED A 30% SHARE!
This has got to be a station record!
This is insane! "Daybreak News"!!!
OUR PHONES, FAX MACHINES, AND E-MAIL ARE GETTING FLOODED WITH CHEERS AND JEERS!
Station Manager
Ha ha ha ha ha!
WELCOME TO OUR PROGRAM. HOW DO YOU THINK THIS IS GOING TO AFFECT BAD LUCK'S CD SALES?
UH... WELL...
ARE YOU LIVING RE NOW, HINDOU-KUN?!
WELL... YOU COULD SAY...
IT'S NO BIG MYSTERY. TO BE HONEST, HE WAS JUST WAITING FOR ME TO COME HOME.
WE, UH... OW SHOULD I SAY THIS? E'RE VERY CLOSE.
Y-YUKI ...?!!

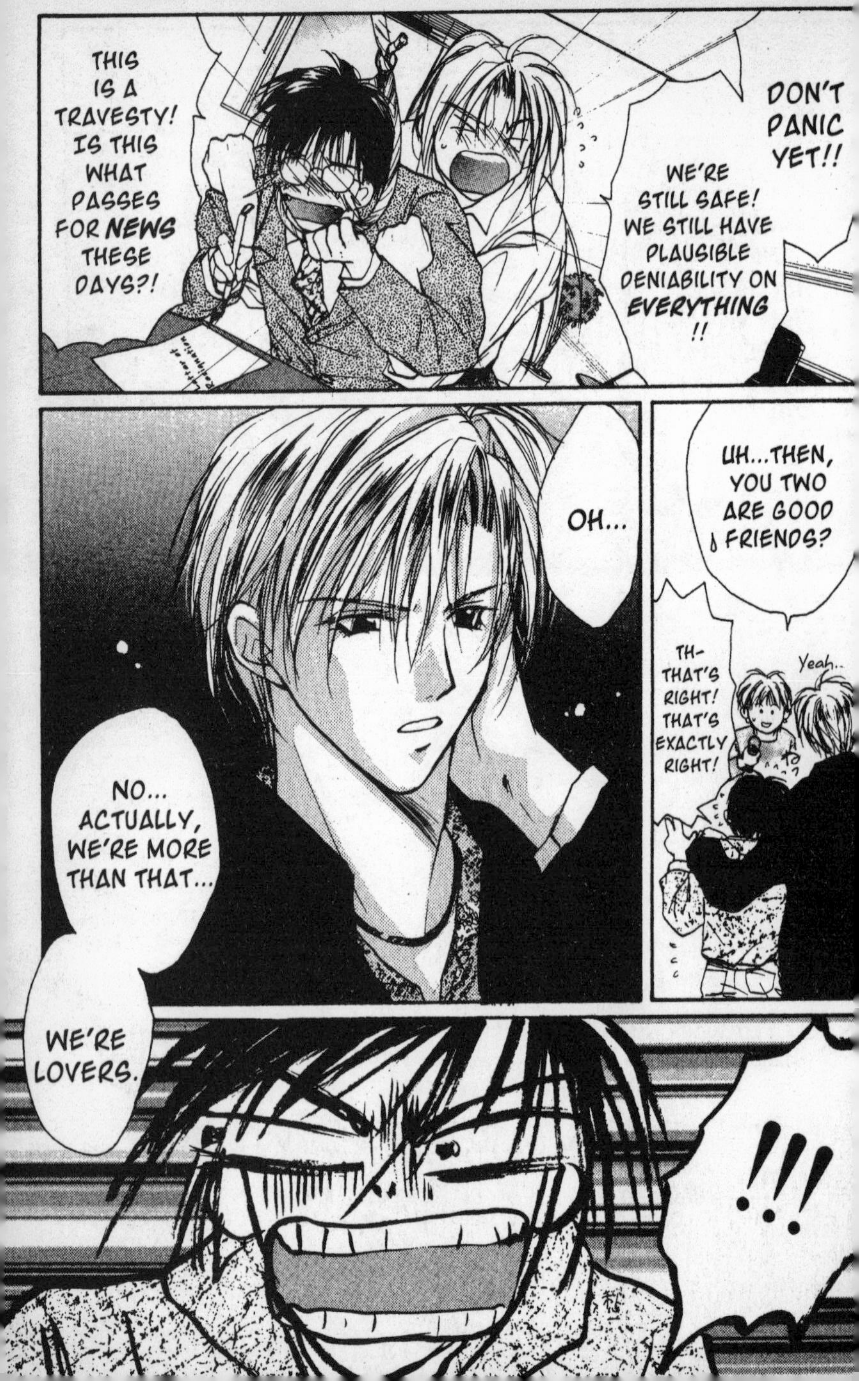
DON'T PANIC YET!!
WE'RE STILL SAFE! WE STILL HAVE PLAUSIBLE DENIABILITY ON EVERYTHING!!
THIS IS A TRAVESTY! IS THIS WHAT PASSES FOR NEWS THESE DAYS?!
UH...THEN, YOU TWO ARE GOOD FRIENDS?
TH-THAT'S RIGHT! THAT'S EXACTLY RIGHT!
Yeah..
OH...
NO... ACTUALLY, WE'RE MORE THAN THAT...
WE'RE LOVERS.
!!!

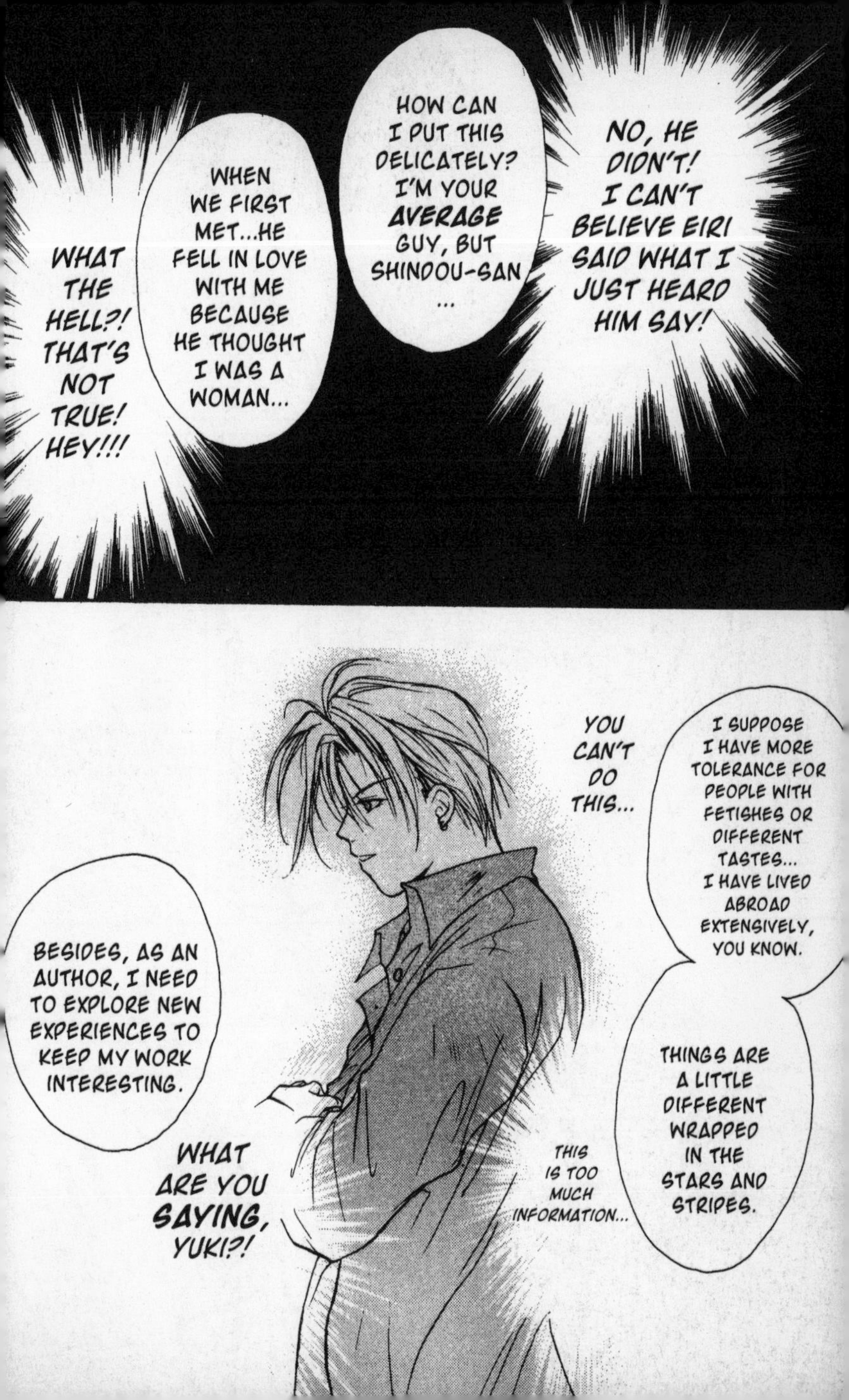
NO, HE DIDN'T! I CAN'T BELIEVE EIRI SAID WHAT I JUST HEARD HIM SAY!
HOW CAN I PUT THIS DELICATELY? I'M YOUR AVERAGE GUY, BUT SHINDOU-SAN ...
WHEN WE FIRST MET...HE FELL IN LOVE WITH ME BECAUSE HE THOUGHT I WAS A WOMAN...
WHAT THE HELL?! THAT'S NOT TRUE! HEY!!!
I SUPPOSE I HAVE MORE TOLERANCE FOR PEOPLE WITH FETISHES OR DIFFERENT TASTES... I HAVE LIVED ABROAD EXTENSIVELY, YOU KNOW.
YOU CAN'T DO THIS...
THINGS ARE A LITTLE DIFFERENT WRAPPED IN THE STARS AND STRIPES.
THIS IS TOO MUCH INFORMATION...
BESIDES, AS AN AUTHOR, I NEED TO EXPLORE NEW EXPERIENCES TO KEEP MY WORK INTERESTING.
WHAT ARE YOU SAYING, YUKI?!

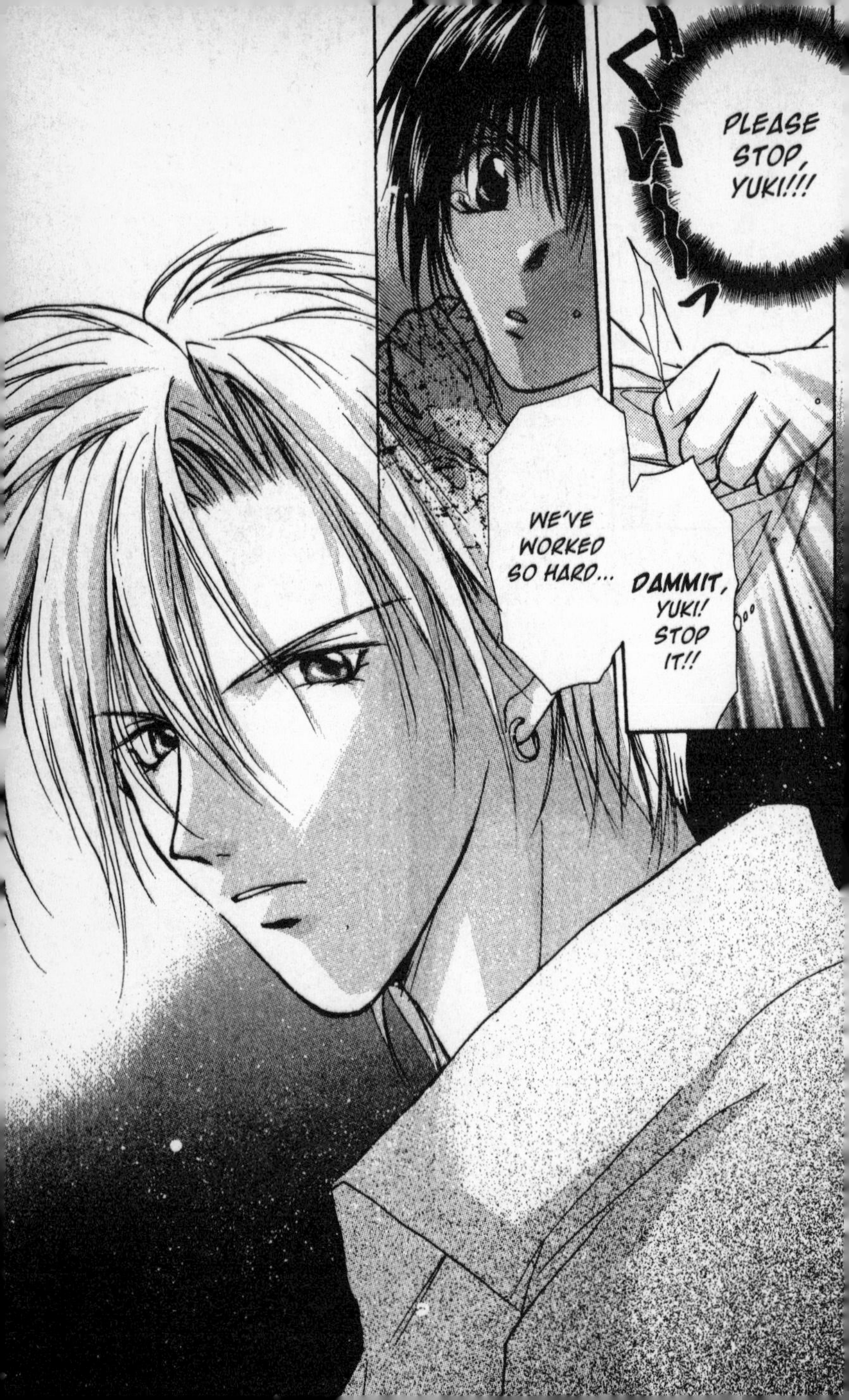
PLEASE STOP, YUKI!!!
DAMMIT, YUKI! STOP IT!!
WE'VE WORKED SO HARD...

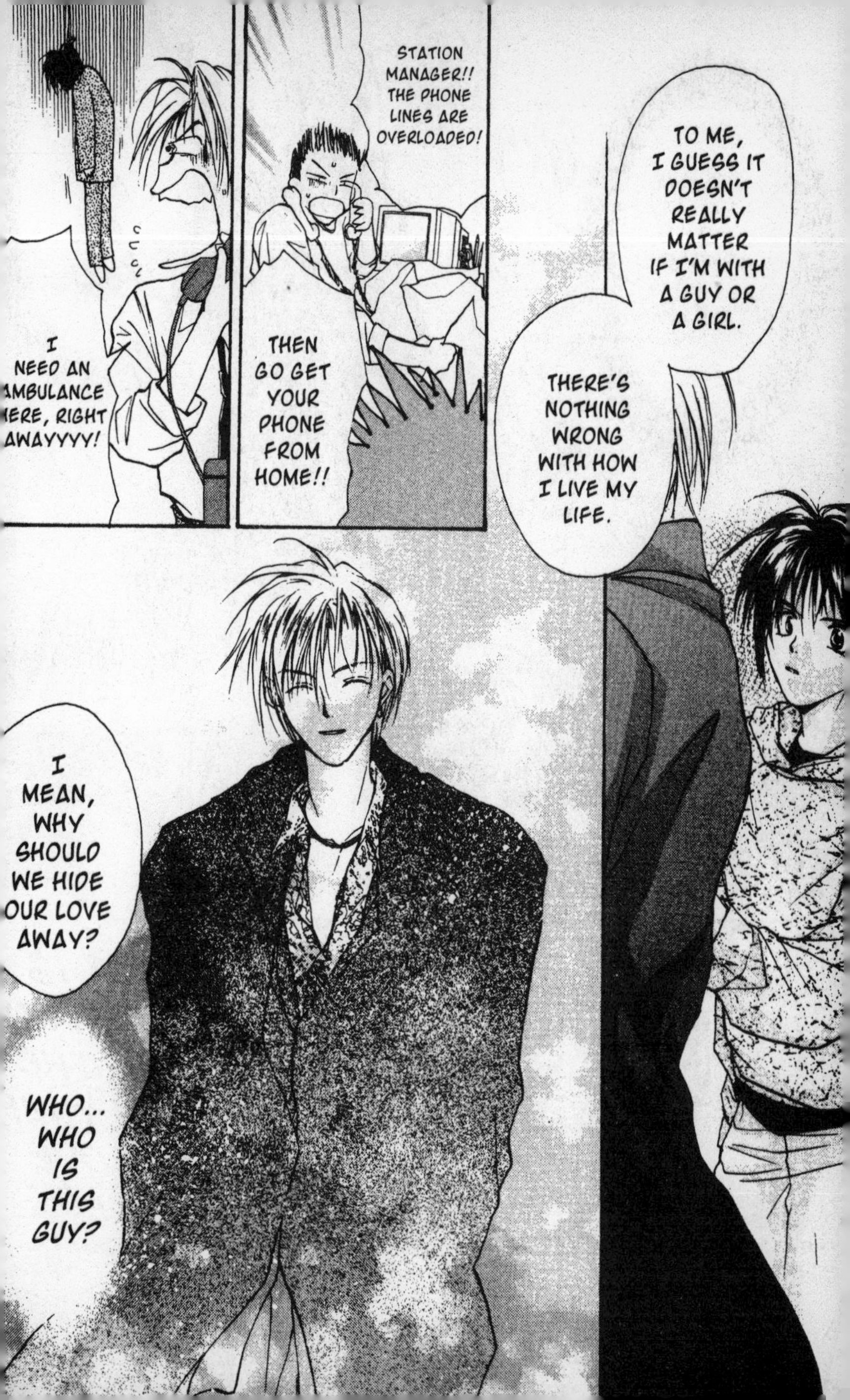
TO ME, I GUESS IT DOESN'T REALLY MATTER IF I'M WITH A GUY OR A GIRL.
THERE'S NOTHING WRONG WITH HOW I LIVE MY LIFE.
STATION MANAGER!! THE PHONE LINES ARE OVERLOADED!
THEN GO GET YOUR PHONE FROM HOME!!
I NEED AN AMBULANCE HERE, RIGHT AWAYYYY!
I MEAN, WHY SHOULD WE HIDE OUR LOVE AWAY?
WHO... WHO IS THIS GUY?

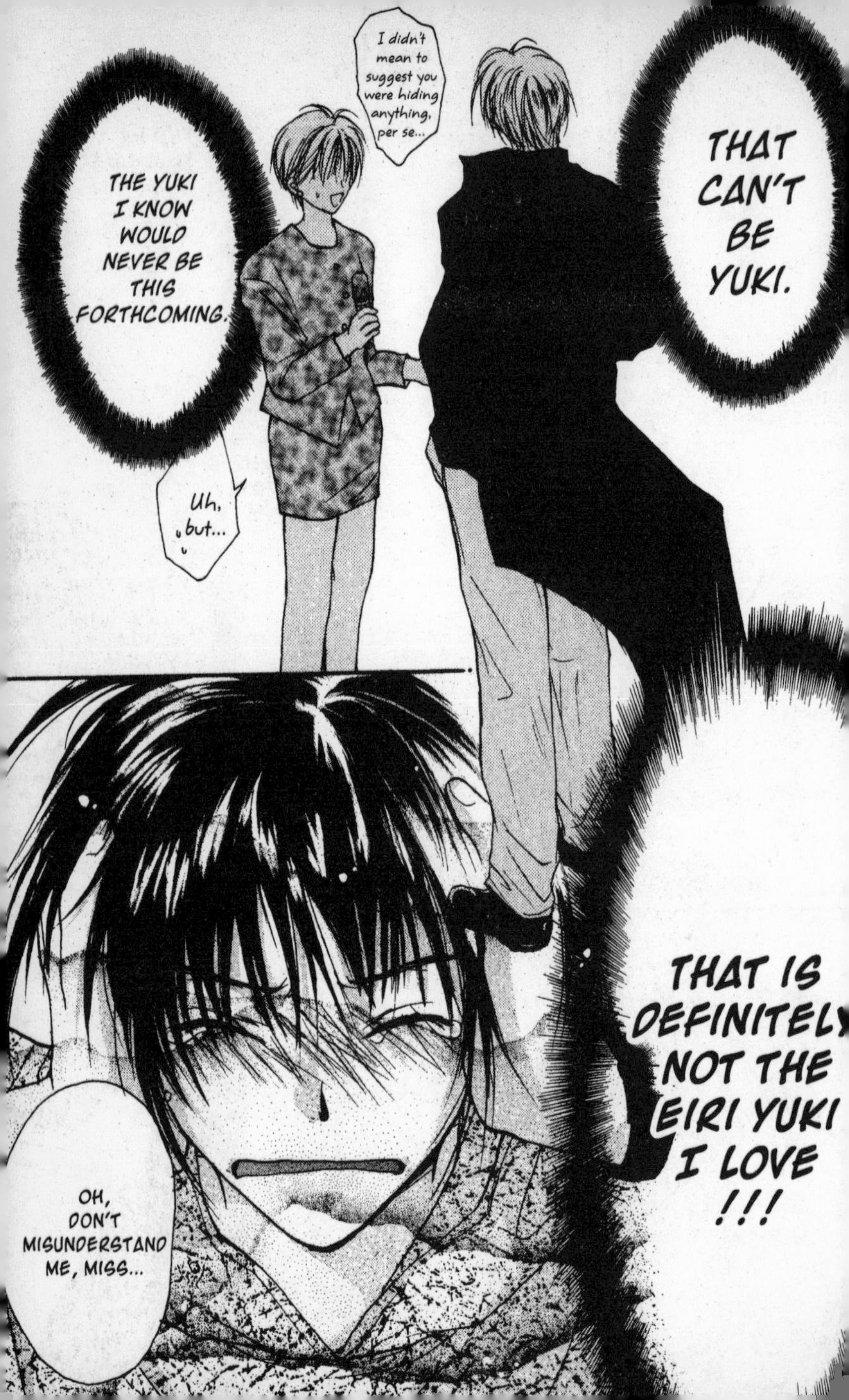

THAT CAN'T BE YUKI.
I didn't mean to suggest you were hiding anything, per se...
THE YUKI I KNOW WOULD NEVER BE THIS FORTHCOMING.
Uh, but...
THAT IS DEFINITELY NOT THE EIRI YUKI I LOVE !!!
OH, DON'T MISUNDERSTAND ME, MISS...

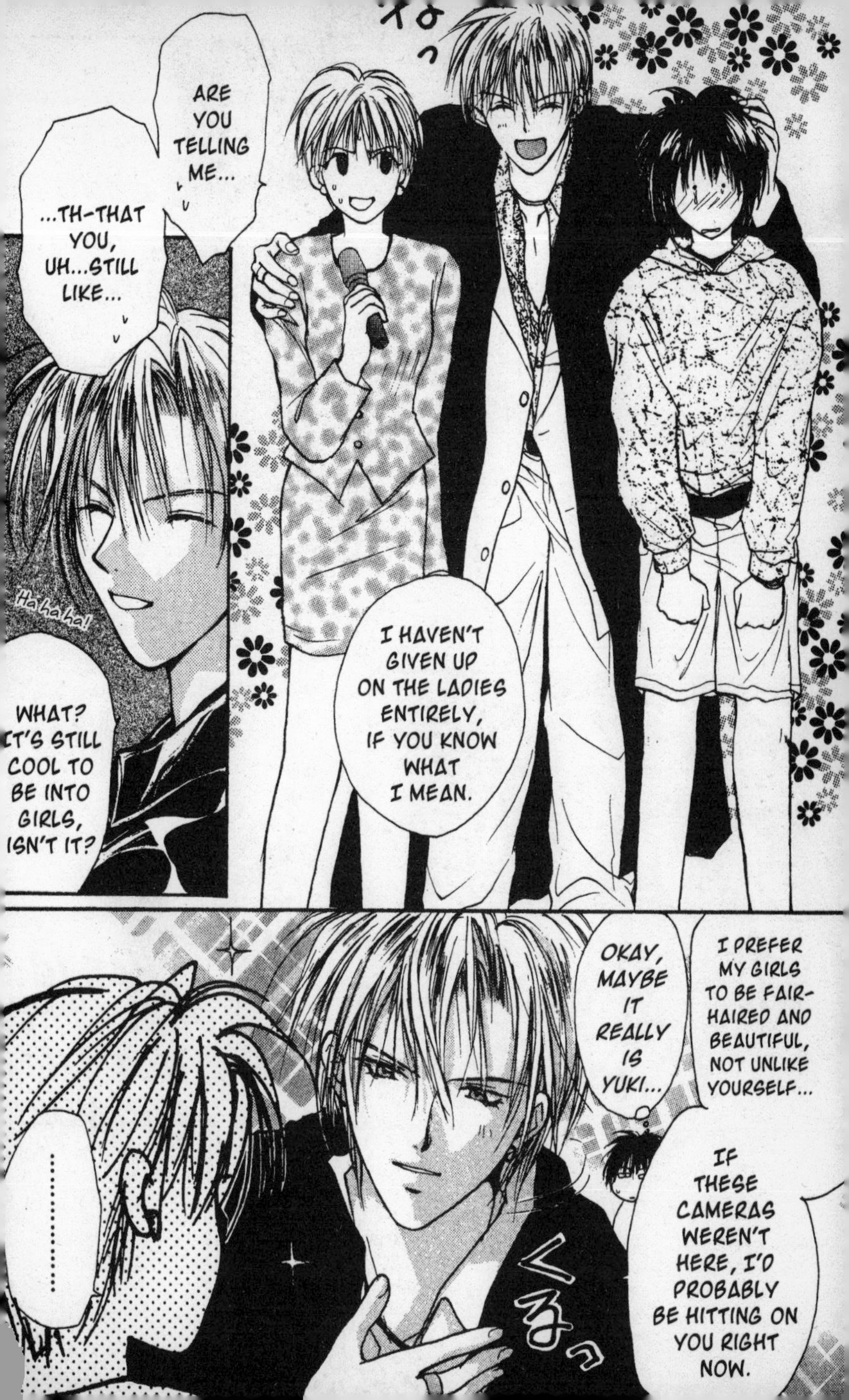
ARE YOU TELLING ME...
...TH-THAT YOU, UH...STILL LIKE...
I HAVEN'T GIVEN UP ON THE LADIES ENTIRELY, IF YOU KNOW WHAT I MEAN.
Ha ha ha!
WHAT? IT'S STILL COOL TO BE INTO GIRLS, ISN'T IT?
I PREFER MY GIRLS TO BE FAIR-HAIRED AND BEAUTIFUL, NOT UNLIKE YOURSELF...
OKAY, MAYBE IT REALLY IS YUKI...
IF THESE CAMERAS WEREN'T HERE, I'D PROBABLY BE HITTING ON YOU RIGHT NOW.
......

ABOUT GRAVITATION TRACK 26!

In every episode of Gravitation, we've been walking the will-he-or-won't-he tightrope. For Track 26, I can only say that something must have happened to our beloved Murakami. What can she be thinking? I can't really say too much at this point, but well...I'm sure this is one of those, "I'm not sure about this..." situations...
This is what happens when you start drawing a manga without thinking about where you're going. But this mafia look on Eiri is definitely coming into its own.
Then again, I'm not sure about this...

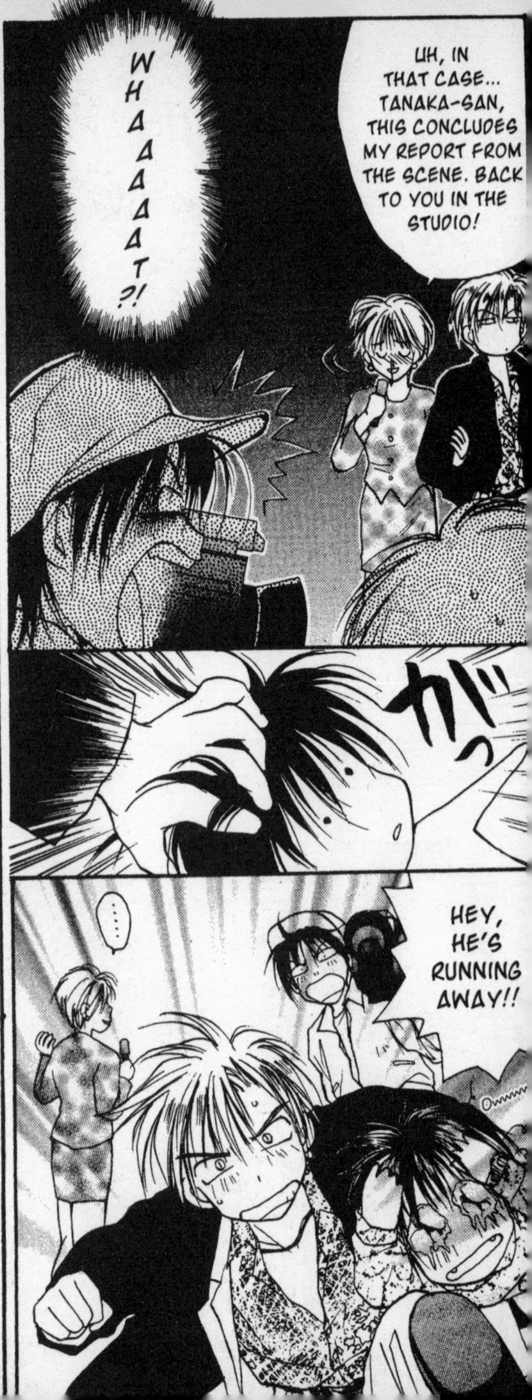
UH, IN THAT CASE... TANAKA-SAN, THIS CONCLUDES MY REPORT FROM THE SCENE. BACK TO YOU IN THE STUDIO!
WHAAAAAAT?!
ガッ
HEY, HE'S RUNNING AWAY!!
......
Owwww

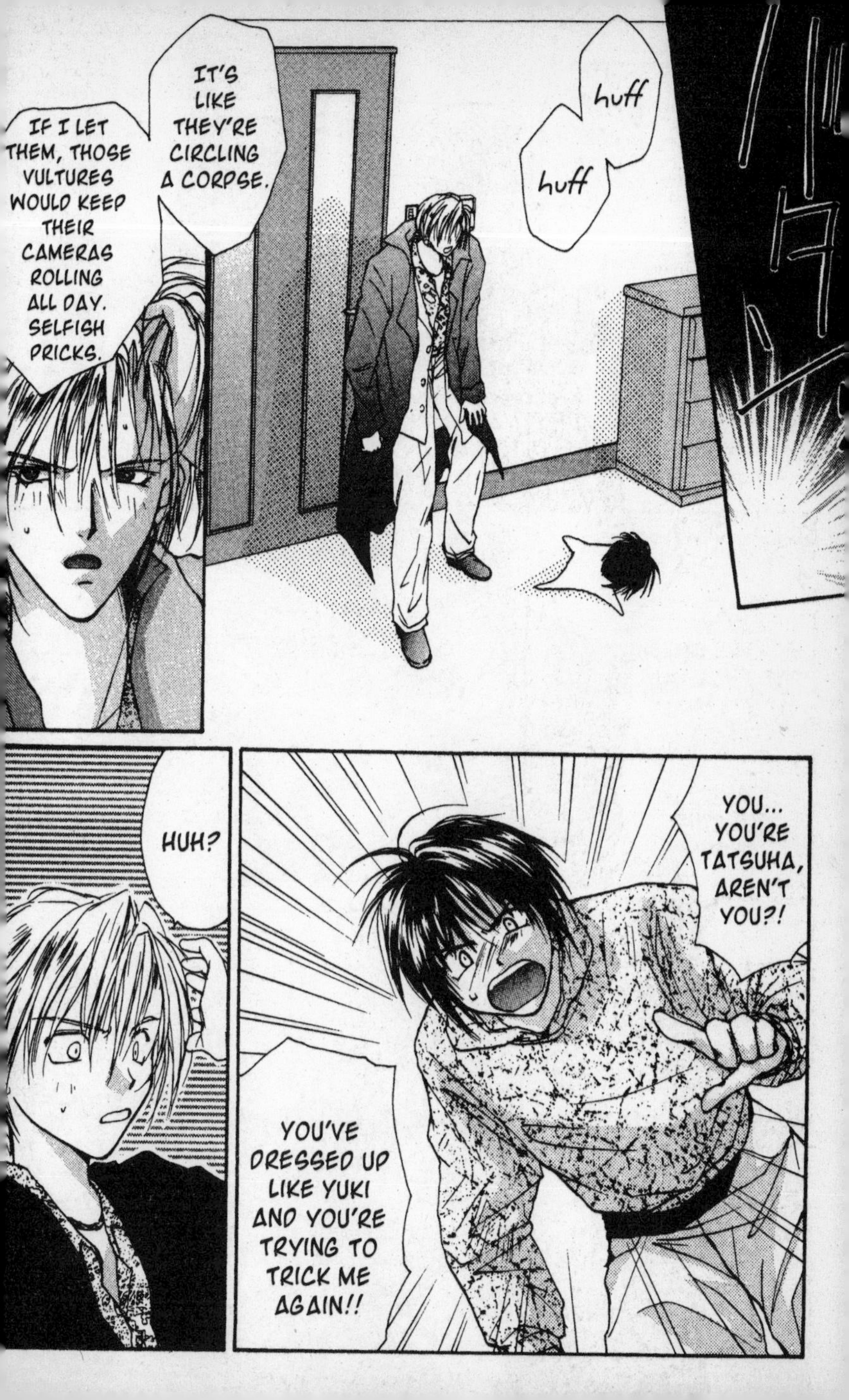
huff
huff
IT'S LIKE THEY'RE CIRCLING A CORPSE.
IF I LET THEM, THOSE VULTURES WOULD KEEP THEIR CAMERAS ROLLING ALL DAY. SELFISH PRICKS.
YOU... YOU'RE TATSUHA, AREN'T YOU?!
YOU'VE DRESSED UP LIKE YUKI AND YOU'RE TRYING TO TRICK ME AGAIN!!
HUH?

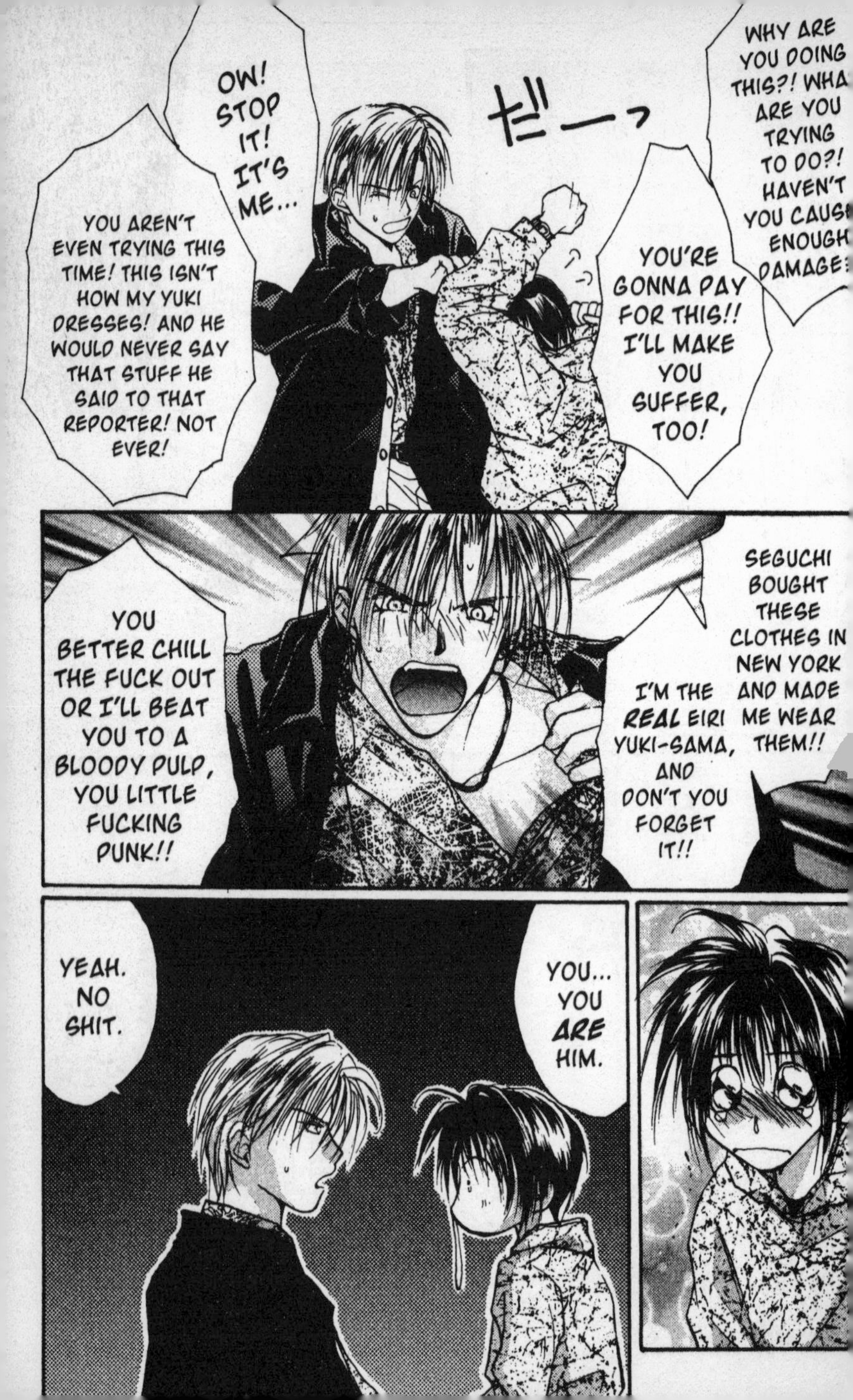
WHY ARE YOU DOING THIS?! WHA ARE YOU TRYING TO DO?! HAVEN'T YOU CAUS ENOUGH DAMAGE
YOU'RE GONNA PAY FOR THIS!! I'LL MAKE YOU SUFFER, TOO!
だーっ
OW! STOP IT! IT'S ME...
YOU AREN'T EVEN TRYING THIS TIME! THIS ISN'T HOW MY YUKI DRESSES! AND HE WOULD NEVER SAY THAT STUFF HE SAID TO THAT REPORTER! NOT EVER!
SEGUCHI BOUGHT THESE CLOTHES IN NEW YORK AND MADE ME WEAR THEM!!
I'M THE REAL EIRI YUKI-SAMA, AND DON'T YOU FORGET IT!!
YOU BETTER CHILL THE FUCK OUT OR I'LL BEAT YOU TO A BLOODY PULP, YOU LITTLE FUCKING PUNK!!
YOU... YOU ARE HIM.
YEAH. NO SHIT.

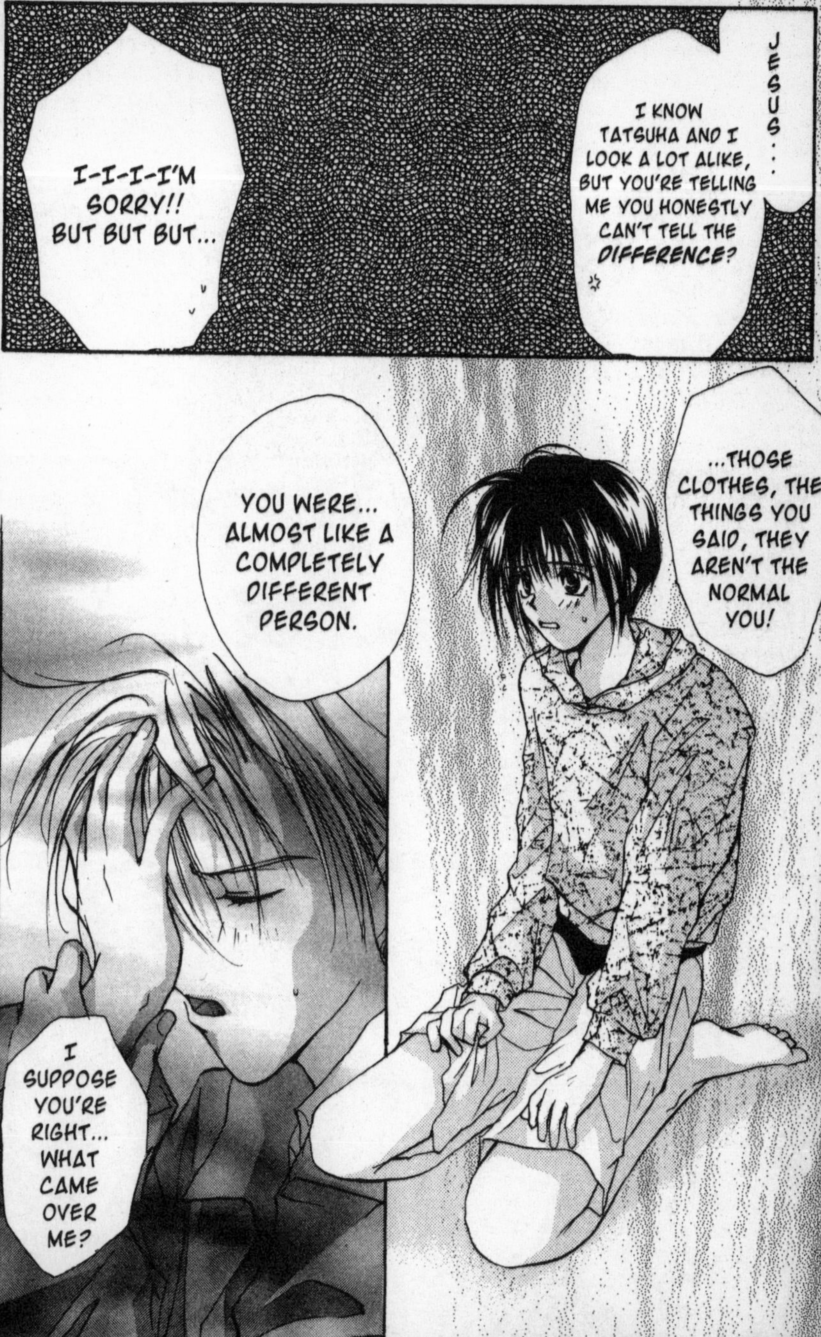
JESUS...
I KNOW TATSUHA AND I LOOK A LOT ALIKE, BUT YOU'RE TELLING ME YOU HONESTLY CAN'T TELL THE *DIFFERENCE?*
I-I-I-I'M SORRY!! BUT BUT BUT...
...THOSE CLOTHES, THE THINGS YOU SAID, THEY AREN'T THE NORMAL YOU!
YOU WERE... ALMOST LIKE A COMPLETELY DIFFERENT PERSON.
I SUPPOSE YOU'RE RIGHT... WHAT CAME OVER ME?

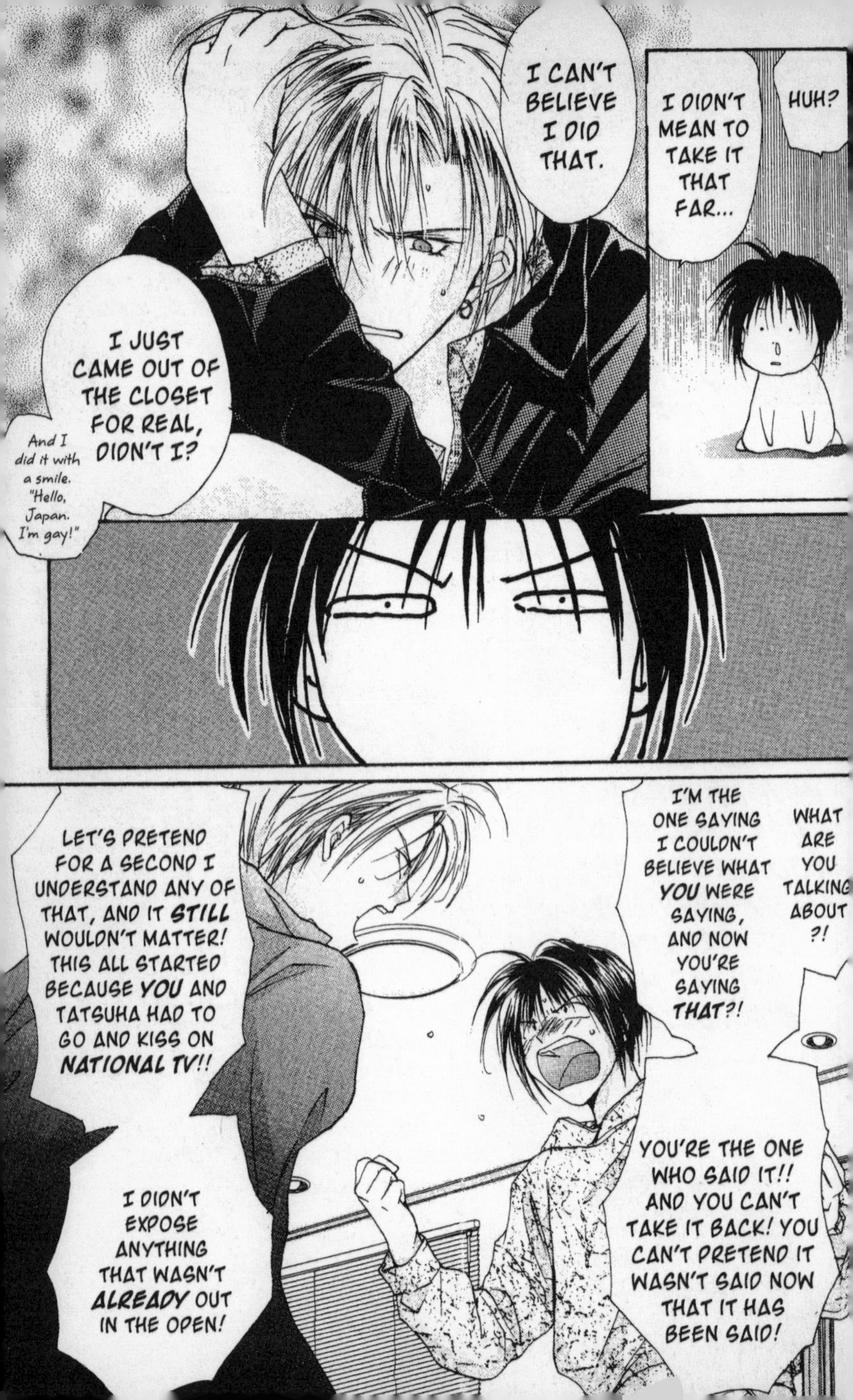

HUH?
I DIDN'T MEAN TO TAKE IT THAT FAR...
I CAN'T BELIEVE I DID THAT.
I JUST CAME OUT OF THE CLOSET FOR REAL, DIDN'T I?
And I did it with a smile. "Hello, Japan. I'm gay!"
WHAT ARE YOU TALKING ABOUT?!
I'M THE ONE SAYING I COULDN'T BELIEVE WHAT YOU WERE SAYING, AND NOW YOU'RE SAYING THAT?!
LET'S PRETEND FOR A SECOND I UNDERSTAND ANY OF THAT, AND IT STILL WOULDN'T MATTER! THIS ALL STARTED BECAUSE YOU AND TATSUHA HAD TO GO AND KISS ON NATIONAL TV!!
YOU'RE THE ONE WHO SAID IT!! AND YOU CAN'T TAKE IT BACK! YOU CAN'T PRETEND IT WASN'T SAID NOW THAT IT HAS BEEN SAID!
I DIDN'T EXPOSE ANYTHING THAT WASN'T ALREADY OUT IN THE OPEN!

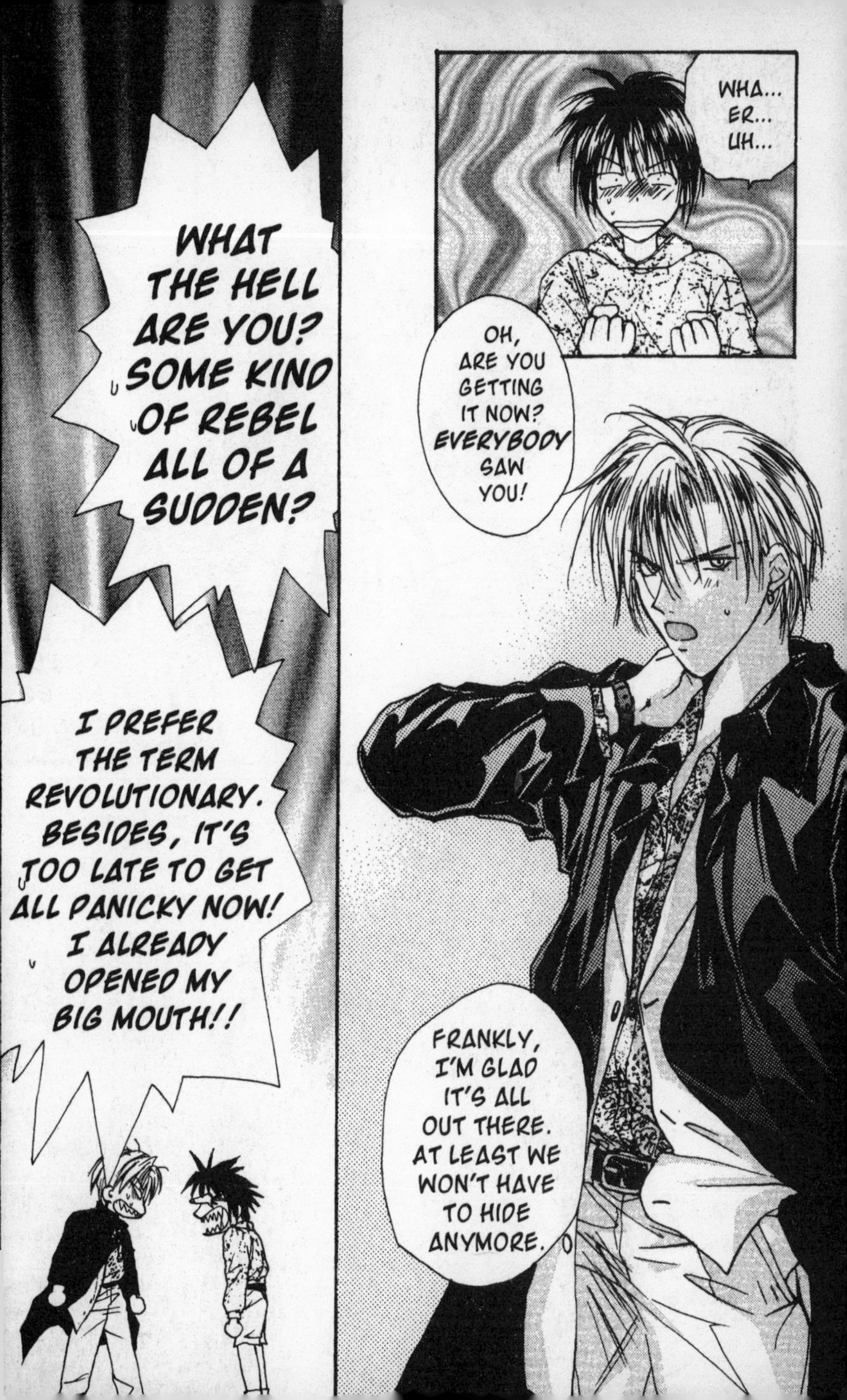
WHA... ER... UH...
OH, ARE YOU GETTING IT NOW? EVERYBODY SAW YOU!
FRANKLY, I'M GLAD IT'S ALL OUT THERE. AT LEAST WE WON'T HAVE TO HIDE ANYMORE.
WHAT THE HELL ARE YOU? SOME KIND OF REBEL ALL OF A SUDDEN?
I PREFER THE TERM REVOLUTIONARY. BESIDES, IT'S TOO LATE TO GET ALL PANICKY NOW! I ALREADY OPENED MY BIG MOUTH!!

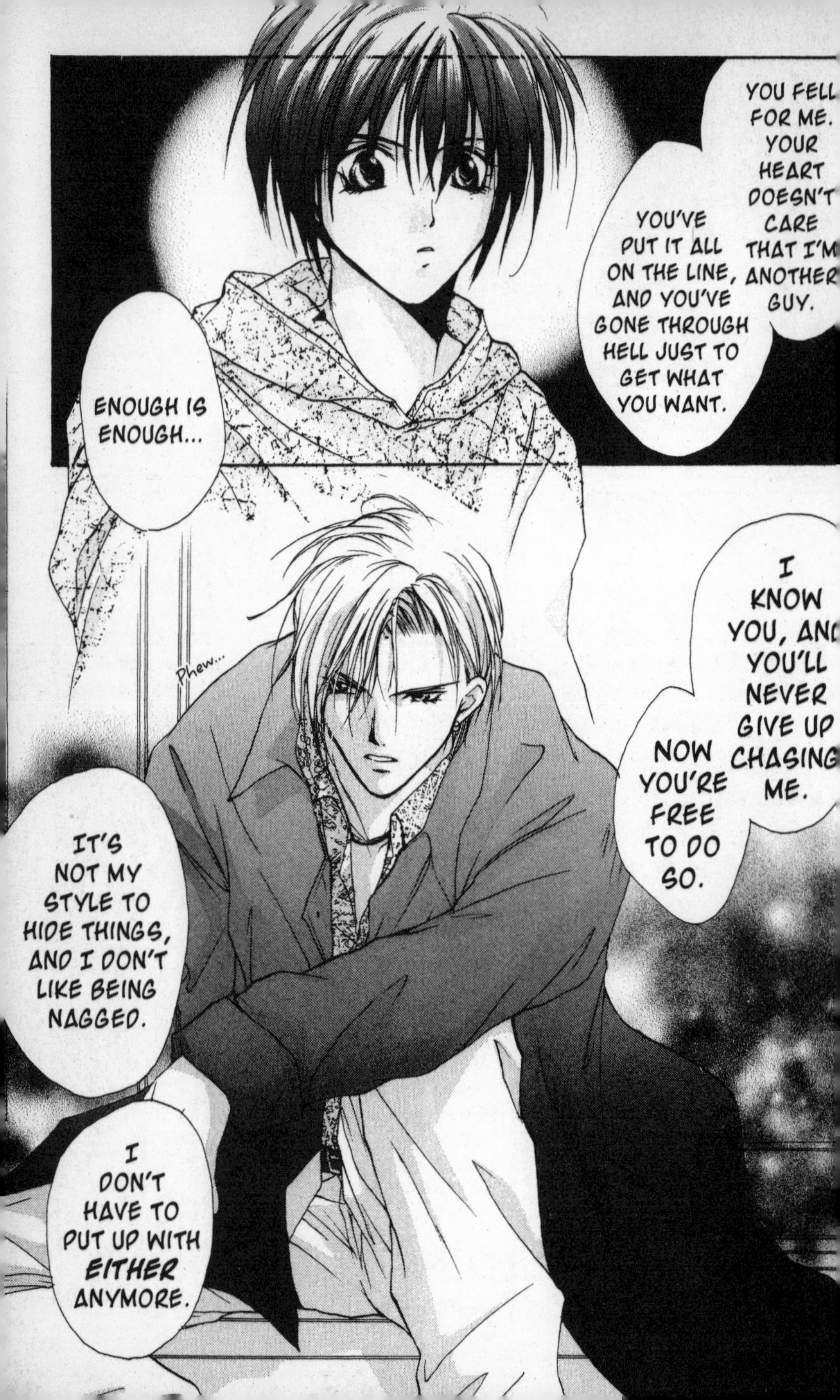
YOU FELL FOR ME. YOUR HEART DOESN'T CARE THAT I'M ANOTHER GUY.
YOU'VE PUT IT ALL ON THE LINE, AND YOU'VE GONE THROUGH HELL JUST TO GET WHAT YOU WANT.
ENOUGH IS ENOUGH...
I KNOW YOU, AN
YOU'LL NEVER GIVE UP CHASING ME.
NOW YOU'RE FREE TO DO SO.
Phew...
IT'S NOT MY STYLE TO HIDE THINGS, AND I DON'T LIKE BEING NAGGED.
I DON'T HAVE TO PUT UP WITH *EITHER* ANYMORE.

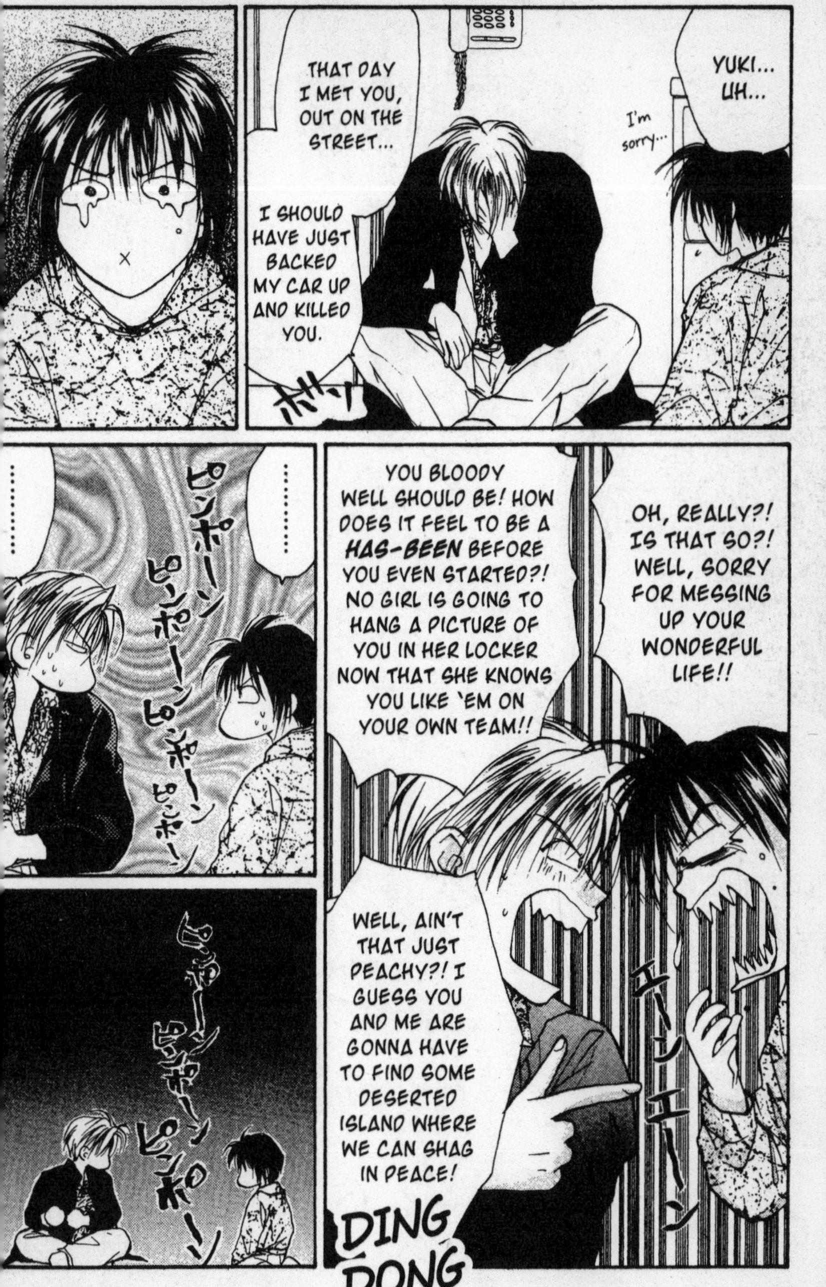
YUKI... UH...
I'm sorry...
THAT DAY I MET YOU, OUT ON THE STREET...
I SHOULD HAVE JUST BACKED MY CAR UP AND KILLED YOU.
OH, REALLY?! IS THAT SO?! WELL, SORRY FOR MESSING UP YOUR WONDERFUL LIFE!!
YOU BLOODY WELL SHOULD BE! HOW DOES IT FEEL TO BE A ***HAS-BEEN*** BEFORE YOU EVEN STARTED?! NO GIRL IS GOING TO HANG A PICTURE OF YOU IN HER LOCKER NOW THAT SHE KNOWS YOU LIKE 'EM ON YOUR OWN TEAM!!
WELL, AIN'T THAT JUST PEACHY?! I GUESS YOU AND ME ARE GONNA HAVE TO FIND SOME DESERTED ISLAND WHERE WE CAN SHAG IN PEACE!
DING DONG
......
ピンポーン ピンポーン ピンポーン ピンポーン
ピンポーン ピンポーン ピンポーン

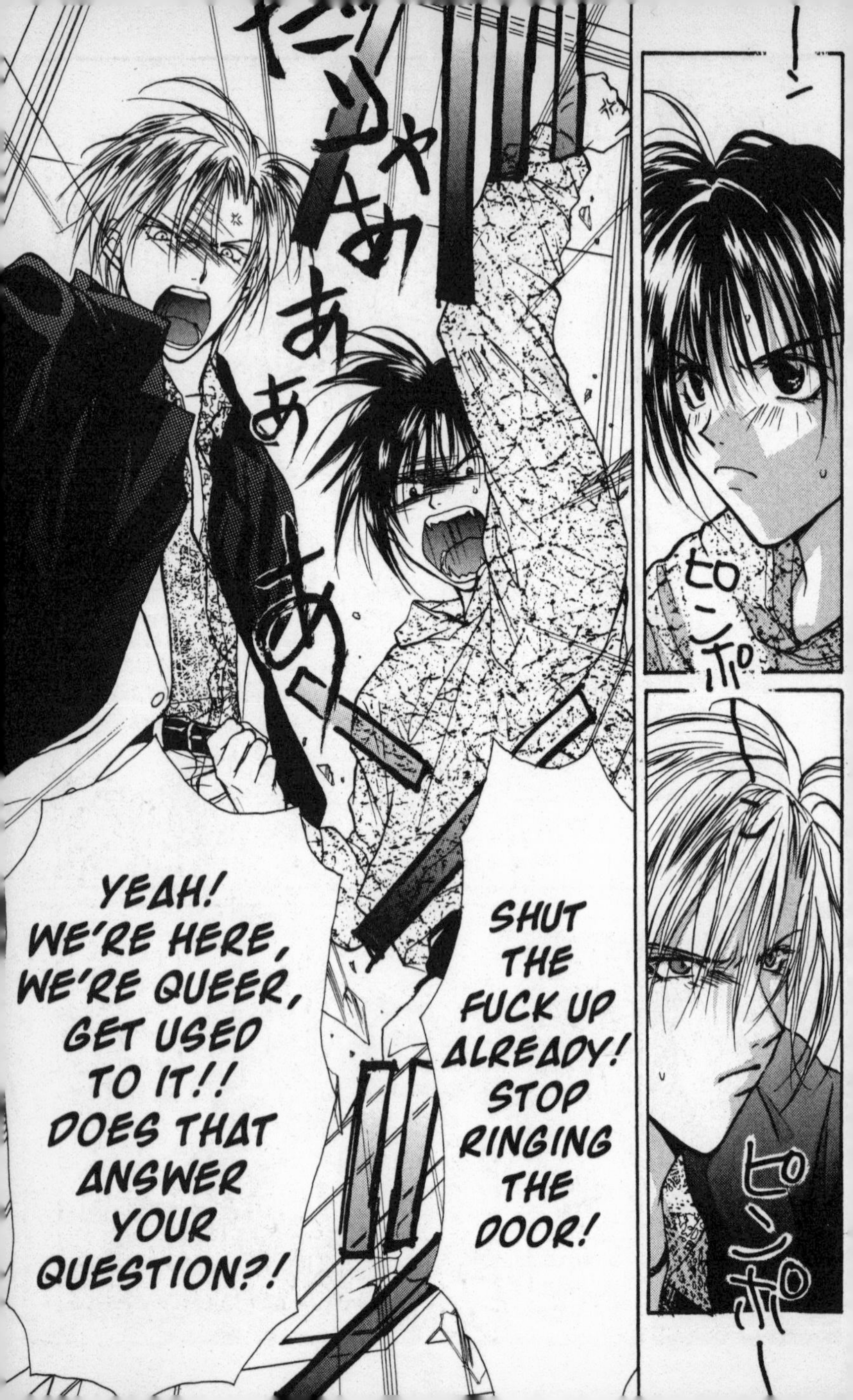

!
ピンポ
ピンポー
だりゃあああああー
SHUT THE FUCK UP ALREADY! STOP RINGING THE DOOR!
YEAH! WE'RE HERE, WE'RE QUEER, GET USED TO IT!! DOES THAT ANSWER YOUR QUESTION?!

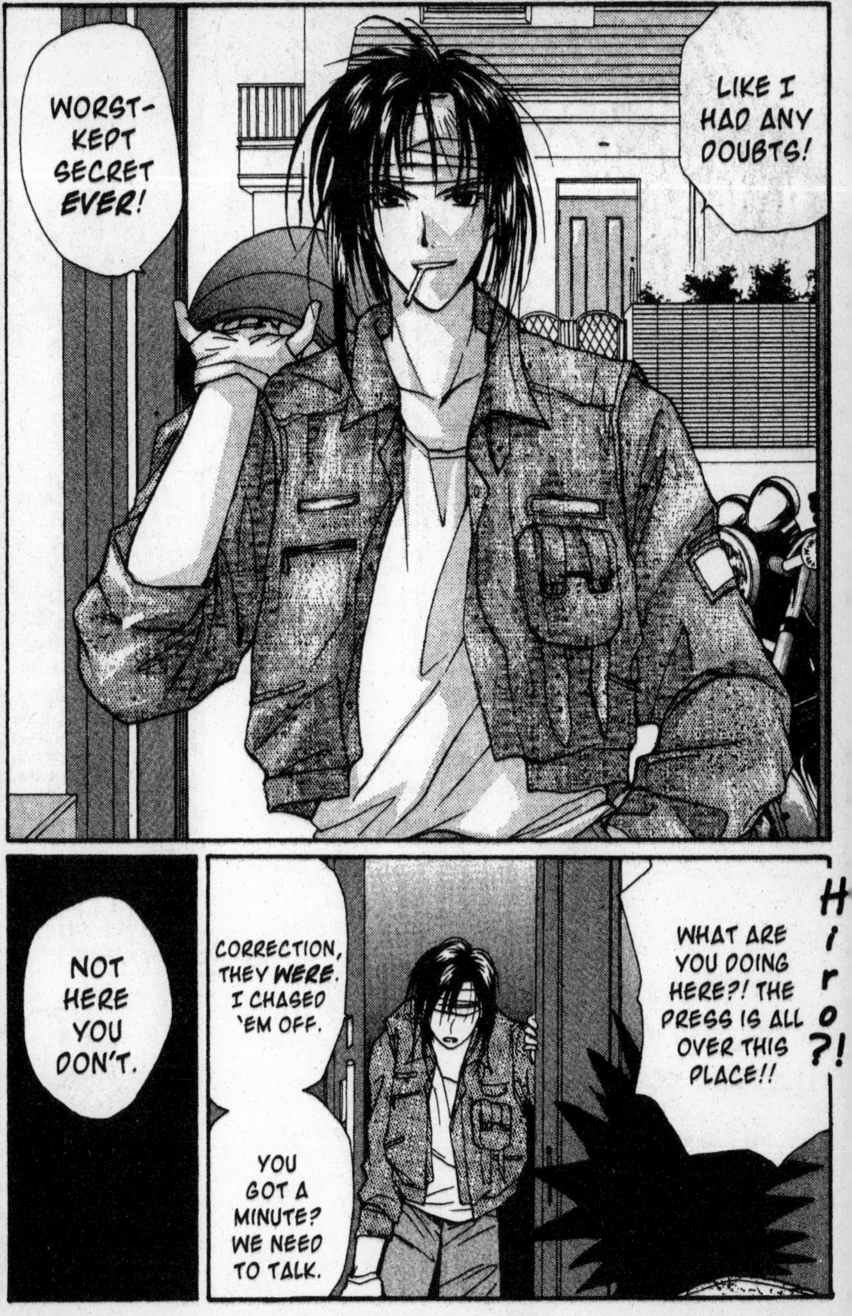
LIKE I HAD ANY DOUBTS!
WORST-KEPT SECRET EVER!
Hiro?!
WHAT ARE YOU DOING HERE?! THE PRESS IS ALL OVER THIS PLACE!!
CORRECTION, THEY WERE. I CHASED 'EM OFF.
YOU GOT A MINUTE? WE NEED TO TALK.
NOT HERE YOU DON'T.

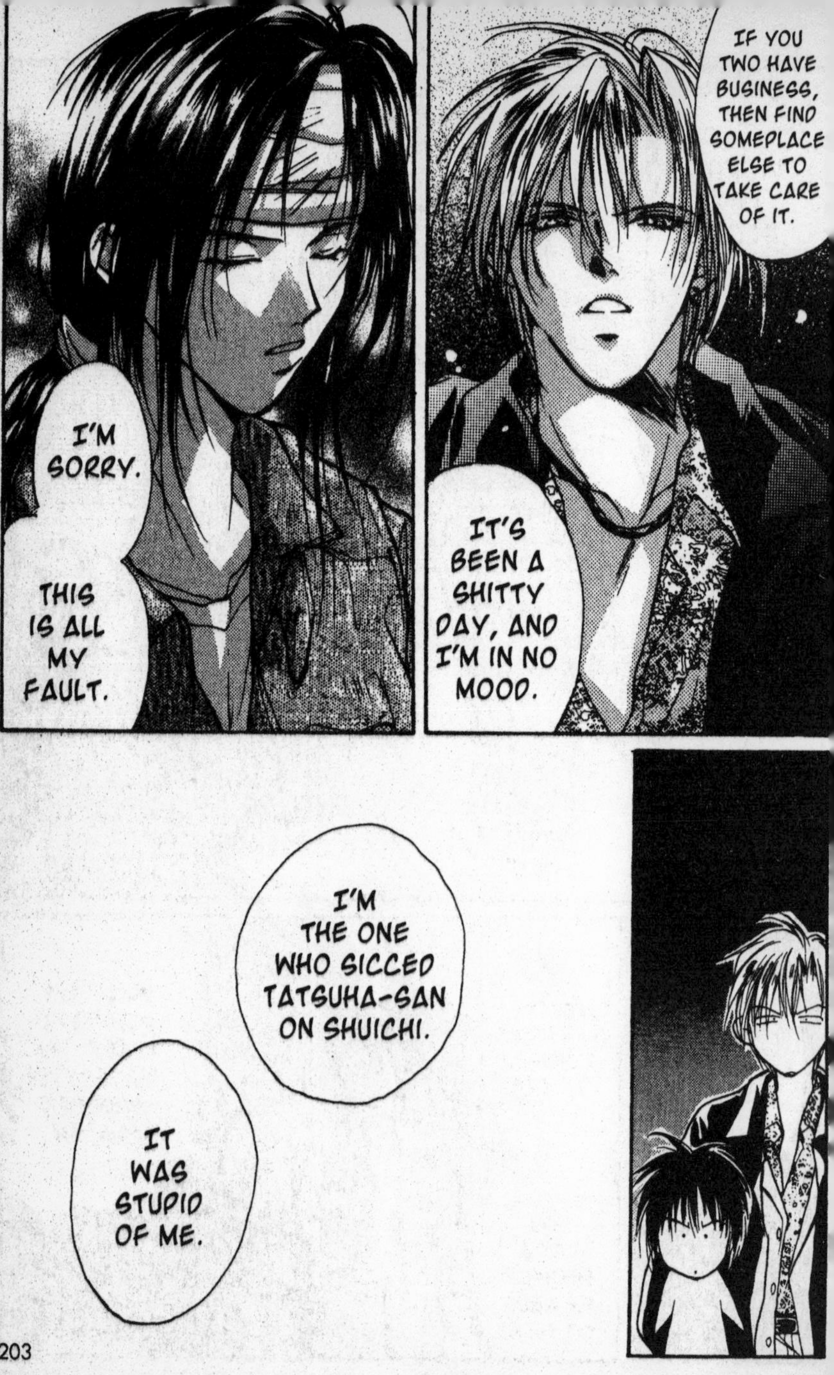
IF YOU TWO HAVE BUSINESS, THEN FIND SOMEPLACE ELSE TO TAKE CARE OF IT.
IT'S BEEN A SHITTY DAY, AND I'M IN NO MOOD.
I'M SORRY.
THIS IS ALL MY FAULT.
I'M THE ONE WHO SICCED TATSUHA-SAN ON SHUICHI.
IT WAS STUPID OF ME.

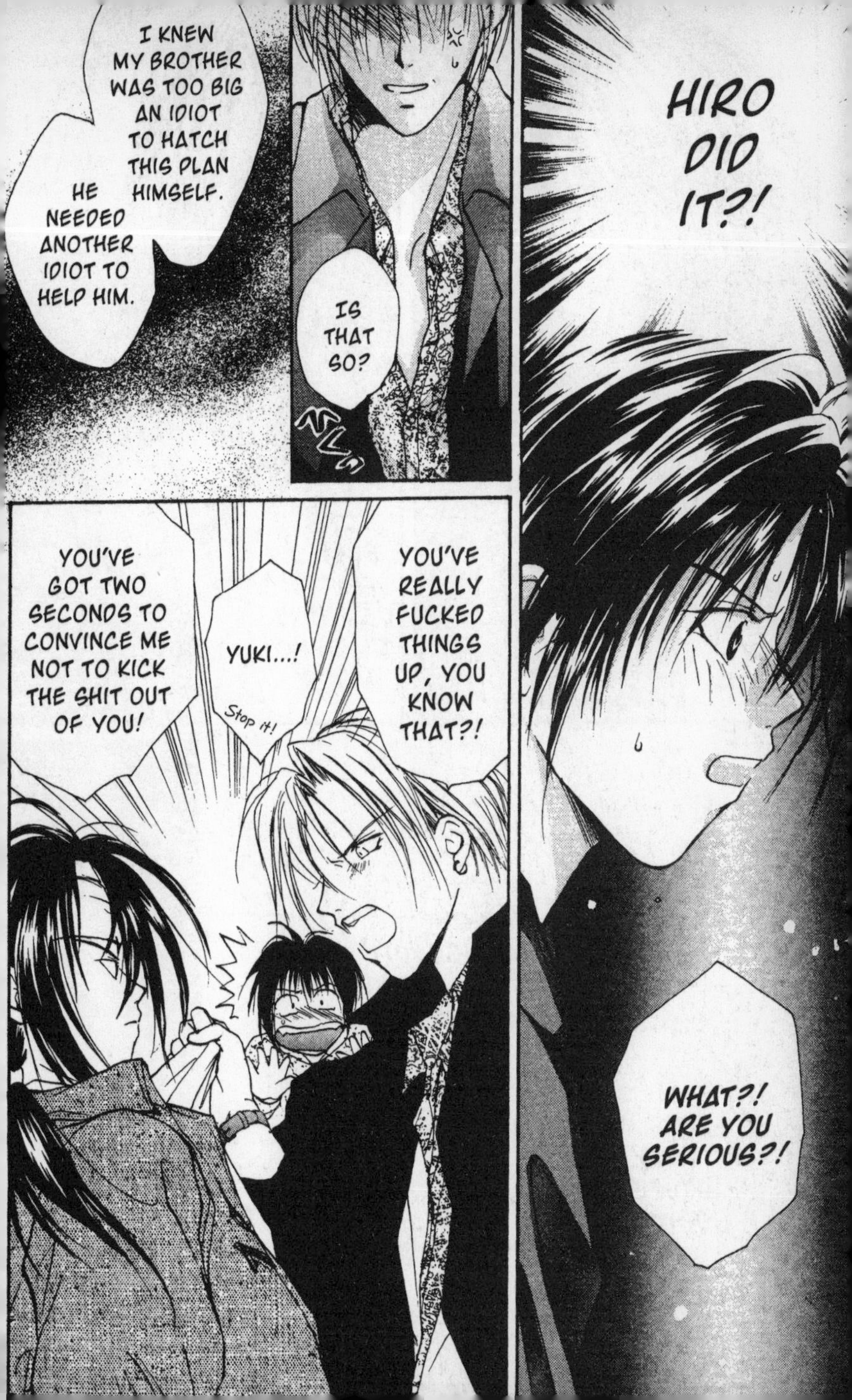
HIRO DID IT?!
WHAT?! ARE YOU SERIOUS?!
IS THAT SO?
I KNEW MY BROTHER WAS TOO BIG AN IDIOT TO HATCH THIS PLAN HIMSELF.
HE NEEDED ANOTHER IDIOT TO HELP HIM.
YOU'VE REALLY FUCKED THINGS UP, YOU KNOW THAT?!
YUKI...!
Stop it!
YOU'VE GOT TWO SECONDS TO CONVINCE ME NOT TO KICK THE SHIT OUT OF YOU!

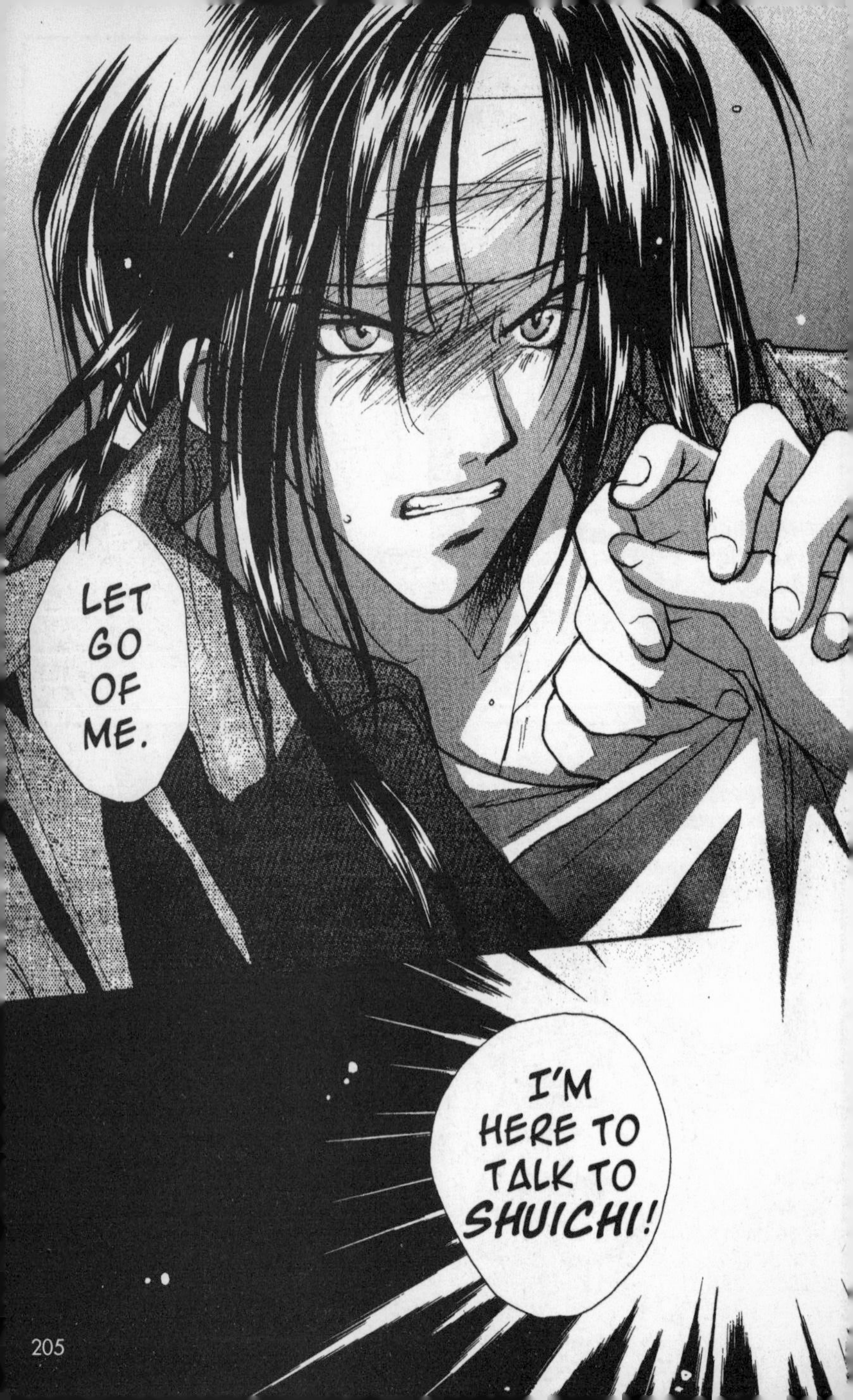
LET GO OF ME.
I'M HERE TO TALK TO SHUICHI!

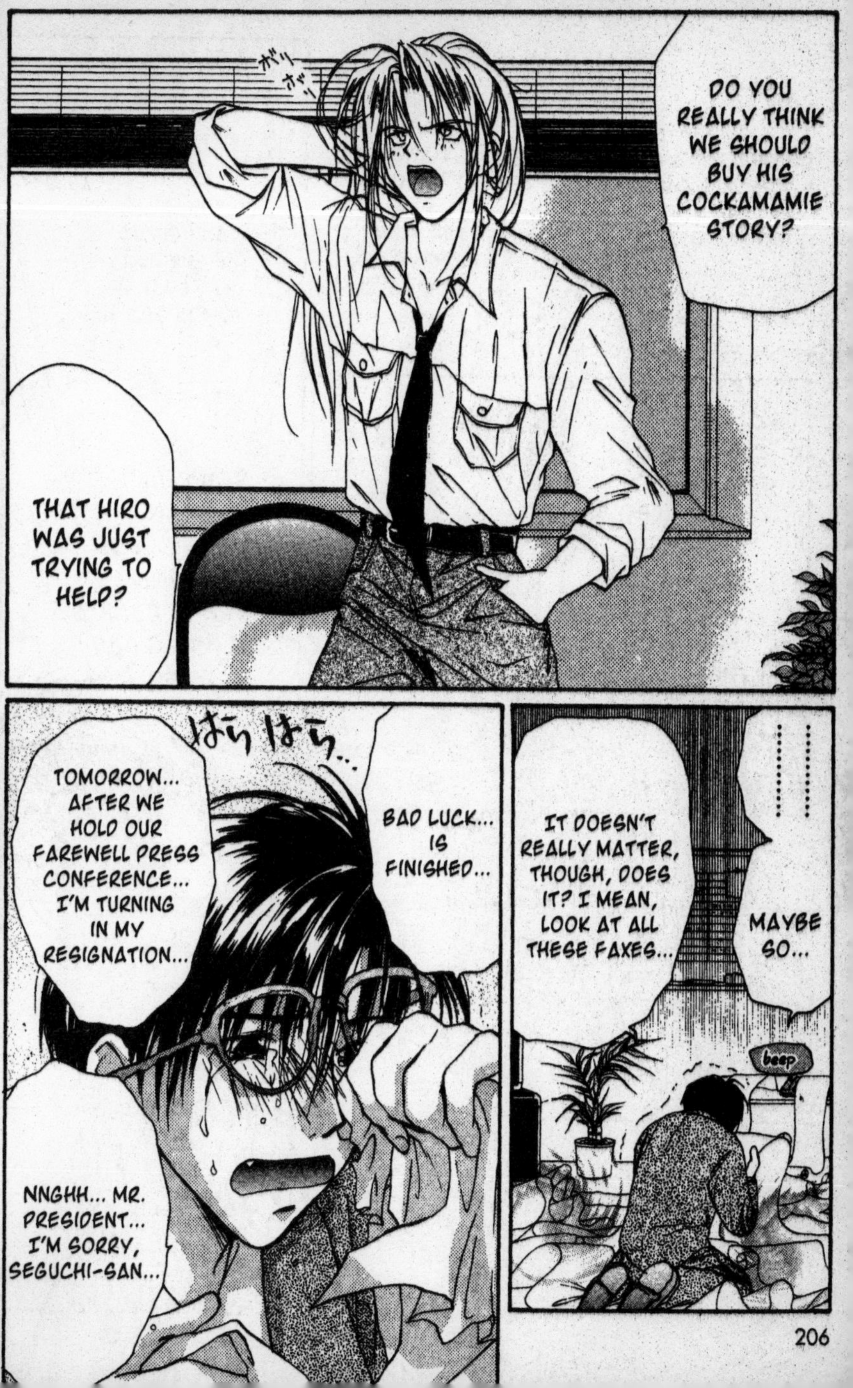
DO YOU REALLY THINK WE SHOULD BUY HIS COCKAMAMIE STORY?
THAT HIRO WAS JUST TRYING TO HELP?
...... MAYBE SO...
IT DOESN'T REALLY MATTER, THOUGH, DOES IT? I MEAN, LOOK AT ALL THESE FAXES...
beep
BAD LUCK... IS FINISHED...
はらはら...
TOMORROW... AFTER WE HOLD OUR FAREWELL PRESS CONFERENCE... I'M TURNING IN MY RESIGNATION...
NNGHH... MR. PRESIDENT... I'M SORRY, SEGUCHI-SAN...

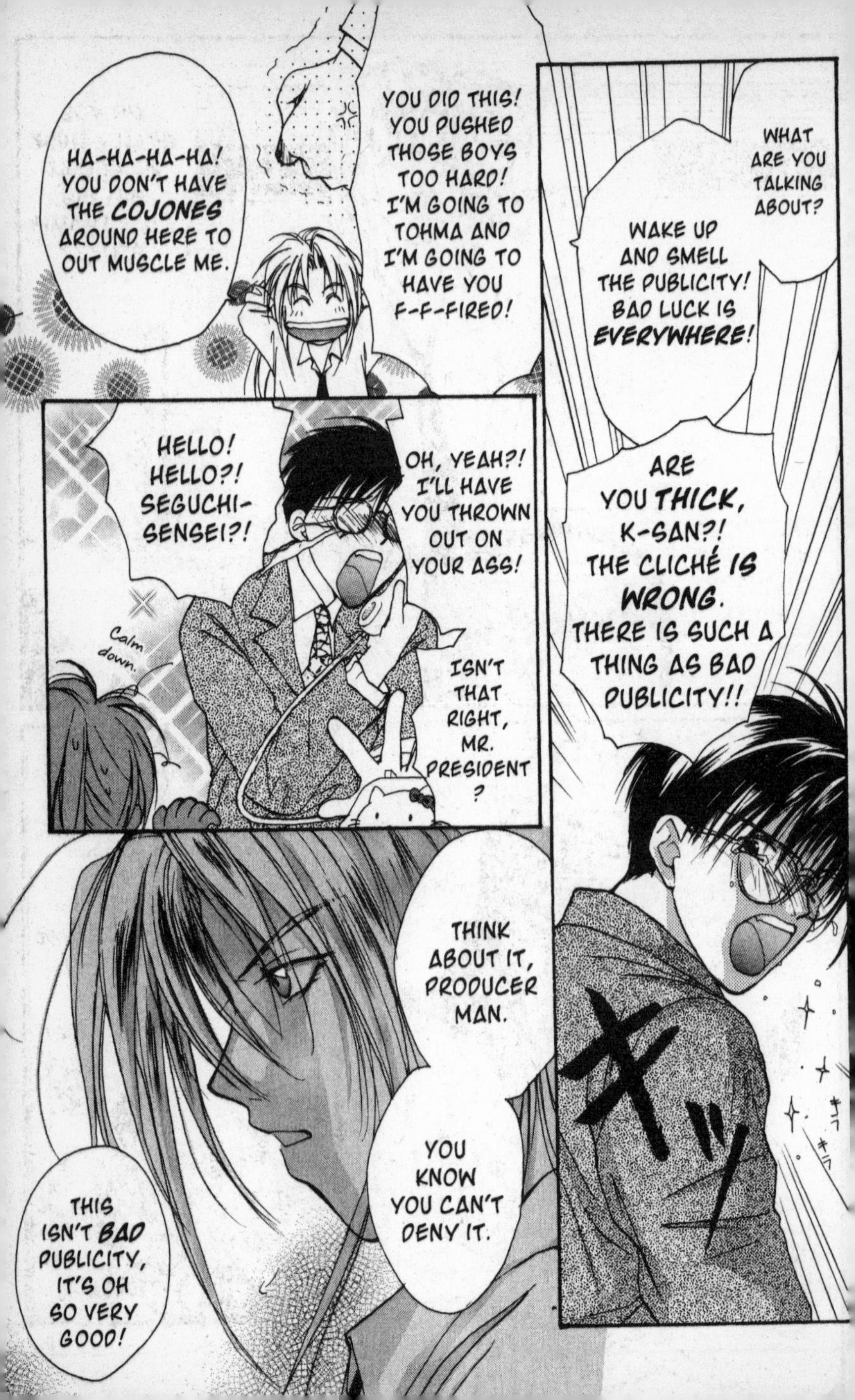
YOU DID THIS! YOU PUSHED THOSE BOYS TOO HARD! I'M GOING TO TOHMA AND I'M GOING TO HAVE YOU F-F-FIRED!
HA-HA-HA-HA! YOU DON'T HAVE THE COJONES AROUND HERE TO OUT MUSCLE ME.
OH, YEAH?! I'LL HAVE YOU THROWN OUT ON YOUR ASS!
HELLO! HELLO?! SEGUCHI-SENSEI?!
ISN'T THAT RIGHT, MR. PRESIDENT?
Calm down.
WHAT ARE YOU TALKING ABOUT?
WAKE UP AND SMELL THE PUBLICITY! BAD LUCK IS EVERYWHERE!
ARE YOU THICK, K-SAN?! THE CLICHÉ IS WRONG. THERE IS SUCH A THING AS BAD PUBLICITY!!
THINK ABOUT IT, PRODUCER MAN.
YOU KNOW YOU CAN'T DENY IT.
THIS ISN'T BAD PUBLICITY, IT'S OH SO VERY GOOD!

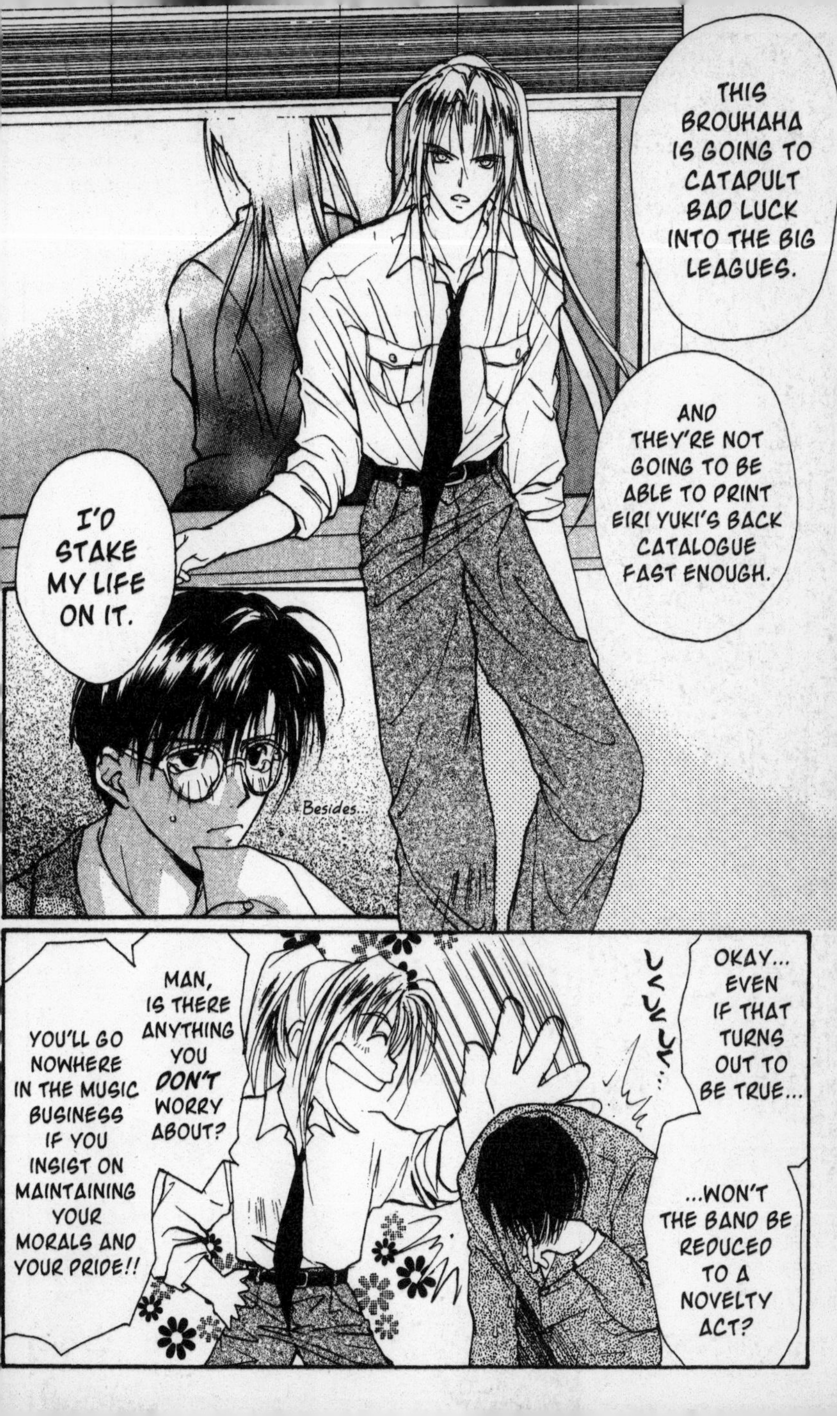
THIS BROUHAHA IS GOING TO CATAPULT BAD LUCK INTO THE BIG LEAGUES.
AND THEY'RE NOT GOING TO BE ABLE TO PRINT EIRI YUKI'S BACK CATALOGUE FAST ENOUGH.
I'D STAKE MY LIFE ON IT.
Besides...
OKAY... EVEN IF THAT TURNS OUT TO BE TRUE...
...WON'T THE BAND BE REDUCED TO A NOVELTY ACT?
MAN, IS THERE ANYTHING YOU *DON'T* WORRY ABOUT?
YOU'LL GO NOWHERE IN THE MUSIC BUSINESS IF YOU INSIST ON MAINTAINING YOUR MORALS AND YOUR PRIDE!!

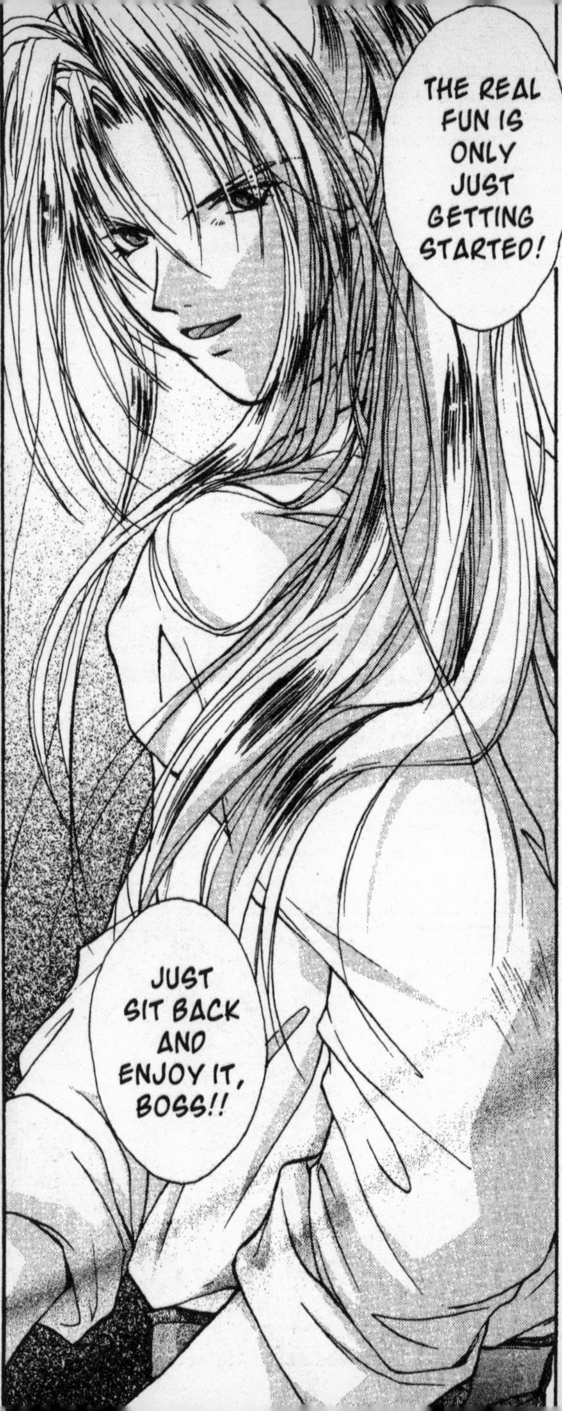
THE REAL FUN IS ONLY JUST GETTING STARTED!
JUST SIT BACK AND ENJOY IT, BOSS!!
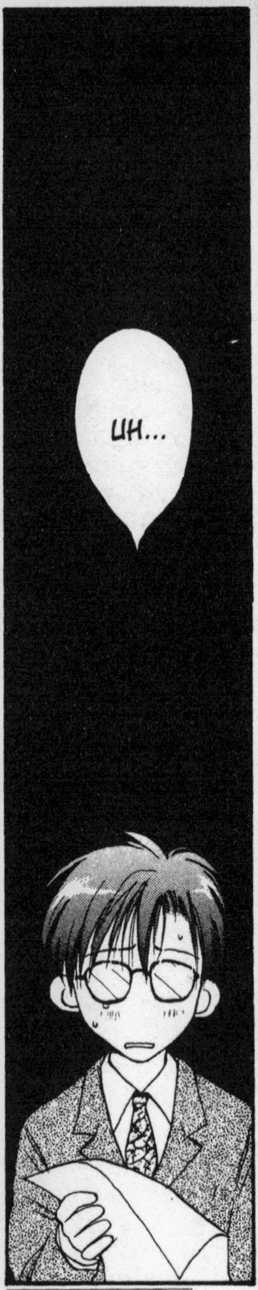
UH...

track26▶END

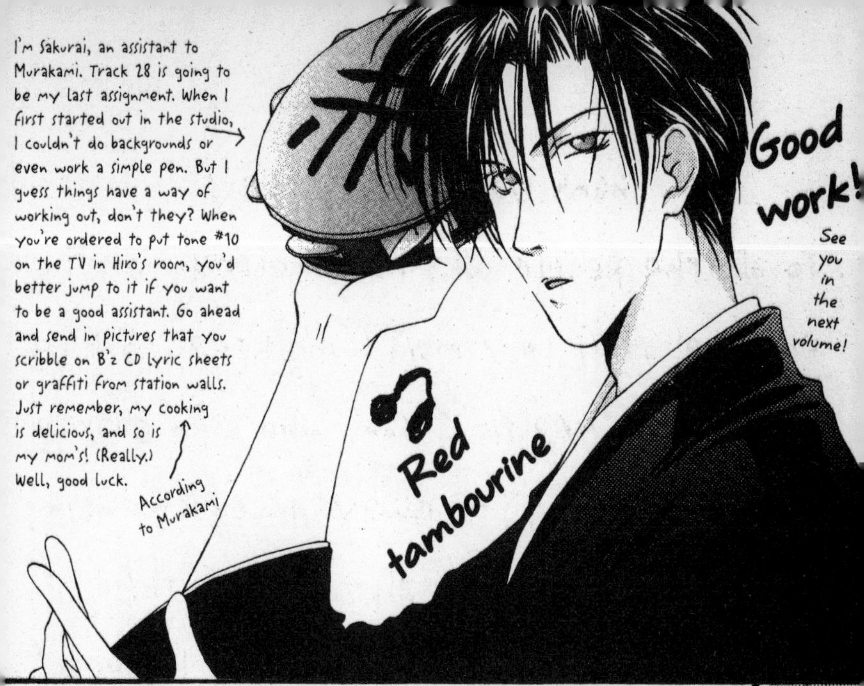
Good work!
See you in the next volume!
I'm Sakurai, an assistant to Murakami. Track 28 is going to be my last assignment. When I first started out in the studio, I couldn't do backgrounds or even work a simple pen. But I guess things have a way of working out, don't they? When you're ordered to put tone #10 on the TV in Hiro's room, you'd better jump to it if you want to be a good assistant. Go ahead and send in pictures that you scribble on B'z CD lyric sheets or graffiti from station walls. Just remember, my cooking is delicious, and so is my mom's! (Really.) Well, good luck.
Red tambourine
According to Murakami

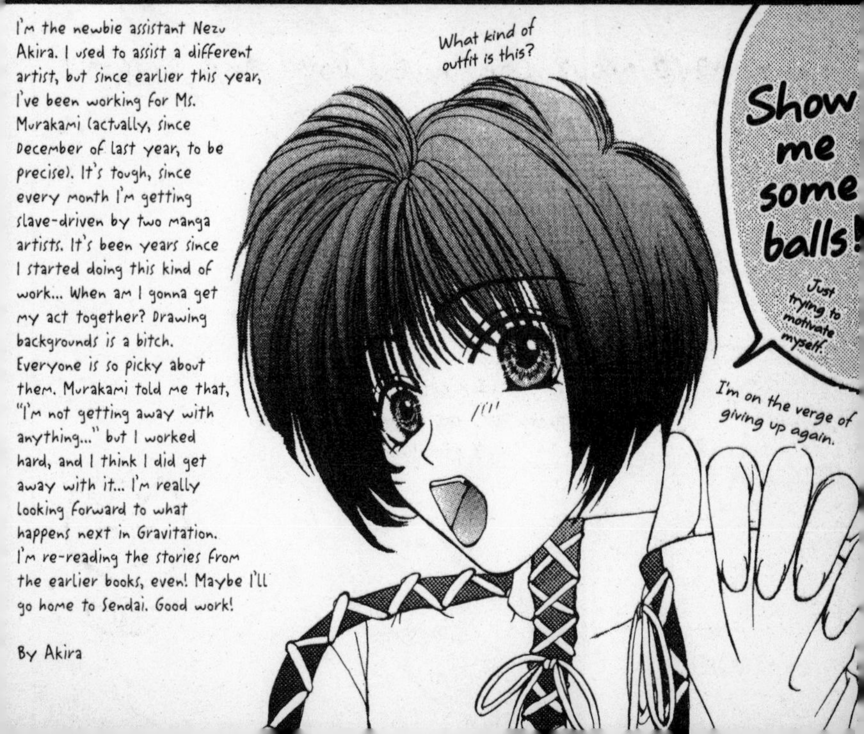
Show me some balls!
Just trying to motivate myself.
What kind of outfit is this?
I'm on the verge of giving up again.
I'm the newbie assistant Nezu Akira. I used to assist a different artist, but since earlier this year, I've been working for Ms. Murakami (actually, since December of last year, to be precise). It's tough, since every month I'm getting slave-driven by two manga artists. It's been years since I started doing this kind of work... When am I gonna get my act together? Drawing backgrounds is a bitch. Everyone is so picky about them. Murakami told me that, "I'm not getting away with anything..." but I worked hard, and I think I did get away with it... I'm really looking forward to what happens next in Gravitation. I'm re-reading the stories from the earlier books, even! Maybe I'll go home to Sendai. Good work!
By Akira

Thank you, dear readers.

To all the people who have helped me: the editorial staff; my mom (who keeps cooking me yummy meals); C-san, who is in charge of me (I'm sorry, I'm always inconveniencing you...), and finally all of my faithful readers. Thank you very much!!! I hope I can have your continued love and support!

See you in Book 7!

– Murakami Maki

P.S. Atsuko-chan, Akira-san, thanks for your comments and illustrations!

Gravitation

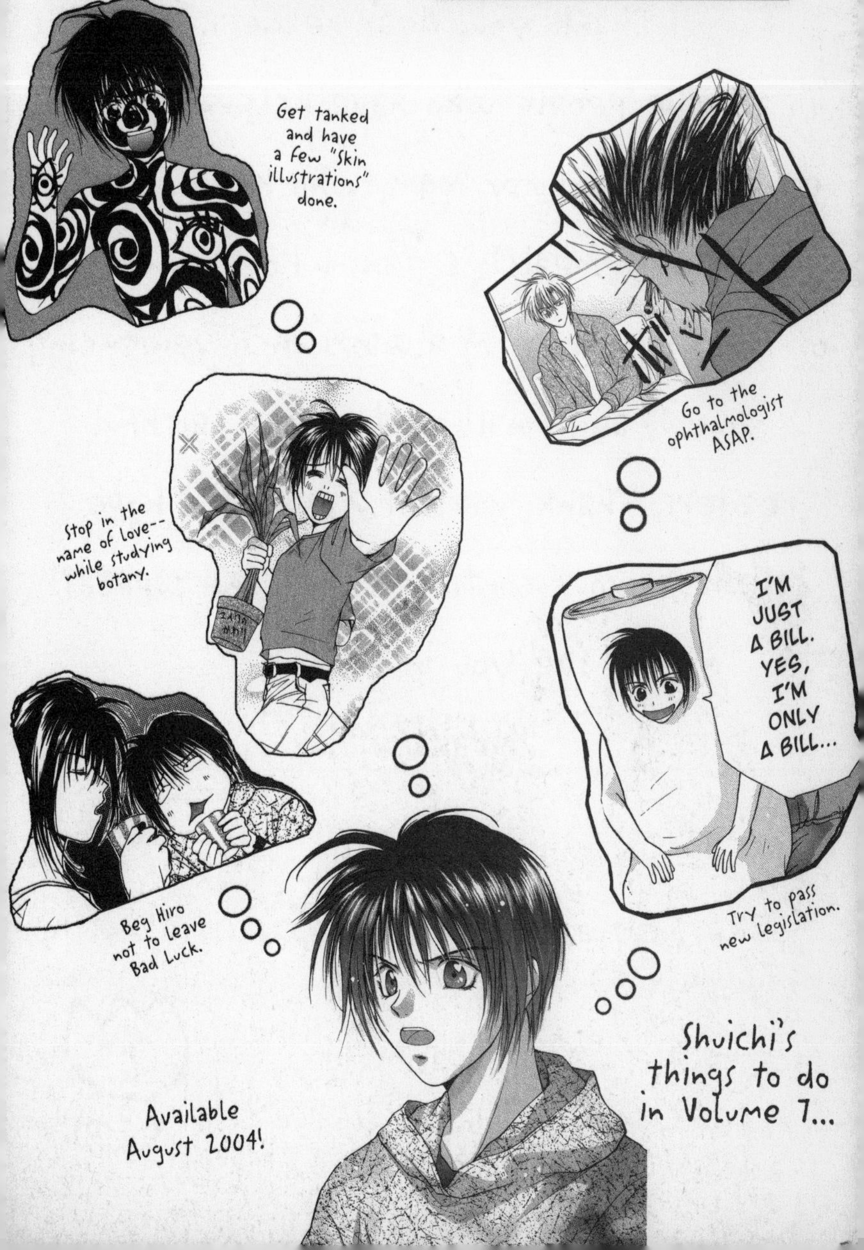

Shuichi's things to do in Volume 7...
Go to the ophthalmologist ASAP.
Get tanked and have a few "Skin illustrations" done.
Stop in the name of love--while studying botany.
I'M JUST A BILL. YES, I'M ONLY A BILL...
Try to pass new legislation.
Beg Hiro not to leave Bad Luck.
Available August 2004!

ALSO AVAILABLE FROM TOKYOPOP®

PITA-TEN
PLANET LADDER
PLANETES
PRIEST
PRINCESS AI
PSYCHIC ACADEMY
QUEEN'S KNIGHT, THE
RAGNAROK
RAVE MASTER
REALITY CHECK
REBIRTH
REBOUND
REMOTE
RISING STARS OF MANGA
SABER MARIONETTE J
SAILOR MOON
SAINT TAIL
SAIYUKI
SAMURAI DEEPER KYO
SAMURAI GIRL REAL BOUT HIGH SCHOOL
SCRYED
SEIKAI TRILOGY, THE
SGT. FROG
SHAOLIN SISTERS
SHIRAHIME-SYO: SNOW GODDESS TALES
SHUTTERBOX
SKULL MAN, THE
SNOW DROP
SORCERER HUNTERS
STONE
SUIKODEN III
SUKI
THREADS OF TIME
TOKYO BABYLON
TOKYO MEW MEW
TOKYO TRIBES
TRAMPS LIKE US
UNDER THE GLASS MOON
VAMPIRE GAME
VISION OF ESCAFLOWNE, THE
WARRIORS OF TAO
WILD ACT
WISH
WORLD OF HARTZ
X-DAY
ZODIAC P.I.

NOVELS

CLAMP SCHOOL PARANORMAL INVESTIGATORS
KARMA CLUB
SAILOR MOON
SLAYERS

ART BOOKS

ART OF CARDCAPTOR SAKURA
ART OF MAGIC KNIGHT RAYEARTH, THE
PEACH: MIWA UEDA ILLUSTRATIONS

ANIME GUIDES

COWBOY BEBOP
GUNDAM TECHNICAL MANUALS
SAILOR MOON SCOUT GUIDES

TOKYOPOP KIDS

STRAY SHEEP

CINE-MANGA™

ALADDIN
CARDCAPTORS
DUEL MASTERS
FAIRLY ODDPARENTS, THE
FAMILY GUY
FINDING NEMO
G.I. JOE SPY TROOPS
GREATEST STARS OF THE NBA
JACKIE CHAN ADVENTURES
JIMMY NEUTRON: BOY GENIUS, THE ADVENTURES OF
KIM POSSIBLE
LILO & STITCH: THE SERIES
LIZZIE MCGUIRE
LIZZIE MCGUIRE MOVIE, THE
MALCOLM IN THE MIDDLE
POWER RANGERS: DINO THUNDER
POWER RANGERS: NINJA STORM
PRINCESS DIARIES 2
RAVE MASTER
SHREK 2
SIMPLE LIFE, THE
SPONGEBOB SQUAREPANTS
SPY KIDS 2
SPY KIDS 3-D: GAME OVER
THAT'S SO RAVEN
TOTALLY SPIES
TRANSFORMERS: ARMADA
TRANSFORMERS: ENERGON
VAN HELSING

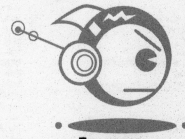

**For more
information visit
www.TOKYOPOP.com**

03.30.04T

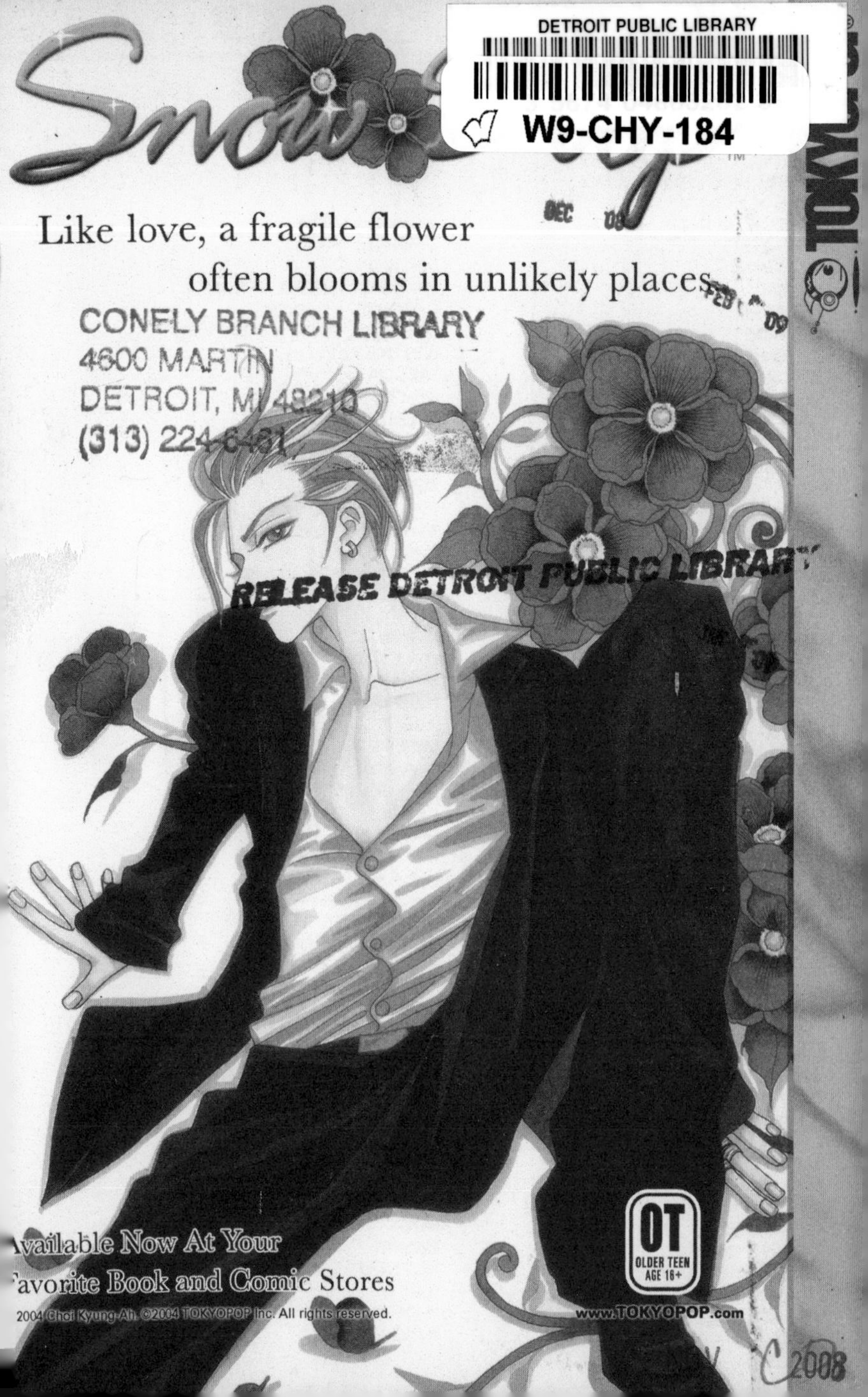
Snow
TOKYOPOP
Like love, a fragile flower
often blooms in unlikely places
Available Now At Your
Favorite Book and Comic Stores
OT
OLDER TEEN
AGE 16+
www.TOKYOPOP.com